MONDAY GIRL'S
REVENGE

David A. Thyfault

Episode two (of four) in the series:
The Making of Detective Neal "Stump" Randolph

ISBN 978-1-943650-33-0

Library of Congress Control Number 2016951332

This book was published by BookCrafters,
Parker, Colorado.

This book may be ordered from
www.bookcrafters.net
and other online bookstores.

DEDICATION

To all victims of other people's choices, especially my patient wife, Patty, for enduring my countless questions ever since I decided to write a fiction series.

ACKNOWLEDGEMENTS

My sincere thanks to these folks for their assistance.

George Andrews
BookCrafters
Rickey Fitzsimmons
Lori Freyta
Deb McLeod
Liz Netzel
Abigail Rhode
Patty Thyfault
Lisa Wiencek

CHAPTER 1

LIKE A MOTHER WHO RUNS WILDLY through the flames of a burning building to save her baby, Detective Delores Sanchez was driven to the most dangerous undercover role of her brief career because she had no choice: She knew from first-hand experience what the rapist's victims felt like and she'd do anything to save them from his hellfire.

A little taller than most Latinas, Delores tucked a small beat-up table under the bare window that overlooked the kidney-shaped pool and a dozen swaying palm trees of the Cal-Vista apartments.

To gather evidence against Dixon Browne, the resident manager, and a man whom she thought of as a serial rapist, Delores was going to have to let him get uncomfortably close.

Uncomfortable because when Delores was a youngster she was fondled repeatedly and had grown to become distrustful of any kind of typical intimacy. The simple thought of somebody's hands, even those of somebody whom she liked, grabbing at her body usually reminded her of her childhood and nearly always freaked her out.

The single difference between this situation and her own experience was that Dixon Browne's victims, who flowed to him with the frequency of waves flopping on the beach at high-tide, weren't children. They were full-grown undocumented immigrants. Regardless of the distinction, Delores knew how helpless Dixon's victims felt and she was the only person who was in a position to do anything about it.

Thus, a few days earlier Delores adopted the role of a naïve and poor immigrant, whom she called Lorraine Martinez, and made up a story about a missing brother. Posing as a financially challenged prospective tenant, she confessed to Dixon that she lacked the full month's rent that was usually required to move in. As expected, Dixon made an allowance and let her move the few bedraggled props she'd brought with her into one of the vacant apartments.

With but a few more minutes until she expected him to drop by for the remainder of the rent, Delores set her recorder pen on top of the fridge and plopped a small black and white TV on the rickety table by the window.

Next, if the very worst thing were to happen, Dixon would probably try to force her into the bedroom, therefore, the best place to stash her hand-sized Diamondback gun was under the matted-down couch pillow she'd already placed on the exercise-mat-turned-mattress that she planned to use for a bed.

After moving a few remaining pieces of beat-up furniture around, about all that was left to do was take a seat at the window and think about how Lorraine might interact with Dixon Browne as she watched for his arrival.

Now, as both the bait and the hunter, Delores was not the least bit confident that both she and Dixon could survive their relationship long enough to slap her magic bracelets on his wrists.

* * *

Freshly showered, Dixon Browne squeezed a glob of paste onto his dentures and jiggled them into place. He ran a brush through his thinning brown hair and moved into his bedroom-turned-office. He passed a shelf full of gambling trophies and opened the desk drawer where he kept two special checkbooks, each holding over twenty thousand dollars.

One account was for a new car. The other held a college fund for his secret daughter, Maria, who lived with her mama, Inez, at the other end of the complex. Proud of his accounts, Dixon pressed his tongue against his uppers, grinned and returned his checkbooks to their proper place.

He crossed the hall to the bigger bedroom and put on his best Bermudas along with a red polo shirt and sandals. That done, he ventured into the kitchen where his current wife, Francisca, was making tortillas. "I'll be back in an hour," he said.

Francisca's English was a little rough, but Spanish was forbidden when Dixon was around. She flipped a tortilla. "What if somebody comes?"

"Dumb question," he said, grabbing the doorknob. "Tell 'em to come back later."

Outside, in the well-maintained courtyard, seven identical buildings, each with twelve apartments, encircled the fenced-in pool. As the resident manager, Dixon lived and worked in building one, which was next to the parking lot where he could keep an eye on the entire complex, including a bicycle rack and a trash area. To his right, the primary cleaning lady had just thrown a large bag into the dumpster. "Juanita," Dixon yelled, while hooking a finger. As usual, Juanita came quickly.

"Yes?" she said, as she pushed her black-rimmed glasses up the bridge of her nose.

"I've got two vacant apartments that need to be painted by tomorrow night."

"But it's my daughter's birthday tomorrow. Can we do them on the next day?"

Dixon's poker skills had taught him how to deal with signs of weakness. He flapped a small piece of paper at her. "There are two apartment numbers on here and somebody's going to paint them by tomorrow. Should I give the money to somebody else?"

Like most everybody around there, Juanita and her husband, Manuel, were always in need of extra money. She bowed her head, indicating that Dixon's bluff had worked. "No, no. We'll do it for you," she said.

It was too easy. "Good. If you hurry you'll have time for cake." Dixon handed Juanita the slip of paper and the standard deal was in place. After the apartments were painted, Dixon would bill the unknowing owner one hundred forty dollars for each apartment and give Juanita and Manuel two hundred, total. Dixon considered the extra eighty bucks to be his finder's fee—half for his car, half for Maria's college fund. His next stop was building three.

As he walked down the sidewalk he glanced across the courtyard to building four, where Maria lived with her mother. Almost sixteen, Maria had no idea that she was the byproduct of a careless fling between Dixon and her mama. Instead, Maria's mama had told Maria that her father was a brave Mexican hero who died while fighting drug lords.

Dixon liked the ruse because his original family didn't know he had fathered Maria and he was able to watch her grow up without the complications of an unwanted marriage or mandatory child support.

But none of that meant Dixon ignored his responsibility or his heart. Quite the opposite. When Inez was pregnant, he regularly slipped her enough cleaning work to pay the bulk of her bills, but he mostly cared about the baby, so he made sure Inez never overworked. Now, all these years later, he had other people do most of the work and only called on Inez once in a while, on Fridays. Thus, he thought of Inez as his Friday Girl and as long as she took care of the only person Dixon loved, he was satisfied. He smiled and kept going.

Upon entering building three, Dixon's nostrils flared at a whiff of refried beans. His saliva glands kicked in as he ascended the half-flight of stairs to Apartment 202. The lease said Juan Hernandez lived there with his wife and their baby girl, which was the maximum number of people allowed in a one-bedroom unit. But Juan and Dixon had a "wink-wink" deal and Dixon was there to collect.

When Juan's wife inched open the door, Dixon could see another woman nursing a baby on an old dark brown sofa. After a brief discussion, the sitting woman passed a sealed white envelope along to Dixon.

The under-the-table price for the three extra people who lived in Juan's apartment was a hundred and fifty bucks per month, in cash, a bargain compared to what they'd have to pay to rent their own place. "Gracias," Dixon said as he stuffed the envelope into his Bermudas. He had one final stop, the one he'd most been looking forward to.

Lorraine Martinez had just moved into building five. He knew her type: humble, poor, intimidated by authority figures. But most importantly, he knew she was afraid she'd get deported.

At Lorraine's door, his first knock yielded no reply, but that wouldn't stop a manager with a master key. He let himself in. The lights were off. There was no music. Two unmatched chairs were backed against the living room wall with a small end-table tucked between them. Two additional chairs were gathered at a wobbly kitchen table, with the little TV he'd loaned her pushed toward the window. "Hello?" he said into the otherwise empty room. "Señorita?"

Nothing.

He closed the door and wiggled his jaw. "Manager," he said, louder this time.

Still nothing.

He placed his hand on top of the TV. It was warm. He moved toward the hall where he looked through the crack by the hinges of the bedroom door. Lorraine was standing behind the open door, undoubtedly scared. "Señorita?" he said again, as he tugged gently on the knob and stood before her. "Come on out. You don't have to be afraid." The tips of her dark brown hair draped delicately across her shoulders as she cautiously stepped forward. Her dark eyes shone in a beautiful, unblemished face. He took her hand and led her back to the living room.

Saliva oozed off the back of Dixon's tongue as he and Lorraine sat face to face. He leaned in. "I looked closer at your application. It says that you're twenty-six. How old are you really?"

"Twenty-six," she said sheepishly.

Dixon shook his head and pointed a thumb toward the center of the complex. "There are only six white families and two black families who live here. The rest are Hispanic. I've been doing this for a long time. If you want my help you have to be honest with me." He smiled. "I'd say you're about nineteen. That's closer, isn't it?"

Lorraine scooted back in her chair, then looked up and nodded.

"Good." He placed his hand on her knee, shifted his teeth with his jaw. "You just tell me the truth and I'll keep you safe."

"Gracias," she said as softly as before.

"You said that you got a job at the restaurant a couple miles up. If they're still paying forty dollars a day for a five-day week you won't have enough money to pay your rent and other bills. Can somebody else help you?"

Her gaze fell toward the floor. "My brother had to go away."

Just as he often did when playing poker, Dixon stared at her until she blinked. Then he said, "Let me guess. He got picked up. Now you're all alone and don't know who to trust." He lifted her chin and bobbed his head up and down the way salesmen do when they want people to agree with them. "That's it, isn't it?"

It took a moment but eventually Lorraine mirrored his head-bob.

Dixon sucked at the air and scooted his chair closer. "Alright. Since you were honest with me, I'm going to help you out. First off, Immigration won't deport you if you make enough income to support yourself, so we have to get you a little more money."

She lifted her head and looked him in the eye.

"I want you to tell the owner of the restaurant to shift your schedule around so that you can have Mondays off. That way you can work for me, just on Mondays. Then, I'll pay three hundred-and-fifty dollars a month of your rent."

She smiled. "You will?"

"Sure. Other women do the same thing for me, only on different days." He laid his hand on her shoulder. "But let me make something perfectly clear. You'll have to do whatever I want. That might mean you'll rake leaves or pick up trash along the fences or cook some food for my police friends." Dixon leaned in close. "And that's not all. When I say you have to do *anything*, I mean *anything*." He placed his hand under her chin and leaned in to kiss her innocent lips.

She crinkled her nose, pushed him away. "No," she yelped as she bolted to her feet, ran into the bedroom and slammed the door.

Dixon smiled. He could have gone after her but there was no need. He'd seen her kind before. Her full rent would be due soon and if she didn't miraculously find the money, she'd be out of options. It was as if she were drawing to an inside straight. "Think it over Señorita," he said as he moved toward the door. Let me know if you change your mind."

Dixon left and hurried back to Francisca. She wasn't allowed to say no.

CHAPTER 2

Out of nowhere, scorching flames flashed high and wide. Then Stump felt the heat. The guilt was back. His stomach felt as if a bunch of boots were kicking him around. Another flare made him gasp for fresh air. "No. No. Not again," he yelped. "Oh my God. Mom! Please! Please!" He tried to run for help but his legs wouldn't move. "Mom!" He thrashed his head wildly from side to side. "Gimme another chance, Mom! Please! Please don't die. MOM. MOM!"

"Stump. Wake up," somebody said from afar. "You're dreaming again." Then Stump felt a hand on his head.

"Huh? What?" Stump paused, opened his eyes and sucked in several quick breaths. Safely in bed, he raised his sweaty head off the pillow. "Oh. Myles. Thank God."

"Same thing, huh?"

Relieved to be back in the present, Stump nodded. It had been three years since his mother's death but he still had nightmares about his role in her passing. If only he'd done what she asked. He wiped a tear from the corner of his eye. "I killed her, Myles."

Myles shook his head. "We go over this every time, Stump. You didn't put the paint thinner in the laundry room nor the bars on the windows."

"I know, but if I didn't—"

"You've got to stop beating yourself up over it. You'll have your chance to do something about it in a couple days. In the meantime, you'd better get a shower. I'll wait."

A short hour later Stump and Myles were in Myles's truck at the local shopping center and embroiled in their most frequent topic. "But what good does it do to have three million bucks if I can't spend any of it?" Stump asked.

"You just worry about what you're doing." Myles pointed out the windshield. "If you wreck my truck, you won't get your license for at least another year."

As adoptive fathers go, Myles's was sorta cool most of the time, but at moments like this the dude was a giant buzz kill. First off, nothing could go wrong on the outskirts of an empty mall parking lot this early on a Sunday morning. Secondly, the driving conditions had nothing to do with what he wanted to talk about. "But, you keep ignoring—"

"I'm not ignoring anything. Young people don't respect money. As long as I'm in charge of your trust, I'm not going to let you piss it away."

"Dammit, Myles," Stump said, smacking the steering wheel. "I don't want to piss it away. I just want enough to buy one stupid car." He pulled up to a stop sign, turned right and swung into the second lane.

Myles smirked. "No way. You may have aced the online driving exam, but you're still not responsible enough. You forgot to signal and you can't even hit the correct lane when you turn a corner."

"For crying out loud, Dude. Nobody's around."

"Don't care. You don't get to change the laws when they're inconvenient."

"Alright, alright. I get it, but I bet there are lots of people who—"

"You might as well get used to it. You're not going to use your trust money for a car, and based on what I'm seeing today, it could be a long time before you get a license. Now, circle around and do it correctly this time."

Stump squeezed the steering wheel as hard as he could. The only way to get Myles to take his request seriously was to complete the two-mile loop around the mall precisely the way Myles wanted it. Below 10 MPH. Proper signals. Correct lanes. Watch the mirrors. No friggin' radio.

Several minutes of silence accompanied them around the parking lot, perfectly this time, then back to the starting point. Stump pulled into a parking spot on the outskirts of the lot and turned off the engine. "Now can we talk about that car?"

Myles tilted his head. "Do it again, going the other direction."

Stump sighed. No use fighting it. Myles had all the power. Foot on brake. Check mirrors. Put in gear. Look over shoulder. Roll eyes.

They were on the fifth perfect trip in a row when Stump detected motion in his left side mirror. A Palmdale squad car was racing across the lot in his direction. He frowned and swerved slightly.

"What the hell are you doing?" Myles asked.

Stump checked again, just as the red lights flashed in his mirror. "Oh, shit." At least Myles was indifferent to Stump's sometimes-colorful language.

Myles spun around, then back. "Interesting. What are you going to do now?"

"I dunno," Stump said, pressing the brake pedal so hard that the truck stopped more abruptly than he intended. He wide-eyed the mirror again just as the cop car pulled to his bumper. There were two officers inside. "What now?"

Myles shrugged. "You got yourself into this mess."

In the left mirror, a tall middle-aged lady cop approached. Stump didn't usually fear cops, but he hated being on the defensive. He rolled down his window.

"Hands on the wheel, where I can see them, please," the officer said from over Stump's shoulder.

Stump turned his head toward Myles for some guidance.

Myles pointed his chin in the officer's direction. "Better do as she says."

The blue-shirted cop reached the window, bent slightly and glanced across at Myles, then back to Stump. "What's going on here?"

"My dad's teaching me to drive."

"Oh, I see. Do you have a permit?"

"Yes, ma'am." He reached in his back pocket, produced a crumpled paper and handed it to the officer. It was the first time he realized Myles was correct about that other matter. "I'm sorry, ma'am. I don't have a wallet."

She shook her head, looked at Myles again and moved toward the fender where she laid out the wrinkled wad and tried to hand-iron some of the creases away. She finally studied the paper and returned to the window. "Neal Joseph Randolph?"

"Yes, ma'am. But they call me Stump."

She nodded. "An alias, huh? How'd you get that name?"

"My Aunt Gerry said it when I was learning to walk."

"I see." She looked back at his permit. "You don't look sixteen."

Stump swallowed. "I just had my birthday. Honest. I'm just a little short. Just ask my dad, he's a detective."

The officer bent over, looked at Myles once more. "That correct?"

Myles reached in his pocket, flashed his badge. "Myles Cooper. Sergeant. L.A."

She nodded, smiled slightly and turned back to Stump. "I watched you go around the lot a few times. Most people don't do that unless they're staking the place out."

"My dad said this was the safest place to practice."

"Do you have your registration and proof of insurance?"

Stump hadn't thought about those things. Fortunately, Myles had already mined the glove compartment. Stump's fingers shook as he took the papers from Myles and passed them on.

"You wait here." The officer said before returning to her squad car. She slid in and closed the door. The officer sitting in the rider's seat was talking into a corded cop microphone. "What are they doing?" Stump whispered to Myles.

Myles shrugged. "Probably checking to see if you have any outstanding violations."

"Are you going to take away my permit?"

Myles tilted his head. "You did make that *lame* lane-change. Remember?"

"This sucks," Stump said just as a new set of cop lights flashed in the other mirror. His eyes widened, "Oh no. There's another one."

Myles looked over his shoulder but said nothing.

As the second squad car parked behind the first, a third one, from the front this time, blasted around one of the buildings, it too with flashing red.

Within mere seconds the third car pulled right to Myles's front bumper, making it impossible to get away. Doors swung open. More blue-shirted uniforms jumped out. Scary officers glared at Stump before walking past him and joining their peers in a cop-cluster behind Myles's truck. Stump's armpits oozed sweat into his clean T-shirt.

The lady cop's arms flailed, as she explained Stump's orbits around the mall. Then the cop who came in the second car said something back to her and just like a football team breaking a huddle, the whole group of officers came to the front of Myles's truck, with the woman now holding a clipboard.

She bent again. "Okay, Mr. Randolph. We talked it over. I'm afraid we're going to have to give you an SDC."

Stump couldn't see the paper, but the oldest officer looked pissed off. "A ticket?"

She waited a few seconds, then, "We don't usually see dads and their sons working together like this, but we like it." She handed Stump the paper. "We're giving you a Safe Driving Certificate. Congratulations."

Stump's eyes widened. He looked at the certificate and back at the officer. "Really?"

"Sure thing. I watched closely and you were doing everything just the way you're supposed to. Good job."

"Wow. Thanks." Stump quickly scanned the now grinning faces of the officers then handed his award to Myles.

The lady cop tapped the bottom of Stump's window frame. "You keep driving safely, Neal." She nodded respectfully at Myles and turned away. Within moments the cops were back in their vehicles, and had turned off their lights and driven away.

Apparently stunned, Myles scanned the certificate and shook his head. "I don't know what to say, but I think that's enough for today. Let's trade seats, and I'll take you to breakfast."

If Stump's grin were any bigger, it might have broken his face.

CHAPTER 3

How COULD COFFEE SMELL SO GOOD and taste so gross? After taking their initial order, the waitress, who was about Myles's age, with lots of jewelry, brought their drinks. "Juice for you," she said to Stump, "and coffee for you," she said to Myles as she slid his cup before him.

Stump paused a long moment, then stared right at Myles.

"What's up?" Myles asked.

"Her rings."

"The waitress? What about them?"

"They were all scratched up." Stump pointed out the window. "Just like that lady cop who gave me that award. They've both been married a long time."

"So?" Myles lifted his cup to his lips.

"That officer kept smiling at you. She was way too friendly for a married person." Stump leaned to the side to see around Myles's cup. "And you've got a big ol' grin on your face. Admit it, Dude. You put them all up to it."

Myles set his cup down, beamed. "You think you're pretty smart, don't you? Alright. You caught me. I wanted to teach you a lesson about taking driving seriously. As far as I could tell, you seemed to get the point."

Stump shook his head. "I can't believe you."

"Speaking of not being stupid," Myles said. "Your mid-term grades came in the mail."

Stump felt like a balloon that had just lost its air. "Probably not straight A's, huh?"

"Hardly." Myles unfolded the paper, slid it across the table. "An A in math, but everything else is a disaster."

"I don't like school this year. It's a waste of time. I don't need to know most of that shit."

"Can't help that, but I do know one thing. If you don't get your act together, you might have to repeat the tenth grade."

Stump looked out the window. "That'd suck."

"Glad you see it that way 'cause I expect you to fix this on your own." He picked up a napkin. "Or I'm going to have to take your license away before you even get it."

"Okay. Okay. You've made your point. Now can we talk about my car?"

"That depends. You got anything new to say?"

"Just that it would be a lot easier on both of us. You won't have to take me to so many places."

"That's not new and you know the answer. Not unless you've got your own money and can pay for insurance and gas."

"But I do have my own money. Three million dollars. Remember?"

"You know what I mean. Your trust money doesn't count. You've got to get a job and earn the money you need. All I'm willing to do right now is loan you the money to buy new tires for Ol' Ug'."

Stump snorted. "That piece of crap bicycle in the storage room? You've got to be kidding me. The last time that clunker saw any action was before cavemen tamed fire."

"It was good enough for my paper route and it still has lots of miles left in it."

"Dude. There's a reason you gave it that stupid name."

"Maybe so, but it's cheap and reliable."

"The handlebars look like goal posts."

"And with a little practice you'll be able to ride your girlfriends around on them like I used to do."

Stump rolled his eyes. "Great, if I happen to see a grandma waddling along the side of the road, I can offer her a ride down memory lane. It's dorky, Dude. If you want me to use a bike we should get a cool racing bike like Lance Armstrong."

"If you want a cool bike, get a job and save your money."

Stump paused. Then, "Knowing you, you'll make me install seatbelts."

"Don't tempt me, but I'd like you to wear a helmet. I'll loan you the money for that too."

Stump banged his elbows on the table, dropping his shaking head in his hands. "Why not get me George Washington's leather football helmet?"

Myles grinned. "If we're done arguing, I got a call from that commercial real estate broker I spoke with last week. He found a building we should drive by when we're done here."

Stump pursed his lips. "An investment for my trust? Those buildings are in the millions."

"Seven million. If we put two million down, we can get a loan for the rest and the rents will pay for it."

"I can't believe this crap." Stump took a swig of his O.J., then plopped his glass on the table. "I'm the only person I know who is both filthy rich and dirt poor at the same time."

"I'm not saying we should buy it, but the right investment might provide some income."

"Income? Who cares about income if Daddy won't let me spend any of it?"

Myles let out a deep breath and sat back. His eyes were vacant. It meant he was thinking something over. Looks went back and forth. Finally, Myles shifted. "I've got a compromise for you. You get a job and save as much as you can. Then, when you have enough money for a decent car, I'll match however much you save, and just to give you an extra incentive, I'll authorize the trust to match it too. That way for every dollar you save, you'll have three dollars to spend on that car. How's that sound?"

"Not bad. But there ain't no jobs. The economy. Remember?"

"I didn't say it would be easy, but a smart fellow, who can triple his money, would probably try a lot harder than somebody else. And I can guarantee you there's an employer out there somewhere who will appreciate that type of enthusiasm. You just have to find him."

Stump shrugged. "Okay, I gotta admit that's a pretty good deal, but I'm telling ya, there's no decent jobs around."

"Now that we've got that out of the way, I've been meaning to tell you that I won't be able to go to that City Council meeting with you Tuesday evening. I've got an obligation at work, so it's okay if you want to wait until next month when I can go along."

Stump bit his lip. He didn't like the idea of facing the whole gang of authority figures by himself.

CHAPTER 4

THE EARLY MORNING AROMA of chorizo made Dixon's mouth water. The fifth of the month was the last day the tenants could pay their rent without a late fee—and at least half of them waited as long as possible. The avalanche of activity that was to follow would be a royal pain in the ass, but afterwards, the only tenants left to deal with were the late-payers, and they were the ones who were most willing to play "Let's Make a Deal."

A significant percentage of the renters were still getting accustomed to America. Some had not yet landed steady jobs, nor established relationships with banks, nor learned how to deal with regular rent payments. A few others simply couldn't resist the liquor-store-on-every-corner temptation.

Whatever their reasons, Dixon had developed several furtive techniques to fatten his checkbooks at their expense. To keep track of it all, he kept coded records in a green spiral notebook in his desk.

The bulk of this secret activity began when Rodger Kraft, the building's owner, was diagnosed with cancer. Prior to that, Rodger had kept track of the day-to-day operations, but his disease led to fatigue and sloppiness. Bottom line was, Rodger wasn't going to live a lot longer and he already had all the money he'd ever need.

There was no reason for Dixon to ignore the window of opportunity that would surely close after Rodger was out of the picture. Besides, Dixon deserved a little extra juice. He was the one who had to be there around the clock, while Rodger Kraft just dropped by for a few hours each day. Dixon had to deal with the squabbles among tenants, and evicting drunks, and making sure the apartments got painted. For that alone he and Maria deserved a bigger slice of the pie, and today the Last Minute Gang would fill his plate. He barely got his teeth tucked into his jaw before Francisca knocked on the bathroom door. "Somebody to see you," she said. "They're looking for an apartment."

Dixon sucked at his teeth. It happened every month at this time. Struggling renters from other buildings had fallen behind on their rent the previous month and now that a new month had arrived, they didn't have enough money to both catch up on the old debt and pay for the new month. Instead, they'd look for someplace else to start all over. Fortunately for Dixon, struggling renters were walking bags of cash.

After a little friendly negotiating, they would be allowed to move into one of the vacant apartments at a big discount for the first month, but they had to pay in cash and they had to take the apartment "as is" even though it had not yet been cleaned or painted. Later, Rodger Kraft would be told that Dixon had to give them some free rent as an incentive to move in. "Tell them I'll be right there."

Dixon considered the exercise to be a win/win for everybody: The tenants beat their former landlord out of the previous month's rent and paid only half-price for their first month at Cal-Vista; as for Rodger, if the new tenants lasted for a few additional months, he'd pocket some cash he wouldn't have otherwise gotten; and best of all, the Dixon-Maria matching checkbooks would be enlarged by several hundred bucks.

As the day unfolded, Dixon collected most of the outstanding rents and made several special arrangements with people who were naïve enough to think their financial problems were temporary. "Just pay half of the rent in cash," he said. "If you can't get the rest, I'll let you stay until the end of the month for free." Of course Dixon pocketed the bulk of the cash and told Rodger Kraft they were going to get caught up on payday.

That night, Dixon slipped into his office to count his rewards. Like bananas, they came in bunches. A half-dozen mini-scams netted him and Maria nearly two grand to split. What father wouldn't do the same thing?

After he updated his notebook there remained a handful of people who still hadn't checked in, including young Lorraine Martinez, whom he hoped to make into his Monday Girl. She and some others would be more desperate the next day when late fees would be added to their debt.

Just then, one of Francisca's gentle knocks interrupted Dixon's thoughts. "The lady from building five is here to see you," she said.

Monday Girl! "Tell her to wait." Dixon hurried across the hall to the bathroom and sucked in some mouthwash and swished it around before he inserted his teeth. Then a comb found his hair and he dabbed his face with Old Spice. Lastly, he popped into the bedroom and threw on some clean clothes.

A minute later Francisca escorted Lorraine into the office and Dixon closed the door. Lorraine's slender body was hidden behind a faded tan blouse that was loose for her frame and hid breasts that were undoubtedly too young to have been affected by gravity. Her thick hair and golden skin were alluring enough, but whenever she spoke, perfect white teeth peeked from behind full innocent lips that were just begging to be kissed. He swallowed the excess saliva that had already accumulated behind his teeth. "Did you bring your rent?"

The slow head-nod answered his question. "Most of it," she said, reaffirming his suspicions. He thought about candy and babies, and taking one from the other. "How much do you have?" he asked, knowing nearly every word that would follow.

Lorraine reached in her blouse pocket and pulled out a wad of crinkled-up bills, including ones. She laid it on Dixon's desk. "Four hundred. I can get the rest in a few days. The restaurant is going to let me wait tables on the weekends."

Her words were simple enough, but he knew she was bluffing. They all had stories like that. He also knew that the best way to beat a bluffer was to come right back at her with an enormous raise. "I doubt your tips are all that good," he said while he stuffed her cash in his desk drawer. "You still won't have enough to avoid eviction. You understand that, don't you?"

Lorraine's eyes confirmed that Dixon had essentially won the pot as he always did. He immediately dealt the next hand. "What about next month?" he asked.

She wrinkled her brow. "What about it?"

"Even if you get this month figured out, you're going to come up against the same situation in a few weeks. You also have to pay for utilities and groceries and bus fare. Correct?" He waited until she nodded. "I guess you could take on a roommate, but you only have one bedroom. Do you know anybody else who'd want to live with you?"

Her brown eyes sought the floor. "What about the job you mentioned?" she asked.

He hid his grin, but his chest throbbed like a beginner with four of a kind. "On Mondays?" he said. "I suppose we could still work something out."

"What would I have to do?"

He shrugged. "Easy things, mostly. Clean vacant apartments, run errands, cook meals. Anything I need."

She looked off to the side. "What about what you tried to do last time? I don't want to do that."

Dixon rose, took her hand and urged her to stand. He gently touched her chin and lifted her head. "You've kissed a boy before, haven't you?"

"Just Ricardo. In Mexico."

"Well, Ricardo's not here to help you pay your rent." Dixon leaned forward to taste her luscious lips. This time she didn't run away.

CHAPTER 5

Playing her role and dressed in second-hand clothes, Detective Delores Sanchez, AKA Lorraine Martinez, caught the 9:15 bus toward her bogus job. From the rear of the bus she verified that she wasn't being followed before she pulled the overhead cord.

Two blocks later she departed, walked one block down the side street, made a right, then walked another half-block back toward Cal-Vista. A final look over her shoulder confirmed she was all clear. She grabbed a key from her purse and slithered behind the wheel of a near-new, grey Audi. Ten minutes later she pulled into the driveway of psychiatrist Jeanine Moreno.

Delores had been a cop a few years, and she'd already experienced more than her fair share of stress, but it wasn't until Dixon Browne dumped a baleful of last straws on her shoulders that she actually sought professional therapy. This would be her first meeting with her shrink.

She was escorted into a private office where Dr. Moreno stood behind a beautiful, but cluttered, antique desk. "Come in, Detective," the doctor said, brushing aside a few strands of her streaked blonde hair. "I'm so happy to meet you." About ten years Delores's senior, the doctor pointed with long, multi-colored fingernails toward a sitting area, near a large window. "Please take a seat."

Delores nodded and curled her own boring fingernails deep into her palms.

At the sitting area, two high-backed leather chairs, each containing a large purple velvet pillow, sat face-to-face. The tidy area looked like a well-planned island of sanity amid a sea of madness. Delores snatched the pillow from the left chair for no particular reason and eased into the soft leather. "I've never been to a psychiatrist before," she said. "You're going to think I'm screwed up."

"First off, Detective," the doctor said as she kicked off her shoes and tucked her feet up under her rear end, "you can call me Jeanine. It's usually a lot easier to talk with a friend," she said, making air-quotes.

Whew! The feeling was mutual. "And you can call me Delores."

"Alright then, Delores, now that we've got all the yucky stuff out of the way—"

Delores grinned and set her pillow aside. She uncurled her fingers and gestured toward a framed picture next to a bottle of hand lotion on Jeanine's desk. "Is that your family?"

"Yep. Two daughters. One husband, but sometimes he can be more challenging than both the girls combined. How about you? Married? Children?"

"I've met a few guys, but nothing has worked out."

"I see. Do you mind if I ask how you heard of me?"

"Oh, sure. I'm from a little two-person department, out in Palmdale. We don't have many resources so when I decided I wanted to talk with somebody I called the L.A. office. They had a couple people on contract. I picked you because, well—"

"I'm a woman."

"Well, yeah, but I hate to admit it, considering all the crap I give men about being sexist."

Jeanine waved a dismissive hand in the air. "I get that quite a bit. Who else knows you're here?"

"Nobody. I don't want anybody to know I'm a head case."

"A head case, huh? The reason I asked is, the county might pay my fee if your supervisor recommends the meeting."

"But then everybody would know I'm a weirdo. I don't think I'm ready for that. If I can just meet with you a couple times on my own, I'll pay you myself."

"Good enough. When you first sat down, you claimed to be 'all screwed up.' What did you mean by that?"

Delores sighed. "Everything. My personal life. My work. All of it. It's stress everywhere I go."

"A common problem in law enforcement. But something must have changed. What was it?"

Delores hesitated a moment. Then, "I guess it was Dixon Browne."

"A boyfriend? A boss?"

Delores smirked. "Neither, but he thinks he's both. He manages an apartment building. I have reason to believe he's a rapist and I'm in an undercover role to gather evidence. That's why I'm dressed like this."

"Sounds dangerous."

"As far as we can tell, he doesn't attack women physically. It's more of a psychological matter. He knows they're vulnerable so he manipulates them into sleeping with him. It's part of a new crime called rape by deception."

"Never heard of it. So, if you're not particularly concerned for your safety, what's the problem?"

Delores clucked her tongue. "Dinosaurs."

"I assume you mean that metaphorically?" Jeanine said.

"Yeah. I'm mostly talking about the DA. He thinks the rape by deception idea is a farce. As far as he's concerned, if a woman gives consent, there's no rape. He wants me to work on other cases, so I'm basically forced to drop the matter or work on it on my own time."

"What's so bad about working on something else? I'm sure there are plenty of people who could use your help."

"I wish I could, Jeanine, but I'm the only one who understands the victims. If I don't stop that animal, nobody will. And that's the problem. I'm damned either way. Now, I'm doubting if I really belong in police work."

"It sounds as if you want me to tell you to quit your job."

Delores looked Jeanine square in the eyes. "Is that what you think I should do? 'Cause I sure don't know."

"Sorry," Dr. Moreno said shaking her head. "I can't make your decisions for you. All I can do is help you think things through."

Delores sighed. "I dunno; maybe this is what I needed to remind me how tough other people have it."

"It never hurts to keep that kind of thing in mind. Tell me something about your personal life. I believe you said it was 'all screwed up' too."

Where to begin? Delores could have gone on for hours about the resentment she carried around over the loss of her sister, but she wasn't ready to discuss any of that with a stranger. Fortunately or unfortunately, depending on how she looked at it, she had other woes she could discuss. Of those, one was somewhat benign. "For one thing, I never should have bought my car. I was doing okay when I just had my condo payment, but I thought I needed a status symbol. Now the payments are too high, my credit cards are maxed and I'm barely getting by." She gazed downwards. "I should have known better. What the hell was the matter with me?"

"I wouldn't be so hard on yourself," Jeanine said. "These things usually have a way of working out." She rested her hand on her ankle. "I have a little mental exercise that might help you. I call it IMT, for Innermost Thoughts. Would you like to give it a try?"

Delores sighed. "Why not? I'm up for anything that will make some sense out of my life."

"Okay, then," Jeanine said. "I'd like you to remove your shoes, pick up your pillow and lay your head back. Get comfortable. I'll present you with a simple question that most women face and you tell me what you think about it. Can you do that?"

"Sounds fun," Delores said while she toed off her shoe with her other foot, "but I'll probably mess it up."

"Can't. There are no wrong answers. Just relax and tell me your thoughts when you ponder this question: If you had to choose between a career or a family, which would you pick and why?"

Comforted by the easy topic, Delores cocked her head to the side and shrugged. "Both situations have appeal. I'd like to have children, but I'd also need some adult interaction to keep me sane. I'd probably be like you and try to do both."

Jeanine pressed her fingertips together in a colorful steeple. "Those are good surface-level thoughts, but we're looking for something deeper. Your innermost thoughts. Let's try again. This time, I'd like you to think about living out in the country with a good hubby, three kids and all the rewards and sacrifices that come with being a mom and housewife, but where there aren't many adult things to do. Compare that to you and hubby living in a more active community where you can have a career and join clubs and a church and do anything you want with adults, but you won't be able to have children. Got it?"

"I think so."

"Okay then, close your eyes and imagine what your life would be like in one of those situations. Consult all your senses. How does it look, sound and smell? What are your innermost thoughts?"

Delores nodded. For the next twenty minutes she played a grownup version of make-believe, much like she had done with her sister, Simone, when they were kids. She let her mind wander and shared all sorts of particulars of what she thought each fantasy life might feel like. Finally she opened her eyes, lifted her head and set her pillow down. "You know something, Jeanine. I think I'd prefer to be a happy mom."

Jeanine grinned. "Okay then, I think you've got it. You found a way to find your deepest thoughts. This should help you to make tough decisions, both personally and professionally. Just get in a quiet place and concentrate on the specifics, rather than vague generalities. That's all there is to it."

PING!

Suddenly, both heads turned toward Jeanine's desk. Jeanine patted her pillow. "Oh, darn. I'm sorry, Delores, but our time is just about up. I don't know about you, but this hour flew by way too fast. Shall I expect you again next week?"

Delores rose and inched toward the window. High up, and off in the distance, a lone gray cloud appeared to be lost. She could relate because far off, in the back of her mind, she had an ugly black cloud of her own. An IMT-like secret that she'd never, ever, ever told anybody. Not her family, not her friends, not her priest. Nobody. And with her finances as they were, she couldn't possibly afford to keep paying psychiatrist fees out of her own pocket. She faced Jeanine. "We'd better find out if the department will pay for me to come back."

CHAPTER 6

Soon after Delores took on the role of Lorraine Martinez she resigned herself to the likelihood that she'd have to spend a fair amount of her time at Cal-Vista. It was boring as hell. TV sucked without cable, and she couldn't read any books or magazines that might suggest she was somebody other than a struggling young Latina. And she sure as hell couldn't have any quests that might contradict Lorraine's image.

The sleeping arrangements were especially uncomfortable. She converted an old exercise mat into a mattress and scrounged an old sofa pillow she had. When she was hanging out, she kept her badge and a small gun under the pillow in case of an emergency, but sleeping like that caused her to wake up with an aching neck. Meanwhile, about all she had to do was think about her past and why she was there in the first place. Sometimes she employed the IMT technique that Dr. Moreno taught her.

Every morning, Delores acted just as she thought Lorraine would. She dressed in old but decent clothes, boarded the 9:15 bus and disembarked a few blocks later and wiggled through a couple side streets to her Audi. From there she drove to her real apartment, took a shower, downed some ibuprofen, put on some eye makeup and dressed for her cop job.

Fortunately one good situation eventually revealed itself.

After a handful of all-nighters, she concluded that Dixon Browne had meant what he said about seeing Lorraine only on Mondays. The rest of the time, he simply didn't come around. But that was the rest of the time. Now it was indeed Monday and she fully expected him to drop by a little later.

She literally rolled out of bed before she stretched out the kinks she'd gotten from balancing her head on a gun-padded pillow. While taking a quick shower she thought about how much she loathed men like Dixon Browne and her stepfather, who had a history of his own.

She may not have been able to do much about her stepfather, but she hoped that today she could gather some evidence that would eventually put an end to Dixon's abuse of innocent women. It was half past eight when he first entered the yard. She flicked on her recorder pen and double-checked her pistol.

*   *   *

Each part of the month lent Dixon Browne different opportunities to grow his fortune. When the last half of the month rolled around, the owner, Rodger Kraft, was aggressive about renting out the vacants. "This is when they like to move," he'd say. "If we don't get them while we can, somebody else will and we'll be stuck with a vacant apartment for another month."

To induce a prospective tenant to sign a one-year lease, Kraft was willing to give them up to two weeks free rent. He might as well have given Dixon the combination to a private safe.

There were plenty of potential tenants who were willing to pay a bargain basement price for the very days Kraft was willing to give away for free. If said tenants had cash, which many of them did because they weren't stable enough for checkbooks and banks, Dixon would grab a wad here and there, then tell Kraft that they took the "incentive plan" and paid nothing. Once again, in Dixon's eyes, it was a big win for everybody, especially for Dixon and Maria. Most months he snagged over seven hundred bucks.

The latter part of the month also presented Dixon with certain nonmonetary opportunities. Nearly all the rents had been collected and the workload was lighter, which afforded him extra time to visit people such as Lorraine Martinez. At half past eight, he grabbed some hand tools and scurried across the courtyard and through the early morning fog to building five. Just outside Lorraine Martinez's apartment, he wiggled his jaw, sucked in his gut and tapped the door.

*　*　*

When the knock finally came Delores reminded herself to act like Lorraine. She slowly opened the door.

"Good news," Dixon said instantly. "I got your name off the eviction list for this week."

"Just for a week? I thought you were going to take care of the whole month."

"Not all at once. I need to see if you're going to do your part before I pay the rest." He held up a sheet of paper. "I've got two apartments for you to clean."

Cleaning? She frowned.

"Relax," he said, putting his hand on her shoulder. "My other people only take about four hours per apartment."

Delores would have preferred to do something that kept him close by and hopefully talking about some of his shady activities, but Lorraine would be more submissive. "Is that all I have to do? Clean two apartments?"

"All I want is to get my money's worth. I'll show you where everything is." He held up a pair of pliers and a screwdriver. "While you're doing that, I'm going to come back here and fix it so you won't have to pay for electricity. That'll save you at least forty bucks a month, more in the summer when you use the air conditioning."

Huh? This sounded suspicious. "How are you going to do that?" she asked as she drifted a couple casual steps toward the recorder.

"No big deal. First, I turn off your electricity in the meter room. Then I come back here and crosswire your electrical box with the one just behind it that services the apartment next door, and Bingo, you get each other's bills. Since that other unit is vacant, it doesn't use much power. Meanwhile, your usage will be charged to the other apartment and paid by the building."

"Is that safe?"

"No problem. I've done it several times. If you treat me right, I treat you right. That's how it works."

While Lorraine would probably appreciate such a clever money-saving tactic, Delores suspected that wires weren't meant to be shifted around like that. "But what if somebody moves into that apartment. Then we'd both be paying a full amount. Maybe it's not worth it?"

"Don't worry," he said in a near whisper. "I've got other vacants I can show to new prospects." He put his hand under her chin. "I know lots of tricks."

She would have liked to call off the wire-switching scam but Lorraine Martinez would likely have a different response. "Thank you," she said, faking a grin.

"God. I love your smile," Dixon said. "Okay then, let's get you set up for a day of cleaning."

A couple hours later, Delores came to realize that cleaning other people's toilets and stoves was more unpleasant than she would have guessed. It made her appreciate the pros. In spite of a reasonable effort, she had fallen well behind.

Another forty minutes ticked by. Sweaty and dirty, she was inside a bathtub, scrubbing some of the grout around the edges when she heard Dixon open the outer door. He scooted right in and shook his head. "At this rate, you're going to be here all night."

She slumped her shoulders. "This is harder than it looks." That was one thing Lorraine and Delores would agree on.

"My other people would have been done by now."

She wiped the sweat off her forehead. "I'm sorry, but it's the best I can do."

Dixon clucked his tongue. "Not good enough considering all the freebies you're getting."

He deserved a quick kick in the groin, but Delores had an objective to keep in mind. "But I need this job," she said.

Dixon put his hand on hers. "I know you do. How would you like to go back to your place and wash up? Then we can go out for a bite to eat. On me. And we'll call it a day."

"Really? You'd do that?"

"Sure I would. I fixed your electricity, didn't I? Just remember, if I do nice things for you, you have to do nice things for me."

Figures. She brushed some loose hair out of her eyes. "Like what?"

"Just a kiss. That's all. But this time it has to be real. You have to kiss back."

She tilted her head, scanned the dirty grout around the base of the toilet, and wasn't exactly certain which option was worse. "But if I do that, I'm done for the day. Right?"

"Yep. That's the deal. I'll get somebody else to finish up both apartments."

Both Delores and her character, Lorraine Martinez, hesitated. A lone kiss might not sound like a big deal to somebody else, but most women hadn't endured a past like Delores's. "Okay," she said, being sure to close her eyes.

CHAPTER 7

Stump would have preferred to avoid the City Council meeting altogether but the sensation of boots in his gut wouldn't go away. Alone and apprehensive, he soldiered his way into the meeting room.

Inside, the Palmdale City Council members sat high and mighty behind their twenty-foot desk that was elevated on a throne-like stage. They resembled a family of royalty, anxious to pass judgment on their lowly subjects. Stump sat near the back with the other peons. Except for a couple children, he was the youngest in the room.

He'd practiced what to say, but it didn't matter. His fingers shook anyway. He might say something stupid. They'd probably reject him. Worst of all, he might cry.

Mayor Curtis, fiftyish and balding, sat at the center of the gang-throne, barking out orders while two council members sat on either side of him. Off to Stump's left, at a separate table, there were additional officials with files, apparently anxious to give the thumbs down signal when called upon. Stump gulped. In this room, where the ties and dresses ruled, he would have to play the game their way. Among other things, he'd have to use his legal name. "Neal Joseph Randolph," Mayor Curtis said into his microphone.

Already? Oh crap. Stump's butt seemed stuck to the bench. Did he really want to do this? What if he were ridiculed? Seconds passed. Then a few more. Heads pivoted while the council members scanned the attendees.

The mayor leaned closer to his microphone. "Is Neal Joseph Randolph here?"

Stump grabbed the back of the bench before him and forced his legs to lift his body. "Yes, sir. That's me." Dozens of rubbernecks twisted Stump's way.

Mayor Curtis pointed to a lectern in the center aisle. "You're first."

Snooping eyes measured Stump as he moved toward the stand. He didn't belong. He wished he were older. Wished he were taller. Wished he hadn't killed his mom. Unsure of what to expect, he laid his shaking hands on the wooden stand. "I'm me," he said, leaning into a small microphone. Snickers from behind him indicated he was already a spectacle.

"Are your parents with you?"

"No, sir. My mom's dead, and I've never met my dad."

"Well, you don't live by yourself, do you?"

"I live with my adoptive father, Myles Cooper."

"Okay then, is he here?"

"No, sir. He had to work tonight."

"Well, I'm sorry, Mr. Randolph, but you have to be sixteen to address this—"

Not that again. "But, I am sixteen, honest."

"Do you have a driver's license?"

"Just a learner's permit," he said, probing his back pockets, but they were empty. So were the others. His brain flashed him an image of earlier, before the meeting, when he threw his permit on his dresser. "I forgot to bring it."

Snorts of doubt came from Stump's back. He could almost hear their thoughts: How can you expect adults to take you seriously when you don't even remember your driver's license? He knew his face was red. He glanced at the door, but he had to stay—for his mom.

"Do you have your plans?" the Mayor asked.

Finally. An easy question. "Yes. I'm planning to get you guys to make my old neighbors fix their homes, so they're safe."

From the Mayor's right Councilwoman Hennretti rolled her eyes. "Not that kind of plans," Mayor Curtis said with a tightened face. "I'm talking about reports. Studies. Time estimates. Stuff like that. You need to show us exactly what you want from us. Do you have any plans like those?"

Stump shook his head and motioned toward the side table. "I called Mrs. Crumpler's office quite a few times to find out what I needed, but nobody called me back."

"Really?" Mayor Curtis turned toward the side table. "Is that right?"

An overweight woman in her late 40's, wearing earrings the size of bracelets, rose. "I talked to him a few weeks ago. That's how he got on the schedule, but I don't remember getting any calls lately."

Stump's eyes shot back to the Mayor. "That's not true. Her number is 619-244-2869." He hoped that knowing her number proved that he'd called it a lot, but the truth was the last seven digits, when converted to letters on a phone pad, spelled out *b-i-g b-u-n-z*. He couldn't forget something like that in a million years.

"I don't know if you noticed," the Mayor said, "but we've got important people in here." He pointed to a distinguished gentleman in the front row. "That's Owen Tosco from the local newspaper. People of his ilk don't have time to waste so—"

A light crackle came over the speakers. "May I make a comment, Mr. Mayor?"

The Mayor glanced to the farthest seat to Stump's right. "The chair recognizes Councilman Michael Barella."

Mr. Barella was perfectly groomed and wore a classic blue suit, complete with white shirt and red tie. "If you all don't mind," he said, "I believe that Mr. Randolph here lives in my district. Before we do something hasty, I'd like to ask him a couple questions."

The Mayor nodded.

Mr. Barella smiled at Stump. "I think I recognize your name. Do you have anything to do with the Jean Randolph doggie park in my district?"

Stump unclenched his fingers. "Yes, sir. Jean Randolph was my mother."

"I thought so." Mr. Barella twisted his head toward the Mayor and the rest of the City Council members. "I'm familiar with this young man. I can vouch for his age. I think he deserves to be heard."

The Mayor shrugged. "Anybody opposed?" There being no protests, he pointed his gavel at Stump. "Okay, Mr. Randolph. What did you want to say?"

A flood of relief swooshed over Stump's body. He wouldn't need notes. The story had both haunted him and motivated him for the past three years. "I'm here in honor of my mom," he began. "I was an unplanned baby and my biological father disappeared. She could have chosen abortion or adoption, but she didn't. We never had much money, but we had each other and that was enough for us. Then she bought our home." Stump smiled. "She loved to take bubble baths in the back bathroom." His eyes wandered among the big shots. Amazingly, they were all paying attention.

"About three years ago she met Myles and they were going to get married. So she hired somebody to paint the inside of our house. I was supposed to clean out our messy laundry room so it could be painted too, but I went somewhere instead. That evening, while I was gone, Mom came home and found the paint supplies in the hall. She had to move them into the laundry room, next to the hot-water heater, so our dog wouldn't spill them."

Stump's pace slowed as the back of his mind fed him images of the worst evening in his life. "Later, she took a bath and the hot water heater kicked on, igniting the fumes from the paint supplies. Everything caught on fire." Tears began to form in Stump's eyes. He tried to shake them away, but couldn't. "By the time Mom smelled the smoke, the fire had filled the hallway, making it impossible to get out." His mind's eye flashed him the horrid mental video of that night. "She tried the windows. But there were bars." Stump lowered his head, paused, tried to hold back his tears, but it hurt too much. It always did. He wiped his eyes with his sleeves.

"Do you want to stop?" Councilman Barella asked softly.

Stump sniffled and shook his head. "No, sir. I want people to know what happened."

A woman in the front row handed Stump a tissue.

With tear-filled eyes, Stump mouthed a thank you and turned back toward the front. "I got home just after a neighbor called the fire department. The smoke was really thick. We tried to find another way for Mom to get out but the windows were her only chance. She pushed the bars from the inside while a bunch of us yanked on the outside, but we couldn't budge them. She kept coughing and coughing. We all were." His brain brought an image of his mom just before she went down for the final time. He whimpered and wiped his dripping eyes.

"When she couldn't take it anymore, she tried to say she loved me but she couldn't even breathe. She fell to the floor and it was too late." He wiped at his eyes again.

The room was silent. Councilwoman Hennretti wiped her eyes. Councilman Goode dabbed the corner of his eye too. "Later, they said the fumes from a spilled bucket of paint thinner caused it all and she died from the smoke." Tears gushed down Stump's cheeks as he buried his face in his hands. "If I would've cleaned up that room like I was supposed to, there would have been enough room for the paint supplies and the thinner wouldn't have spilled." He whimpered. "I wouldn't have killed my own mother."

Other people dabbed their eyes. The tissue woman rose and wrapped her arm around Stump while he wept and didn't care who saw him. For the moment she was the mother he so desperately missed.

"We're sorry about your bereavement, Mr. Randolph," the mayor said. "It sounds as if the bars didn't meet current safety codes."

Stump released his temporary mother and wiped his eyes with his already-soggy tissue. "She could have gotten out."

"Excuse me, Mr. Mayor."

"The chair recognizes Mr. Barella."

Barella looked at the audience and back at his fellow council members. "As touching as Mr. Randolph's story is, there's more you need to hear." Barella turned his attention to Stump. "Would you mind telling my associates about the dog park?"

Stump nodded and wiped his nose. "A couple weeks after my mom's death the assistant principal of our school was found at the bottom of a cliff. Everybody thought it was suicide, but I remembered a license plate number and figured out who did it. Her grandmother gave me a reward, which I used to build the park. We named it after my mom and my assistant principal."

Oohs and ahs replaced the skepticism that previously filled the room.

"I remember that case," the Mayor said before pointing his gavel in Stump's direction. "So, what is it you want from us?"

Finally. "All the houses in that neighborhood are old. You should make those people fix their homes so they don't die too."

The Mayor cocked his head. "We know our older homes don't meet current building codes, Mr. Randolph, but we can't force people to do anything like that. They're grandfathered in. If you want to get something like this accomplished, you'll need to find out if the neighbors agree with you. Then, you'll need some specific plans. That requires a community planner or an attorney."

"But you're the government. I thought that's what you're supposed to do. I thought you cared."

A chorus of sarcastic scoffs sang from the crowd.

"I can assure you we care, Mr. Randolph," the Mayor said, "but we don't have people just sitting around waiting for projects to work on. I suggest you call Mrs. Crumpler's office again. Maybe she can help you figure something out."

Stump turned his head toward BigBunz, who sat motionless. "Is it free?" he asked as he turned back toward the mayor. "'Cause I don't have any money."

The gang-giggles from behind Stump's back answered his question.

CHAPTER 8

The next afternoon Myles and Stump gathered to follow up on a previous discussion about investing some of Stump's trust money. Stump drove them to the Cal-Vista apartments where a commercial broker, Clay Clayborne, and the grandfatherly owner of the property were waiting by the curb when Stump parked the truck.

"Right on time," Clay said before turning to his right. "Rodger Kraft, meet Myles Cooper and his son, Stump. They're the Milky Way Trust."

During the handshakes, Kraft held Stump's hand a split-second longer than people ordinarily do. "Clay here tells me you solved a couple murders. That's quite an accomplishment."

Stump tugged in his hand and shifted his feet. "Thanks."

"If you don't mind my asking," Myles said to Kraft, "Why are you selling?"

"Good question. When the economy went bad, construction jobs in the area dried up and a lot of our tenants had to go back to Mexico where they'd have lower overhead." He rubbed his throat. "More vacancies mean less income and more work for us. I'm just tired of it."

"It's the same story for nearly everybody," Clay said. "When the cash flow is down, some owners will ride it out but the ones who sell can't get as much as before."

"The market always comes back," Kraft said. "When it does, you can easily bump the rents back up by at least twenty-five bucks a month and the property's value will go right back up."

"By a half-million dollars," Stump said.

All three adults turned their heads. "Sounds about right," Kraft said. "How'd you know that?"

"Simple. We looked at several marketing brochures. The asking price usually equaled about twenty times the profits. It's just multiplication."

Myles wrapped his arm around Stump's shoulder and gave him a playful squeeze. "He's always been a numbers whiz."

"I'd say so." Kraft turned toward Stump. "Too bad you've got your own money. I could use a clever fellow like you around—"

Stump rose to his tiptoes. "A job?"

"Yeah. After school and on Saturdays. Odd Jobs. Painting. Things like that. I didn't think you'd be interested."

"I sure am. I want to buy a car."

Kraft pointed toward the parking lot. "What's wrong with your truck?"

"That's mine," Myles said. "He gets to drive it for practice until he gets his license. I told him if he wants a car he has to get a job."

"Good idea. It'll make him appreciate his money more." To Stump, "Do you have a way to get here?"

"I can use my dad's bike. It's just six or seven miles. I can make it in twenty minutes." He crossed his fingers behind his back.

Kraft nodded. "I guess that'll work. How's ten dollars an hour sound?"

"It's a deal," Stump said, shoving his hand at Mr. Kraft.

"When you count my money and what you get from the trust," Myles said, "that'll be like making thirty dollars an hour."

Stump smirked through a king-sized grin. "Yeah. I already figured that out."

"Okay, then," Kraft said. "You can begin on Monday, after school."

"Hello, Rodger." The new voice came from behind Stump. Coming was a middle-aged man with messed-up hair, Bermuda shorts, sandals and a deep-red polo shirt. The only thing missing was black argyle socks.

"The manager," Kraft said. He introduced everybody to Dixon Browne and then asked Dixon for a small favor. "Can you show these guys around? I've got a doctor's appointment in fifteen minutes."

"I guess so. What's up?"

"Oh, they're just thinking about buying an apartment building like ours."

"And I get to work here," Stump added.

Dixon looked Stump's way and then at Mr. Kraft. "We don't need any help. I've got all that covered." Stump's heart sank. He looked toward the bigger boss for support.

"There are a few extra things I want to get done," Kraft said. "I already gave him my word."

Dixon's jaw pumped up and down as if he were chewing gum.

"Regardless of what happens today," Kraft said, looking at Stump, "I'll expect to see you on Monday."

"About three-thirty," Stump said, resisting the urge to jump up and down like a kid.

Kraft tipped his head approvingly to Stump. "Nice meeting you all."

Myles faced Dixon. "What are we going to see today?"

Dixon glared at Stump. "I guess I can show you the common areas, and a couple vacants."

"What about the ones people are living in?" Myles asked.

"Not a good idea. Strangers scare these people."

Stump and Myles exchanged glances.

"Follow me," Dixon said. He walked briskly and slightly

bent over as they all moved alongside the pool fence, to building three. At the main entry a powerful whiff of ammonia danced up Stump's nostrils.

"Whew. Somebody die in here?" Clay asked.

"Just doing some cleaning," Dixon said, leading them down a half-flight of immaculately carpeted steps. He pointed in the laundry room, where there were several washers and dryers and a pop machine. Everything was spotless.

"Very nice," Clay said.

"Let's go upstairs," Dixon said. "I just had an apartment cleaned by a new lady. I want to see how it came out."

Clay flipped over his brochure as if he was looking for something. "How many cleaning people do you need?"

"Juanita handles the common areas. But she and her husband also do most of the painting, so I let other women clean the vacants."

"Do you have anything that's not all cleaned up?" Myles asked. "So we can get an idea of how rough they can get?"

Dixon's face tightened. "There's one down the hall I've been working on. I suppose we could look at it."

The apartment was darker than Stump expected and had some dust on the windowsills and counters. As the adults discussed painting costs and other trivialities, Stump drifted toward the kitchen, where the stove was pulled a few inches away from the wall. He flicked one of the burner knobs causing a loud snap and a huge flash ball to pop out. His hand recoiled and he jumped back.

"Damn it." Dixon rushed over and returned the knob to its rightful place. "This stove has a short. I knew I shouldn't have brought you guys in here."

"You okay?" Myles asked.

"Yeah," Stump said, catching his breath.

"We have to leave," Dixon insisted.

After a brief walk the entourage reached building two. Dixon stopped and pointed to the parking lot where two men were leaning up against a parked car. "Dammit. I've already told those guys that it's illegal to drink beer out there." He handed the key to Clay. "You go show these fellows Apartment 202. I'll catch up with you."

When they reached the second floor a tenant with a basket of dirty clothes stepped out of her apartment. "Excuse us," Myles said. "We're inspecting the building. Would you mind if we took a quick look through your apartment?" It was immediately obvious that the woman didn't speak English, but Stump had taken enough Spanish in school to gain her approval.

In the living room, another woman stood by a crib, changing a child's diaper. A bunch of toys were packed underneath it. The kitchen had a stack of clean dishes on the counter. The bathroom was clean and a pile of towels teetered on the vanity. There was no bed, just two double mattresses, piled one on top of the other. The closet door was open, revealing shoes and boxes on the floor. The whole exercise only took a couple minutes. Then they regrouped in the hallway.

"That's what I'm talking about," Myles said. "You get a completely different impression when they don't know you're coming." He turned to Stump and pointed to another unit on that same floor. "See if you can get us in that one."

Once more, the renter graciously complied. The two-bedroom model had very little furniture. Myles and Clay went toward the bedrooms while Stump looked in the kitchen, which was cluttered with dirty dishes. A large bowl on the counter contained a newly dated deposit receipt. As before, it just took a couple minutes to complete a quick visual inspection.

As they were leaving the apartment Dixon startled them from the landing. "What the hell's going on? You weren't supposed to do that." He held out his hand to Clay. "Give me my key."

"Sure. Here ya go." Clay said before turning to Myles. "Anything else you guys want to know?"

"Yeah. I've got a few more questions," Myles said, "but you don't have to stick around. We can touch base a little later."

After Clay left, Myles and Stump followed Dixon to his office where Myles asked several general questions about the building and operations. Then he turned to Stump. "What about you? Anything on your mind?"

Dixon looked at the clock on his desk.

Stump ignored the disrespect. "How much is the damage deposit?"

"Five hundred," Dixon said abruptly.

Stump pointed at a checkbook-sized pad on Dixon's desk. "Is that a receipt book? Can I look at it?"

"Be my guest." Dixon handed him the book.

Stump flipped through a few pages. "Do new people have to pay all of their deposit before they move in?"

"Yes. If they start out behind, they never get caught up."

"So you don't accept partial payments?"

Dixon sighed and shook his head. "That's what I just said."

"This book is for the last three weeks and the receipts are numbered from 651 to 700?"

"Yeah? So?"

"Well, there was a receipt for two hundred bucks in that apartment we just looked at. It was numbered 126 and it was dated a few days ago. So there must be another book. One that shows the partial payment."

Dixon shifted his feet, jiggled his teeth. "Oh, yeah. I had one left in an old book, which I used that day."

"What about the partial payment? You just told us you don't take those. Can I see that other book?"

Dixon rolled his eyes and smiled. "My wife threw it out. Anything else?"

Stump scratched his head. "The broker told us you don't allow more than three people to live in a one-bedroom apartment. Is that true?"

"Unless three people already live there and a woman has

a baby. Then we let them stay a few months before they have to get a two-bedroom or move out. Why?"

"We looked at another apartment before you got there. There were six toothbrushes in there."

Dixon glared at Stump. Waited several seconds. "Maybe they brush their teeth a lot."

"But there were extra mattresses on the floor and two different sizes of men's shoes in the closet."

Dixon smirked. "Sometimes people have guests, you know."

Before Stump could ask another question, Myles's cell phone squawked. Myles glanced at the readout. "It's about my mother," he said, mostly to Dixon. "We'll get back to you if we have any more questions."

Dixon rose and glared at Stump, who caught the scowl and suddenly realized he was going to have to work with this man and probably shouldn't have pushed so many buttons. "You keep this place really nice," he said.

CHAPTER 9

A DAY LATER STUMP WAS THINKING about the City Council meeting and was so confused he could have hidden his own Easter eggs. When it came to making older homes safe, he expected more cooperation out of the government, yet the Mayor threw the bulk of the problem right back in Stump's lap. How the hell was a sixteen-year-old kid supposed to make adults fix their homes?

Thankfully, the Mayor had instructed the City Planner to help Stump out, so Stump asked a fairly new friend, James, for a ride to BigBunz's office.

Stump liked James because the guy was an oddball. His dark-rimmed glasses and pale skin lent him a misleading Clark Kent-like nerdish image. They became friends earlier in the year when they registered for tenth grade. James suggested Stump substitute James's phone number and email address for those of Myles's on Stump's registration card. That way if Stump wanted to ditch school, which Stump had only done a couple times in his whole life, the robo-call of the attendance office would go to James instead of to Myles.

James went on to say he would provide Stump's contact info in the same way and as long as they didn't overdo it they could ditch school from time to time and cover for each other. A few weeks later James tested his concept and it worked perfectly.

As Stump and James got to know each other, Stump discovered that James was born in South Africa and had immigrated to America with his parents when James was a toddler. That meant that, in spite of his pale skin, James was both technically and literally an African American. Predictably, James was totally willing to exploit his status. For instance, the previous spring he had snail-mailed a job application to the Parks and Recreation Department. On it he indicated he was an African American student in search of summer work. Apparently, they were interested in diversity because they hired him, sight unseen, to work at the pool for the summer. When he arrived, they were surprised, but he hadn't lied so what could they do?

Now at the municipal building, Stump and James popped out of James's Subaru and headed for the City Planner's office, or BigBunz, as Stump remembered her.

At the reception area a woman was working behind a large, thick window with a hole cut into it. "Help you?" she asked.

"The mayor said I should talk with Mrs. Crumpler," Stump said, assuming that a little namedropping wouldn't hurt. "I'm Neal Randolph."

"Have a seat. I'll tell her you're here."

Stump and James joined a few others in the waiting area, "Just watch," Stump said. "Now that the Mayor's on my side, this woman is going to take me more seriously."

"I dunno, Dude. You said you ratted her out. She might want to teach you a lesson."

They watched people come and go for quite a while until finally James tossed a brochure on the table. "I ain't impressed no more. It's been a half-hour. You'd better check to see what's taking so long."

Stump rubbed the top of his head and approached the check-in window for the second time. "Excuse me," he said more humbly than before, "I asked for Mrs. Crumpler a long time ago."

"I know," the receptionist said, "but she's in a conference. You'll just have to wait."

Back behind the receptionist, a man walked out of a hallway, followed by BigBunz who had a cup of coffee in her hand. Stump pointed. "That's Mrs. Crumpler right there."

The woman checked. "Sure is. Hang on a second. I'll go see if she's free now."

Stump watched as the lady explained the situation to BigBunz, who rolled her eyes and then walked off. The clerk returned to Stump. "She said she'll get to you as soon as she can."

"Did she say how long that'd be?" Stump asked. "My friend has to get home."

"I'm sorry, but she didn't say."

Another fifteen minutes dripped by. Then, "Too bad we don't know which car is hers," James said.

"It's the green one by the entrance where we came in," Stump said. "License plate says *Crumpy*. Has to stand for Crumpler."

James smiled that goofy grin of his. "I have an idea. You sure her phone number is *BigBuns*?"

"Yep. With a Z. Why?"

"You go wait by the back door out of sight so she can't see you and I'll deliver her right to you."

Stump's hands lifted to his waist. "How you gonna do that?"

"You want to talk to her or not?"

Stump sighed. "Nothing else is working. I just hope you know what you're doing." He shuffled out the main entrance and moved to the corner of the building where he could see the employees' entrance on the other side.

It only took five minutes before Mrs. Crumpler darted out the back door and headed right toward her car. At the halfway point, she stopped and looked around like she was lost. Stump had his chance. "Mrs. Crumpler," he said from behind her. "I need to talk to you, like the Mayor said."

James came around the corner grinning and swaggered over to join them.

Crumpler glared at Stump. "Is this your idea of a joke? 'Cause I don't like to be ambushed."

"Well I'm sorry, but people shouldn't have to trick you just to talk with you."

"And I don't have to deal with idealistic children. This is precisely why we changed the regulations so that only serious, older people can address the Council."

"If you would have returned my calls, everything would be easier for both of us."

"I had you on the agenda. That's all I had to do. Now what do you want?"

"I just want to help those people, for my mom, but I don't know how to go about it."

She shifted her weight to one foot. "I was thinking about helping you, but after what you guys just did I'm having second thoughts."

"Please. There has to be something we can do. People are going to die," Stump said, hoping a little hyperbole would reveal how important this was.

Crumpler glanced at James and back to Stump. "You obviously loved your mother. That's the only reason I'm going to tell you this. There might be some small things we can do."

Stump rose to his tiptoes. "Really?"

"Yes, but I'm not going to invest one minute of my time into this unless you get an attorney or a professional community developer to help you. I won't return your calls or meet you in the lobby or anything. I'm not going to hold your hand. Got it?"

"But won't that cost a lot of money?"

"Welcome to the real world, where mommies don't do everything for you. If you want my help, you're going to have to get an attorney and you'll have to do most of the work yourself. If you're like my kids, I'm betting you won't do a damn thing." She stuck a finger to within inches of James's face. "And don't you ever trick me again. Got it?" She turned to walk away.

"You're just a power-hungry bully," James said loud enough that she was sure to hear.

Stump grabbed James's arm. "C'mon, Dude. Didn't you hear her? She's disappointed in her kids. That must suck."

James smirked. "Bullshit. Her kids probably ain't no worse than you or me."

Stump laughed. "That's my point, Dude. How would you like to have a couple kids like us?"

James laughed too and they headed for the Subaru. "How'd you do it?" Stump asked.

"Get her to come outside? Easy. I told her I was a tow truck driver and I was hired to haul her car away for not making payments."

"How'd you know she didn't make a payment?"

"That wasn't the point. I just had to convince her that there was a problem, so I agreed that there must have been a banking error. I said I couldn't leave my truck, but if she'd come show me a payment receipt or a copy of a check, I'd give her a couple days to straighten it out with her bank. You know the rest."

Stump smacked James on the arm. "Wow. That's pretty cagey, Dude."

"Yeah. My mom had one of her co-workers pull that same trick on my dad once, to serve him divorce papers. Asshole deserved it, but what was he going to do, have the guy arrested for impersonating a tow truck driver?"

Stump laughed out loud. "Good for her. I like it when moms win for a change." Stump rubbed the back of his neck. "BigBunz was right, though. I'm in over my head. She ain't going to help me, and I sure as hell can't afford an attorney. The whole thing has gotten too complicated. I think I'm just gonna have to forget about it."

James lifted a fist in the air. "Now we're getting somewhere. Now we can focus on more important things—like this." James lifted his leg and let out a loud fart while simultaneously belching.

Stump about lost it. He'd never heard anybody's orifices work in unison before. "Dude! We should totally make a video of that and put it on YouTube."

CHAPTER 10

After her most recent meeting with her psychiatrist, Delores was feeling more optimistic about her career and more motivated to reel in Dixon Browne. Given that there were going to be high demands on her time and there was still some uncertainty whether Dixon Browne might be dangerous, she asked her boss, Sergeant Byrdswain, who was often referred to as Birdman, what he thought of bringing Myles Cooper into the case strictly as back-up.

It had been three years since the trio met in a professional capacity. At the time, the ink was not yet dry on Delores's criminology degree and most of her time was spent reviewing old case files. Then Myles Cooper called Birdman and said his newly adopted son, Stump, had solved a double murder. Further investigations by the detectives uncovered two additional murders, leaving plenty of good press to spread around.

Now, Birdman welcomed the idea of having another seasoned detective close by, just in case Dixon Browne proved to be violent. Both Birdman and Cooper were at the police building in one of the meeting rooms sucking down coffee when Delores, soda in hand, arrived. Even though protocol was always a concern, she gave Myles a warm hug.

"Well, Sergeant Myles Cooper. How the heck have you been?"

"Not bad for an old dude, Detective. Good to see you again."

"How's Stump?"

Myles snickered. "He's growing up too fast for my liking and too slow for his. He's just about ready to get his driver's license."

"The young ladies better watch out," Byrdswain said.

Delores grinned. "I see he got the doggie park up and running."

"It took all of his reward money but he hung in there. The same woman who donated the money was so impressed she put him in her will. She had no other heirs so she gave him ten percent of her estate. Three mill."

"Well, he deserves it," Delores said.

"I guess so, but he thinks he should have the money anytime he wants it and I'm trying to hold him back so he doesn't get the impression that money is easy to come by."

"Nice problem," Byrdswain said.

Myles shrugged and turned to Delores. "How 'bout you, Detective? You like being a cop?"

"Sometimes I wish I didn't look so young. Certain people don't take me seriously."

Myles grinned. "Is Birdman giving you guff?"

"Naw. He ain't half-bad. I'm talking about the public."

"I assume that has something to do with why you called me?"

"Sure does," Byrdswain said. "Last month a Hispanic woman, named Yolanda Vigil, got pulled over for speeding. She told the officer he had to leave her alone because she had been married to an important man and was about to become a citizen. She handed the officer some suspicious papers, including a crude divorce decree that looked like something a couple entry-level college guys might draw up. So the officer brought her to us for questioning."

"Fraud, huh? That's right up my alley."

Delores scooted some papers aside. "Ms. Vigil wouldn't

say a lot, just that everybody had to leave her alone because she was almost a citizen. I know about the naturalization process and sensed that she had been misled. We had her old address so I popped on over there and spoke with a neighbor. Turns out Ms. Vigil was talking about the manager of an apartment building and the guy had done the same thing with other women. It smelled suspicious so I pretended to be a potential tenant and signed a lease so I could meet the guy and find out what he was up to. There's something really evil going on in that place."

"Evil? Like what?"

Byrdswain tapped a file jacket he'd brought with him. "There's a new rape law—Penal Code 261 says a guy can't coerce or trick a woman into giving consent."

"It's called rape by deception," Delores said.

"You guys lost me," Myles said. "Lots of fellows tell white lies to get women into bed, but what does that have to do with Yolanda Vigil's marriage and divorce?"

"Yolanda is undocumented," Delores said. "Most women in that situation only have a couple ways they can stay in the U.S. *legally*. One is to have a baby. The other is to marry another citizen."

"So you're saying she married the dude so she could stay here, legally. What's wrong with that?"

"It takes three years to become a citizen that way," Delores quickly added. "Yet hubby gave her those bogus walking papers before the first year was up. In spite of all that, Yolanda was convinced she was still on track to become a citizen."

"Hmmm. If there's any crime there, it still sounds like fraud to me."

Delores raised a finger. "But what if we turn things around and look at this from hubby's perspective? He could have been the one who promoted the marriage idea, knowing full well that he'd close out the so-called marriage long before she'd ever become a citizen."

"Why would he do that?"

"We don't know yet, but we can assume he and Yolanda were intimate and if that was the result of him intentionally misleading her about the citizenship issue, her consent doesn't count."

"But, if she married the guy, she surely knew there'd be bed action."

"At least for six friggin' months," Byrdswain said with a scowl on his face.

Myles snickered. "That sounds like the voice of experience, Birdman."

"You don't want to know."

"But it was all under false pretenses," Delores said to Myles. "Now he's got another woman living with him who fits the same profile. Maybe he's pulled the same scam on her. Either way, we've got multiple counts."

Byrdswain leaned in. "Detective Sanchez thinks that makes it 'serial' rape by deception."

"I've never heard of such a thing."

"Like we said," she went on. "This whole concept is new. Only twelve states have laws like it. We're having to figure it out as we go along."

"I gotta admit it's interesting. What does the DA say?"

Delores scoffed. "That's the rub. If you listen to him, you'd think we have no more chance than a worm in a chicken coop. He says it would be impossible to prove that a wife, who knowingly and willingly gives consent, doesn't actually mean it."

Byrdswain nodded. "He prattled on about the hundreds of other cases on our shelves, complete with DNA results, just waiting to be solved."

"But those cases went cold for a reason," Delores said. "And we know who our dirtbag is and what he's doing." She slid her can aside. "I need some time to build our case and to determine if there are accomplices or other bad guys doing the same things."

"I can see you're fired up," Myles said, "but why'd you call me in? I don't have much expertise in this kind of case."

"The DA doesn't think this guy's worth our resources, but I don't want to give up. Birdman is sticking with me so he's going to work our other cases and I'll have to work off the clock sometimes. That leaves us thin. Since you live close by, it'd be nice to have somebody else I can call on if need be."

"As back-up, huh? Sure. What have you done so far?"

Birdman leaned in. "For starters, the dude said he had 'friends' in the department but I checked with the Sheriff and the officers in that district. Nobody has any reason to do extra favors for this guy."

"It was all a bluff," Delores said. "We figured he preys on the naïve and timid ones, so I took on that persona, using an alias and rented one of his apartments. I fed him some crap about a missing brother, and told him I had a low-paying job."

Byrdswain grinned. "He thinks she's 19."

Delores pursed her lips. Then, "See what I mean? I put my real age on the application, but the bastard didn't believe it. Like I said, people don't take me seriously."

Myles lifted his cup. "The fools."

"He's already begun hitting on me. He calls me his Monday Girl. God, he makes me cringe."

"Monday Girl?"

"Yeah. I'm supposed to do whatever he wants on Mondays in exchange for some help with my rent."

"Just Mondays?"

"Apparently. He said he's got somebody else to do his bidding on Wednesdays and Fridays and maybe other days too."

"Wednesday Girl and Friday Girl?"

Delores smirked. "You got it. So far, it's as if I'm auditioning to get laid. I've already had to kiss him but I doubt he's going to stop there." She wiped her mouth. "Gross. Gross. Gross. I gotta fry this damn pig!"

"While Detective Sanchez is doing her homework, we could use another small favor," Byrdswain said. "You L.A. boys have better equipment and more resources than we do. We'd appreciate it if you'd do a background check on him for us. Ours isn't very thorough. See if we've got a Code Five."

"Outstanding warrants, eh? Sure," Myles said, taking his iPhone from his pocket and readying his fingers to take notes. "Who is this bad boy? Where's he live?"

"Name's Dixon Browne. He's at the Cal-Vista apartments."

Myles stopped dead in his tracks and set his iPhone on the table. "No friggin' way. I know that guy. Stump and I were there the other day. We suspected he was cooking the books, but didn't suspect anything like this. The owner of the building even offered Stump a job."

Both Byrdswain and Delores perked up. "Did he take it?" she asked.

"You don't know the half of it."

CHAPTER 11

IN THE OFFICE OF DR. JEANINE MORENO, Delores eased into the same high-back chair as before. She removed her shoes and observed Dr. Moreno's fingernails. "I looked forward to this meeting because it's one of the few places I can drop the formalities and simply be Delores."

"Welcome back," the doctor said. "How are you doing this week?"

"A little better, but I'm still confused about some things."

"Have you had an opportunity to work on the IMT technique we learned?"

"Undercover work can get pretty boring, so I tried it a few times. It was both helpful and scary."

"How so?"

"It made me face some things that I didn't really want to think about?"

Jeanine nodded. "Sometimes that's what we need."

"You know something, Jeanine? I hope you don't mind if I change the subject, but the last time I was in here, I noticed your fingernails. Now, they're completely different but equally as beautiful. Do you mind if I take a closer look?"

"Of course not," Jeanine said, holding out her hands.

Delores delicately cradled the doctor's remarkably smooth hands in her own scruffy cop-hands. The left thumbnail was pearl white with a small red heart painted in the center. All the remaining nails were of the same deep red, but two nails had small pink hearts painted in them. Delores shook her head. "They're lovely. Who does them for you?"

"My girls and I work on them together. The red heart is my husband. The pink ones are the girls."

"You're so lucky to have such a special family."

"Well, thank you. I'm glad you like them. Getting back to where we left off the last time you were here, you said you were the only person who could understand Dixon Browne's victims. I wanted to ask you what you meant by that but we ran out of time."

Delores cringed. She'd been hiding a couple big secrets from everybody for a long time. She didn't like to think about either one of them, let alone discuss them. On the other hand, Jeanine was both smart and easy to talk to. Delores rose and stared out the window for a long moment. Finally, she said, "I suspected we'd get around to my childhood sooner or later, but I didn't think it would come up so quickly."

"You didn't come here just to examine fingernails, right?"

"I dunno, Jeanine," Delores said while pressing her hand along her thigh. "Maybe down deep, that's really what I wanted to talk about."

"It's up to you."

Delores grabbed her pillow, leaned back into her chair and sighed. "When I was young, everything was bad. I lived with my older sister, Simone, and Grandma, along with Mama and Tio."

"Tio? Doesn't that mean *uncle*?"

"Technically he was our stepfather, but when Simone was little she couldn't say *padrastro* so mama just said he was Tio—but that wasn't correct either because we should have called him Tio Carlos—which still wouldn't be correct because he's a stepfather, not an uncle. See what I mean when I say everything is screwed up?"

Jeanine smiled. "People frequently assign convenient nicknames to family members. So, did you all get along?"

Delores's clammy fingers trembled as if she were a witness in a high-profile case and had just been asked to betray God, himself. She pulled her pillow toward her. "Tio molested Simone and me."

Jeanine's eyebrows squeezed down. "I'm so sorry, Delores. That must have been awful."

"He started sneaking into our room at night when Simone was ten and I was seven. He must have thought I was too young at first, because he'd been groping Simone for a long time before I knew about it."

Jeanine clucked her tongue.

"He told Simone that everybody did the same thing but nobody was allowed to talk about it. Naturally Simone believed him. Then one night when I was eleven and Simone was staying with friends, I felt his hands on me." Delores's tear ducts activated. "I still remember how ugly he looked with his ultra-thick eyebrows. I tried to pull away, but he held me down and told me to keep quiet or he'd hurt Mama."

Jeanine rose and retrieved a tissue box from the cluttered side of the room. "I'm so sorry, Delores," she said, holding out the box.

Delores snagged several tissues and patted both her eyes. "I pretended I was being examined by angels so they would recognize me when I got to heaven. When I finally got the nerve to say something to Simone she said the same thing had been happening to her."

"That must have been absolutely horrific for both of you."

"It wasn't over yet," Delores said, wiping away more tears. "Simone was ashamed of herself. She said if she'd said something to Mama earlier maybe Tio would have left us both alone. The next morning we confronted Mama."

"How did that work out?"

"Mama said even if it were true, there wasn't anything

she could do about it because Tio was the only person who could support us. Mama made us promise not to bring it up again, so we mostly pretended it never happened. After that, Tio slowed down some but he still came around once a month or so. Finally, about two years later Simone woke me in the middle of the night. She was fourteen and crying. This time Tio had raped her. Simone said if she didn't leave, he'd keep doing the same thing to her, and sooner or later he'd want me. She decided to run away and wanted me to go with her, but I was only eleven, Jeanine. I was too scared to leave and too scared to stay. The next morning when I woke up, my beautiful sister was gone." Delores lifted her hands to her face and sobbed.

"Let it go, Delores. Let it go."

Delores squeezed her pillow and cried tears she'd been holding back for too long. Finally she lifted her head and blew her nose. "Tio stopped touching me after that. Mama must have figured out what happened, but nobody talked about it for all the remaining years that I lived there."

"Simply awful," Jeanine said softly.

"I still don't know where my sister is. I've tried to find her but she didn't have a social security number. She could have a new name now."

"What about your grandmother? Did she know what was going on?"

"I don't think so. That's another one of my problems. Nobody has ever told me anything. All I knew for certain was Tio had all the power and I felt helpless and lonely. I cried myself to sleep lots of nights. I told myself over and over again that if I ever had a chance, I would get even. I think that was one reason I became a detective."

"Where are your mama and Tio now?"

"Grandma is in heaven, but Mama and Tio live in El Centro. I don't see them very much. Too many deep wounds and I don't want to hurt Mama. I've tried to get over what happened, but I never could, especially losing Simone."

"I'd guess not. Can you tell me how all this affected you in your later years?"

Delores sucked down another deep breath. Discussing her past actually made her feel a little better. "I've always had a difficult time trusting men, which isn't fair to them or me."

"That must be difficult, especially considering the last time we met when you said you'd like to be married and have children someday."

Delores scoffed. "Who'd marry a train wreck like me? Whenever I find a nice guy and we begin to get serious, all those horrible memories haunt me and I sabotage everything in ways I don't even want to talk about."

"We can get back to that later. For now, I'm still curious about how all this came to a head. I take it Dixon Browne reminds you of Tio?"

"He's even worse."

"Worse?"

"I don't think he molests children, but he's been doing bad things to several vulnerable women that I know of and I'm the only one who knows how it feels to be manipulated like that."

"So you plopped yourself right in the middle of the very activities you hate so you could protect other women from the exact same feelings you had?"

Delores nodded her head. "Dumb, huh?"

"Noble and unselfish where the words that occurred to me."

PING!

"Darn," Jeanine said. "That bell always seems to go off too soon. Would you like to know what I think before you go, or did you just want to vent?"

Delores sighed. "Am I totally hopeless, Jeanine?"

"You're like the string in a beaded necklace. You're trying to hold everything together but the beads are too heavy. Meanwhile you can't get revenge on Tio without hurting your mother so you've found an alternative. We call that *transference*."

"Transference? I'm a disaster."

"Another thing. You keep blaming yourself, but none of this is your fault. The first thing you need to do is get your self-loathing under control."

"I'll try, Jeanine, but it won't be easy."

"It never is, but as challenging as your work situation is right now, I'm more concerned about the pent-up feelings you've never faced regarding your family and your personal life. Unlike your cases, which come and go, these issues are going to be with you until you fix them. Until then, I don't think you'll ever be able to function properly in any phase of your life. Does that make sense?"

"Are you saying I ought to level with Mama about Tio raping Simone? 'Cause, I'm not even sure she'd believe me."

"Could you do that?"

"I don't exactly know, Jeanine. How do you tell your mama something like that?"

"I'll leave that up to you, but remember this: Regardless of what you choose to do, it's usually better to be kind than correct."

Delores's skin tingled. As before, she'd been at Jeanine's office less than an hour and somehow Jeanine helped her understand some of her core thoughts and feelings. Maybe someday she could confide in Jeanine about her other issue: the black cloud behavior that couldn't possibly be healthy.

CHAPTER 12

Stump was well on his way to the fifty practice-hours he needed to convert his driving permit into a full-blown license, and Sunday enabled him to knock off another big block. He and Myles were twelve miles from the canyon where Stump's assistant principal died several years earlier before Myles had to issue any pointers. "Keep a closer eye on the speedometer," Myles said. "It's easy to go too fast on highways."

Stump let off the gas. "You still going to Oklahoma to see Grandma Pauline?"

"Yep. Tomorrow. That is if you can get by without me."

Of course he could. He'd probably have James come over and they could call some girls. "You've gone on short trips before and it always worked out."

"Alright then, but I want you to be extra careful, especially on that job of yours. If you find it dangerous for any reason, just get out of there. Okay?"

"Dangerous? Why would that job be dangerous?"

"I'm just sayin'." Myles pointed to the speedometer. "You're going ten over, again."

As they moved up the hills and around curves, Myles offered Stump fatherly pointers about driving on curves and near big trucks. Stump doubted if all dads taught their sons those things.

After they reached the top they drifted along for a few quiet miles before Stump said, "There it is," and pulled into the small parking area. They walked the gravel path that led to the viewing platform from which Ms. Johnson was pushed. From the far corner, they could see half-way to forever where the early morning clouds rested on the horizon like a stack of giant cotton balls. Down below, a pair of red-tailed hawks lazily glided in the upwind along the canyon wall. On the desert floor a blend of cacti, green foliage and sandstone seemed to be modeling for a painting. "This is the exact spot," Stump said as he leaned over the edge of the handrail.

"Let me ask you something," Myles said. "What would you say if I suggested you forget about that job and look for something else?"

"No way. I need that money," He turned his head. "Unless you'll let me grab a few grand from my trust."

"You know better than that. But there must be something else you can do."

"There's nothing out there, Dude, except drive-through joints and they don't pay as much." Stump spit over the handrail and watched his saliva ball race to the bottom. "Why are we having this dumb conversation, anyway? The other day, you thought that gig was thumbs up."

"I know, but I got to thinking you might learn more somewhere else."

"Learn more? I'm looking for big bucks, not more school."

"Well, okay. But I want you to be careful. I don't trust that Dixon guy. And keep looking, just in case something better shows up."

"Yeah, yeah. You know something? All you government people are weird."

"Just because I want you to be safe?"

"Not that. James and I tried to get some information from the City Planner. She made us wait for over an hour before she finally said she wouldn't even help me unless I hire an expensive attorney. She was purposely making it harder."

"It seems like that sometimes. Maybe it's for the better. Even if you get your program approved, most of the people in that area will be grandfathered in."

"Yeah. They said something about that. What is that anyway?"

"Usually, new rules only apply to remodels and new homes. They don't go back to existing homes and make those people do anything. It's not fair."

"What? Then what good is it to go through all this shit if they're not going to fix the houses that need it the most?"

"You never know. After you bring the matter to everybody's attention some people may do just what you want on their own. Sometimes you have to travel the road before you find out what's at the end of it."

"That's just stupid. Besides, they're changing the rules in a few months so I'll be too young to address them again until I'm twenty-one. I don't need their bullshit." Stump spat again, watched his spitball splatter off jagged rocks.

"What about your particular councilman?" Myles asked. "He might be able to help."

"That Barella guy? He looked like a penguin in his black suit and white shirt. How's he gonna help?"

Myles shrugged. "Zig Ziglar said you can get anything you want if you just give enough other people what they want. What would you think a councilman would want?"

"I dunno. They looked like they wanted power."

"Bingo! And you're in his district."

"So? I can't vote."

Myles grinned. "No, but all those people in that neighborhood can. Maybe you can get him some good will in the area in exchange for what you need."

"Me? How'm I supposed to do that? It's all gotten too hard. Not worth it."

"Suit yourself. At least you're starting to figure out that life isn't always easy."

The pace back down the winding road was slower than it was coming up. Even if Stump could get the laws changed, the grandfather thing would kick in so there was no telling if anybody would make their homes safer or not. Who wanted to piss away all that time and energy if nobody gave a damn? It was no use. He might as well face it. The whole idea was stupid. If his mom were alive, she'd understand why he decided to forget the matter. Besides, BigBunz made a good point: Moms don't expect much from their kids. Screw it. He exhaled and felt enormous relief knowing he could move on and focus on making money.

Eventually, they reached the edge of Palmdale where Myles said, "We have a few extra minutes. I need to talk with one of the neighbors over by your mom's old place for a bit."

"Sure," Stump said, newly contented. A few minutes later, he made the final turn onto his old block. "Which neighbor?"

"The Murphys."

Stump nodded. The Murphys lived right next door to Stump's old home. He drove past their house and the vacant lot where his house used to be. Then he turned around and parked in front of the lot. Just as they got out Myles's phone rang.

"Cooper, here." Myles listened. Then, "Can you hold for a second?" He turned to Stump. "It's about my mom. I'm going to have to take this." Stump nodded.

As Myles walked slowly down the street discussing his mother's situation, Stump looked back toward the weeds that had overtaken his former front yard. He eased toward a thin glimmering object that was poking up through the weeds. He kicked at it and loosened a mangled lid to a shoebox-sized metal box that his mom had kept in the laundry room.

The crumpled box stirred up memories of his mom and the laundry room where the fire started. None of that would have happened if he'd removed all his puzzle magazines and the other old papers out of there like he was supposed to, but he couldn't be bothered. If he'd just done that one simple thing, she'd still be alive. That lone mistake was the key link in a chain reaction that sent flames into the center hall and blocked his mother's only escape route. The bars on the windows foiled her last chance, and...

Unwanted tears crowded the corners of Stump's eyes. Boots of guilt stirred inside him. Ashamed once again, he walked deeper into the lot where the living room once was. His mind flashed to when he was in grade school and stole a Christmas tree and plunked it right in front of the picture window so the neighbors would know that the Randolphs had a tree, too. A half-smile visited his lips as he remembered how mad his mom was when she made him take that tree back. Now, he was proud of her. The tears in his eyes escaped and rolled down his cheek.

He took a few more steps toward where his mother's bedroom was. Still more tears dripped down his face as he thought about how much she loved her private bubble baths surrounded by lilac-scented candles. Candles reminded him of flames and flames reminded him of that damn sky-high inferno again.

He commanded his mind to stop sending those God-awful images, but the more he tried to forget, the more he remembered. More tears reminded him of her smoke-stained cheeks when she eventually choked to death right before him. He'd never forgotten the horror in her eyes as she mouthed "I love you" as she fell for the final time, just two feet away, on the other side of unforgiving bars. Her last gasps must have been pure torture and it was his fault. He kicked the weeds. God, how he missed her. A stomach full of angry boots stomped harder than ever. Stop thinking about it. Can't. Thump. Thump. Thump. Louder. Louder. He covered his ears but the damn boots kept marching.

Stop it. Stop it. Stop it. But it kept getting worse. He fell to his knees and wept openly. "I'm so sorry, Mom. I'm so damn sorry."

A hand gently rested on his shoulder. "It wasn't your fault, Stump," Myles said softly.

Stump shook his head and faced the only man he'd ever

loved. "Yes, it was, Myles," he said through sobs of regret and all that was left to do was embrace and cry together in the weeds over the special woman they'd both lost.

CHAPTER 13

Yesterday's visit to the vacant lot had ripped the scabs off Stump's heart. The only way to escape his perpetual guilt was to draw something substantial from the ashes of his mother's death. Last night he called James and advised him to expect a robo-call from school.

Now it was Monday morning and Myles had taken the bus from Palmdale to LAX, from which he planned to fly to Oklahoma to see his mom. When the business day began, Stump placed a call.

"*Michael Barella's office.*"

"Hello, this is Neal Randolph. I need to meet with the councilman today if possible."

"*Regarding?*"

"He knows me. I've got a plan to help him in the upcoming elections."

"*Please hold. I'll see if he's available.*" Moments later she returned. "*He's pretty busy today, Mr. Randolph, but he said he can squeeze you in for a few minutes between ten and ten-fifteen. Will that do?*"

"Totally. Tell him I'll be there." Thrilled, Stump scanned his phone records before he called Mr. Irv Wedlock, a reporter for the local TV network. Mr. Wedlock had run a brief news story about Stump after Stump solved the murder of his assistant principal.

"*KCLA TV. Can I help you?*"

"Yes. I need to speak with Irv Wedlock. This is Neal Randolph. He might remember me as Stump."

"*He's busy right now, Mr. Randolph,*" the receptionist said, "*but I can get a message to him.*"

"It's very important that he calls me later in the morning, at exactly ten-ten."

"*Exactly ten-ten?*" She chuckled. "*Alright. I'll let him know, but no promises.*"

"Tell him it's important."

"*Okay. I get it.*"

With those issues resolved, Stump did a quick Google search for a lame store that sold lame bicycle tires for lame bikes named Ol' Ug'. He'd have to get by there after his meeting with Barella.

After a quick shower, Stump slipped into Myles's bedroom and borrowed the spare keys to the truck. He'd never done anything like that before, but somebody once said you have to break a few eggs to make an omelet. He was supposed to have an older licensed rider with him whenever he was behind the wheel, but he'd just have to sit up tall to avoid attracting attention.

The cab seemed bigger and colder without Myles. Stump's hands shook as he inserted the key. Let's see. Slide the seat forward. Adjust the mirrors. Turn the key. Instant noise. Country music sucks. Turn radio off. Thank God. Twist key again. Nothing. What the hell's the matter? Oh, yeah. Foot on brake. Try again. It started. Cool. Ready for his very first solo ride, he shifted into Drive and grinned as the transmission engaged.

Alright now. Keep foot on brake. Both hands on wheel. Check side mirror. All clear. Here goes. He cautiously lifted his foot off the brake and inched out of the parking lot and onto the street where he gracefully accelerated. The nearest car was fifty yards back. Cool. Cool. Cool. He'd made it.

Ding! Ding! Ding!

What the—Ding! Ding!

Damn. Flashing light on dash. Ding! Ding! Can't pull over here. Ding! Ding! Need a driveway. Ding! Ding! There's one. Ding! Pull in. Ding! Damn it. Ding! Stop the truck. Ding! Ding! Buckle seat belt. Whew!

Back on the street, it all came back to him. He stayed within the speed limit, used his blinkers, checked his mirrors regularly and looked over his shoulder when changing lanes. At the next light he rolled down his window and turned the radio to something decent. Gotta remember to turn it back to the stupid country station.

He checked himself out in the mirror. Driving was cool. Too cool for school.

At the councilman's office, it took him a few gyrations forward and back to wiggle the truck into a parking spot. More confident now, he checked his phone. Eight minutes early. He found the suite and the receptionist. "I'm Neal Randolph. I've got an appointment."

"C'mon in, Stump," he heard from off to his side. As before, Councilman Barella was dressed sharply. "No school today?" he asked as they sat on opposite sides of Barella's desk.

Stump shook his head. "I got to do a couple things."

The councilman raised his eyebrows. "I don't have much time. What's on your mind?"

"Yesterday, I visited the lot where my mother passed away. Now, I'm more determined than ever to make something good come from what happened to her."

"I'm already inclined to vote for your idea, if that's what you're wondering."

"Thanks, but my problem has to do with the procedures. They keep making a big deal out of the paperwork. Is it really that important to get an attorney?"

Barella nodded. "Afraid so."

"That's the problem. My dad said an attorney might charge three thousand dollars to do all the work. I can't afford that much money."

"I can't pay it for you, if that's what you're getting at."

Stump shook his head. "I have another idea. I was hoping you'd run an ad on Craigslist and get me a probe bonel attorney."

Barella grinned. "It's called *pro bono*, but why would I do that?"

"'Cause you'll both get exposure. I already know what to say in the ad. '*Pro bono attorney wanted for community project. Make a name for yourself around City Hall. Better than free advertising*'."

Barella nodded. "I can see how that helps you and this mystery attorney, but what's in it for me?"

"There's an election coming up. I was thinking you could make up some brochures that tell people that we're making homes safer and mail them to everybody in the area. Show them that you're fighting for them. Then they'll vote for you."

Barella crinkled his brows. "I don't—"

Stump's ringtone interrupted. "Oops, sorry. I should've turned off my phone." He looked at the readout and back to Barella. "It's a reporter from KCLA TV."

Barella sat back in his gigantic leather chair and locked his hands behind his head. "Then you'd better take it."

"Thanks." Stump pressed the button, "Hello?"

He paused. "Good to talk to you again too, Mr. Wedlock." He listened again. Then, "Trying to get better safety codes where my mom lived, but it's not a good time to talk right now. I'm with Councilman Barella. Sure will...Okay. Yes, sir. Will do...'Bye." Stump hung up and turned to Barella. "Mr. Wedlock said hello."

Barella nodded. "What was that about?"

Stump had learned when he and James met with BigBunz that sometimes a partial fib was needed. "Phone tag. He saw my name in the newest Gazette after the previous meeting and remembered me from three years ago. He wanted to know what I'm up to—for a human interest story."

"Oh really? That's interesting."

"They're thinking of sending a camera crew to the next meeting. He wants me to keep him posted."

"I see." Barella tapped the newspaper on his desk. "Getting back to our discussion, I understand how much your mother meant to you and I want to help out, so here's what I'd be willing to do. I'll see if I can get you a free attorney. I'll also get some brochures printed up like you suggested, but instead of mailing them, I'd like you to hand-deliver them, door to door."

Stump groaned. "But I have school—and a job. I don't have time—"

"Has to be that way," Barella said. "It's a lot cheaper and marketing is way more effective when it's face-to-face."

"But my time? I'm already too busy."

"We all are. That's the deal, Stump. Take it or leave it." Barella rose and rested his hand on Stump's shoulder. "It's your mother's honor we're talking about here."

Indeed it was. "Deal."

After his meeting with Barella, Stump had one more project. He stopped by a bicycle shop and grabbed a pair of pudgy all-black tires for Ol' Ug'. At home, he returned the truck's radio to the stupid country station and imagined people stomping through fields of cow pies and saying dumb-ass things like dad-burned.

He dragged Ol' Ug' out of the storage closet and shook his head. The three-speed clunker used to be maroon, but it had faded down to a combination of rust and flat gray primer paint, making it uglier than a show dog's anus; on the other hand, it could get him to his job where every hour meant ten bucks, times three.

After he straightened out the bulbous fenders, which looked like something that a nine-year-old girl would use, it took him all afternoon to get the rusty bolts loosened and everything slammed back together. Finally, he stood the two-wheeled mass of ugliness right-side up, set the kickstand and stepped back. It couldn't have looked more ridiculous if it had a white wicker basket, a ringer bell and pretty pink tassels.

CHAPTER 14

Later that afternoon Stump and Ol' Ug' rolled into Cal-Vista. He used an old pair of Myles's handcuffs to attach the bike and his helmet to the rack.

Mr. Kraft's office, which was actually a one-bedroom apartment that had been converted, was on the lower level of building six. Kraft was behind his desk in what was once the living room when Stump arrived. Cell phone at his ear, Kraft motioned for Stump to have a seat.

A collection of folders, legal pads and magazines laid claim to the top of Kraft's desk. The remainder of the room had some bookcases, a sofa and a couple small tables. About all Stump could see in the former bedroom was some file cabinets and a copier.

A crumpled, not-very-clean pillow leaned up against the arm of one end of the sofa, suggesting that Mr. Kraft used the sofa for naps. Stump laid his backpack on the floor and sat at the other end. On the coffee table there was a single medical magazine with a lead article titled "Dealing with CINV." Stump's mind automatically converted the letters to the digits on a phone pad—2,4,6,8—and grinned, thinking, *who do we appreciate?*

While he waited for Mr. Kraft, Stump wondered what he would have to do. Mow the yard? Pull weeds? Didn't matter much, just so long as he got ten bucks an hour, times three, toward a car.

"I'll see you then." Kraft said to his caller before hanging up. He turned to Stump. "Right on time, I see. How was the trip?"

"The bike's lame, but it's better than walking."

"Good attitude. Someday you'll appreciate what you had to do to get a car. Did you guys find a building to buy?"

"Not really, but we weren't in a hurry. We liked this one, but to be honest, there were a couple things that bothered us."

"Oh? Like what?"

Stump kicked lightly at his backpack. "I'm not sure I should say."

"Go ahead. You won't hurt my feelings."

"Well, for one thing, we think there's extra people living in some of the apartments."

"What gives you that idea?"

"Too many toothbrushes and mattresses. We asked the manager about it, but he didn't have a good answer."

Mr. Kraft lifted his shoulders slightly. "Anything else?"

"My dad was wondering about the open account at Home Depot. What stops the manager from buying things and then taking them back for cash refunds and keeping the money?"

"Dixon wouldn't do that. We've known each other too long." Kraft cupped his hands around his mouth and lowered his voice. "Don't tell the broker I told you this, but I think you made the correct choice. It's difficult to manage apartments in this economy. Gets harder every year."

Stump's fingers dug into his palm. "What happens if you sell your building? Do I still have a job?"

"I wouldn't worry about that. There's always plenty of work for smart and energetic people."

"What about the manager? I don't think he likes me after the things I asked him."

"You just report to me. I come and go, but I'm usually here around this time. I'll work up a list of projects I want you to do, but if I'm not here and he asks you to do something, go ahead and do it. But if neither of us gives you anything specific to do, you can always refer to the list or pull weeds out by the fence." Kraft grabbed a key from his desk drawer. "This'll get you into this office. There's nothing special in here, but you can drop off your backpack or use the restroom."

"When's payday?"

Kraft grinned, "Every other week." He handed Stump a legal pad. "Use this to keep track of your hours. You know anything about painting?"

"A little." Truth was, all he'd ever done along those lines was remove some graffiti when he got caught stealing liquor. Oh, well. He'd just fake it.

A half-hour later, Stump had a new tarp under a section of wrought iron fence encircling the pool. He dunked his three-inch brush deep into the can so it could absorb as much paint as possible; then, he quickly flung the drenched brush to the top of one of the bars and essentially slapped the drooling paint on the bars as it raced to the bottom, ending up with more polka dots on the tarp than a leopard's hide.

He dipped again and again, slopping just as much paint on the tarp as the bars. Then, just when he was making some decent progress, "That's a weird way to paint," a female voice said from behind him. He pivoted his head to see a Hispanic girl, about his age.

"You scared the heck out of me," he said.

"I'm sorry. I didn't mean to."

He wiped his hands on his pants. Looked closer. She was sorta cute. Dark hair, honey-colored skin, lady-parts big enough to need a bra.

She pointed toward the corner of the parking lot. "You have a funny-looking bicycle."

Who the hell does she think she is? He would have liked to tell her off but he'd said worse things about Ol' Ug'. "Better than walking."

She pointed to building three. "I just put our last load of clothes in the dryer. I thought I'd say hi while I wait."

"I can't talk now. I'm supposed to get this fence painted."

She rested a hand on her hip. "If you'd slow down a little, you'd get more paint on the rails and less on your clothes and everything else."

What the hell did she mean by that? Then he felt it. His belly was wet and sticky. There was a shiny black spot about the size of a basketball covering the front of his shirt. Most of the rest of him had accumulated a collection of shiny blobs and splatters too. "You think you could do better?"

"At least I know you don't hold a paintbrush like a hammer. You got a smaller one?"

Stump clucked his tongue and pointed to the box he'd placed across the sidewalk on the grassy area. "Yeah, the wimpy, girly ones are over there."

She crossed over and glanced in the box. "Your brush should only be a little bigger than the bars." She pulled out a one-incher. "Like this one."

Stump nearly laughed in her face. He didn't need no stinking girl telling him how to paint. His way was good enough. The paint was getting onto the bars. That's the important thing. He looked at his shirt again and his spotted legs and his shoes and the hundreds of paint droplets he'd left on Mr. Kraft's new tarp. Dammit. Just as before, when she said his bike was funny looking, she was right. He'd made a mess of it all.

"If you use a lighter one like this," she continued while approaching one of the bars, "you can hold it in the tips of your fingers, more like a pencil. Then only dip the lower third of the bristles into the paint."

Stump raised his hand to examine the black brush-of-death he'd been dipping all the way to the top of the bristles. He recalled the excess paint that swooshed over his hand like a shiny black waterfall when he held the paint-filled brush with the bristles facing up and hurried the brush down the bars. "I like to go faster, so I put more paint on my brush."

She grinned. "And everywhere else. Here, let me show you." She knelt down and dabbed a modest amount of paint on the bottom of one of the bars. "After you've got it started, you add new paint to the dry area just above the wet paint and drag it toward the wet area that you already painted. Always go from dry to wet. That way you cut down on brush strokes, get an even distribution, and it dries properly." She looked up.

He had to admit she knew more about it than he did. "I guess your way is almost as good."

"No mess either."

Wow. She didn't even need a tarp. He smiled. "My name's Stump."

"Stump? Is that your real name?"

Was she going to criticize that too? "No. It's Neal if you must know."

She tilted her head toward her shoulder, "Well, I like Stump better. It's original. My name's Maria."

Flirting! She was actually flirting. Just when Stump looked his absolute worst a rad girl came out of nowhere and went out of her way to put some moves on him. He already hoped he'd have another chance to see her when he didn't look so ridiculous.

Before he could think of what to say he heard sandals flapping towards them. He turned to see Dixon Browne march right into their space and glance at Stump's clothes and the tarp. "You call that painting?" he said. "It's a good thing you don't work for me 'cause I'd fire your ass and give this job to somebody who knows what they're doing, not some spoiled rich kid."

"I gotta go," Maria said as she set down her brush on Stump's paint can.

"Good idea," Dixon said. He turned back toward Stump then aimed his jaw toward the bike rack. "That your bike with the handcuffs on it?"

Maria stood behind Dixon's back, facing Stump. She opened and closed her mouth like a ventriloquist's dummy, mocking Dixon's loose-fitting false teeth. Stump damn near laughed out loud. "My dad said I could use them to lock the bike up."

"That's a laugh. Who'd want to steal that pile of rust?" Dixon spit some goo onto the grass. "The way I see it, you're the one who's a thief for taking a job that somebody else needs."

Dixon was clearly trying to provoke Stump, but Stump couldn't risk losing thirty bucks per hour. He ignored the bait.

"Don't you know there are people around here who could have used that money to feed their families?"

"Well, I need money too."

"Oh, yeah. Did your rich daddy refuse to buy you some Gummy Bears?"

One good uppercut would airmail those teeth of his back to wherever they come from, but he said, "I need money to buy a car."

"Yeah. Good luck with that. How much the old man paying you anyway?"

Stump picked up the brush Maria had placed on the paint can and dipped it into the paint as Maria suggested. "That's personal."

"Whatever it is, it would have made a huge difference to a workingman trying to pay his rent and feed his babies. Now he won't have that chance. How's that make you feel?"

Stump shifted his weight. For the third time in fifteen minutes somebody else's version of the truth made him uncomfortable. Dixon was right. Considering the deal Stump had cut with Myles, he was making way more than a family man would get to do the same job. On top of that, he had several million bucks stashed away in the Milky Way Trust. For the first time in his life, Stump felt guilty for having too much money, especially compared to people who had kids to feed. On the other hand, he only had a quarter in his pocket. "I'm sorry for those people, but I need this job too."

Dixon scoffed. "This ain't no place for children." He pointed to Stump's shirt. "The old man deserves what he gets for hiring a pig."

As Dixon walked away, Stump looked toward building three. Maria was standing behind one of the lower windows. She waved. Stump grinned and delicately dipped the smaller paintbrush in the can. He held it up to show her it wasn't dripping and mouthed the words *thank you*.

CHAPTER 15

THE NEXT COUPLE OF DAYS Stump painted more and more of the wrought iron fence and chatted with Maria whenever she swung by, but he was fed up with Dixon Browne's snide comments.

Then, on Wednesday, Maria must have watched for him to finish his work for the day because she was waiting on one of the picnic tables near the pool when he checked out. "Well. I see you didn't get as much paint on that T-shirt as you did on the one you wore the other day."

Happy to see her, he wondered why women paid so much attention to other people's clothes. "I had a good teacher," he said as he sat across from her.

"By now, you're probably planning on becoming a professional painter."

"I haven't really thought about a career all that much, but I'm pretty good with puzzles."

"Puzzles? Like what?"

"License plates and phone numbers. When I look at either one, I can convert the numbers to letters and see hidden words."

"What good is that?"

He snickered. "One time it helped me catch two killers, that's all."

Maria smirked and put her hand to her chin. "You know something? I think you're just making that up to impress me. You're hoping I'll let you kiss me."

"Wrong."

"So, you don't want to kiss me?"

"What? No. Wait. I didn't mean that. Of course I want to do what you said, but I was talking about the murders. You can look it up or talk to my dad or even Mr. Kraft. They all know about it. I saw some bad guys dump a big crate in a dumpster and remembered their license plate. It was Oreo cookies."

"That's silly. What did cookies have to do with anything?"

"Easy. Silly things are easier to remember. Sometimes I change numbers into letters and see words that are easier to remember than the numbers."

She was staring at him as if he were one of those wacky nerds on *The Big Bang Theory*. "Honest," he said. "I really did memorize their license plate and told the cops. They used my tip to arrest a lady who was in on four murders altogether." Now that he thought about it, it sounded sorta unbelievable to him, too. "You have to believe me. I wouldn't lie to you."

Maria gazed at him. "I guess that is pretty good. You're smart. You should go to college."

Whew. She believed him. "Is that what you're going to do—go to college?"

"I think so," she said, tilting her head from side to side. "Mama says it's okay, but we don't have no money."

"Well, there are community colleges and grants and scholarships."

"I was thinking about becoming a community organizer, like the President, only I don't really know what they do. I'd just like to help people."

"I don't know if you have to go to college for that. What about your dad? Can he help?"

"I never got to meet him. Mama said he died fighting drug lords in Mexico just before I was born."

"Wow. A real hero. That must make you proud."

"Sure it does. What about your papa?"

"That's something you and I have in common. I never met my dad either. Mom said I was an accident. You know a mistake that some women make. She didn't know much about him and never really wanted to find out. She said it would just complicate things. Finally, she met Myles. After she died he adopted me."

"I like people who are nice to children."

Children? Is that what she thought of him? "I wasn't no child. I was already thirteen, and I'm sixteen now and getting a car real soon."

Maria straightened up "You are? That's rad. When can we go for a ride?"

"As soon as I save up the money."

Her head lowered slightly. "Oh."

"You sound disappointed."

"I am. You said you're getting a car *real soon*, but you're not. You have to work first. Save up the money. That's going to take a long time. You know something? I think this is just another one of your made-up stories to impress me so I'll let you kiss me."

"No it's not. I promise. I'm working to get something that will just get me by for a while but after that I'll have a really, really, really cool car, and lots of money."

If her rolled eyes had gone any higher they might have spun into orbit.

"I mean it," he said. "I own the Milky Way Trust."

She shook her head mockingly, "What's that?"

Time to really impress her. "Just millions of dollars. That's what." Her eyes flashed over his shoulder, indicating she hadn't even heard about his mysterious fortune.

"I hate that guy," she said.

"What guy?" Stump turned to see Dixon Browne across the courtyard. "Oh. I get it. I don't like him either."

"Really? We're a lot alike. I think I'll make you my crushboy."

"Crushboy? You're not going to try to crush me are you, because I might hurt you."

"Not that, silly. It's a term girls use to explain their relationships. First you meet somebody, then you get a crush on him, then you let him kiss you, then he becomes your boyfriend, then you get engaged, then married, then one of you has an affair and then you get divorced."

Divorced? Jumpin' Jesus!!! Stump didn't even know this girl's last name yet, and already she was planning their divorce.

"Okay. You can kiss me, but make it quick. Mama's waiting for me."

CHAPTER 16

ALONE, STUMP CLOSED THE BATHROOM DOOR and turned on the fan so nobody in the nearby apartments could hear him. He considered turning off the light too just to enhance the mood, but that would be too dark. He slid the stepstool to the front of the vanity and climbed up one step where the middle of the mirror was within easy reach.

He assumed that other people had practiced kissing mirrors too, but even if they didn't it had to be the kind of skill that girls, especially Maria, would appreciate if their kisses were to escalate beyond the quick peck by the pool. He straightened his shoulders.

From a foot back he focused on his lips, imagining he was kissing Maria as he alternated between relaxing his lips and then pressing them together. Relaxed lips equaled fluffy; pressed together lips looked like he'd just choked down some broccoli. Relaxed was better.

Still back from the mirror, he tilted his head to the side. Then farther. Then back to center. What if he got into some super-serious Frenching? He opened his mouth all the way. If he looked back there far enough it reminded him of a miniature cave with a single stalactite hanging down. What was that thing for anyway? He'd check Google later.

Okay, he'd made a decision. If he opened his mouth in mid-kiss, it wouldn't be all the way.

He stuck out the pointy tip of his tongue, swung it slowly from side to side like a horizontal dimmer switch. Not that much, dummy, she'd never have her tongue way over there. He crept it forward a little and rolled the edges upwards. Couldn't imagine why Maria might like that—unless she rolled her tongue too. Did girls do that? Why was he salivating? He grinned.

Just how far could he stick his tongue out there anyway? He inched it out a bit, then a little more until his stalactite thing hurt. He stretched his tongue upwards, tried to touch it to his nose—then back toward his toes. Touch it to my nose, then touch it to my toes. Cute rhyme, but he had more erotic things to think about.

Ready for some genuine practice, Stump leaned forward and touched his lips and nose to the mirror. He couldn't avoid seeing his eyes. Movie stars usually closed theirs, but wouldn't they want to see what was going on? He compromised, closed one eye and watched his head tilt from side to side. As his lips puckered and his head swirled in perfect sync with the matching head in the mirror, he moaned. MMMMMM!!! Not that loud, dummy. It sounds like you hurt yourself. Mmm. Yeah, like that.

With one eye open and lip-locked with his mirror buddy, he looked down his cheek to the tongue in the mirror. It reached for his own and they touched for a second before they spun around like ice-skaters. The guy in the mirror needed a breath mint. He smiled and made unintended eye contact with the slobbery-faced, one-eyed gay partner who was licking his own tongue. He giggled and accidentally drooled down his chin, causing him to laugh and pull back.

Conclusion: Frenching was sorta gross, but aside from the fact that he felt like a wet-faced fool, there was a certain comfort in knowing a few things not to do should he find himself in a round of saliva-trading with Maria; like, don't open one eye. If she happened to be doing the same thing, he'd probably laugh so hard something would squirt out his nose.

Finished, he used a bath towel to wipe down the mirror, then flicked the switch and swung the door open just as he heard a key in the front door. The knob turned. Oh shit, Myles was back.

Myles stepped in and glanced at the footstool "What's going on?"

Hmm. Stump couldn't admit to slurping mirror syrup. "Just finished changing a light bulb. How's Grandma Pauline?" he asked, smoothly changing the subject.

"Not good. I think she's going to have to move."

"I hope you don't mean to an old people's home."

"Well, sometimes she needs company and my sister can't take her."

"Then bring her here. She can live with us."

"You don't know what that means," Myles said while wheeling his suitcase to his room. "There's daily supervision, bathing schedules, a special diet. You and I aren't exactly health bugs, you know. Then there's all her pills—somebody has to take her to the doctor."

"Don't matter. I know how bad you're gonna feel when your mom is gone. You'll miss her more than you think. I'd love to supervise my mom now, or help her with a diet or any of those other things you mentioned. When your mom goes away, you'll be thinking the same thing. I say we should welcome her, even if that means we have to move again and get me a car to drive her around."

Myles raised a finger. "You had me going there for a while."

"Okay, I admit I was just throwing that last part in to test the waters, but I meant the rest of it. We could get one of those assistants you told me about."

Myles put his hand on Stump's shoulder. "You know something, Stumpster? You may only be 16, but sometimes you're pretty darn wise. Thank you for saying all of that. In fact, you've made me feel better. I'll look into this a little more."

"She can have my room if she needs it."

Myles pointed a finger-gun at Stump and shot him a bullet of respect. Moments later, and alone in his room, Stump checked YouTube for some kissing videos.

CHAPTER 17

IT HAD BEEN A FEW DAYS SINCE Dr. Moreno successfully forced Delores to visit her memory bank. Now, an hour and a half into a scheduled trip to El Centro to clear the air with her mama and Tio about how their actions all those years back still affected her, Delores realized she'd always looked upon her youth with the same trepidation that she experienced when she played with a jack-in-the–box. As predictable as the outcome was, she was always surprised when the puppet-monster ultimately sprang into her face. Now, in her adult life, all that turtle-headed hiding from her past was making it difficult to have any kind of normal romantic relationship.

When fifteen minutes from El Centro, she was haunted by that other comment Dr. Moreno had made about choosing kindness over being correct. How the hell was she supposed to *kindly* clear the air with a child molester and the woman who had enabled it? She could think of a half-dozen emotions that defined her attitude about her ugly past and ultimately losing her sister, but kindness sure as hell wasn't among them.

Ultimately, Delores turned onto the final street and parked in their empty driveway. She opened her glove box and stashed both her .38 and her cell phone. She looked in her rearview mirror. It was time these people learned they were no longer dealing with innocent little Delores. She'd become a skilled detective and deserved respect. Most importantly, they needed to understand the long-term damage they'd inflicted on her.

Delores marched to their front porch, straightened her clothes and rang the doorbell. As she waited, she caught the scent of lemon furniture polish. She smiled. Mama was always a clean woman. If nothing else, that was one reason to exhibit some of that kindness Dr. Moreno spoke of.

It took but a minute for Mama to get to the door. "My sweet Delores," she said, a grin lighting her small face. A brief hug reminded Delores how much taller she was than her mama. "Come on in," Mama said, tugging Delores's hand.

Until that moment Delores hadn't realized how tight her stomach muscles were. As they moved to the living room she looked over her mama's shoulders. Most of the lights were on. It didn't appear as if Tio or anybody else was there. Mama turned around. "We don't get to see you very much."

Delores nearly responded with, *"Well there's a reason for that, Mama,"* but it was too early for belligerence and Tio wasn't there to hear what she had to say.

Mama pointed to the table at the corner of the room. "Did you see my birthday card? Tio had it delivered to me."

A chill swooshed up Delores's back. She'd been so engrossed in her own problems, she'd forgot to stop and get something. What kind of daughter doesn't even bring a card on her mama's birthday? Delores hoped that her face wasn't nearly as red as she assumed it was. "Very nice of him," she said while glancing through the card and trying to hide her embarrassment. "Where is Tio now?"

Just then two car doors slammed. "That's probably them," Mama said. "He went to pick up two women from our church."

Delores didn't know what to think about the paradox of a pervert's involvement in a church. Nor was she pleased with the dynamics of strangers around when she had such an important topic to discuss. All she could do for now was exercise patience.

A fairly long period lapsed before Tio pushed in the front door and held it open. His other hand held what looked like a small gift. Slowly, an elderly woman, probably in her eighties, employed a walker to help her breach the threshold. Once she made her way in, another similarly aged woman followed, holding a cake with chocolate icing. "Hello, Delores," Tio said happily, as if he'd always been her good friend. "This is Carmen and Araceli."

Araceli placed her cake on the dining table before addressing Delores. "It was so nice of you to drive all this way for your mother's birthday."

It would have been if that were what happened but now, bloated with guilt, Delores didn't have the nerve to divulge the truth. "Thank you," she said, noticing that Tio's eyes darted to the table with his card on it and then to a couple other places.

After Tio helped Carmen sit down, he extended the small gift to Delores's mama. "Here ya go, Anna. It's from Delores and me."

Mama's face lit up and Delores's eyes shot to Tio. He must have figured out that she hadn't brought anything and the S.O.B. wanted her to be indebted to him. Part of her wanted to tell him what a presumptuous a-hole he was, but another part of her was trying to follow some sound advice about being kind. She didn't want to disrupt her mother's moment, but she damn sure planned to write him a check on her next payday.

"What is it?" Mama asked Delores.

There was only one possible answer. "You'll just have to open it to find out."

Tio grinned and nodded while Mama tore into the wrapping, opened the box and squealed. "It's an iPhone."

"A nice one," Tio said. "Now we can take pictures of you

and Delores and she can show us how to forward them to everybody we know."

It all made the important Detective Sanchez feel like irrelevant Delores again. She obligingly posed for a couple pictures with her mama and wished that Simone could have been there. Then Tio handed her the iPhone. "Now take a picture of me and Anna so we can show everybody how happy we are." Good God. What a con man.

Over the next couple hours Delores suffered through dismal things like happy faces, birthday cake, and too damn many pictures. She forced herself to smile while she showed her mama and Tio how to take selfies and send pictures to their friends. The entire mood was the exact opposite of what she had wanted. Then she ran out of time.

CHAPTER 18

ADULTS WERE FRUSTRATING. Half the time they'd tell Stump to grow up and the other half the time they treated him like a kid. Take Myles for instance: Myles didn't mind if Stump had his own car, but Stump wasn't allowed to use his own trust money to buy it. Then there were the people at Cal-Vista. Mr. Kraft treated Stump with respect, but Dixon was always comparing Stump to "real" adults.

The City Council and BigBunz were the same way. For the moment he was permitted to present his ideas for improving home safety, but nobody would tell him how to do it. Thus far, Councilman Barella was the only exception. At least he'd called to say he'd ordered the brochures and found an attorney, named Danielle Delgado, who agreed to help Stump put his project together.

Then on Sunday morning, after a couple hours of practice driving, Stump and Myles dropped by the printing company to get the brochures and there it was: another smack-down. "That selfish asshole," Stump said, examining the brochures and handing one to Myles. "He took one whole side for his picture and didn't even mention Mom or me on either side."

Myles glanced at the brochure and cocked his head to the side. "The important thing is to get people to come to your meeting."

"I know, but just when I thought Mr. Barella was an okay guy for getting me an attorney, he pulls this bullshit."

"Well, people will be back from church and moving around by now so you can tell them all about your plan face-to-face."

Shortly thereafter, they pulled into Stump's former neighborhood and parked. "You ever do anything like this?" Stump asked.

"Canvassing? Yeah, a little, but the Violent Crimes Division does it more. Sometimes they bang on doors all day just to get one good lead." Myles handed Stump about fifty sheets. "There's a trick to it. We want to keep moving so we can get to as many people as possible, but if you find somebody who wants to learn more about it, stay with them and answer their questions. On the other hand, some folks will talk your ear off if you let them, especially older people. Just excuse yourself and tell them you have lots of other people to see."

"What should I say?"

"We'll go together on a couple calls. You'll get the hang of it."

They walked up the closest driveway and knocked on the door. "Go ahead," Myles said to Stump as a middle-aged mom-type tugged the door open.

Stump swallowed. "Your house is dangerous. You wouldn't want to come to a meeting, would you?"

She glared at him as if he was nuts. "What?"

Myles stepped forward and held out one of the brochures. "Hello, ma'am. We're handing out these invitations to come to the City Council meeting in ten days. There's going to be a discussion about making homes in this area safer. We thought you might like to come."

The lady took the brochure, peeked at it, then looked back at Stump. "My husband never does nothin'."

"No problem," Myles said. "If you have any questions, our number is at the bottom."

At the next home an eight-year-old boy answered. Caught off-guard, Stump looked at Myles for guidance.

"Is your mom or dad home?" asked Myles.

The kid turned and screamed toward the center of the home. "Daddy. Some men are at the door."

A man? Rad. Stump hadn't been called a *man* very often.

A toilet flushed, the dad-dude came to the door and Stump tried again. "Hello. My name is Stump ... er, Neil Randolph." He held out a brochure. "We're working with Councilman Barella to make homes safer. We'd like to invite you to our next meeting—in 10 days."

"This better not cost me no money. I'll be in the front row raising hell if it does."

Stump shrugged. He hadn't really figured out the numbers yet.

Minutes later, Stump was on one side of the street knocking on doors, just like Trick or Treat, and Myles was on the other side. Eventually, they met at the end of the street. "Let's go to the next block over," Myles said, "and head back toward the truck for more brochures."

By the time the morning disappeared, Stump had the hang of it and Myles pointed down the block where a woman was watering her flowers. "Let's ask her if we can rest for a bit in the shade of one of her trees."

Once settled, Stump removed his tennis shoes. "That Barella was right about one thing," he said. "This is pretty effective. Several people said they'd come to the meeting."

"Mine too," Myles added. "One woman wanted to know if I could get her a street light for the front of her house."

"I met a lady who said she remembered the fire," Stump said as he rolled a few blades of grass though his fingers.

Myles nodded. "I've been meaning to ask you about your job. How's that going?"

"I'd put up with just about anything for thirty bucks an hour."

"Glad you got that figured out. Anything else?"

"I met a cute girl, named Maria. She's got a cat, and her mom's nice."

Myles's eyes widened. "Oh, that's right. Those kids go to a different school, don't they?"

"All the girls at my school are lame."

Myles chuckled. "It seems like that sometimes. What about that manager? Dixon. You getting along with him?"

"He's a jerk. But Mr. Kraft is pretty cool. He said it was smart not to buy his building."

Myles nodded. "He should know what he's talking about. Maybe we should put that whole investment idea on the back burner for a while." Myles ripped a few blades of grass out of the ground. "You know, it still wouldn't bother me if you looked for some other job."

Stump turned his head, snickered. "What? You're always telling me once I start some—"

"I know, but sometimes I can go to extremes, and I just want you to know I'm flexible on this, so feel free to move on if you'd like."

"Not unless I find something better, and I don't have time to look."

"Well, don't get in a pissing match with that manager. Just walk away if he gets pushy."

"Yeah. Yeah. First you wanted me to get a job, now you tell me I can quit." He shook his head. "Adults are weird."

Just then a familiar Subaru turned the corner. "There's James," Stump said. "He said he'd drop by to help but I wasn't sure he'd make it."

"Good, we can use him if we want to get to the halfway point today."

James parked and joined them with one of his mischievous grins. "Sorry, I'm late, but I had to go to the cleaners to *drop my pants and jacket off,*" he said, making air quotes.

Stump shook his head, looked at Myles who obviously didn't get the joke. "C'mon, Myles. Think differently. First he had to drop his pants, then he had to—"

"Oh, yeah," Myles said. "Never heard that one before."

CHAPTER 19

"How do you like it?" Dixon asked the woman he believed to be Lorraine Martinez. Another Monday had arrived and he'd obviously assumed a Caddie would impress her. "It's brand new," he bragged.

Delores poked her head inside the fire-engine-red beauty and checked the lower right corner of the brake pedal. A hint of wear indicated that Dixon was bullshitting her about the age of the vehicle; nonetheless, "It's pretty," she said.

"It's an SRX with all the bells and whistles, including OnStar. Do you know what that is?"

Of course she did, but Lorraine probably wouldn't. "Something in outer space?"

"It's the best music system money can buy. I know you haven't formally agreed to be my Monday Girl but you do still need my financial assistance, so I figured you'd rather go for a ride than work your ass off around here. The choice is yours."

Lorraine would be cautious but Delores recognized an opportunity to get some dirt on him. She'd play it as Lorraine would. "How long will it take?"

"What difference does it make? Would you rather spend the day scrubbing toilets?"

"But no kisses?"

He smirked. "Just one. A good-bye kiss, when we get back."

She hesitated before she sighed, "Okay, but I have to go to the bathroom first. I'll be right back."

"Hurry."

Once in her apartment, she seized her cell and placed a quick call.

"*You okay, detective?*" Myles Cooper asked, having obviously seen her name on his read-out.

"Yeah. Dixon bought a red Cadillac and wants me to go for a ride."

"*A Caddie? Scamming people must be more lucrative than we thought. You going to go?*"

"Yeah, I might be able to get some dirt."

"*Where you headed?*"

"Not sure exactly, but I'm shooting for one of the beaches, where it's nice and crowded."

"*Good idea. I could tail you.*"

"I don't think that's necessary. He's trying to act like a gentleman."

"*A gentleman, huh? Don't be so sure. His background check just came in. No warrants now, but years back he had a run-in with his original wife. She charged him with sexual assault, but he must have made nice with her 'cause she withdrew the charges.*"

"That's not much help. Anything else?"

"*Just a couple traffic issues. You have a gun with you, don't you?*"

"Yeah. My trusty Diamondback."

"*That little pea shooter?*"

"Don't scoff. It'll do man-sized damage if I need it too. Got a small recorder too."

"*Good. Keep me posted and ditch him if it gets dangerous. I'll come get you.*"

She smiled. Myles sounded like a big brother. "Thanks for being there, Myles. It makes me feel a lot better knowing you're available when the Birdman gets bogged down." She hung up, grabbed her only blanket off her bed and returned to Dixon.

Once there, she raised the blanket slightly. "Can I put this in the trunk?" Dixon obliged and the trunk appeared to be clear of any potential weapons. He then opened her car door, whereupon she slid in and quickly checked under both seats while he circled around the car. Clear.

Dixon slid in. "Can I put some tissues in the glove box?" she asked. It too was clean.

"There are some beautiful places in the desert," Dixon said.

"Could we go to the ocean instead? I haven't been to a beach since I was a little girl."

"I'd rather go inland. We can get to know each other better. That's why you brought the blanket, isn't it?"

"But I was raised in the desert. It's boring. I'd rather see the water."

Dixon grinned and tapped her knee. "One of the things I like about you is you have a mind of your own. How 'bout Venice Beach? We could get there in a little over an hour."

Good choice. It'd be safe and give her time to probe for information. "Is it nice?"

"One of the best," he said. He flicked on some soft music. "Did you know I had a tenant hauled off to jail yesterday?"

"No. What'd he do?" she asked, anxious to get him talking.

"Disobeyed me. I've told him before not to drink beer in the parking lot, but he didn't seem to get the message."

"I don't like it when they whistle at me and say nasty things."

He touched her knee. "That's why I had some of my cop-buddies take care of it. Sometimes I gotta remind people who's the boss."

Cop buddies? What a liar. She and Birdman already checked that out and nobody considered him worthy of special treatment. Nevertheless, she was glad he was in a bragging mood.

"Don't you worry, though," he said, bumping her knee again. "If you take me up on my offer, I'll teach you how the game is played so people can't jerk you around."

She reached in her purse, secretly turned on her pen-recorder and pulled out a tissue to fake-wipe her eye. "It would be easier to decide if I didn't have to do nasty things."

Dixon grinned. "It's not nasty. It's more like a friendly business deal. All sorts of people trade money for services. That's all we're really doing. Think of it this way. If we make love, it just takes a little while and that's all you have to do for the whole week. There are only a few Mondays a month so even if I call on you every week, which I probably won't, that's a lot of compensation for very little on your part."

"But I'm a lot younger than you. Do you do this with other women my age?"

"Not usually. They're not as stable, but you're more mature than others your age. I saw that the first time I met you."

Whew! It would have been much more difficult to keep her cool around him if he were fondling underage girls. "But you're married. Does your wife know what you're doing?"

"Sure she does, but we have an *understanding*."

"I've never heard of that. How long have you been married?"

"Look, this isn't about her. It's about you and me."

Damn. Delores was hoping she could lead the conversation to his other marriages and divorces, which might shed some light on the wacky papers he'd given Yolanda Vigil. "Could I talk to those women, just to see how it worked out for them?"

"That wouldn't be a good idea. But, I can tell you about Victoria. We meet every other Wednesday. After we have a little fun, she gets help with her rent. That's all there is to it. She likes our deal. You could do the same thing, only on Mondays."

"So all I'd have to do is be with you twice a month, no cleaning toilets?"

"You have to be available every Monday, but that's the basic idea."

"Does that cleaning lady do things like that too?"

"No way. I don't mess with married women." He turned off his sound system. "Look, I've leveled with you. I'm offering you something you need and you just might enjoy yourself. I think you ought to go along with it."

Delores sensed that she'd pumped Dixon enough for the time being. Among other things, she had learned he was confining his activities to single, adult-aged women who appeared to be fairly loyal to him. That meant the best way to gather more info in the near future was to focus her investigation off-site.

Another key point was, if Dixon's relationships were really as he defined them, there wasn't any rape by deception because the women pretty much got what they bargained for. Furthermore, none of this had anything to do with bogus marriages and divorces. As husbands went, Dixon was no prize, so there had to be a decent explanation for why those women would agree to marry him and then move on down the road so quickly.

For now it was probably best to back off, act like Lorraine would. Avoid raising suspicions. In the meantime, she'd best touch base with Myles. "Can we pull over?" she asked. "I have to find another bathroom."

CHAPTER 20

SEVERAL HOURS LATER DELORES had been to the beach, walked the pier and made several stops at the ladies restroom. After lunch, she and Dixon drove a few miles north and rode the nine-story Ferris wheel at Pacific Park. Overall, he was mostly a gentleman. If he had been anybody else she might have actually enjoyed herself.

Afterwards, while headed back to Palmdale, she had activated her recorder and they were jammed into the never-ending crowd of bumper-to-bumper traffic where she wanted to get him talking again. "Did you have a family before you worked at the apartment building?" she asked, knowing that most people like talking about themselves.

Dixon turned off the music. "That's an odd question. Yeah, I was married once. Had a couple kids."

"Do you still see them?"

"Not often. Speaking of living arrangements, it's time you and I have our talk about your rent and security."

Perfect. She'd like to talk about that too.

"I wasn't sure I wanted to tell you this," Dixon said while glancing her way, "but I have another option besides that Monday Girl idea we talked about. I think it might suit you better. You could even quit your restaurant job if you want to. What do you know about anchor babies?"

Anchor babies! Now Delores was getting somewhere. "You mean if you have a baby, they don't deport you?" She discreetly adjusted her purse on her lap so the microphone was better positioned.

"That's part of it. New babies are automatically citizens and INS won't split the family up, so the mom and dad can stay too. But there's something even better. If you marry an American, you automatically become a citizen, which is much better because you can get a good job and social security. You'd like those things, wouldn't you?"

What a crock. Delores knew quite a bit about the naturalization process and there was nothing *automatic* about it. Regardless, this conversation was promising. "That sounds real good, but I don't know anybody like that."

"Sure you do. Me. I've married several women like you and it worked out real well."

Several women? "Isn't that illegal?" she asked, anxious to hear more.

"Not really. You just have to do it the right way. Then, after enough time has passed, we'd get a divorce. After that, you could meet other people and get married again, for real next time, and have a real family or a real job. That would be nice, wouldn't it?"

Delores avoided smiling. "What would I have to do?"

"There are two ways we can do it. The first way is easiest. All you have to do is move in, pay $2,500 and sign some papers. Then you live like a real wife for six months. After that we finalize the papers and it's done."

So, that filled in the blanks. Dixon was essentially selling a phony fast track to citizenship. The cost was $2,500 plus a bunch of housework and all the bed action he wanted. In the meantime his wives were fundamentally confined to his apartment where he could brainwash them. Once he was confident they'd keep it all a secret, he could dump them and go get somebody else. But there had to be more because Dixon only preyed on poor women. "But I don't have any money."

"That's why there's a second option. Instead of paying the fee, you just live with me six additional months. I figure all the housework and everything is just as valuable. Either way you won't have to pay any rent and you end up better off."

It sounded more like a jail sentence than a pathway to a better life. "What would I have to do?"

"It's easy," he said. "You just live like a real wife. Cook and clean house and consummate the marriage."

"Consummate? What's that?"

"You know. Adult relations."

She said nothing.

"I know what you're thinking," he went on, "but married people do things for each other all the time. It isn't always about love. Other things are important too. Security. Convenience. Sex. Everybody is trading something they have for something they want. That's all."

"Then do I get papers?"

"Not quite. We have to wait a little while, so it looks like we lived together for a longer period, then we go to a final interview and it's over. So what do you say? Should we give it a try?"

If Delores weren't in character she may have laughed in his face. That was the most pathetic marriage proposal she'd ever heard of. Still, it seemed to have worked on several women. "Is that what Francisca is doing?"

He nodded. "Yep. She's smart. Just like you."

"How many other wives have you had?"

"That's not important."

"It is to me. I'd feel better if I knew other people had been through the same thing."

"Let's just say Francisca is not the only one."

"What do you do if Francisca doesn't want to make love when you want to?"

"She doesn't do that. It's the deal."

"But that doesn't seem right."

"It doesn't matter anymore. I can cut her loose any time. She won't care. She's already got what she wants."

They reached Cal-Vista, pulled in and parked. "How often?" Delores asked as they walked toward her building.

"How often what?"

"You know. Making love. How often do I have to do that?"

Dixon opened her door with his master key. "Whenever I want." He closed the door behind them and lifted her chin. "Either of the things I'm offering you are a lot better than what you're doing now."

Her eyes narrowed. She walked over to the window, then back. "How long before I have to decide?"

Dixon put his hands on her waist and pulled her to him. He was obviously ready for that end-of-the-day kiss they had discussed earlier. She still had a lot more to do to strengthen her case and had to string him along. As awful as it was on a couple of levels, she had to allow it.

Almost instantly he pushed his tongue towards hers. She would have preferred to bite the damn thing off but she did the best she could before he lowered his hands onto her buttocks. She pulled back. "Just a kiss. You promised."

"Hugs and kisses go together. Everybody knows that. It's part of the deal." He kissed her again then forced his hips to hers. "I want you right now."

She had visions of Tio and Dixon's other women. So many victims. She damn near kneed him, but instead shrank back and away, barely keeping her wits. She had to calm him down and maintain her role. "I'm sorry, but there's something I should have told you. I can't right now. I have cramps and er...lady problems. That's why I've been going to the restroom so much."

He took a step back, dropped his arms and then exhaled. "Okay. We'll put it off." He put his open hand on her cheek. "But I want you to listen to me. I'm tired of our little one-way street. If you can't pay your bills on your own you gotta move out or let me help you, but that means you gotta be nice to me too. Understand?"

She sure did. Much better than he realized.

CHAPTER 21

IF LORRAINE MARTINEZ WASN'T going to smooth Dixon's ruffled feathers somebody else sure as hell was. He checked his watch. Midafternoon. Maria's mother, Inez Quintana, or Friday Girl as Dixon thought of her, should be home, alone, and she'd gotten away with way too much for way too long.

Inez was Dixon's earliest Cal-Vista conquest. Some sixteen years earlier she came to the country with her husband via the southern border. They basically wanted to lie low, start a new life and avoid the wrath of the INS. But her husband went home and never came back.

That left Inez alone and in need of help. Dixon said he could get her some work if she was willing to show her gratitude and almost instantly Inez was with child.

After she gave birth to Maria, Inez needed Dixon more than before, but Dixon, who was legitimately pleased with the idea of watching his daughter grow up, already had a family and his ex would ridicule him endlessly in front of his other two kids if she learned of his carelessness. All of this led to a mutual understanding. Dixon and Inez agreed to keep their fling a secret. She'd stay in the complex where he could watch Maria grow up and he'd provide Inez with enough of the ongoing work to pay her bills. As it played out, Inez liked most of the arrangement. She could raise Maria on her own terms and all she had to do was attend to some routine chores and accommodate Dixon's physical needs from time to time.

As far as Dixon was concerned, he didn't have to be involved with a crying kid or diapers, and just as importantly, he was free to dip his noodle in other pots. Over time he reduced Inez's responsibilities to Fridays only and he pretty much got his physical pleasures elsewhere. No doubt about it, Inez owed him more than anybody else on the planet and it was time for her to pay some of her debt.

Still frustrated from the abrupt conclusion to his day with Lorraine, Dixon let himself into Inez's apartment. Thanks to him, the décor was nicer than most around there. She even had a few colorful pictures of the old country and a crucifix on the walls. On the dining table, dancing flames of two coconut-scented candles swayed innocently.

Inez came from the kitchen. Not much more than five-one and in her late thirties, she had gotten a little chubby. "It's not Friday," she said.

"Don't matter," Dixon replied in a no-nonsense tone. He shifted his teeth and observed her dark red toenails on bare feet and a faded dark-blue T-shirt that was incapable of hiding her braless, full-sized breasts.

He tapped her breast. "Turn around."

Her eyes shot to his. He returned an intimidating glare, pressed the same breast. "Do it," he insisted.

Inez pursed her lips and slowly did as she was told. When half-way around, Dixon put both hands on her shoulders and stopped her. Sixteen years and thirty pounds had replaced her hourglass figure.

He dropped his hand to her butt and then slid it inside her shorts and undies. "Kinda let yourself go, haven't you?" She said nothing.

He squeezed her butt until she yelped, causing an unauthorized cat to scurry from behind the couch into one of the bedrooms. "When I ask you a question," he said, "I expect an answer. Got it?"

"Yes, yes, yes," she said quickly, obviously in pain.

"That's better," he said, letting go. He reached around her with both hands. Her breasts were soft, much fuller and droopier than those of the other women he was accustomed to. From outside her flimsy cotton T-shirt, his fingers explored her now-firm nipples. "You know you're not supposed to have pets in here, don't you?"

"Maria found it. I'm sorry."

He clucked his tongue, palming her breasts tightly. "You women are all a bunch of selfish, rule-breaking bitches, aren't you?"

"Uh-huh," she said sheepishly.

Dixon shook his head. "What kind of answer is that?" He pinched her nipples and her shoulders instantly curled forward. "I want you to admit that you're all a bunch of selfish bitches."

"We're selfish bitches. We're selfish bitches," she said, quickly and emphatically.

Dixon nodded, softening his grip, but not enough that she might relax. "I expect you to get rid of the cat by tomorrow, got it?"

"Yes. I'll do what you say. Just don't hurt me anymore."

"Okay, then," he whispered into her ear. "Now that we have an understanding, I'm going to talk to you about a few things that are on my mind, and you're going to let me know if you agree with me. Got it?"

Her head jackhammered up and down. "Okay."

He gently tugged on her tee. "For starters, take this off."

Without hesitation Inez did as she was told. Topless, she dropped the shirt to her feet and stood rigid. He spun her around, grabbed her shoulders, glared down her torso and then back to her face. "How do you suppose a fellow feels when he does nice things for a woman but she takes advantage of his kindness and doesn't give him much in return?"

"He must feel bad."

He pursed his lower lip and then lifted her head. "It's even worse when they never even say thank you."

She looked him in the eyes and nodded, "I'm sorry—"

"Too late," he said as he removed his leather belt and tongued his uppers. "All you women are the same. You'll take advantage of good ol' Dixon if you can get away with it. He shoved her toward her bedroom. "I'd say you deserve a damn good spanking. Wouldn't you?"

There was no need for her to reply.

CHAPTER 22

WHILE STUMP PEDALED OL' UG' to work a call came in from Danielle Delgado, the attorney who had agreed to help with the upcoming City Hall meeting. *"I need you and your dad to drop by tomorrow,"* she said. *"We've only got two weeks and we have a lot to do."*

We? "But I thought that's what you do?"

"I'll do the paperwork, but I need you to do the rest of it—to complete the package."

"But I have a job. I have to earn money."

"Money? It must be nice. Maybe you forgot I'm working on your case for free. I'm happy to help you but you have to help me help you."

Stump sighed. "Okay, I'll try."

"Good. Be here no later than four."

Damn. Nothing was ever easy. After he reached Cal-Vista, he handcuffed Ol' Ug' to the bike rack and hustled toward Mr. Kraft's office where he heard Mr. Kraft arguing with Dixon. He poked his head in the office. "I'm here, Mr. Kraft."

"Ah, Stump. Great." Kraft said before he coughed and spit into a tissue. "You're good with math; you can settle an argument for us. We want to install a flower garden in the courtyard. Do you know how many cubic feet of mulch we need to fill a landscaping circle that's about sixteen feet across?"

Stump plopped his backpack on the floor. "How deep do you want the mulch?"

Kraft looked to Dixon, then back. "About two inches."

"You'll need thirty-four cubic feet," Stump said without hesitation.

"Told you," Kraft said to Dixon. Back to Stump, "How'd you figure that?"

"Simple. Pi times the radius squared, divided by the depth as a decimal."

"Dixon thought it was close to a hundred feet."

Stump would have liked to make a smug comment but guarded his tone. "You'd have to take some back." Tone or no tone, Stump enjoyed one-upping the dude again. Dixon merely shrugged.

"I'm sorry, sir," Stump said to Mr. Kraft, "but I have to have tomorrow off to meet my attorney."

"Legal problems, huh?" Dixon said sarcastically.

"No. I have to get ready for the next City Council meeting."

Kraft wiped the corner of his mouth with his tissue. "No problem. I hope it works out."

"Unless you have something else you want me to do, I'm going to get after the weeds by the dumpster now."

"Good enough. I'll catch up with you before I leave."

A little while later Stump discovered that pulling sticker weeds was a lot easier if he trampled them over first so he could get to the bottom of the stems. "Can you talk?" A familiar voice, softer than usual, came from behind him. He turned to see Maria rubbing puffy eyes.

"What's wrong?" he asked touching her hand.

She looked back toward the buildings. "When I got home from school Mama had been crying. I tried to get her to sit down and talk to me, but she just kept saying she *felt so dirty*." Maria took Stump's hand and pulled him toward a red mini-van. "We need someplace where we can talk," she said while sliding the door back. "Get in. It's Juanita's."

Stump shrugged and followed Maria into the back seat where he observed the lock assembly on the door had been removed.

"I promised Mama I wouldn't say anything," Maria said, wiping a tear from her cheek, "but I have to talk to somebody. I think somebody beat her, maybe worse."

Stump's brows clamped down. "No shit? That sucks. He grabbed for his cell. "Want me to call the cops?"

Maria slapped his arm. "God, no! That's the worst thing we can do. Mama's scared of the police. Nearly everybody is."

"Then how about Mr. Kraft? I can tell him."

Maria shook her head. "We can't. He'll just make us talk with Mr. Dixon."

"Well then, let's go talk to Dixon."

Maria squeezed Stump's hand. "That's what I suggested to Mama but she turned away. I think he might be the one who hurt her."

Dumbfounded, Stump's jaw dropped.

"Mama won't tell me what happened."

"Maybe I could get my dad to help? It's not his department, but he's a detective."

She glared at Stump and grabbed for the door handle. "You're not listening to me. I should have known you wouldn't understand. I'll go find somebody else."

Stump's hand pulled at hers. "Don't go. I'm sorry. I know you said she's afraid of the police, but I don't know what else to do."

"We have to work on it ourselves. Together. In secret."

"Work on what? This is none of my business."

"I know, but somebody has to figure out what happened and turn him in. The police will listen to you. You're smart and white."

"White? I don't know what that has to do with anything. I think the cops would listen to you, too. You're her daughter."

"I would but if Mr. Dixon is the one who hurt Mama, and if he sees me asking questions, he might hurt her again, or hurt me, or throw us out of the building and Mama says we can't afford to live anywhere else. That's why I need you to do it. You work here so it won't look suspicious if you talk with some of the people."

"I wouldn't know what to do and it would take a lot of time and I already have too much to do. Besides I don't want to make waves either. I might get fired."

"Please!" She scowled right at him. "What if it was your mama?"

Ouch! She might as well have taken a giant bite out of his heart. Stump remembered exactly how he felt when his own mother had been slipped a date-rape drug and ended up in the hospital. He didn't need coaxing to fight then. Maria's mother deserved the same respect. "Okay. You're right. I'll try."

Maria squeezed Stump's neck so hard it hurt. "Thank you, thank you. I knew you'd do it."

"Do what, exactly? I don't really know what you want me to do."

"Maybe you can talk to some other people and see if they know anything. Dixon has had a lot of women live with him. He may have done bad things to them or somebody else. If so, you can turn him in without dragging Mama into it." She touched his chin. "I'm sorry, but I have to get back to Mama. Let's meet again tomorrow and I'll introduce you to a friend who can help us."

"Tomorrow? I can't. I'm meeting somebody else."

"Another girlfriend?"

"Not a girlfriend. An attorney. I already promised her. I'm sorry, but it can't be helped."

"So you do like me?" she asked, smiling gently.

"Well, yeah. Sure I do."

"Okay then. Just promise me you won't tell anybody what we're doing. I could never forgive myself if Mama got hurt again."

"Okay. I promise." Stump said softly. "I'm really sorry about what happened."

Maria grabbed Stump's face and gave him his very first serious non-family kiss on the lips. "You're so sweet," she said, pulling away quickly. "You're my boyfriend."

CHAPTER 23

IN HER MID-TWENTIES AND VERY SHORT, Danielle Delgado wouldn't intimidate a grade-schooler, but she had one big thing in her favor: She was willing to work on Stump's case for free. Stump and Myles met her in her office as she'd requested.

"I've spoken with Mrs. Crumpler at the City Planner's office," she said while tapping some papers. "I have the list of everything we need to do right here."

Shocked, Stump glanced at Myles, then back to Ms. Delgado. "How'd you do that so fast? It took me lots of calls just to get a straight answer out of that office."

She shrugged. "Apparently the best thing we can do to improve the safety codes is get the residents to vote on it. If we give them a couple years to get it done they might go along with the idea."

"What if they don't want to go that route?" Myles asked.

"But I want to force them to do it," Stump said. "It might piss some of them off, but it's for their own good."

"I know what you mean," the attorney said, nodding. "Older people are always using that line on us, but I'm afraid there really isn't any realistic way to force them to do what you want. As good as your idea is, some people will fight you because they don't have the money or don't think the risk is all that great."

Stump swallowed. If he were to be completely honest, he'd heard some of the residents make comments along those lines when he handed out brochures with Myles.

"If the legal process fails," she continued, "about all you can do is try to inspire them to upgrade their homes on their own. That's why you should be sure to deliver those brochures Mr. Barella made for you."

"We'll be distributing the last half real soon," Myles said.

"Good. In the meantime we should be able to get everything you need and you can present your idea at the next meeting. From there, you should know fairly quickly what you're up against."

Stump's gut rumbled. "I guess nobody cares as much as I do, but I ain't quitting."

Myles said to Delgado, "His mom always said he's no quitter."

"Okay, then. First, I need a neighborhood map that shows the exact houses we're talking about. You can probably get something from an escrow or title company." She turned her page. "Oh, yeah, I could use pictures of individual houses that appear neglected or unsafe. I'll upload the best ones into a packet."

Myles turned toward Stump. "James would probably help you."

"I also need a written report from a professional, stating the common safety problems in the area. I've got a list of home inspectors here who can do that."

"Are they free?"

"Hardly. It'll probably take a couple hours to create a good report. I'm not sure what an expert would charge."

"I'll try to cut a deal with somebody," Myles said to Stump. "You might have to paint their house or something."

Stump raised his brows. "This pisses me off. All I wanted to do was help make homes safer so other people don't die like my mom did. Now I've got to do damn near everything and I don't get anything out of it."

"Hold it there, Stumpster," Myles said. "You're taking out your anger on the wrong people. Ms. Delgado is trying to help you, for free no less, so am I, and some others."

Stump hadn't really thought of it like that. "Sorry. It's just that I've got school and a job and homework and I'm trying to get my driver's license and I still have to deliver a bunch of brochures." Then there was Maria and her mama and his desire to get back in the kissing van, but nobody needed to know of those complications.

"You should know where you stand in a few days," Delgado added. "And it's only going to cost you about sixty dollars for office supplies and copies. You can pay me later."

"Wait a minute," Stump said. "This was supposed to be free."

"I'm sorry. I can waive the legal fees, but I can't pay any of the out-of-pocket expenses for you."

Stump bit his lip. It was always the same damn thing. "But I don't have any money."

"I suspected that. Can you mow my parents' lawn for them? They just live a few miles from here. I've already spoken with them. If you can do that a couple times, they could pay the incidentals for you."

Stump groaned. "Mr. Kraft might let me use the Cal-Vista mower."

"There ya go," Myles said. "We can throw the mower in the back of my truck."

Danielle Delgado tapped her folder. "Okay, then. Get me what I need by Monday and I should be able to get your packets together in time for the meeting."

Stump made an arm-nest on his attorney's desk and laid his egghead, complete with his scrambled brain, right in the middle.

CHAPTER 24

It wasn't that much to ask. Stump only wanted two things out of life: to get his own car and to eliminate the overwhelming guilt he'd been hosting ever since his mother's passing. Neither issue should have been very damn complicated, but they'd both become quagmires.

To get a car he had to get a job, which started off okay, especially when he met Maria, but then Dixon Browne had injected himself in the mix. Now, Stump was expected to figure out if Dixon really hurt Maria's mama, or anybody else, without Maria's mama knowing what he was doing. How the heck could he do that?

Now at Cal-Vista Stump dipped Ol' Ug' into the bike rack. He looked across the courtyard where a Hispanic woman was sweeping dirt off the sidewalk near a pallet full of mulch bags and a newly-dug flower garden. He wondered why anybody would wear sweatpants and a sweatshirt this far inland, especially in the afternoon.

On the other side of the pool Dixon flung open the door of Kraft's building and walked quickly toward Stump. "You've done it again, you twerp," he said as he blew by. What the hell was that about?

As Stump entered the office, Mr. Kraft came out of the restroom. "I don't know what's worse," he said while setting a small plastic bottle of meds on his desk. "The disease or the medicine. Sometimes I wonder if it's all worth it."

"I've still got some work to do back by the fence," Stump said, trying to change the subject.

"That reminds me," Mr. Kraft said as he slipped slowly into his chair. He opened his drawer and pulled out an envelope. "You got a few days into this pay period."

Oh! Cool! It was about time something good happened. Stump almost snatched the envelope right out of his boss's hand. "Thank you, sir."

"You want to know something?" Mr. Kraft said. "Some people should be ashamed for the way they approach their jobs. They do the least they can to get by. That's like stealing."

Uh-oh. A lecture. Dixon must have seen Stump and Maria in the back of Manuel's mini-van and said something about it to Mr. Kraft.

"But then there are the other people," Kraft went on. "They put in their best effort, whether anybody is watching them or not. It's a matter of character to them. You're like that. I can tell by how much work you've done already. A guy like you approaches his payday differently. He holds his chest out, walks right up to the boss and grabs his money, like you just did."

Whew. Apparently Mr. Kraft thought Stump was doing okay after all. "Thank you. I'll try to remember that." He started to turn around but thought better of it. "Can I ask you something, Mr. Kraft? I don't really know how to ask this, but do you think it's possible that the manager is hurting people around here?"

Kraft lifted his head. "Dixon? What made you ask that?"

"I'd rather not say. You know, in case it's not true."

"Alright. I'll respect that, but he doesn't have to hurt anyone. He has the authority to get rid of people if they cause trouble."

"Never thought of that. Thanks. I'm going to get after that back fence area now."

Once outside, Stump squeezed his envelope and thought about the things he'd accomplished around Cal-Vista: the painting, the weeds, the trash, the scraping of the wooden fence along the back of the lot. Mr. Kraft was correct. He had earned that check.

Savoring the moment, Stump slowly opened the envelope to admire his very first real paycheck. Forty-six dollars? He busted his ass for a friggin' forty-six bucks? That wasn't even enough to pay Myles back for Ol' Ug's tires. To make matters worse, it would be another two weeks before the next payday and he'd be broke the whole damn time, just like he'd always been. Why work at all if you're going to be broke all the time?

He recalled how his mom sighed when she'd been paid. He remembered her clipping coupons and scraping coins out of the bottom of her purse just to find a tip for the pizza delivery driver. He understood her better now. Wished he could thank her for all she'd done that he'd taken for granted. He shook his head and stuffed the check in his pocket.

CHAPTER 25

Pulling weeds sucked. "Hello, Stump."

Huh? He turned. Somehow Maria had wandered all the way to the back of the lot without his seeing her. She held out a napkin. "This is for you."

She had a large cookie in one hand and a glass of lemonade in the other. Stump wiped his forehead with the back of one of his gloves. "Wow. Thanks." Somehow, Maria knew how to make difficult moments better. He plopped his gloves on the ground, took a big bite and washed it down. "Chocolate chip is one of my favorites."

"Mama made them for Dixon, but she let me pick out the biggest one for you." Maria pointed back toward the new flower garden. "That's her sweeping the sidewalk. I told her that you're my boyfriend."

Boyfriend? There it was again. He'd clearly surpassed the crushboy level. "How's your mama doing, anyway?"

"Not too good. She wears hot clothes and won't tell me what's wrong." Maria puckered her lower lip. "We both cried when Señorita left."

"Your cat? Where'd she go?"

Maria lowered her head. "Mama said she snuck out the door when I was at school. I just hope she'll come back." Maria poked Stump's arm. "Hey. Mama's going inside now. Let's get in Manuel and Juanita's van where we can talk better."

The kissing van! Even though the back seat would be awfully hot Stump could take a few minutes to be alone with the girl who thought of him as her *boyfriend*. They climbed in and Stump propped the door open with his foot.

"Mama's been working really hard the last two days. She barely stops to sit down and keeps the bathroom door closed when she's in there. I think I heard her cry."

"I'm really sorry, Maria. I know what it's like when something awful happens to our moms."

"I still think Dixon did something to her because she won't talk about him."

"But Dixon doesn't need to get mean," Stump said, recalling Mr. Kraft's earlier comment. "He can just throw people out if he wants to."

Maria clucked her tongue. "He's not going to beat people up in the courtyard where everybody can see."

True that. "So I suppose you still want me to help?"

"Of course I do. Mama is the sweetest woman I know. You have to find out what he did and then we can figure out what to do to him."

"I'll try, but I've got so much to do. Report cards are coming out before long and I ain't doing too good. On top of that, I gotta get ready for my next big meeting and mow some old people's lawn. And I still have to get some work done when I'm around here. If I lose this job, I'll never have enough money to—"

"You know something?" She kissed his cheek. "You amaze me. You're doing all of the things you just mentioned but you're still going to help me."

"I still think you should just call the police. Let them figure it out."

"I already told you if the cops make Dixon mad he might make everything worse. Mama doesn't want to risk it. You should come by tonight before you go home. Then you'll see how sweet she is." Maria's eyes were pathetic, her tone desperate.

"To tell you the truth, I remember how I felt when somebody hurt my mom."

Maria clapped her hands. "I knew I could count on you." She laid her head gently on his shoulder and turned her lips toward him. It was the moment Stump and his mirror-buddy had anticipated. He closed his eyes. As their lips met he swirled his head slowly around, like the movie stars. He rubbed her shoulders and felt her bra strap. It was an incredibly natural moment, unlike the goofy giggle-kisses he once got at a party, even different from when Maria had kissed him a couple days earlier. Was it too early in the relationship to stick his tongue out? Is that what a full-blown boyfriend does? How far? Oh damn. He had a cookie crumb in the back of his mouth.

As if on cue, he detected the tiniest tip of Maria's tongue. Somehow all of his other questions went away. His tongue matched hers. He was doing it. For real kissing. French kissing. His heart pounded and his penis stiffened. An incredible memory embedded itself in his mind.

Suddenly the van door blew open. "What the hell's going on?" Dixon asked, glaring. Under other circumstances, Stump and Maria's private game of tongue tag would be none of Dixon's business, but Stump was supposed to be working. "Sorry," he said, shifting his shorts.

"You think you're smart," Dixon said as Stump got out. "But I know your game. You wait until the old man isn't paying attention, and then you chase innocent girls. I know what you're after, and it ain't going to happen while I'm around." He faced Maria. "And you. Your mother would be ashamed. Besides, you can do better than this twerp."

"That's not a nice thing to say about my boyfriend."

Boyfriend! There it was again.

"Now get out of here," Dixon said to Maria, "before I make you wish you'd never met this guy."

"Okay, I will, but you're not nice." She turned to Stump. "Come see me when you get off work. He can't stop us then."

Wow! She'd just defended him. Girlfriends were rad.

As Maria walked off, Dixon returned his attention to Stump. "Let's get something clear. I don't like you. You're nothing but a spoiled rich kid."

"I'm not rich."

"Oh, bullshit. I know about all that money that was handed to you."

"But I don't get it for five years."

"Boo hoo! On top of everything else, the old man says he wants you to paint the lines in the parking lot, but I was going to give that job to somebody who's raising a family. But that's no sweat off your balls. Right, rich boy?"

"I keep telling you, I'm not rich. I gotta work just like everybody else." Sort of. While it was true that he needed to work, Stump's situation wasn't at all similar to somebody who had to feed a family and had no way of tripling his or her money. Maybe he really was taking advantage of people around there—except Maria who kept calling him her boyfriend. He couldn't help it if he was so darn charming. He bent for his gloves. "I gotta get back to work."

*　*　*

After his shift, Stump knocked on Maria's door as agreed, but Dixon answered instead. Maria stepped in front of Dixon and into the hallway. She tried to close the door but Dixon stuck his foot in the way. "I like the fresh air," he said.

"Whatever," Maria said before moving down the hallway and turning to Stump. "I can only be a minute. Mama's making me be nice to that man, but I don't like him."

"Me neither."

Maria whispered, "You should ask Juanita about the notebook."

"The cleaning woman? What notebook?"

"It's in code. She thinks Dixon has other wives and makes them all do it with him."

"Do what?"

"Make love, silly. I really gotta go now."

Maria kissed her fingertip and touched it to Stump's lips, then stepped inside.

Stump turned and headed for Ol' Ug' with another lesson to ponder. Girlfriends were more complicated than fighting City Hall.

CHAPTER 26

Delores waited until the end of rush hour to begin a two-hour trek south around the backside of L.A. via I-15. Yolanda Vigil, the woman who'd initially tipped off the cops about Dixon's antics in the first place, had given an address in the beach town of Carlsbad. Other than her feisty attitude, Yolanda fit the profile that Dixon seemed to prefer—undocumented, not yet middle-aged and vulnerable.

Now, Delores wanted to have another meeting with Yolanda. The open road, a cold Pepsi, and steadily moving traffic lent her a much-needed lift.

Carlsbad was similar to other beach towns—large million-dollar homes by the water, with older, more modest homes inland. Yolanda lived in the latter where lush foliage was commonplace. At the home in question two giant red rose bushes climbed proudly like palace guards up either side of the front door while countless other healthy flowers decorated other sections of the mature landscaping.

Yolanda was supposed to be in a finished-off garage to the side and back of the property. Delores had seen the arrangement before. The family who owned the property usually lived in the main house and provided newly arrived undocumented immigrants and other homeless Hispanics with a relatively safe place to live until they could get acclimated. After a few months, the temporary boarders would move on and somebody else would take their place. Yolanda was simply one of the links in the chain.

Along the side of the house, Delores marveled at hundreds of delicate pink and white pansies that fluttered in the breeze like excited butterflies that were happy to see her. She tapped at the appropriate door and Yolanda answered. "Hi. Do you remember me?" Delores said. "I'm Detective Sanchez. We met in Palmdale a few weeks back. I'd like to ask you a few questions about your former husband if you don't mind."

Yolanda didn't answer.

Even though Delores was young, she'd been taught how to bond with apprehensive witnesses. "It's been a long drive. I'd be most grateful if you'd let me use your restroom."

Yolanda looked her up and down and then opened the door. "Oh, thank you," Delores said as she stepped inside. "I really appreciate it." Inside, two single beds lined the outside walls and presumably doubled as sofas. Across the small room, two chairs and a small kitchen table butted up to some very limited counter space. All of it was nicer than the dilapidated items she'd been using at Cal-Vista. She moved into the only other room and closed the door.

A couple minutes later she washed up and joined her hostess. "Do you mind if I sit down?"

Yolanda gently nodded.

"I know you're afraid," Delores began, pleased to have broken the ice, "but you don't need to be."

Yolanda remained rigid.

Delores pulled a few papers from her purse. "I've been investigating Mr. Browne. I think he's purposely misled several women about what it takes to become a citizen and I'd like to find out just what he told you and what your relationship was like. It would be a big favor if you'd help me."

Yolanda hesitated but then said, "He knows policemen."

"I know he's threatened you, but I'm an officer and if we

really wanted to harm you, we wouldn't have let you go the last time we saw you." Delores glanced toward the small kitchen counter. "Could I bother you for a cup of water?"

Yolanda nodded and moved toward the kitchen. "He told me they were watching me," she said.

Delores nodded. "I know he says things like that, but he doesn't have any authority over you or anybody else. You can believe me. We don't have anything against you."

Yolanda laid two glasses of lukewarm tap water on the table and sat down. Delores took a look at her water. As was typical around there, it had tiny floaty things in it. "If you don't mind my asking," she said, before taking the smallest sip possible, "how'd you meet Mr. Browne?"

Still hesitant, Yolanda eyed Delores before answering. Then, "I came up here with Claudia and Luis."

"Friends?"

"Claudia is my cousin. Luis is her husband. Luis had a job in L.A., but rents were lower in Palmdale so we moved into Mr. Dixon's building."

"But they must have left," Delores said, knowing that Dixon wouldn't get entangled with anybody who had family nearby.

Yolanda nodded. "Luis got a better job. He and Claudia moved in with Luis's new boss, but there was no room for me."

Delores could just about fill in the blanks from there, but the important thing was to keep Yolanda talking and eventually ask her to testify against Dixon. "So you were all alone. What happened next?"

"Mr. Dixon said I had to pay all of his rent by myself, but I had no money."

"So he offered to help you?"

"He said I could work for my rent," she said, nodding.

"Did you agree to do that?"

Yolanda stared at the ground. "He said there was something else."

"Get married?"

"He said he'd help me learn English and get a green card so I could get a better job and take care of myself."

"What about citizenship?"

"That too. He said the government would help pay my bills."

"Did he make you pay him some money too?"

"He wanted me to, but I didn't have no money so he said I had to live with him longer." She hung her head. "I thought that was what I wanted because I wouldn't have to move again."

Delores scooted her chair right in front of Yolanda's. "I have to ask you something personal, but it's very, very important. Did you have to have sex with him?"

Yolanda's head bobbed downward. "He said we had to or they wouldn't give me my papers."

"Well, that part is true. There's an interview where they want to make sure people aren't lying about their relationships. How long did all this go on?"

"Many months."

"Did he keep making you do those things?"

Yolanda scrunched her nose. "Yes. Other women too."

Delores shook her head in disgust. "Would you have done that with him if it weren't for the agreement you had?"

Yolanda's lower lip pressed upwards. "No. He's way older than me, and I like my own people."

Delores paused. "Just so I'm clear, Yolanda, are you saying that you only let him do those things with you because you thought he was going to help you stay in the U.S. and get you citizenship?"

"That's what he told me."

Although it was precisely the news that Delores hoped to hear, she sure as hell wasn't happy about it. She knew from her own experiences how ashamed and helpless Yolanda must have felt. God, how she hated men like that.

Yolanda sniffled. "I just hope Jesus will forgive me."

Delores placed a hand on Yolanda's knee. "Jesus knows that you only did what you had to do."

Yolanda's saddened eyes made contact, as if to say *thank you*. "He said if I told the police what we did I would go to jail. And now, you're here. Am I going to get deported?"

"Not if I have anything to do with it." Yolanda may have sneaked into the country illegally, but she was a gentle woman who didn't deserve to be exploited. "What you did was wrong, but you didn't know that. I have a big favor to ask of you. It would really help me if you'd be willing to press charges against Mr. Dixon. Do you know what that is?"

"No. I don't want to be around him. He might do something bad to me."

"Well, he can't really do that."

"That's what he told me you'd say."

"Well, what if I got some other people to start the whole thing? Would you be willing to tell the judge about your situation too?"

"A judge?" she shook her head wildly. "I don't want to do that."

"You won't get in trouble. Dixon is the one who's bad."

"No. No. No. I already told you too much."

Yolanda reminded Delores of Simone. Both were a few years older than she and both had been manipulated and abused by a man they'd trusted. "Do you know any other women who did the same things with Mr. Dixon?"

"Just Inez."

"Inez? Where can I find her?"

"Still at the building, I think."

"Would she talk to me without telling Dixon?"

"No. No. She and her daughter have been there for many years. They're loyal to him."

"I see." Delores said while she put her pen away. "What are you going to do now? Where are you going to live? How are you going to support yourself?"

"I met a nice man. He's got a job, but I'm afraid to tell him I slept with a man I didn't love."

Delores squeezed Yolanda's hand. "If you want my opinion, you should tell this new man the truth. If he's a good man, he'll understand." She reached in her pocket, handed Yolanda her business card and her only cash—a fifty-dollar bill. "I want you to have these things. If you ever need to talk to someone, you can call me. I promise not to tell anybody else without your permission." Yolanda's face contained both tears and a smile as they rose.

As Delores walked back past the flower field, she soaked up the outdoor beauty that contradicted some of the indoor ugliness she'd just left behind. Once back in the car, she noted that her tank was near empty. She opened her purse and peeked in her checkbook, knowing full well she'd already maxed out her overdraft protection. Ditto her credit card. All she had was a partial roll of quarters in the glove box that she kept for parking meters and emergencies.

Of course all of that would get worse in a few days when both her condo payment and Monday Girl's rent would come due. "Fuck!" she screamed as loudly as she could.

CHAPTER 27

THE NEXT DAY, DELORES PUMPED a handful of quarters into a parking meter and followed a couple skate boarders toward the beach. A gentle breeze blew her a warm kiss through a row of palm trees. The peace was literally just what her doctor ordered.

After her recent meetings with Dr. Moreno, Delores made some progress with some of her challenges but every frustrating meeting with Dixon Browne and his trail of victims set her back. And none of that addressed Delores's biggest, darkest secret—the black cloud matter.

When with her shrink, Delores had admitted to suffering with long-term intimacy problems borne out of the things Tio did to her and Simone when they were children. But Delores had never told anybody—not her shrink, not her mama, not even her priest during confession—how she learned to overcome her inadequacies. Why would she? She barely believed it herself.

Moreover, as long as she was making progress on her lesser issues, such as finding time to relax, she had reason to hope that her black cloud of shame would eventually dissipate on its own. Until then, she elected to remain focused on the present, and at the moment there was a delightful row of unique shops along the beach area to check out.

A couple minutes later Delores reached the boardwalk, stepped past the walkway to the asphalt and turned left, toward her primary destination: The Happy Place Bookstore. She'd seen it from afar some days back when she and Dixon were in the area. It was at the end of the next block by the Skate Plaza, which was abuzz with boarders, and wedged right between the bookstore and that impressive puddle of rumbling blue water on her right known as the Pacific Ocean.

As Delores followed the crowd, she expected to enjoy the scent of fresh-brewed coffee from the sidewalk cafés, but when she drew to within a few paces of the bookstore she was surprised by the earthy scent that had also pierced the salty air. A busy window display of unfamiliar titles bragged of the type of odd reads one could find inside.

The store itself was smaller than the cookie cutter chain stores but the classy wooden floor-to-ceiling bookcases lent the place much more charm. Original paintings, probably the work of locals, were packed onto every spare inch of wall space, most with price stickers on them. The lights were dim, and a half-dozen readers of eclectic ilk occupied randomly scattered, comfy chairs.

A short line of anxious buyers waited for their turn with the lone cashier who was a long-haired hippie-type wearing a sleeveless jean shirt and a touring cap. "Can I help you?" a woman said from behind Delores. The woman was too wise looking, too formal and too mature to be a clerk.

"Your place is so charming," Delores said, grinning.

"We try. I'm Millie Skater. My husband and I opened the place a long time ago. Are you looking for anything in particular?"

Delores glanced outside to the skaters in the ramps and resisted the urge to say that Millie's last name matched their activities. "I hear you have a nice section of travel books."

"Sure do." Millie said, pointing toward the back corner. "On the wall just past the restroom. Let me know if you need any help."

After thanking the learned shopkeeper, Delores glanced in the general direction of the travel books and slowly worked her way past several homemade displays. Considering the internet and the competition from the bigger book companies, it must have been tough to keep up a small shop like this.

When she reached her section, Delores scanned the titles of several dozen interesting hardcover possibilities. Since she had done very little traveling, part of her wanted to see pictures, but pictures took up pages where fascinating information could be revealed through the words and experiences of well-traveled authors. There were so many delicious prospects she already knew she'd be coming back.

She picked up a large white book, simply titled *Great Britain*, and gave it a quick thumbing. Loaded with pictures and stories, it seemed like a bargain for $17.50.

"You ever seen Coca-Cola London Eye?" a male's voice came from her side. She turned quickly to see a tall, thin, blonde man, wearing gorgeous maroon suspenders and smiling through a piano's worth of perfect white teeth.

"Well, no. I don't think I ever heard of it. A Coca-Cola store?"

He grinned. "It's no store. You Yanks call them Ferris wheels. It's much taller than the one in Pacific Park, up north a bit."

This time she detected his delightful British accent. "Sorry. I've never traveled very much."

"Me mum likes it," he added. "So it has to be good." He looked to be about thirty. No ring and was getting cuter by the minute.

"I've never heard of it."

"I used to work there, as a tour guide. It's always been my favorite attraction."

"Even better than Big Ben and the changing of the guard? I heard those were the best."

"They're nice. So are the museums. But nothin' beats the view from 135 meters high in the chilly London sky—

particularly when you're sitting in your gondola with a special friend, overlooking a dozen sights all at once."

"Oh, I get it. That's why they call it the *Eye*."

"The eye in the sky, it is. Day or night, it's just as good. Maybe I can show it to you sometime." He extended his hand. "My name is Gordon."

She tilted her head and took his hand. What a delightful stranger. "I'm Delores. What does Coca-Cola have to do with it?"

"They have sponsor rights and put red lights on it. Some locals don't like it but I think it's romantic."

So was this unexpected moment.

He smiled. "What does a lass such as Delores do when she's not reading books?"

Hmm. Some guys were intimidated by her career. Others were weirdly aroused by it. She hoped Gordon would be different. "I'm a constable," she said, trying to sound at least vaguely familiar with his lexicon.

"Are you on holiday?"

"No. Why would you ask that?"

He waved a gentle hand in front of her. "No uniform."

"I'm not that type of officer."

"Oh I get it. You must be an inquiry agent?"

Inquiry agent? Delores smiled and nodded. "I forgot that term."

He pointed toward the sidewalk café. "I've never met an inquiry agent before. Could we take a spot of tea?"

Delores was more inclined to go for an espresso, but what the hell. This was the kind of guy that had real promise and she was getting a little more confident about her ability to deal with nice men. She paid for the white book with a couple crumpled ten spots she'd found in her old purse the night before, caught a wink from Millie and eased outside where they grabbed a small table at the nearby café. Before long they were laughing about their language differences. "Another one," Gordon said. "No British lass would refer to her bum as a fanny."

"Why not?" Delores quizzed while grinning.

He leaned forward and whispered. "It means the other lady-thing. You know. The vagina."

"Oh, my gosh," she said, raising a hand to her lips in mocked surprise. "I'm glad you said something before I said something really embarrassing."

Gordon laughed. "That would not be good." He tipped his cup of tea her way. "Would you have time to go for a walk?"

Delores preferred to know people a little better before going anywhere with them, but Gordon had the pleasant ability to ask questions without being offensive. Probably something he picked up as a tour guide. And now that she'd had a couple conversations with her shrink, she was feeling more confident in her ability to deal with men. What harm could possibly come from a trek down a well-traveled boardwalk in the daylight? "Why not?" she said, faking a British accent. "An inquiry agent ought to be able to protect herself from a handsome lad with suspenders if she has to."

Gordon smiled, grabbed her hand and led her across the pavement to the sandy side where there were jugglers and mimes and every sort of street merchant scattered amongst the palm trees. She and Gordon strolled a hundred yards before they reached a gray-haired man sitting on the sidewalk with his back to the base of a tree.

An upside-down fedora rested at his side for donations while he strummed a beat-up acoustic guitar and a tender version of "Puff the Magic Dragon" floated past his yellowed teeth. Delores wondered if the wrinkled hippie had any grandkids as she tossed her last three quarters into his hat.

A quarter-mile further, they crossed back to the boardwalk side where they inched their way past an endless chain of window displays. At one point they drifted into a gift shop where they were told the local government was making serious rumblings about replacing the street vendors with a row of hotels—an idea nobody seemed to like.

Finally, still hand–in-hand, they reached a small vacant shop with a hand-made For Rent sign in the window. They tucked into the breezeway to get out of the flow of foot traffic for a moment. Then after a few more semi-private moments, Gordon gently pulled Delores to him. "I'm going to be in the states a few more months and I'd love to get to know you," he said, leaning in for a kiss.

Her eyes shot toward the water and back. A familiar horrible chill raced up her back. She flashed thoughts and images of her youth and Tio rubbing his hands all over her. Did Gordon really like her or was he just another pervert? The chill intensified as she recalled all the other men she'd rejected at impromptu moments like this. It was too much, too quick. "I can't," she said, while shoving her new book in Gordon's chest. "I've gotta go." She turned and ran all the way to her car without looking back.

As she drove away she wiped her tear-covered cheek and cursed herself. She knew from past experience that now she had two choices: either suffer through days and days of self-flagellation or be rid of her angst the usual way: revert to her black cloud personality. At least that way she could pass her rejection, like a hot potato, along to somebody else.

CHAPTER 28

Prior to her trip to the bookstore, Delores thought she was gaining ground on her intimacy issues, but her run-away moment from Gordon proved the opposite. She still couldn't trust decent men.

It wasn't new. Delores had always had boyfriend issues. She gave her virginity to a high school classmate who promptly dumped her. Other experiences were equally disappointing. It seemed as if she had no more value than an old coat. Just try her on for size and cast her aside when done.

Then she met Dr. Jeanine Moreno and after Delores discussed some of her intimacy issue she began to understand herself better. She'd had deeper thoughts and hoped she could handle her romantic encounters better. Then she met Gordon.

Once again, the love coward inside Delores took over, and if her knees buckled in fear every time she faced a simple kiss, how could she be certain the dangers at her work wouldn't lead her to the same type of crippling impotence? A cop had to be much stronger than that.

For better or worse, she had learned from experience that the quickest way to overcome her weakest moments was to be even stronger in similar situations—only in these alternate situations she was the one who had all the control. It was time to balance things out.

Delores had to find a man. Just about any man would do. That was the point. Get him alone and prove that when it came to the love act, she could be just as devoid of emotion as any cold-hearted man. In short: Cowardly Delores was out; Don't-Give-a-Damn Delores was in.

The first step was to cake on enough make-up to impress a clown. Follow that up with a pair of four-inch hoop earrings and a dozen mists of perfume in all the right places. Then she donned a pair of tight-fittin' jeans with bangles.

She'd already picked out a bar. Buckaroos was back toward L.A. and away from everybody she knew. She'd driven past the joint a few times and seen the pickup trucks and the big ol' hats. Perhaps she'd call herself Lorraine. She hadn't decided yet. All she knew for certain was she'd never ridden a cowboy before.

Nearly an hour later, Delores pulled into the parking lot. As she reached the front porch, the stench of yesterday's beer suggested she was about to step fifteen decades back in time. She half-expected a saloonkeeper to throw a drunk cowboy out on his ear for making lewd comments to an upstanding saloon girl.

Inside, Buckaroos was dark as midnight, but Delores could make out a dozen good ol' boys in cowboy hats, and half that many ladies. Except for several booted dudes at the bar, nearly everybody else was sitting at tables. Against the far wall, a jukebox took up a spot where a player piano and a bare-armed dancing girl with a colorful ruffled skirt would've fit right in.

Delores eyed a seat at a table away from the speakers. A mustached bartender, with a white towel tucked in his belt, damn near beat her to her seat. "What can I getcha?"

"Just a Bud," she said.

A moment later, a tall cowboy from the bar, maybe in his mid-thirties, headed her way with two Buds in one hand and two cold mugs in the other. If she were a movie producer casting for a Western, she wouldn't have to change a thing.

Along with blue jeans, boots and a white cowboy hat, he wore a light blue shirt with snaps instead of buttons. He had to have a name like Luke or Austin or Bart. "M'name's Clint," he said, pouring her a beer. "This one's on me." He dropped his hat on the chair, revealing short, curly brown hair. "What would your name be?"

Delores grinned. When it came to picking up men, it couldn't have been much easier. "They call me Delores," she said, tipping her beer his way as if to thank him for the freebee. "What do you do for a living? Ride bulls?"

"Me? Naw. When I ain't in this joint, I'm in another one jest like it. I sell boots." He pointed a knuckle her way. "How 'bout you? You got a job?"

"Yeah, I'm a cop." It was always fun to watch their eyes when she said that. "Does that intimidate you?"

He grinned and raised-up his beer. "Hell, no. Why should it? I ain't done nothin' wrong."

"Most guys get nervous around cops."

"Well. I ain't most guys. You lookin' to bust somebody?"

"Nope. I'm on my own time, just looking to have a little fun. That's all." She sipped at her beer.

"Oh, yeah. What kind of fun can a lady-cop have in a place like this? There ain't no bad boys in here."

"Cops are just like anybody else, ya know."

He turned partly around. "Hey boys. Looks like we got us a Sheriffette."

Several heads turned her way but nobody seemed to be shocked or impressed. Delores looked him in the eye. "Was that a tip-off to somebody?"

"Why would I give a damn about these cowboys? If they done something wrong they can fend for themselves."

Delores tipped her near-empty beer mug his way and he ordered another round.

For the next half hour Delores and Clint discussed their ages and lack of spouses and kids. Then he headed for the men's room and she scoped out his butt. Not bad.

After they downed another beer, Clint pointed his chin her way. "Mind if I ask you something personal?"

"Guess not. I don't have to answer if I don't want to."

"Did you ever get it on in a jail cell?"

She'd heard that question before. "Nope. Too many other people around."

"So you would have done it if nobody was around?"

She tipped her head down in mock shame and then glanced flirtatiously his way. "I'll never tell."

"What about doing it with your uniform on? You ever done that?"

"Does that type a thing turn you on?"

"I dunno. Never thought about it much, but I heard ladies like to do it with guys who wear uniforms. That true?"

She sniggered and pointed at his hat. "Like phony cowboys?"

He sat back, then smiled and took a swig from his beer mug. Then, "You saw right through me, didn't you?"

"It took a few minutes," she said. "Some of your language was a little too sophisticated for a simple cowboy."

"Oh, yeah?"

"Another thing. Nearly every guy in here has a can of chewing tobacco in his back pocket, but you don't."

"I never liked sitting down with a can in my pants."

"Then there were all the questions. That's what a salesman does. So I reasoned that when you're not working, you aren't really a cowboy. It's just an act. However, you're pretty good at playing the role and you've probably hooked up a few times, so you don't fight it." She stared him in the eye. "Is that about right?"

He nodded. "Close enough. But here's something this salesman figured out about you. You ain't been looking around at the other guys very much."

"So? Does that boost your ego or something?"

"What it really says is, you were telling the truth when you said you're not here to bust anybody. If you were, you would have approached the bartender because he's the most likely person to know the people in here."

Delores smiled.

"So that means you were probably also telling the truth about wanting to have a good time. And more importantly, you haven't eliminated me."

"It appears salespeople are just as good at reading cops as cops are at reading salespeople."

"And all of that means you're open to getting out of this place. I've got a nice hotel room just a couple miles down the road. I'd like to drop by and take off these damn boots. Then we can put all the bullshit aside and get something to eat."

Delores grinned. "I guess I roped me a cowboy."

CHAPTER 29

WHAT WAS MARIA DOING ON THE SIDEWALK, two blocks from Cal-Vista and waving Stump down? He pulled Ol' Ug' over. "I want you to meet Mama," she said.

"Okay, but why are you out here?"

"If Dixon sees you or your bike he's going to butt in again."

True that. Whenever Stump and Maria had something private to do, good ol' Dixon always seemed to show up. "Okay. I guess I can lock my bike to a sign post."

Since Dixon usually paraded the courtyard they hurried to the back of Maria's building before they scooted down the hall to her apartment. Maria opened the door. "I'll get Mama."

While Stump waited he noticed a pink theme in their apartment. The curtains, lampshades, a sofa and several candles seemed like part of a team. "Mama. This is Stump," Maria said from just behind him.

Stump pivoted. "Hello, Mrs. Quintana. Maria gave me one of your cookies the other day. It was delicious. Thank you."

Mrs. Quintana walked right over to Stump and hugged him, then took his hand. "You loved your mama. You are welcome in our home."

Wow. Stump had barely met the woman and he already understood why Maria was so fond of her.

"You sit down. I get you another cookie."

"Maria tells me you've lived here longer than anybody."

"Since Maria was born. Then we lost her papa."

"He was a hero," Maria said.

Stump nodded. "I know what it's like to lose somebody. I lost my mom and my dog." Stump smiled. "I called him *Dogg*."

"You made a park for your mama. You're a good man."

Stump glanced at Maria. She'd obviously told her mama about the doggie park. It was difficult to believe that anybody, even Dixon Browne, would push this gentle woman around. Maybe she'd verify something else that was on his mind. "Can I ask you a question? Do you like the manager? 'Cause I sure don't."

"He lets me work. I do what he wants." Her face was devoid of emotion, as if she were afraid, just as Maria had said. Maybe a mild push would confirm it.

"I think he's been taking money from some of the people around here. Do you think I should call the police?"

Her head swiveled back and forth. "Jesus says to forgive."

"But stealing is one of the Ten Commandments."

"No police. We just do what Mr. Dixon wants."

Maria tilted her head toward Stump as if to say, *I told you so.*

"You'd better get to work now, but come back when your work is done? I'm making posole."

"That's Mexican soup," Maria said. "Mama is the best cook anywhere."

Stump usually ate fast food so how could he refuse? "Maybe for a little bit, but I have to get home early. I'm working on another project."

"Something else for his mama," Maria said before turning to Stump. She led him back to the hall and whispered. "Juanita and Manuel are expecting you after you get off work."

He nodded and hurried off to get Ol' Ug'. No wonder Maria was so protective of her mother. Mrs. Quintana was a tender woman who deserved the same type of protection from bullies, particularly Dixon Browne, as his own mother.

After reaching his bike Stump realized he had a big problem. Aside from Goggle searches, he didn't know much about doing research. Furthermore, he was supposed to do his sleuthing without certain people knowing what he was up to. On another level, it was exciting as hell to enter into his first-ever investigation. He thought of it as, *The Case of Did He or Did He Not?*

If Stump lucked out, he'd discover that Kraft was correct: Jiggle Jaw had so much power there was no need for violence, in which case, there was some other explanation for Maria's mama's strange behavior. That would allow Stump and Maria to "*sync their devices*," as James called it.

Unfortunately, Stump had a hunch that the investigation would likely take a route closer to what Maria suspected. He knew first-hand that Dixon was an intimidator. It wasn't difficult to imagine the man doing other sleazy things.

Together, it was an interesting puzzle that Stump might have appreciated more if he didn't have to get ready for the next City Council meeting, which was less than a week away and he still hadn't attended to the things his attorney wanted. With so many demands on his time, something had to give.

After his shift he threw his backpack over his shoulders and cycled three blocks to a convenience store where he handcuffed Ol' Ug' to the bike rack. After that, he jogged right back to Cal-Vista and sneaked around to the back door of building seven so Dixon wouldn't see him. Inside, he scanned the nametags on the mailboxes and found Manuel and Juanita Alvarado in Unit 102.

Stump had seen enough detective shows on TV to have a rough idea of what he was supposed to do, but when it came to the details he wasn't exactly sure. Should he take notes? Use his iPhone recorder? Take pictures? He wished he'd made a list of potential questions before he got there.

Oh, well. He'd just have to wing it. He gently rapped on their door. A few seconds later a big scary-looking guy answered—presumably Manuel.

"Hello. I'm Stump. Maria asked me to speak with Juanita."

Manuel let him in and they all sat in their nicely decorated living room. "You have a nice apartment here," Stump said.

Manuel sat forward and glared at Stump. "Mr. Dixon said you got our line-painting job." His tone was intimidating.

Stump shifted his feet, glanced at Juanita then back at Manuel. "I didn't know it was going to cause a problem."

"But you're rich. You don't need no money."

Stump's jaw muscles tightened. Why did people keep saying that? "I'm not rich. Someday, I might get some money, but that's a long time away."

"What are we supposed to do?" Juanita asked. "Live on the streets?"

"No. No. I'm sorry. Honest. I didn't even know they were thinking of painting the stripes. If you'd like, I can ask Mr. Kraft if I can do something else."

Seconds passed before the corners of Manuel's mouth curled upwards. Then Juanita broke into a big smile and Manuel laughed and pointed at Stump. "We're just joking you. We know that a rich boy wouldn't ride that old bicycle around."

Stump hesitated, then grinned and pretended to wipe his brow. "Whew! That's a relief. For a minute there, I thought Maria was crazy for sending me up here."

"We've wanted to do something like you're doing for a long time," Juanita said, "but we couldn't afford to get caught."

"Why don't you just go to the owner? He's the real boss."

"No good," Manuel said. "Mr. Kraft leaves everything up to Dixon."

"We need the money and Dixon knows it," Juanita added.

Manuel raised a finger. "Besides, we heard Mr. Kraft's days are numbered."

Stump's brows jammed down. Naturally, he knew that Mr. Kraft was ill, but this sounded more imminent. He gawked at Juanita. "Are you saying he's dying?"

"According to Dixon, it's six months tops. Poor thing."

Manuel nodded. "My uncle got like that. He just wanted to die in peace, but everybody dragged it out. It was stupid."

"But you're different," Juanita added. "Mr. Dixon can't fire you or make you move away or threaten to deport you."

Stump swallowed. Naturally, he'd heard terms like "white privilege" before, but this was the first time he understood that he'd actually caught a few breaks in life.

Manuel spoke next. "We've always known Dixon steals money from us, but after he got that fancy car he takes even more."

"Really? How?"

"Lots of ways. Mr. Kraft bought enough carpet to redo three apartments, but they only carpeted two. Then Dixon had me help load the rest in a pickup. The driver handed Dixon some money, but I don't know how much it was."

Juanita pointed her jaw toward her husband. "Tell him about the paint."

"That too. Two weeks ago Home Depot delivered fifty gallons of paint in five-gallon buckets. We painted some apartments and then I noticed three of the buckets were missing. That stuff is twenty-four dollars a gallon."

Stump automatically did the math. "Wow. That's three-sixty."

"He's got girlfriends and wives too," Juanita said.

"Four wives that we know of," Manuel added, the veins in his neck bulging.

Juanita tapped Manuel's knee. "Girlfriends too. He's always hitting on women." She made a tightened face. "Some of them go along with him."

"Gross," Stump said, matching Juanita's expression. Then, "Do you think he'd hurt anybody, like Maria's mama?"

"Wouldn't surprise me," Manuel said. "He used to drink a lot and throw his weight around. One day he threatened me, but we both knew I could rip his head off, so he backed off."

"That's when he started giving us odd jobs," Juanita said.

"He's lucky I didn't kill him," Manuel added, red-faced.

"Aside from a long time ago, is there any sign he's beaten up anybody lately?"

"I've seen bruises on his wives before," Juanita said. "And Francisca told me he pushed her down. Now, Inez is sweeping sidewalks again. I don't know why he'd hit that sweet woman."

Stump had had those exact thoughts. He nodded toward Juanita. "Maria mentioned a notebook?"

"Dixon keeps it in his desk. I clean his office and sometimes he leaves it out. I looked at it once, but I couldn't tell what it said cause it was messed-up letters and numbers. One of his previous wives, Elizabeth, said that he does so many bad things he has to write them down so he doesn't forget anything."

"Could be a code."

"That guy's always up to no good," Manuel said with a scowl. "I told her to steal the notebook and mail it to the police."

"I told you I don't want to get in trouble for stealing. And we could lose our jobs if I got caught."

"If you could get it tomorrow," Stump said, "I might be able to make copies in Mr. Kraft's office after he goes home."

"No, no, no," Juanita said, shaking her head. "It would be too risky. If Dixon caught any of us, he'd blame me and throw us out."

"What if you give it to me when I first get here? I can go up to the Fed/Ex store and make copies. Then we can put it right back."

"I'd rather do that. But you have to promise that if you get caught you won't say anything about us."

"Of course not. I'll just say I found it."

Having no more questions, Stump excused himself. Outside, he realized he liked poking around. It was like solving a complicated math problem, only this problem actually had a legitimate purpose. He couldn't wait to update Maria about *The Case of Did He or Did He Not?*

CHAPTER 30

Following Myles's advice, Stump used his paycheck to open his first checking account. By the time he paid for new checks and peeled off ten bucks for spending money he remained nearly broke. On top of that, he'd lost a chunk of work time for the privilege of establishing said account and money not earned was just as costly as unwanted expenses.

The only good thing to come out of the irritating exercise was Myles had agreed to deposit another thousand bucks into the account to avoid monthly service charges. Disgusted, Stump mounted Ol' Ug' and pedaled off to Cal-Vista where he hurried to Juanita's apartment for the notebook.

"You're late," she said. "I'm supposed to be working, not waiting around for you."

"I'm sorry, but I had to—"

"Here it is," she said, handing him the notebook. "Now hurry, I want to get it back into Mr. Dixon's desk before he notices it's gone."

Stump sighed. "I'm really sorry but I haven't checked in with Mr. Kraft yet."

The muscles in her face stiffened. "But you said you were going to get copies right away."

"I was, but something came up. I'll get 'em right after I find out what he wants me to do today. I promise." Stump lifted the flap of his backpack and tucked the notebook inside before he hurried toward Rodger Kraft's office.

"I'm sorry I'm late, Mr. Kraft, but I had to get to a bank." Stump adjusted his backpack. "How you feeling?"

"Been better. You're going to clean out some gutters today, but it's really hot on the roof so go in the kitchen and get yourself a large bottle of water, then check with Dixon. He'll show you how to do it."

Dixon? Ah, crap. That guy was always a pain in the butt. "Okay, we'll take care of it," Stump said, already in the kitchen area.

Kraft nodded. "I'm not feeling well, so I'm going to go home for the day."

"I'll walk you to your car," Stump said.

As Kraft drove off, Stump considered using Mr. Kraft's copier to copy Dixon's notebook, but Dixon was always lurking in the weeds and Stump already promised Juanita he wouldn't do that. Instead, he threw the water into his backpack, returned to Ol' Ug' and biked to the Fed/Ex store.

There, a woman in a red jogging outfit was busily working at the copy machine. "Excuse me," Stump said. "How much longer are you going to be?"

She pointed to a full canvas sack on the floor. "About five minutes. I've got a few more things to copy for a party."

Thirsty, Stump gulped down some of his water then noticed the Dollar Store just a couple doors down. He returned the bottle to his backpack, which he plopped next to the copier before heading outside and down the sidewalk.

Inside the Dollar Store he rushed to the greeting card section, perused a few cards, found one he liked for Maria and hurried to the checkout area where he penned a comment inside the card before rushing back to Fed/Ex.

At the copier he swapped the card for the notebook in his backpack, set the backpack aside and proceeded to copy nearly forty pages. Some minutes later he paid for the copies before opening his backpack to lock away the notebook and copies. Oh, crap. The water bottle had leaked and drenched both his schoolbooks and Maria's card. The only items that weren't wet were the copies and notebook.

He shook his damn head, went outside, dumped out the damn water, threw the damn bottle away, and dangled the damn backpack, wet books and all, over his damn handlebars. He threw Ol' Ug' on the ground and maneuvered Dixon's notebook and the sacked copies behind his back, under his shirt and inside his belt.

As he made the return trip to Cal-Vista, his eyelids narrowed to slits. An hour ago, he had ten bucks, which he planned on using judiciously until the next payday, but he'd blown nearly all of it on the copies and the card. On top of everything else he'd just lost another half-hour, for which he could have earned five bucks and tripled it, and he'd probably have to pay for his damaged books. How the hell was he going to get a car if he kept pissing away his money and time on everybody else?

An irritating return trip to Cal-Vista ended at the bike rack where Dixon was standing, arms folded. "At it again, I see," he said, in a snarky tone.

Careful not to reveal the bulge under the back of his shirt, Stump wiggled his bike into position. "I don't know what you're talking about."

"Oh bullshit, rich boy. Your pattern is as predictable as gravity. You waited 'til the old man drove off and then went for a joy ride." Dixon held out his hand, "Give it to me."

"Give you what?"

"You know what, rich boy. My notebook. It's missing and I'm betting you're the one who has it."

Stump might have crapped his pants right then and there if Dixon's word choices had been different. The words, *I'm betting* meant Dixon wasn't sure where the book was. "I don't know nothing about no notebook," Stump fibbed.

Dixon pointed at the backpack. "Then you won't mind showing me what's in there."

Stump felt like the cat that ate the canary, but he played it straight. "I don't have to show you nothing."

"What you afraid of, rich boy?"

"I ain't afraid. It's just stupid to play games. I'm going to go put my stuff away, then I'll be ready for work." Stump flung the still-damp backpack over his shoulder to hide the bulge under his shirt before walking off.

In Kraft's office, he quickly dragged a chair to the bookcase and hid the notebook and copies on top and out of sight. He then laid his backpack on the floor and perfectly aligned it with the edge of the center cushion.

He grinned and returned to the courtyard, where Dixon had leaned a twenty-foot extension ladder against the side of building two. "You're going to clean out the gutters," Dixon said. "I want you to scoop out the debris with your hands and drop it over the edge to the ground. When you're done, go around and clean up your mess."

Sounded easy enough except for one thing: Stump had never used an extension ladder. He grabbed ahold of a rung and looked skyward. The damn thing reached half-way to the sun.

He sturdied it as best he could and apprehensively stepped on the lowest rung. Once there he brought his other foot to the same rung. Only a bajillion more steps to go.

"What's the matter, rich boy? You scared?"

Damn right he was but he wasn't about to admit it. "I'll be alright. I just have to get used to it. That's all."

"Well, get going. The old man ain't paying you all that big money just to suck your thumb."

Stump's fingers shook. If other people could do it, he could too. Just raise one foot and keep going. He squeezed the next rung so Dixon wouldn't see his fingers quiver. He took another step and followed it with a few more before the ladder began to pulsate. Why would it do that?

Another up-glance revealed he'd barely begun. His toes went numb but he forced himself to continue. The next few steps took him a full eight feet off the ground where the pulsation had become more like a vibrating jackhammer. Dixon had to be screwing with him, but a look out of the corner of Stump's eye revealed that Jiggle Jaw was off to the side.

"This is great," Dixon chortled. "I ain't seen knees tremble like that since the last earthquake."

Screw him. Stump took another rung. Then the next. Keep going. It got a little easier. Finally, he'd made it to the top, some two stories above ground. He leapt from the ladder onto the roof and stepped back out of Dixon's sight before letting out a deep breath of relief.

"Good news," Dixon yelled from below. "You'll be up there the rest of your shift. Now you won't be distracted by your girlfriend."

What a strange effin' dude.

CHAPTER 31

THE VIEW WAS PRETTY COOL, up there where the birds spied upon the land creatures. At the same time Cal-Vista's roof was hotter than Satan's oven. Stump attempted to kneel down near the edge of the building, but when his hands hit the roofing asphalt he sprang back and had to regroup.

He removed his shirt and folded it to make a mat. He knelt before one of the over-sized gutters that were packed with three inches of black grossness, presumably rotted palm leaves. Dixon must have known this was a disgusting job, but complaining would only lend the bastard extra pleasure.

As instructed, Stump shoved his bare hand into the near-scalding gooey mess and stirred up a roof-stink that would have humbled a sewage plant. He wished he'd brought gloves. With a handful of gutter-gunk, he peeked over the edge and dropped his first stink bomb, which splatted violently on impact. It was sorta neat, until he recalled that there were windows down there. He'd better avoid messing them up or Dixon would make a stink of his own.

Stump scanned the ground, found a space between windows and dropped another glob but it splattered on the building itself. After a couple more messy experiments he settled on making bigger piles but fewer of them and a little further away from the building.

Before long he made a game of it. With each new handful of goo he pretended to be a precision dive-bomber, who dropped bombs on bad guys without causing collateral damage. He made a whistle trail as the gunk-bombs fell. Then when they hit their target he made an explosion sound and waved his arms around as if to swat away dangerous shrapnel.

After that, he became a rescue worker as he dropped supplies out of a helicopter to starving children. Then he was God himself punishing the sinners with a brand-new black plague that no bad man could possibly survive. Before he knew it, he'd made it half way around the building and to the corner. His hands were pink from the heat and disgusting but he'd killed all the bad guys in the entire world.

He rose, opened his combination T-shirt and kneepad and picked the least dirty spot to wipe his dripping brow. He wished he'd brought another bottle of water. He turned to get to the next gutter just as Dixon came out of Mr. Kraft's building. Stump grinned. No doubt Jiggle Jaw had checked out his backpack. The beauty of it was Dixon would find nothing while the very thing he wanted was hiding just inches above his head. Served him right.

Stump finished cleaning out the other sides of the building and rose. There were six more buildings to go. He bopped around to the ladder and suddenly all of that dive-bomber courage he'd experienced earlier had evaporated. God, it was a long way down. How do you get around to the front of a ladder without falling on your ass? What if it slides to one side? His knees began to quiver again. He paused a second, wiped off his hands and snagged his cell out of his pocket. Even the best fighter pilots called in the reserves when needed.

While he waited for Maria to come hold the ladder, he reminded himself that the next City Council meeting was just days off and he still hadn't completed the work Danielle Delgado requested. There was only one way to get everything done. He texted James. *Gotta cut school tomorrow. Watch for robo-call.*

"Hey? You up there?" Thank God. The Cavalry had arrived.

The ladder was remarkably stable with Maria holding it and half-way down the jitters were gone. Stump wanted to kiss her for a couple different reasons. Instead he asked a favor. "Can you get me an old towel to replace my shirt while I get a drink out of the hose and move the ladder to the next building?"

"Only if you're still going to see me and Mama later."

He was already looking forward to it.

After two more buildings Stump cleaned up his messes and had used up his workday, but he still had some personal business to attend to. Back in Mr. Kraft's office, his backpack was at least six inches away from where he'd left it. Obviously Dixon had checked for the notebook just as Stump suspected. "Screw you," Stump said out loud. He washed his hands and face; then, he retrieved the notebook from the top shelf and hurried to Juanita and Manuel's apartment.

Juanita flung the door open before he even knocked. "Where've you been? Dixon knows his book is missing and he thinks I did it." They joined Manuel in the living room.

"I've got it right here," Stump said, tapping his backpack.

Manuel shook his head. "You have to get out of here. If Dixon catches us together, he'll know what happened. You can keep the copies but get rid of the notebook so he can't catch any of us with it."

"Will do." Stump hurried out the back door and circled around the back of the parking lot so he could come in the back door to Maria's building.

Maria must have been watching for him. She stepped into the hall wearing a lovely tight blouse and blue shorts atop those long, honey-colored legs. "Let's go for a walk," she said.

Stump grabbed her hand. "Are you sure? My clothes are so dirty, you must be embarrassed to be with me."

"That's silly," she said as they moved through the hall.

"You're a working man. You have to get dirty. I'm proud of you."

Stump beamed, silently. He wanted to hug her—and more.

As they marched up the street, Stump filled her in about Dixon, the notebook and the water leak in his backpack. "It even ruined a card I bought you."

"A card for me?" she said, letting go of his hand. "Nobody ever bought me a card, except for my birthday."

"I've still got it, but it's all messed up from the water. You can see it if you want to."

"Yes. Yes. Show it to me."

Amused, Stump retrieved the water-damaged envelope from his backpack. An ink stain had drooled all over her name on the outside. She grinned, opened it and read it out loud. *Violets are blue, Roses are red. I'm glad you're my girlfriend, the young dude said.* She viewed the handwritten part. *You're one of my favorite people. Love, Stump.* She pulled it toward her chest. "I love it."

"But it's all messed up."

"I don't care." She threw her arms around his neck. "I love you too." The kiss that followed was long, tongue-fun and sloppy. Stump's mirror buddy would have been proud.

CHAPTER 32

IF ADULT LIFE TAUGHT STUMP ANYTHING it was that the benefits, such as long, late-night phone conversations with Maria, came with a high price. Among other things he had ditched school several times to catch up on his other obligations. Now it was Saturday morning and he was pooped.

He stuffed a couple pages of copies from Dixon's notebook in his pocket and forced himself to get his ass to work. He mounted Ol' Ug' and felt as if the pedals were pushing back.

A mile up, he stopped at a convenience store, snagged a Red Bull and kissed his last three bucks goodbye. He threw down the first gulp, climbed back on his bike and thought about Maria. He wasn't sure if they were actually *in love* but she'd mentioned people making love a couple of times and if he was reading her correctly there might be opportunities along those lines in the very near future.

One of the best ways to get her to play lip-lock was to have something new to tell her regarding his investigation of Dixon. Maybe the papers in his back pocket would serve that purpose.

At eight-thirty he flushed down the last of his energy drink and coasted into the bike rack. Across the courtyard Juanita's cleaning cart sat parked on the sidewalk. Good, he had some news for her.

Juanita was scrubbing down the washing machines. "What did you find out?" she asked the second he entered the noisy laundry room.

"I threw out the notebook, but I've been too busy to look through the copies."

"Everybody's busy. Try being a mom and cleaning an entire complex." She had a good point. People like her and Manuel obviously had it much rougher than he did. "Before you leave today," she said to him, "you should go next door. The man who manages that place hates Mister Dixon."

"Oh really?"

"He says we have too many people here and nobody controls them. He doesn't like it when the kids get noisy." A huge, unexpected smile stretched across Juanita's face. "Last night, he banged on Dixon's door. It had something to do with broken beer bottles somebody threw over our fence into his parking lot. Before I knew it, they both came running out of Dixon's apartment. Dixon was chasing him and waving his gun in the air and yelling like a wild man." She stopped and raised her hand to cover her grin. "He was wearing his bathrobe and slippers, but nothing else. Not even his teeth."

Juanita's happy mood was contagious. Stump smirked too.

"Then his bathrobe flew wide open like a cape, and his *thingy* was flopping up and down while he ran." She held her thumb and forefinger about an inch apart and laughed so hard she snorted, which made her laugh even harder and snort again.

Stump envisioned the 50ish Dixon; toothless, caped, and running around waving a big ol' gun in the air while little ol' Johnson flopped in the wind. "I gotta admit," he said, and joining her giggle, "That's pretty funny alright. I wish I'd seen it."

After they'd both calmed down, Stump shook his head one last time and pointed his finger in the direction of the neighbor's building. "I gotta get to work, but I'll get over there later." Then he recalled the first night he'd met Juanita and Manuel and how unprepared he felt. He snagged his cell. "Do you know the guy's name?"

"Connors. Mr. Connors."

After making a few notes, Stump hustled over to Mr. Kraft's office where the boss was resting on his sofa. "Morning, Mr. Kraft," Stump said, while pulling his timesheet off the bookshelf. "What do you have for me today?"

"Before we get into that," Mr. Kraft said while sitting up, "I've got something I need to talk to you about." He rubbed his eyes and sat up. "Dixon tells me that after I leave here each day you're doing things besides your work, like talking to girls and leaving the property. Is that true?"

This wasn't good. At the same time, Mr. Kraft seemed more exhausted than angry. "Yes, it's true. I've had to do some things for school and the City Council project I told you about. For instance, last night, I wrote part of a report that I have to give to a building inspector tomorrow. I didn't get to sleep until two in the morning."

"You're working on a Sunday?"

"Have to. The big meeting is Tuesday evening, right after I get done working here."

"You're not charging me for the time you're spending on those extraneous activities, are you?"

"No sir. That wouldn't be right." Stump showed Kraft his timesheet. "I keep track of my time, just like you told me. Look here. Today, I wrote down that I started at eight forty-five even though I was here a little earlier."

Kraft waved off the timesheet. "I already looked that over. I wasn't sure why a fellow with such a short shift would break his day into several blocks, but now I get it. What about this girlfriend I heard about? She's not going to interfere with your work, is she?"

"I admit that we like each other. I like some of the other people around here too, but I work a little extra to make up for any time I spend with her. You can tell that I've been getting my work done."

Mr. Kraft nodded. "I noticed that too. Between us, I don't blame you. She's pretty charming, but don't get too distracted—and just make sure you don't bill me for time you spend on something else. Okay?"

"I won't. I promise."

"Alright then, now that we've got that settled, I want you to get a large push broom from the maintenance room and sweep the back part of the parking lot, especially the lines, so we can restripe them next week."

As Stump made his way to the parking lot he scratched his head. He'd heard comments at school and on TV about rich people in general taking advantage of other people, but Mr. Kraft sure didn't fit that description. He was a nice man who went out of his way to be fair. Stump was more determined than before to do a good job for the man.

As the morning and afternoon passed, the desert sun bounced non-stop off the parking lot pavement and stole more and more of Stump's energy until finally he needed a serious break. He scrounged a few coins from the bottom of his pocket and bought a Pepsi from the vending machine, then drifted toward Mr. Kraft's office where he took a few pages from Dixon's notebook and had a seat in the bathroom.

His previous glances at the pages revealed a mishmash of letters and digits that didn't make sense. This time he looked for patterns. Then he saw the letters *EJJ*. That had to be a clue.

CHAPTER 33

A DAY OF REST? What a crock. Sunday or not, Stump had just gotten thumped in the head with a pillow. James came by as agreed to help deliver the last batch of brochures. Stump hoped to squeeze in a couple driving hours after that and if there was any time left over, he wanted to catch up on any loose ends for his upcoming meeting with the City Council. Oh, yeah. And mow the lawn of Danielle Delgado's parents and talk with Maria.

After a piece of toast, Myles, James and Stump packed into Myles's truck and Stump drove to his old neighborhood. There they waited for home inspector Geoff Harrington per Danielle Delgado's suggestion. Harrington was to drive the neighborhood and issue an official report about the general safety of the homes as compared to those in other communities. His findings would be included in information packages at Tuesday's meeting.

"Did Geoff decide how much he's going to charge me?" Stump asked Myles.

"He usually gets four hundred to inspect a home, but this is a little different, so he was going to ask his boss if he could reduce it to a couple hundred."

Myles might as well have punched Stump in the belly. "But that'll take most of my next paycheck."

"I guess it will, but I think we can add his fee to the money you already owe me for the bicycle tires."

James jabbed Stump in the ribs. "Ya can't beat that."

Stump shook his head. "I feel like an effing mother bird. As soon as I catch a juicy worm, the chicks all want it."

"Just wait until you get a car," James said.

Myles nodded as if he totally agreed. "Speaking of the tires, when you going to pay me back?"

Fortunately Stump had anticipated this topic. "Don't creditors like to make loans to people who they know will pay them back?"

"Sure. Why?"

"I got a small pay check but after I paid the damn bank fees and kept a little for spending money, I don't have much left, and it's two more weeks to the next payday."

"Common problem," Myles said. "It's called living beyond your means."

"I can write you a check for the whole sixty dollars I owe you, and you can lend it right back to me—like the banks do."

Myles chuckled. "First off we're closer to a hundred when we consider the helmet. And second, you'll never get me paid back that way. Why don't you pay me five bucks for now and pick up the rest from your next check or two?"

Stump glanced heavenward. "Okay. But that only leaves me with a few bucks for spending money over the next couple weeks."

"Spending money for your girlfriend?" James asked, obviously trying to embarrass Stump.

"Good question," Myles said. "I've noticed you've been taking more showers and using my cologne. A guy doesn't have to be a detective to put all that together."

"Her name's Maria," James said.

Stump would have preferred to avoid the topic altogether but the toothpaste was out of the tube. "She's just a girl who lives at the apartment building."

"She a looker?"

"I guess so," Stump said, being careful not use up his entire vocabulary.

"I see." Myles hesitated a moment. Then added, "Do I need to worry about what you're doing?"

Oh, crap. This was getting uncomfortable. Stump couldn't say anything about a kissing van, nor admit that two nights ago he and Maria sneaked into Mr. Kraft's office and actually had a discussion about going all the way. Just then a car turned the corner and pulled in behind them. Thank God. "Looks like Mr. Harrington's here," Stump said as he pivoted and rushed toward the newcomer.

Grateful to have escaped the third degree, Stump waited for the end of the intros before asking, "How much are you going to charge me?"

Geoff glanced at Myles and back to Stump. "I'm sorry, but my boss says the best we can do is three hundred."

It was like being slapped in the face. "But my dad said you'd only charge me two hundred."

"Wait a minute," Myles jumped in. "I was just guessing. I think you ought to be grateful that Geoff's working on a Sunday and giving you a discount."

Stump took a deep, pained breath and turned to Geoff. "He's right. I'm sorry. It's just that I don't have much money."

"Welcome to the club," Geoff said. "I'll try to get the boss to come down a little more, but don't count on it."

* * *

While the desert wind blew warm air into their faces Stump, Myles and James handed out brochures and urged neighbors to come to the meeting. When they observed a home with a noticeable safety flaw, they took pictures. It was mid-afternoon before they were finished.

After dropping James off, Myles and Stump drove an hour and a half north on CA-14 to Bakersfield and had just begun the return trip via I-15, when Stump got to thinking about something that had been bothering him. "Can I ask you something, Myles?"

"If it's about dinner I was just thinking about that too."

"No. It's about Maria and her mother."

"Oh. You can ask, but since I've never met either one of them I don't know if I can be much help."

"From what I can tell, Maria's mother is basically passive. She stays at home, does all the right things and simply tries to be nice to people."

"Sounds like a very nice person."

"She is, and so is Maria. But Maria's completely different. She's more confident; she has goals and tends to stand up for herself and her mother. Why aren't they more alike?"

"Well, we have to be careful about lumping people together, but it's not uncommon for the children of immigrants to be more independent than their parents."

"I know what you mean. James's folks came up from Africa, but he's a lot crazier than they are. Why is that?"

"Good question. According to Maslow's hierarchy of needs, people first have to concern themselves with the necessities like food, clothing and shelter. Then once they feel secure they can pursue other things. Sometimes that can take generations. I suspect Maria feels a lot more secure than her mother ever has. That enables her to take more chances."

"Hmm. That's interesting. Maslow, huh? Remind me to look that up later, would ya?"

"Sure. If I don't forget."

"Speaking about forgetting, how's Grandma Pauline doing?"

Myles sighed. "Not good."

"I still say she should live with us."

"If we did that, we could consider you to be one of her caregivers and slip you a few dollars from time to time."

"I don't want no money for being nice to Grandma Pauline."

Myles stared straight ahead for a few seconds. "You know something, Stumpster? For a fellow who has his own financial woes, that's one of the least selfish things I've heard in a while. You make me really proud sometimes."

"Sometimes? I'm so cool I don't even feel the desert heat."

"Yeah, right. I'll keep your offer in mind. Thanks." Myles tapped the seat. "There's something else I want to talk to you about. This is important so I want you to pay attention."

Stump raised his eyebrows. "'Sup?"

"Since I'm a law enforcement officer, I'm considered an officer of the court. Among other things, I'm supposed to report any under-age people who I know to be engaged in intimate activities."

"But I haven't done that."

"I'm not saying you did or even that you will. But the society wants guys like me to protect young women, especially from older guys, predators. If those guys get caught messing with the young ones, it's a felony and they can go to jail for a long time. If younger guys like you get caught messing around with somebody your own age he can be charged with a misdemeanor. It's not as bad, but it's still a crime."

It sounded serious when he put it that way.

"I know that lots of people your age do it anyway," Myles continued. "Of those, some of them get in a lot of trouble including pregnancy and courts. That's why I think it's better to wait until you're older."

"I told you, Dude, we ain't done nothing like that."

"Yeah, I know, but I'm not stupid, so if it happens anyway I hope you'll be respectful of the girl and use condoms." He raised a finger. "And whatever you do, don't let me know about it 'cause I sure as hell don't want to have to decide between turning you in and shirking my responsibility."

Hmm. Stump nodded. He appreciated the tone, and being treated like an adult, and the predicament that Myles was in. "Okay, I get it. If anything like that happens, I promise to be careful and not to tell you about it."

"Just play it smart, okay? That is unless you like the idea of changing dirty diapers."

GROSS! 'Nuff said.

CHAPTER 34

Do unto others before they do unto thee. Prior to her cowboy incident, Delores had several occasions when she overcame her cowardice by turning the tables on somebody else. It was all about control and the loss thereof.

She would not have been so stressed were it not for the countless nights she and sister Simone had endured Tio's wandering hands and the physical pain of his pinching and probing. She remembered his threats and the liquor on his breath. Just as bad were the noises he made just before he was done. Surely, she was good for something besides that.

When she got older she desperately wanted to find a man who would genuinely love her. She would give every ounce of her being to such a man, but it always ended the same way. When things got serious she thought about how she felt when Tio's hands explored her. The only way to avoid the risk was to say no, and run away.

But then the guilt set in. Guilt for not trusting her partner. Guilt for leading him on. Guilt for being such a damn coward. Guilt for being a cop. People can't trust cops who run away from trouble. Whenever she got to that point, she had to find a way to regain control in the bedroom or she'd drive herself nuts. She didn't have to give a damn what her partner thought, or if he wanted to see her again. The whole idea was to dismiss any emotional connections. Do unto others before they do unto thee. At least that way the coward inside her could temporarily go away, leaving her with a chance to deal with her other issues.

She'd employed her switch-game a few times over the past couple years and learned to tuck away what she did in a forget-it place in her head. But then came the cowboy moment. At the time, she was fully willing to ride the dude for all he was worth but when it came right down to it, she backed out. That was the first time she'd done that and she didn't really know why. Nor did it help her with her self-confidence about dealing with Dixon Browne.

Today being Monday, Delores was at Cal-Vista and expecting a visit from the human octopus. In a twisted way, she almost hoped he'd force himself on her and thereby give her the proof she needed to send him to a bad-ass prison where he'd discover that cons hated sexual predators as much as she did. But the truth was, she'd kill Dixon Browne before she'd let him actually rape her. For now, she needed to bring him down with routine police work and one way to do that was to exploit his weaknesses.

Although Delores wasn't particularly vain, she knew that Dixon considered her counterpart, Lorraine Martinez, to be something akin to his gambling trophies. She still had a few days until the rent would come due again, so she figured she might be able to keep him at bay until then by treating him like a driver in bumper-to-bumper traffic. As long as he was inching toward his destination, he'd probably hang in there and put up with short-term frustrations, giving her more time to gather enough strong evidence to lock him up, preferably for life.

She gathered her purse, and placed her pen recorder on top of the fridge, then arranged two chairs so one had its back to the recorder. She draped her purse on that one and left the other facing the mic. Then, she slipped into the bedroom and hid her Diamondback DB9 pistol under her pillow. That done, she called both Myles and the Birdman in case she might need backup.

One final look in the mirror. One final pep-talk and Delores, along with her aliases, Lorraine Martinez and Monday Girl, was ready. As expected, the knock came just before nine.

Delores paused a moment before she pulled the door inward. Dixon Browne quickly stepped inside, looked around, plopped right where she'd hoped he would and clasped his hands behind his head. "I never did get you any better furniture, did I?"

"I saw a couch at Goodwill," she said, taking her own seat.

Dixon shook his head. "You may not need it. I've got some good news for you. Francisca is moving out. You can take her place."

Uh-oh. "Why? What happened?"

"Mutual agreement. This means you and I can be together and you won't have to worry about paying your bills."

This could be good news, but not for the reasons Dixon thought. If Francisca was moving away, she might be willing to testify about her relationship with Dixon. The important thing was to get to her before she moved away. "But it's not nice to be with a man in that way while he's already married," she said trying to sound as Lorraine would.

Dixon rose and scooted his chair directly in front of hers. "Francisca won't care. That's the way the deal works. Once we agree to split up, it's easy on everybody."

"What about that woman you see on Wednesdays? Won't she want to move in with you? She was here first."

"Victoria won't care either. She likes things just the way they are. Besides, I don't want her kid underfoot all the time."

Delores was glad she had asked the question. She'd planned on talking with Victoria when the time was right, but now she was having second thoughts. A mom would be reluctant to rat out the one guy she needed to make ends meet. "But if I move in with you, will you want to keep sleeping with her?"

Dixon moved his hand to her chin. "Look. None of us are in love or anything like that. We're just a bunch of people who do certain favors for each other. That's all."

"But you said I might have to marry you."

He shook his head. "If we only get together on Mondays, you aren't a wife and you can't become a citizen. That's why you want to move in and get married. It's much better for you."

"Are you sure you can get me citizenship, because a lady at work said you have to be married for three years and take a test. If I have to wait for three years after Francisca gets her citizenship, it would take too long for me to get mine."

Dixon shifted his teeth. "That's true for most people, but I have a special friend who works in the immigration office. He streamlines things for me. Once he stamps the papers, you're in."

Keep lying, you sack of manure. "But what about the money? Do you still want me to pay you, 'cause—"

"I've got that figured out too. You still work at the restaurant and pay me a few hundred each month. That's less than half of what you're paying in rent now. That'd work, wouldn't it?"

"But if I have to give you that much, I'll never be able to save enough money to start over on my own."

Dixon hesitated and exhaled. "Look. This isn't about the damn money. You and I belong together. You're going to be powerful and important around here. If it'll make you feel any better, you can forget about the money and move out in eight months. Now, that's the best I'm going to do."

"I just don't think I should sleep with you."

"Has to be part of it. That's what I get out of the relationship. You want to be fair, don't you?"

"But I don't know very much about making love."

"No problem. Most of it will come naturally but I can show you videos of me and Francisca. You can learn what to do by watching that."

Her eyes widened. "You take pictures?"

"Sure. You'll figure it out in no time."

"You wouldn't take pictures of me, would you?"

"All you gotta do right now is decide if you want to be my Monday Girl or get your citizenship. Either way," he said, reaching for the bottom of her shirt, "this is the next step."

"Not now," she said pushing his hand away. "I need more time. Can't we just go for another drive?"

"No way. I've waited long enough."

"But I haven't actually agreed to anything."

"Look. This is Monday and you already owe me. If you want my money, it's your day to do as I say."

"I know I owe you, but—"

Dixon ground his jaw, then swallowed. "Your only other option is to clean dirty apartments all day. The choice is yours."

Indeed it was. In fact, Delores had several choices including one or two that Dixon didn't know about. Of the three options he presented, she knew which one he wanted but she couldn't even make love with guys she liked. She sure as hell wasn't going to bump uglies with a sicko. She looked at her not-so-smooth cop hands and imagined them in a bucket of hot water. "I guess I'll have to clean apartments."

CHAPTER 35

THE NEXT MORNING, Delores's hands were sore from a day of scrubbing other people's toilets and stoves, but at least she'd wrested some time and damning confessions out of Dixon Browne, especially regarding his claim to have a shortcut to citizenship. Sadly, it still wasn't enough.

Before she could convict Dixon, she had several obstacles. First off, she had to have proof, beyond a reasonable doubt, of what he had done. Then there was the newness of California Statute 261. Rape by deception hadn't been tested very much and nobody had elevated it to a serial status.

If that wasn't enough to worry about, there was a potential entrapment issue. If a court were to rule that her own actions essentially drew Dixon into crimes he might not have otherwise committed, none of the things that he did to her could be used as evidence against him.

Mercifully, the law wasn't entirely one-sided. The entrapment defense could be beaten if it could be proved that the defendant was predisposed to commit such crimes before being entrapped. Therefore it was important for Delores to have several witnesses who'd testify against him, which was why she was hanging around Cal-Vista on a Tuesday morning.

If Dixon and Francisca we're calling it quits Francisca might be willing to open up and help Delores break her case.

Luckily, Delores had just observed Francisca enter building three, where the laundry room was. A cautious meeting was in order.

Dressed as Lorraine, Delores made her way downstairs where she glanced across the courtyard. It being all clear, she scurried over to meet Francisca.

In the laundry room, Francisca was alone and had just put some change in a washing machine. "Hello," Delores said softly before Francisca swung around.

Francisca's eyes searched Delores's face and then picked a basket off the folding table. "I bet you're real happy."

Even a non-detective could have seen the black eye and the large bruise that encircled Francisca's wrist. "Oh, my. You okay?"

"You don't fool me. I know who you are. You think you can steal my husband just like those other whores."

Delores pursed her lips. She could feel the pain in Francisca's voice. "No, that's not it. Honest."

"Oh, yes it is. You give yourself to him for money. That makes you a whore."

"You have it all wrong. We haven't done anything like that. I promise." Technically, there were a few gross kisses, but there was no need to bring that up. "I just want to talk to you. That's all. Please give me a chance."

Francisca shook her head. "Don't matter, now. He threw me out."

"Threw you out?" Delores sucked some air through her teeth. Dixon had said that Francisca's departure was mutual and Francisca was happy about it. "When? Where you going to go?"

"What do you care?"

Delores took a step closer, gently touched Francisca's black eye. "Believe me. I care a lot more than you'll ever know. I've been in love too, but sometimes the people we love don't have the same feelings. It's very painful when they break our hearts." She lowered her voice. "We both know if this man truly loved you, he wouldn't beat you and throw you out of his home."

A deadpan stare washed across Francisca's face, indicating Delores had hit a nerve.

"Do you have a car? Anybody to help you?" Delores continued.

Francisca shook her head. "Don't need a car."

"I know some good people who you can live with for free until you can figure out what you want to do. They have children and live right by a church."

Francisca turned her head. "How does a person like you know people like that?"

Delores would have liked to level with Francisca and draw out more information, but this was neither the time nor the place. "The important thing is to get you out of here before you get hurt again."

The slight turn of Francisca's head, the scrunched brows and the child-like stare all revealed that she was sizing up the offer. Delores had her chance. "We can leave right now if you want to."

"No," Francisca said, shaking her head. "I have one more day. I want to see if he changes his mind and lets me stay."

"I don't think that's a good—"

"It's none of your business."

As abrupt as Francisca was, Delores knew from her own relationships that love plays mean tricks on hearts. In those moments objectivity and common sense are often overruled by false hope and desperation. Francisca appeared to have reached that point. "Okay, then. I'll tell you what. I'll leave you alone for now. But tomorrow, if you decide you want my help you just stand in the courtyard by the new flower garden at two o'clock. I'll have somebody watching and they'll get a nun and another couple to come by at four to take you to a safe place for as long as you want."

Francisca looked deep into Delores's eyes. "I'll give him one more day."

Delores took Francisca's hand. "Please be careful. If he tries to hurt you again, promise me you'll run away."

CHAPTER 36

When a fellow sweeps a large parking lot, it allows his mind time to wander. In Stump's case his thoughts frequently involved Maria. For instance, if his hunch about Dixon's notebook proved true, Maria might be very, very grateful.

Compared to some of the video games Stump had played, and the advanced Sudoku puzzles he'd solved, Dixon's codebook appeared to be rather sophomoric. A brief examination revealed that the most common three-letter combinations ended with two J's, such as *AJJ* or *EJJ*. Since Dixon routinely dealt with numbers, like 600 dollars for a damage deposit or 900 dollars for rent, the back-to-back J's could easily stand for two zeros. If that was true, then other letters probably stood for the remaining digits and since all the letters came from the front end of the alphabet, the letter *A* probably stood for the number *1*, *B* stood for *2* and so on.

Stump grinned. He was looking forward to getting back into the notebook copies, and the potential reward Maria might offer. Just the thought of kissing and touching her perked him up, both between the ears and between the legs.

At the end of his shift, Stump still had one other thing he wanted to do before visiting with Maria. He checked his iPhone notes, then journeyed next door to meet the neighbor as Juanita had suggested. The lone building was quite a bit bigger than those at Cal-Vista. Based on the three stories and the configuration of the doors and windows Stump supposed there were about 44 apartments.

Both the grounds and the building itself were immaculate. All of the drapes in the windows matched and reminded him of military barracks. Stump pulled open the main entry door to see a mature woman, maybe fifty, cleaning the inside of the windows near the rows of mailboxes. "Excuse me," he said. "Do you know where I can find Mr. Connors?"

The woman grabbed a roll of paper towels. "He's busy now."

"My name's Stump. I work next door. I was told Mr. Connors might have some information about our manager."

"What kind of information?" she asked while wiping a smudge off the window.

Stump paused, then said, "I'm sorry. I don't want to appear rude, but I should probably talk with Mr. Connors."

"I'm his wife. He doesn't like to be bothered."

Hmm. A wife would probably know just as much, maybe more. "My girlfriend thinks Mr. Browne hurt her mother. I'm trying to find out if he's ever hurt anybody else."

"Why don't you ask the people over there?"

"I am talking with a few of them, but most haven't lived there very long. Besides, if Dixon finds out that I'm asking questions about him, my girlfriend might get in trouble or I might get fired."

A shuffling sound came from the lower level. "He's got a good point," a male voice said. "Come on down."

Stump looked at the lady, who nodded.

Stump descended a half-flight of stairs to the garden level. Mr. Connors wore long pants, his shirt was tucked in, he was clean-shaven and his hair was combed. Overall he made a much more professional first impression than Dixon Browne did when Stump and Myles first visited Cal-Vista. Stump offered the man his hand. "Thanks for talking with me, Mr. Connors. My name's Stump."

Mr. Connors shook hands before he climbed up his stepladder to remove the outer cover from a light fixture. "It's good to see a couple people doing something about that crazy manager—even if you are just a teenager." Mr. Connors rested the light cover on the top rung of his ladder. "Hand me one of those swirly light bulbs from that box by your feet, would ya?"

Stump grabbed a fluorescent bulb and traded it with Mr. Connors for the one just removed. "I was told you've lived over here for quite a while and might know some inappropriate things Mr. Browne has done."

Mr. Connors screwed in the bulb. "I can tell you one thing. That guy changes women more often than most of us change underwear."

Stump grinned. "Did you ever talk to any of those women?"

"Just one. A couple years back. Beatriz, I think it was. He chased her away. She stayed with us for a few days while my wife found some people to help her."

Stump added the name Beatriz to his phone notes. "What did he do to her?"

"She wouldn't say. But we saw some bruises and suspected that he beat her pretty good."

Uh-oh. If Mr. Connors was correct, this was consistent with Maria's suspicions and *The Case of Did He or Did He Not?* had just become more complicated. "Do you know her last name or where I can find her?"

"Not really," Mr. Connors said while replacing the light cover. "She talked about going back to Mexico, but it's hard to know."

Damn. "I heard he waved a gun at you."

Mr. Connors stepped off the ladder and squared his shoulders with Stump. "That dumb bastard's going to point that gun at the wrong person and end up eating his own lead. One time he mouthed off to some roofers and got his teeth knocked out. I imagine you've seen him wiggle his dentures around."

Stump nodded. "Has he ever shot it?"

"We suspected so one time, late at night. Coulda been firecrackers though. We were in bed and decided not to get in the middle of it. The other day he chased me out of his apartment when I tried to get him to clean up a broken beer bottle that one of his people threw over the fence onto our property. The belligerent bastard never learns his lesson."

Stump nodded. "A little bit ago you implied that somebody else was asking questions."

"About a week ago. A young detective dropped by. At first I thought she was just a prospective tenant." He pulled a pen from his shirt pocket, pointed it at Stump. "You know something? I've been watching you over there. You're a good worker. Reminds me of when I was a kid. I like that. Why don't you give me your number? If I get overloaded, I might just call you for a little help."

Wow. Another job. A rush of pride proved that Mr. Kraft was correct when he said it was important to do a good job even if nobody was watching. "Glad to," Stump said, "but I won't have any extra time for a while."

"Well, it's always good to know people you can count on. Let me know if you become available."

"Sure will. Thanks."

After they traded numbers, Stump made a gleeful exit. He almost ran back to Cal-Vista, but that would be too kid-like. Instead, he took one quick hop before adding a couple more notes to his iPhone. He could hardly wait to share his findings with sweet-lipped Maria.

Twenty minutes later, he and Maria walked hand-in-hand toward the ice cream store. He could barely contain his enthusiasm as he filled her in on the job offer and what he'd learned about the notebook code and Dixon. Stump was the happiest he'd been in a long time. He jammed his hand in his pocket and damn near got sick. "Oh no! I lost my iPhone."

"Are you sure?" Maria said. "When was the last time you had it?"

Stump thought back. "Right after I returned from the Connors's place. We have to retrace our steps."

They hurried back to Cal-Vista where a cursory search of the most likely areas proved fruitless. They rushed over to Juanita and Manuel's place where Manuel complained that Dixon screwed them out of more money. Finally Manuel speculated that Dixon was probably behind the missing iPhone and said someday somebody was gonna nail that dude.

Stump grabbed Maria's hand and they ran to Dixon's apartment but got nothing more than snarky comments about Stump's irresponsibility. Stump was in no mood for the bullshit.

"We can tape hand-made signs on the outer doors of each building," Maria said as they walked across the courtyard toward her apartment. "Whoever finds your phone can bring it to my place."

Stump plopped onto a picnic table. "Dixon was right. I'm a loser. The biggest damn meeting of my life is tomorrow night and I lose my iPhone. I can't even communicate with anybody."

Maria placed her hand on his shoulder. "You can borrow mine."

"That won't help. None of my people know your number."

"But you probably know theirs. You could call the key people and let them know what happened. Then they could still reach you."

"I guess that's better than nothing. Are you sure you can get by without it until after the meeting?"

"Of course. That's what people who love each other do."

Stump sighed borrowed her cell, pink case and all, and headed home to his other responsibilities. He owed Maria more than ever.

In his apartment, he snagged a bag of chips and slipped into his room, where he grabbed the copies of Dixon's notebook. To test his theory, he wrote out the alphabet on a single line.

Below the letters he wrote the numbers one through twenty-six. Then he examined the first line on one of the pages.

b-bja 15,23,5,19 bjj 15,14 af20,8.

If the number one stood for the first letter in the alphabet and vice versa, as he suspected from his previous examination, there was a good chance that each of the first two b's stood for the number two. He jotted two two's on a separate line. Then, he'd already guessed that the letter j stood for zero, so he wrote that down and grinned. Next, the number one should replace letter a, and that meant the first four characters stood for 2-201 and he knew what that meant. A gleeful chill tickled his neck. He reached for his cell to call Maria, but...oh yeah, he had her phone.

CHAPTER 37

Finally. The day for Stump's presentation had arrived. Given that he'd followed Danielle Delgado's plan so closely, the bureaucrats would surely approve his idea and implement some sort of program to make homes safer in his old neighborhood. After that project was out of the way, he could sleep better and focus on his other pressing issues, like attending to his slipping grades and paying Myles back.

This time he would act more professional. He placed both his painting clothes and his nicest dress clothes in a plastic bag, and then pocketed both his learner's permit and Maria's cell. Ready, he mounted Ol' Ug' and pedaled to school.

During first break he called Danielle Delgado and confirmed that everybody else had finished his or her tasks. Then he acted on one of Myles's suggestions and called Mr. Feldsen at Inland bank. The banker couldn't make the meeting but he offered to drop by some business cards and brochures in case any residents needed loans.

At lunch, Stump wrote out the bullet points of his speech so that he could review them throughout the afternoon. His mom would be proud.

When the final bell rang, he donned his backpack and rode to Cal-Vista for a couple hours of work. On the way, he got to thinking that Maria had changed his life in ways he'd never imagined. Whether it was when she showed him how to paint, or when she made early reference to his being her crushboy, or showing her compassion for her mother or lending him her pink phone, the outcome was always the same: Maria made Stump's life better. Maybe this was love, maybe not, but he was all for it.

A few minutes later Stump and Ol' Ug' pulled into a Walgreens lot where Stump acted on another one of Myles's recommendations. Inside, he found the condom display.

At Cal-Vista, Juanita's cleaning cart was near the entrance to building three. Stump cuffed Ol' Ug' to the rack and then found her in the laundry room, where clothes flopped in noisy machines offering enough background noise to quash any eavesdroppers. "I've got some news for you," he said.

"Me too. You first."

Stump filled her in about his meeting with Mr. Connors. "But the most interesting thing is, Mr. Connors said a lady detective has been asking questions about Dixon."

Juanita's brows drew together. "That's interesting alright. Did he say why?"

"Apparently she mostly wanted to know about Dixon's previous wives."

"Good, maybe the cops have finally figured out what's going on." Juanita glanced toward the hall. "Speaking of his exes, Dixon told Francisca to move out."

A coldness climbed Stump's back.

"I saw her crying by the new garden," Juanita continued. "She said she tried everything, but he wouldn't change his mind."

"Did she say if he ever hurt her?" Stump knew his question sounded insensitive, but Francisca might have some information that would help him in *The Case of Did He Or Did He Not?* "We have to make sure she tells us where she goes, in case she needs us or we need her."

"Okay. If I see her, I'll give her my number."

"I'll watch for her too. By the way, I figured out the code for the notebook."

"Good. Does it say how he screws us over?"

"I haven't had time to figure that out."

"Well, hurry up. Now that he's thrown Francisca out, I really want to see him get arrested."

Their conversation done, Stump hightailed it to Maria's apartment. She answered her door wearing a pretty pink T-shirt and white shorts that accented her long golden legs. "Hi," he said before he gave her back her cell. "I've got something to show you." He reached in his back pocket and pulled out several sheets of folded paper. "I figured out Dixon's code. The first complete sentence says '2-201 *owes 200 on the 16th*'."

Maria's eyelids popped open. "Really? That's great. Does it say anything about him hitting Mama?"

Stump shoved the papers back in his pants. "Not yet. I just got started, but I should be able to figure it all out within a few days, after my meeting."

She clapped her hands "You deserve a reward."

"Yeah, that's what I think too, but not 'til I get off. I'm painting the lines in the parking lot and I want to finish as many as I can to impress Mr. Kraft."

"I love you," Maria said as she planted a lip-peck on his cheek.

There was the "L" word, again. "Would you mind if we meet in Mr. Kraft's office after I get off work? You might be able to help me practice what I want to say at my meeting."

"Okay. But you better be ready for that reward."

She could count on that.

At Mr. Kraft's office, the door was closed, but not locked. Stump flicked the switch, causing Mr. Kraft to lift his head from the desk. "Sorry I woke you, Mr. Kraft. Are you ready for me?"

Mr. Kraft yawned. "You'll find a five-gallon bucket of yellow paint and some supplies next door, in the maintenance room. Take it all to the back of the parking lot. I'll meet you out there in ten minutes, after I slap some water on my face."

Minutes later, Stump had changed into his painting clothes and dragged out the items Mr. Kraft mentioned, which included some traffic cones and a couple eight-foot two-by-sixes that were joined on the end by a strong hinge. He shoved a half-sized roller pad on an extension handle and pried open the bucket. The golden reflection of the paint reminded him of the sun.

"I could've hired professionals with a sprayer for this job," Mr. Kraft said a few minutes later, "but I don't like the idea of paint particles drifting in the breeze. This is the old-fashioned way. First, you'll block off about twenty parking spaces with the cones; then, unfold the long boards so they form one long straightedge for the roller. That'll be sixteen feet."

So that's what the hinged two-by-sixes were for. Stump did as instructed and scooted the long wooden straightedge next to one of the old faded lines.

"That's the idea," Mr. Kraft said, while hanging a heavy-duty screen that was about the size of a small computer monitor inside the bucket. "All you gotta do is dip the roller in the bucket, wipe the excess paint off by using the screen, then use the boards as a guide."

"What about a drop cloth?" Stump asked recalling his earlier work on the pool fence.

"Takes too long to keep moving it around. Just be careful and don't let the roller get sloppy."

Stump dipped the pad just enough to wet the edge of the pad and rolled it up and down the screen until it seemed wet but not drippy. He carefully butted the edge of the pad up against the wooden straightedge and slowly glided the pad forward.

"That's the idea," Kraft said as a fresh new line was born. "You'll get better and faster. Just be careful when you move the boards to the next spot. They'll have paint on the bottom so don't drag them anywhere 'cause they'll smear the stuff all over the place. About every three or four lines you'll need to wipe off the boards. That's all there is to it."

It all made sense. "I'll be careful."

"Good. I gotta get home now and get some rest. Just remember that I'd rather you take a little longer and think about what you're doing than rush through the job and make a big mess that we have to live with forever. You can finish tomorrow if you need to. I'll see you then."

The more Stump got to know Mr. Kraft, the more he liked the man. Mr. Kraft was one of the few people who had faith in Stump. Pleased, Stump moved the traffic cones to the back of the lot where it would be easier to watch for Francisca while he worked.

CHAPTER 38

AFTER MR. KRAFT LEFT, Stump made a game out of painting the lines perfectly and quickly. He'd knocked out nearly a third of them and was humming along with the momentum of a racehorse when a passenger van pulled up near building one, the doors burst open and a priest and two nuns emerged. Curious, Stump watched as the nuns hurried around the front corner of the building toward the entrance while the priest walked briskly toward the courtyard. Almost instantly the nuns came quickly back with Francisca between them. "Father, we've got her," one of them said.

Before Stump could gather his wits, they all hurried to their vehicle and drove away. Stump eyed the courtyard, but nobody else was outside to see what happened. Stunned, he rested the roller on the paint bucket and scratched his neck. It was like a high-speed grand kidnapping from God, and Francisca was the chosen one. Based on the swiftness and furtive getaway, Stump was pretty certain Francisca wasn't coming back.

He considered looking for Juanita, but he didn't want to admit that a priest and two nuns just stole the one person they both desperately wanted to talk to. Juanita wasn't the only one he was worried about. Maria wouldn't be very happy if she knew he'd let a potential ally slip away.

Exasperated, he elected to keep his mouth shut, at least for a while.

The final half-hour flew by. In addition to his curiosity about the divine departure of Francisca, he tried to rehearse what he planned to say at the meeting later that evening, but mostly, he thought about what he wanted to say to Maria.

Finally, just before quitting time, Maria entered the courtyard and motioned that she was going behind Kraft's building, presumably to get to the office without Dixon seeing what was going on. Stump nodded and gathered supplies like he would ordinarily do, and put everything away before he let them both in Mr. Kraft's office and locked the door.

Inside, one more look at her legs and he knew what he wanted to do. "You can't imagine how much you mean to me," he said as he pulled her to him. Their arms encircled each other and the hug quickly progressed to a kiss, then passionate, wet tongues danced like lazy waves between their lips and Stump's heart throbbed in a way it had never felt before.

He nudged Maria onto Kraft's couch and kissed her and closed his eyes. She returned his affection as gentle moans of approval accompanied their hands as they each explored the other's body for the first time. When Maria's hand found its way to the front of Stump's shorts, an unexpected chill washed across the hair on his neck. The moment was right. He pulled back slightly and whispered, "Can we make love? I have a condom."

"Um-hmm."

They peeled off their clothes and Stump admired her nakedness. His heart pounded like a field of bombs as he and Maria progressed to the ultimate act, which was totally wonderful, not just physically but also psychologically.

It ended quicker than he would have liked, but when it was over, they lay naked, wrapped in each other's arms, and Stump knew it was a moment he'd never forget. He felt warmth throughout his body, and a genuine love for Maria. He removed the condom, then kissed her and held her and cherished the special moment. "You were my first," he said, softly.

Maria smiled. "You don't think I'm a bad girl, do you?"

"Of course not. We have real feelings for each other."

"Do you love me?"

"Yeah. I think I do."

"Me too." She kissed him before she brought him back to reality, "I hate to say it, but I think your meeting is pretty soon."

He'd have to hurry to get there on time. "I'd rather stay right here for a little while. They won't care if I'm just a little late."

Maria sat up. "Don't be silly. You've been looking forward to this for a long time." She put on her bra. "Your mom would want you to get to that meeting on time."

Stump blew out a deep breath. "Okay. I guess you're right." He bent over to get his shorts just as a key waggled in the doorknob. Both he and Maria grabbed for their clothes and stood up just as Dixon barged in.

Dixon's eyes shot back and forth, and then to the used condom between Stump's feet. If they were anyplace else Stump could shove the asshole out of there but Kraft's office was neutral territory at best. At worse, Dixon had more right to be there than Stump did.

"Both of you put your damn clothes on," Dixon snapped. He pointed at Maria. "I'm ashamed of you."

"Oh, yeah," Maria scoffed as she turned around and pulled her panties into place. "Whatever I do is none of your business."

Dixon grabbed her upper arm. "The hell it isn't."

By that time, Stump had put his shorts on. "Hey, let go of her," he said, reaching for Dixon's hand.

Dixon spun Maria back far enough to avoid Stump's reach. "You'd better watch it, kid. We both know you don't belong in here." Dixon turned to Maria. "Now, you get dressed. I'll be dealing with you when I'm done here."

"Just don't hurt her, okay?"

Dixon shot his finger to within inches of Stump's nose. "You know something, rich boy? You're no better than a goddam alley cat. Now get the hell off of my property before I call the cops."

Stump reached for his shoes. "This ain't your property."

Still holding Maria's arm, Dixon escorted them both out of the building. "Stop squeezing me, you jerk-wad," Maria yelped just before she yanked free and ran for her apartment.

"I'll be right behind you," Dixon shouted before turning to Stump and repeating the finger-wag exercise. "As for you, all I want to see is ass and elbows. Get on that worthless bicycle of yours and get the hell out of my sight."

Partly ashamed, partly pissed off and almost late for his meeting, Stump hurried over to the bike rack, but as he drew closer, Ol' Ug' didn't look right. Then he saw the flat tires. "Damn you, Dixon," he screeched while spinning around. But Dixon was already gone.

CHAPTER 39

ACROSS TOWN, BERNICE BICKLE, the City Stenographer, was in charge of setting up the City Council's meeting room. She arrived fifteen minutes early, unlocked the large double doors, flicked on the lights and laid out a stack of printed agendas.

Mrs. Crumpler, the City Planner, joined Bernice. "There are quite a few people gathering outside already," she said.

"It ought to be interesting." Bernice handed Mrs. Crumpler a dozen packets of papers that she'd gotten from attorney Danielle Delgado. "Would you mind placing one of these at the seat of each official?"

Crumpler nodded, took the papers. "I understand that Neal went door-to-door and drummed up some interest in his safety cause."

"Probably a good idea," Bickle said. "The more people, the better his chances."

A man stuck his head in the room. "Is this the building codes place?" His voice was slurred.

Crumpler faced the man. "Yes, but we're not quite ready."

"Don't care," the man said loudly as he drew closer to her. "My grandpa built my house and it's been good enough for me. The goddamn do-gooders can pass all the bullshit laws they want, but I ain't changing nothin'."

"Sir, I can smell liquor on your breath," Crumpler said. "If you don't calm down, I'll have to call security."

"You threatening me? I ain't afraid of you."

"I'm not threating you, sir. I'm just asking you to calm down. You'll have time to talk if you want to, so there's no reason to get angry with me or anybody else right now. We'll be underway in a ten minutes. Why don't you take a seat?"

"I don't have to listen to you. When are the big shots coming in? Those are the guys I want to ream."

"I just told you. We'll be starting in ten minutes or so. Now are you going to behave or not?"

"Ah, hell. I gotta take a leak, anyways. Where's the goddamn men's room?"

The drunk guy wandered off and a few minutes later a sprinkling of other people began to join the room, including the Mayor and Anderson Powell, the local newspaper reporter, followed by some additional neighbors and Councilman Michael Barella, who was spiffed up as usual.

Myles came in with the next wave. He waited in a short line and picked up one of the agendas. He saw some familiar faces, but not Stump. "I remember you," a lady said to Myles. "From when you and your son brought a flier to my door. Isn't this exciting?"

"I'm glad you came," Myles said. "Would you excuse me? I have to talk with somebody." He eased into some space between Danielle Delgado and Mrs. Crumpler. "Evening, ladies. Either of you seen Stump?"

"Not me," said Delgado.

"Me either," Crumpler said. "He'd better hurry. He's first up."

Michael Barella joined them and nodded at Myles. "Where's the lad?"

"Don't know. He should've been here by now."

The room continued to fill up while others people waited in a small line to get in. Most seemed curious, but a couple of them were loud and appeared angry. The clock indicated the meeting would begin in just five minutes.

Myles set his papers on a seat in the front row, went to see if Stump was in the hallway or parking lot. He tried Stump's iPhone, but got no answer.

CHAPTER 40

Furious, Stump knew full well who had sabotaged him but he couldn't do much about it. Dixon was probably already at Maria's chewing her out in front of her mother. If Stump were to go there, either to confront Dixon or to borrow Maria's cell to call Myles, there was sure to be a big blow-up over what happened in Mr. Kraft's office.

Meanwhile a bunch of people were counting on Stump to get to that meeting. He had to find another ride. He ran to Juanita's apartment and banged on the door but there was no answer. He knocked again. Still no answer. His ear to the door revealed no noise. Son-of-a-bitch. He flashed down the stairs, then toward the parking lot. No sign of their van, either. Time was running out.

He glanced from one end of the lot to the other but nobody else was moving toward the lot. He needed another option. Anything. He got an idea. If he was lucky Maria might be in her bedroom and he could avoid Dixon. He ran to her apartment and tapped lightly on the window, but no answer. As badly as he felt for Maria, he had to take a chance. He crossed his fingers, went inside the building and knocked on the door to her apartment. As he feared, Dixon answered.

"You got what you wanted," Stump said to Dixon. "Now I have an emergency so I need to borrow Maria's phone."

"Oh, yeah. What emergency?"

"You knew damn well about my meeting." He pointed toward the downtown area. "I'm going to be late. I need to borrow Maria's phone."

"Sounds like you should've thought of that before."

Stump sighed. "Look. I know you hate me and that you sabotaged my bike, but I'll overlook it all if you'll just let me talk with Maria."

Dixon peeked over his shoulder at Maria, who was sitting, hands folded in her lap, on the couch next to her mother. He turned back to Stump. "She's busy." Dixon pulled out his own cell phone, waved it at Stump. "I already told you to get off the property. You want me to call the cops?"

"No. But it's nearly seven miles."

"Boo hoo," Dixon said and closed the door in Stump's face.

Stump's eyes narrowed to tiny slits. "Fuck you, Dixon," he said at the last second. He only had one other option. One day in gym class, he had run a mile in ten minutes. Maybe he could get to a store or somebody who would loan him a phone.

CHAPTER 41

MYLES RETURNED TO THE MEETING ROOM where nearly all the seats were taken. Mayor Curtis sat down, flicked on his microphone. "Can you hear me in the back row?"

Heads bobbed and the chatter subsided.

"Everybody please take your seats," the Mayor said. "We need to get started if we're going to get you all out of here by eight o'clock."

Bernice Bickle closed the doors.

Myles approached his saved seat where the fellow next to him leaned over. "I don't know who the hell is behind all this bullshit, but I'll be damned if I'm going to let any of these big shots force me to make repairs to my home."

A gentleman behind them leaned forward. "Idiots must think we're made of money."

Myles wondered where Stump was.

"It's nice to see so many concerned citizens here tonight," the mayor began. "Due to the size of the group, and in the interest of giving everybody a chance to participate tonight we're going to keep our announcements brief. We just want to remind everybody that next month's meeting will be the last one for this year and it has been moved up one week because the building is scheduled to be sprayed for termites. Then we'll be on break for four months before resuming our meetings. You can find more information on our website." He pointed to the back row. "Or watch for Anderson Powell's articles in the Palmdale Herald." Powell waved nonchalantly to the crowd.

The Mayor proceeded to introduce the Council members and the people at the side table. "If nobody has any other announcements, I want to call Neal Joseph Randolph to the podium. Mr. Randolph wants to discuss safety issues in the older part of town. Would Mr. Randolph please come to the lectern?"

Myles waited a few moments just in case Stump made a last second entrance, but no luck. People began to mumble and look around.

"Is Mr. Randolph here?" the Mayor asked.

Myles rose. "Mr. Mayor, I'm Myles Cooper, Neal's father. I don't know where my son is, but I can assure you this meeting was very important to him. He probably had to work late or something. If you can move his portion to later in the program, I'll go look for him. He has to be on his way."

Moans of frustration permeated the room.

"I can vouch for these people," Councilman Barella said from the mayor's left. "We've been working together on this project."

The Mayor nodded toward Myles. "How long will you be?"

"It'll probably take me ten minutes to get to his work, if I have to go that far, and that long to get back."

"Alright then, I guess we can move on to the next person on the agenda. Mr. Marvin Berkowitz. About rezoning the commercial lot on Highway 14. Is Mr. Berkowitz here?"

While Berkowitz took the podium Myles slipped out the door and Danielle Delgado followed. In the hall she asked, "Do you need another pair of eyes?"

"Thanks, but it might be better if you'd stay here until I know what's going on. I've got your number."

"I'll wait out here. Good luck."

Worried, Myles rushed to his truck.

CHAPTER 42

AFTER HE HAD JOGGED A HALF-MILE, Stump's calves tingled, his breathing was labored and his heart pounded. It would be impossible to maintain that pace for six more miles. He switched to a strategy he used to employ when he lived with his mom: run a block, walk a block, and try to regain his wind in between.

He slowed to a fast walk. His calves and thighs were noticeably weaker. He sucked at the air. A moment later it was time to run again. He had to ignore the discomfort.

Just then, a car whizzed past him. So did another. He had an idea. If he timed it right he could keep going, but turn around anytime a car got close and stick out his thumb. Maybe somebody would stop and take him to the meeting.

Another car was coming. He stuck out his thumb but they didn't even slow down. Back to the plan. Run a block, walk a block, turn around, thumb out, keep going, time to run again.

Another half-mile and Stump's body pulsed from head to toe. His lungs burned. Perspiration trailed down his temples and dampened his shirt. His toes ached from jamming into the front of his tennis shoes. That damn Dixon would be sorry for all of this. It was getting dark. Stump had to keep moving.

Another two-block combination and Stump came to the parkway he'd ridden past many times. A thirty-foot wide riverbed was lined by a six-foot stone wall on each side and both walls were topped by an equally tall wrought iron fence. A convenience store and Stump's bank were directly across the river. The flashing clock on the bank's sign had the time at seven-nineteen.

He looked right. The nearest crossover bridge was six blocks away. It would take too long and his legs were limp and sore. As an alternative, the water in the river looked to be no more than a foot deep. He had to make a shortcut.

He hustled down the embankment and wrapped his fingers around the top crossbar of the closest wrought iron fence. He sucked in a deep breath and pulled himself to the top, where he forced his leg over and pivoted, then dropped down to the other side. The sun had just faded over the horizon and darkness loomed. He had to hurry.

A closer look revealed that the stone wall was a little taller than he'd first thought, about eight feet. He had to get down there and then across the river and up the other side. The riverbed was covered with softball-sized stones and bushes. He sat on the wall, turned around and let go.

Suddenly his left foot crashed onto a loose rock. Excruciating pain shot up his leg as his ankle rolled and forced his knee to bend sideways and take the entire weight of his crashing body. He yelped and crashed to the ground. Instinctively he rolled to his back, grabbed for his knee, rocked forward and back and damn near cried. Suddenly, reality struck him. He had to get out of there while he could still see. He cringed and forced himself to lean against the wall but the pain forced him right back down.

A small opening between the branches of the bushes revealed that across the river occasional vehicles passed by the bank. He watched several of them zip by before a white pickup truck rolled slowly through. Myles!

Stump's heart skipped as he yelled and waved his arms wildly, but Myles had already passed him and there was no way Myles could see Stump in a rear-view mirror.

CHAPTER 43

AFTER MARVIN BERKOWITZ finished giving his presentation, the Mayor had a brief conference with the Council members while the rest of the attendees watched the clock and the door in anxious anticipation.

"Okay, everybody," the Mayor finally said. "Since Mr. Randolph has still not arrived, we're moving to the next matter. We need Mr. and Mrs. Trevor Warren to approach the lectern. They're requesting that the city modify some parking arrangements near South Palmdale Park."

A chorus of moans wafted through the air while a tall, thin man and an elderly woman with a walking cane took the spot behind the lectern. Danielle Delgado used the opportunity to scoot down the hall to call Myles.

"Any luck?" she asked as soon as Myles answered.

"No," Myles said, obviously exasperated. "*I went all the way to his work, but didn't see him riding anywhere. I'm backtracking now. Heading back your way in case I missed him. This doesn't make sense. He's been looking forward to this for weeks.*"

"Well, I hope he's okay. The Mayor didn't sound too happy. He moved on to the next issue. There's only one more after that. You must know what Stump wants to talk about. You could probably speak for him."

"Right now, I'm too worried. Something must be wrong. I've got to find him."

"Okay. What do you want me to do?"

"Just stall them the best you can. I'll let you know when I find him."

CHAPTER 44

WORRIED, STUMP DRAGGED HIS GOOD LEG underneath him and put both hands on the wall by his butt cheeks and pushed himself up. Once standing, he tested his knee. The pain was dull, deep and severe, but he could withstand it if he didn't bend it. Now, how to get out of there? There was no way he could jump up the wall, at least not in that immediate area.

He looked up and down the riverbed and remembered some kids he'd seen playing under the crossover bridge a couple nights earlier. They must have had some way to get down to the river. He gritted his teeth and limped toward the bridge. "You fucker, Dixon."

A healthy person might be able to walk a mile in fifteen minutes, but Stump needed that much time to limp his way along the riverbed to the bridge. A single streetlight on the other side of the river shone on a four-foot pile of softball-sized rocks with a kitchen chair stacked on top, like a throne. That had to be the way the kids got in and out.

Stump wiped the sweat off his face and hobbled toward the shallow, flowing water. Any other time he could have jumped the little brook with ease, but there was no way his bad knee could handle the take-off or the landing. He plunged his right foot into the water and welcomed the coolness of the filthy liquid that filled his shoe. He dragged his left foot to meet his right. He lifted his right foot out of the sucking mud and repeated the process several more times until he finally reached the other side and fell to the rocks.

He crab-crawled slowly and painfully to the rock pile and worked his way to the top, where he stabilized the chair. With his hands on the chair-back and his weight on his bad leg, he slid his good knee slowly onto the seat. But that was the easy part. He gnashed his teeth. It was time to take the more painful move. One. Two. Three. When he folded his bad knee underneath him it was as if the devil plunged a pitchfork deep inside the joint. "Damn you, Dixon," he screamed.

Now kneeling, he had to stand up to get within reach of the top of the wall. Okay. Lean the chair into the back of the wall. Don't fall. He shifted his knee and foot of his good leg so that half his body was squatting. His better leg lifted him to a standing position while his damaged leg eased next to it. He'd made it to a standing position and celebrated with three rapid breaths.

From there he reached for the top of the wall and pulled himself up as if he was doing a chin-up. A thirty-second breather was followed by a dozen slow and agonizing steps and he finally reached the final obstacle: the other wrought iron fence. As he gasped for air, his half-limp arms pulled his mud-soaked body to the top where he worked his way over and crashed onto the grass on the other side. A jolt of adrenalin lent him a momentary reprieve before the throbbing returned. He moaned as he massaged the grapefruit-sized knob that had overtaken his kneecap. A couple deep breaths were followed by a few baby steps up the embankment and he'd finally made it to the sidewalk. Now it was just eight miserable blocks to the convenience store. The shortcut nearly cost him his life.

CHAPTER 45

FOR THE NEXT TEN MINUTES Stump plodded and limped and cursed as he forced his feet to shuffle towards the convenience store. Finally, out of breath, sweating like a marathon runner and covered in mud, he reached a gas pump where an old man with a baseball hat had just pulled in. "Sir, Do you have a cell phone I can use? It's an emergency."

The man obliged just as the bank's digital clock next door flashed eight and two ones. Stump plunked at Myles's cell number knowing that the meeting was probably over.

"*Myles Cooper.*" Myles's voice was rushed, anxiety-riddled.

Relieved to hear Myles's voice, Stump nearly sobbed. "Myles, it's me, Stump. Can you come get me?"

"*Of course. Where are you? Are you okay?*"

"I'm at the Stop and Pop next door to the bank. I can't bend my knee."

"*I'll be there in five minutes.*"

Thank God. Stump returned the cell phone to the stranger, and waddled toward the sidewalk in front of one corner of the store where he sat on the curb, raised his better knee and lowered his head into a wobbly arm-nest.

His bad knee thudded like a base drum until Stump heard an engine and approaching tires. Myles tapped his horn and

Stump pulled himself into the cab. "Is the meeting over?" he asked, as he twisted his way onto the seat.

"Good God," Myles said. "This is worse than I thought. I'm taking you to the medical center."

"Not right now, Myles," Stump said while massaging his knee, "I need to get to the meeting before everybody leaves."

"It's already too late, Stump. I just spoke with Danielle. They already adjourned."

Stump lowered his head. "I want to go there anyway. At least I can apologize to anybody who's still there."

Myles sighed. "Alright. If you're sure you can handle it, but we're going to the center after that."

As they progressed toward City Hall, Stump told Myles about his missing cell phone and that Dixon had slashed Ol' Ug's new tires, and all that happened after that.

Partly because of what Myles had said some time back, Stump left out everything that had to do with Dixon walking in on him and Maria. Instead, he simply lowered his head and rested until they arrived at the City Hall building.

There, a few stragglers were still filing out of the building. Stump limped inside where he found Danielle Delgado and Councilman Barella arguing in the conference room. "There they are," Barella said.

The councilman hurried to Stump and pointed in his face, "I don't know who you think you are, but I stuck my neck out for you, even paid for all those damn brochures. Then, when it was your turn to follow through, you're out making mud pies."

Myles stepped forward. "Back off, Barella, before I bloody up your thousand-dollar suit."

"I'm going to send you people a bill," Barella said before clomping off.

Danielle Delgado wiped some dirt off Stump's eyebrow then dropped her hand to his shoulder. "Something awful must have happened. I'm sorry. I know this was real important to you."

Stump dumped himself onto the bench and grabbed his knee. "Yeah. I'm sorry too."

CHAPTER 46

So MUCH TO TELL. So much more to hide. Delores stopped at the restroom before her next appointment with Dr. Jeanine Moreno. When washing up, Delores looked in the mirror. A detective was supposed to have her act together but how the hell was she supposed to be a leader when her own life was a complicated cobweb of confusion?

In her personal life, she held a life-long grudge against Tio, yet did virtually nothing about it. More recently, she stupidly chased another nice man away for no good reason. Then there was her turn-the-tables exploitation of Clint the cowboy who hadn't really done her any wrong. In fact, she made things worse for herself when she led the dude on, then capriciously changed her mind, thereby earning the self-ascribed label: prick tease.

Her work life was just as bad. She was determined to show her higher-ups how mature she was by playing the role of a naïve teenager. How dopey was that? Not as bad as subjecting herself to a perv like Dixon Browne, as if convicting him would stop the thousands of pervs everywhere. The fact of the matter was there were so many similar cases on the shelves it would take an army of detectives to make a small dent in their number.

With so many misgivings, Delores had serious doubts

whether she was really fit for police work. That's why she needed another healthy dose of Doctor Moreno's advice. Jeanine always made her feel better or at least gave her ways to deal with her anxieties.

"Good morning, Delores," Jeanine said minutes later and directing her patient to the still-tidy sitting area by her big window. As usual, Jeanine snagged the chair to the right, thereby revealing the back of her hand.

"I see you redid your nails," Delores said. "Mind if I look?"

Jeanine folded her feet up under her as she always seemed to do and extended her hands for inspection. This time one thumbnail was sky blue with a polished flat yellow stone glued near the cuticle; the other thumbnail had a darker background with a small pearl-colored button, obviously representing a full moon. Predictably, there were no clouds in Jeanine's skies.

The remaining nails bore images of the toes of four different pairs of tennis shoes, each pair a different size and color. Somebody had painted dainty little laces on each shoe. Delores shook her head in admiration. "You are so creative."

"Each pair of shoes represents a real pair in our family. That's why my husband's look so dirty, and the youngest girl's shoelace is untied."

Delores smiled. "They beat tattoos 'cause you can change your nails whenever you want."

Jeanine put her finger to her lips. "Don't tell anybody, but I have a Sylvester the Cat tattoo on my lower back. My husband calls it his Puddy tatt."

"Puddy tatt?" Delores almost laughed out loud. "Well, I hope I have a family like yours someday."

Jeanine pointed toward her desk. "Before we get going, you'll be pleased to know the department has finally agreed to pay my fee for eight weeks."

Delores raised her eyebrows. "That's a relief. After what happened to me lately, I need every darn one of those weeks."

"Why? Was this week worse than usual?"

"I wouldn't call it worse," Delores fibbed. "Just a lot more of the same conflicts."

"If you don't mind my asking, when you find yourself entangled in these confrontations do you remember to choose kindness over being correct, like we discussed?"

Delores grimaced. "To tell you the truth, Jeanine, most of my conflicts are with some pretty nasty people. It's difficult to choose kindness with people like that."

"Let's start there," Jeanine said, tugging her leg tighter. "Give me an example."

"Sure. I've always hated the groping that Tio did to Simone and me, but now that I can do something about it, I don't want to drop a bomb in the middle of Mama's life. I keep hoping he's changed, but I don't like that guy and it's nearly impossible to be kind to him."

"I see. Along those lines, a while back you told me Tio's actions made it impossible for you to trust men when your relationships become serious. But I've never heard you speak of your interactions with women. Do you think you'd feel the same way about a romantic encounter with another woman?"

Delores wrapped her arms around her pillow. "I admit I've asked myself that same question, but I'm not really attracted to women in that way. In fact, I bet we both know women who can be just as manipulative as any man can, and that's what I don't like. When people say they like you but they are really just looking to get off. Either gender can be like that. I'm definitely not gay."

"Okay. Let me ask you something else. You seem to get along well with men when there's no threat of intimacy. But when you get alone in a romantic or special moment, your wheels fall off. Can you tell me about the transition? What is the trigger that changes everything?"

Delores's mind flashed to how wonderful everything was with Gordon, right up to the moment he said he'd like to get to know her better. But discussing the matter with Jeanine might lead to a very uncomfortable follow-up conversation about a certain cowboy and she wasn't ready for that. She glared out the window, where a swaying palm tree looked as if it were trying to dodge the breeze, much like she was trying to dodge the truth. She hesitated for what must have been a full minute, then, "I wasn't really ready to talk about this," she said looking down, "but the fact is, well, I'm a coward."

"A coward? That's a term I wouldn't have ascribed to you. If it makes any difference, I think it takes incredible bravery to subject oneself to people like Dixon Browne. There aren't many people who could pull that off."

"I guess not, but what if I make things worse for somebody, or fail and make a fool of myself?"

"Well, you can't control everything and everybody, but I can tell you that people who get bogged down in self-doubt don't accomplish as much as the ones who plow forward and take their chances."

"It's still scary."

"I'm sure it is, but our problems, be they cowardice or anything else, are often byproducts of our early years. Based on our previous discussions and how animated you've been today, I'm guessing something dramatic happened recently along those lines. Can you tell me about it?"

Delores's eyes sought the company of the swinging palm tree. Finally she rose. "His name was Gordon."

For the next half hour, Delores informed her friend of a delightful suspendered guy who wanted to get to know her better. Finally, a tear took possession of the corner of her eye. "It was like love at first sight, Jeanine, until I shoved that stupid book in his face and ran away. Now, I'll never see him again."

"That must have been disappointing," Jeanine said with heartfelt compassion. "What happened after that? Did you go back and look for him?"

Delores dug her nails into her chair. She wasn't about to get into the cowboy event where she'd have to admit she'd done something so irrational she could have been nominated for Idiot of the Year. Just then a welcome ping announced their meeting had neared the end. Thank God.

"We can get back to this next time," Jeannie said, "but before you go, I have something I'd like you to try when you're alone. It's along the lines of IMT. I call it Project Out and Reflect Back. Would you be willing to give it a try?"

"Can't hurt," Delores said, happy to talk about anything but her turn-the-table tactics.

"Okay, then," Jeanine said. "Here's how it works. Get in a quiet spot and lay your head back. Close your eyes, get comfortable and imagine what your life will be like twenty years from now. Get to an older and wiser version of who you are now. Does that wiser you have gray hairs or wrinkles? What's your home like? Are you married? Have children? Where's your mom? Things like that. Then once you've projected yourself into that mindset, you're going to ask your smarter self to reflect back. Ask that knowledgeable version of you what she thinks you should have done differently during the previous twenty years."

"Oh, I get it. It's like a do-over, without having to make the mistakes first. Sounds interesting." Of course, anything was better than discussing a certain cowboy.

CHAPTER 47

After seeing Sergeant Myles Cooper's truck pull into the police lot Delores worked her way to the conference room. The night before Myles had called her to request a meeting regarding Stump and Dixon Browne. While she waited she listened to her most recent recording of her and Dixon. Most of it was difficult to understand, so she made notes.

"Okay. I'll get back to you," Myles said to a caller as he entered the conference room and ended his call. He nodded toward Delores. "First Stump, now my mom."

"We can reschedule if you need to," she replied, while flicking off her recorder.

"Naw. That won't change anything. She fell and bruised her arm. She needs a little more supervision. It's looking as if I'm going to have to go get her and let her live with us."

"Moms don't always know how much we worry about them." Or about our careers or our personal lives.

"Agreed, but right now I've got to deal with Stump. He had a run-in with Dixon and I had to take him to the medical clinic."

"Oh, no."

"It's nothing permanent. His big meeting was supposed to be last night but Dixon sabotaged Stump's bike and he ended up in a ditch with a severely sprained knee. He damn near didn't get out of there. I don't know what I'd do if I lost him."

"Oh, my God. What happened?"

Myles sat forward and told her the whole story to the point when he found Stump sitting on a curb at the convenience store. "He had mud all over him and could barely walk. Now he's home in bed, doped up on Percodan."

Delores pursed her lips and recalled what Dixon did to Francisca's wrists. Now this.

"We don't have any proof," Myles added, "but Stump has been a thorn in that guy's side from day one so—"

"I gotta admit, Stump's always been a good judge of character. Now what? You going to make him quit his job?"

Myles hesitated for a second, then, "I don't know, Detective. He wants to get a car, and now he's got a girlfriend. The last thing he needs is for his daddy to pull the carpet out from under him."

"Yeah, I know. I've seen them talking." She'd seen them climb into a van too, but didn't see the point in mentioning it.

"If I drag him away from there, he'd resent it and they'd still find ways to get together. I'm just hoping they're being careful. A hasty accident would change their lives forever."

Delores smiled wistfully. If her own mama had been more open about sexuality, maybe they could have talked about Tio's behavior and stopped it before Simone ran away. "Sounds like you're going to let him hang in there."

"It's a tough choice, but regardless, I think Dixon needs to be stopped before he does any serious damage."

Before he does any serious damage? It was antiquated comments like that that constantly reminded Delores that she was at odds with an entire gender that seemed oblivious to how people like Dixon completely destroyed lives. Either all of them were mistaken or she was. "Really? Are you saying serial rape isn't serious?"

Myles paused, twisted his head and said, "I'm sorry, Detective. I have to admit that up until now, I pretty much thought your rape by deception argument was a reach. After all, it's a new concept and hard to prove, and when it comes to relationships both genders do a lot of misleading."

Maybe there was a ray of hope with Myles. "But now, some light in your head has gone on?"

"Yeah. I think so. When Dixon puts unnecessary obstacles in Stump's way, he's messing with me too." Myles squared up to her and lowered his voice. "You're in a similar boat. Dixon's wives aren't just women to you—they're like family—just as Stump is family to me and we both want to protect our families. Up until now, you understood that better than a dunder-head like me. I'm sorry I didn't put all that together sooner."

Delores allowed herself a Mona Lisa smile. There was no telling how complete Myles's epiphany was, but it was as if she'd reached the top of a tall hill and could finally go downhill for a change.

"Let's start over," Myles said. "What can I do to help?"

"Well, Dixon threw Francisca out and he wants me to move in with him; I'm running out of time." She tapped her recorder. "He admitted to defrauding women, but he wasn't very specific and he could always say he was just making it all up to impress me."

"You're keeping a gun close by, aren't you?"

"Just my little pistol. Anything else would be too bulky and conspicuous." She cleared her throat. "There's another thing. Dixon said he'd taken nasty videos."

"Uh-oh. Did she go along with it?"

"I doubt it, but even if she did—"

Myles raised his hand. "She wouldn't have consented to anything like that were it not for his lies."

It appeared as if Myles really was catching on. "It would be nice to get in his apartment to confiscate or even steal those videos, to spare those women from embarrassment."

"That's illegal seizure. You wouldn't be able to use them as evidence."

"I know, but at least I can prevent him from spreading

them around. At the same time, I don't think I want to risk tipping him off that somebody is paying attention to him."

"So I take it you have some other angle?"

"I need something stronger. I'm going to see Francisca this afternoon in Carlsbad. You can come with me if you want to."

"I'm not sure that's a good idea. If you're thinking of asking her intimate questions, she'd probably be more at ease if I wasn't there. You got anything else I can do?"

"I'm glad you asked. Dixon told me about a woman named Victoria who he likes to see a couple times a month, just on Wednesdays."

"A Wednesday Girl? You mentioned her before."

Delores nodded and ticked her tongue behind her teeth. "Exactly. It's the same kind of relationship he wants me to have with him on Mondays. I'd like you to have a non-threatening chat with Victoria, maybe about something unrelated, just to find out how loyal she is to him. But the important thing is to keep it low key, so she doesn't get spooked and tip him off that we're on to him. If she's willing to sing, she might know how we can reach his exes."

Myles nodded. "Got it. What else?"

"Well, our preliminary background check on Dixon included criminal, credit and phone records, but you guys have more resources. I'd like you to do a broader search. Get a national criminal check and see if you can find any other bank accounts, maybe out of state. You just never know what we might learn."

"Sure."

"Social media too. I once heard a woman say she found some information on Ancestry-dot-com about an old boyfriend that didn't come up in Google. It wasn't the kind of thing that would have been on a police record either."

"Okay. Anything else?"

"Not for now, but I'm going to try to figure out how Dixon gets so many marriage licenses. There's no telling how deep this goes or who else might be in on it."

"Good idea. It sounds like we have a plan. Before I get out of here, can I ask you something else? Would you be interested in meeting somebody? I know a nice guy about your age who works at the ME Office."

A set-up with another cop? That couldn't possibly end well. "Not really, especially not another cop. And that medical stuff can get sorta gross. I already see too much of that. I don't want somebody else's cases haunting me too."

Myles shrugged. "Well, if you change your mind, let me know. I think he'd like you."

"Thanks anyway."

As Myles walked off, Delores stood tall and flipped her hair back. She may have been surrounded by quite a few "dunder-heads," as Myles called himself, but at least she finally had a symbolic victory with somebody. Only 10,000 more cops in L.A. to go.

CHAPTER 48

ONCE AGAIN, STUMP AND MARIA were alone and naked. At least it seemed that way. He wasn't touching her, nor could he see her. But none of that counted as long as they were together and this time nobody cared. He was happy, at peace, in love. His erect penis seemed happy too.

His muzzy mind sent answers to unasked questions. Oh, yeah. It was Wednesday. He'd seen a doctor, taken powerful drugs and just had a dream. His bedside clock reflected eleven-thirty.

More alert, he had to take a leak and it wouldn't be simple with a severely sprained knee and a powerful case of morning wood. He scooted carefully to the edge of the bed, eased his legs to the floor and rose to his feet. He'd never taken pain pills before, but the throbbing in his knee assured him it was a damn good idea.

He leaned into his dresser and then the wall as he hobbled toward the bathroom. At the stool he elected to sit down to pee. Ahhhh. If only all his problems were that easy to solve.

While sitting there he removed the elastic knee brace that he'd gotten from the doctor's office. The damn knee looked like a war zone—swollen, bruised and ugly. He wished he could check in on Maria, but she'd be in school. Damn Dixon.

Call it an awakening. Stump now knew how dangerous Dixon could be, and somehow, someday, he'd get even. He rubbed his knee for a couple minutes before he rewrapped it and shuffled into the kitchen. He snagged a half-full bottle of OJ from the fridge. He wouldn't need a glass.

Since Dixon was always trying to bust Stump's balls, there was a good chance that Mr. Kraft already knew what happened in the office. If so, Stump's job was toast. It would be easy to verify. He grabbed the hardline, had the number memorized. Two rings and the boss answered.

"Mr. Kraft, this is Stump."

"It's early to hear from you. What's up?"

Hmmm. Kraft seemed surprisingly calm. "I'm sorry, but I'm not going to be able to come in today."

"Oh?"

"I sprained my knee and the doctor said I should take it easy for a few days. I wouldn't be able to do much anyway."

"It must be serious."

It didn't make sense. If Dixon ratted Stump and Maria out, Mr. Kraft would surely tell Stump not to bother coming in. "My dad's going to take me over there tomorrow to get my bike. I might be able to see you while I'm there."

"That'd be good," Mr. Kraft said before a dial tone ended the call. If Kraft knew what happened, it sounded like he was going to give Stump another chance, but why? There were plenty of other people who wanted the work, and those people didn't sneak into his office and romp on his sofa with their girlfriends. Stump vowed to himself that he'd never do anything like that again. He dialed another memorized number and rubbed his knee while he waited.

"Law offices?"

"Hello, Danielle Delgado, please. This is Neal Randolph." Stump couldn't blame his attorney if she refused to take his call. After all, she did a lot of free prep work for the meeting and wasn't obligated to put up with Dixon Browne's bullshit. He heard the faint click. *"Hello, Stump. How's your leg?"*

"The doctor says I'll be okay after the swelling goes away. You have a minute?"

"*I guess so.*"

"I'm not going to let Dixon Browne prevent me from implementing my program. Can you get me on the schedule for the final City Council meeting in three weeks?"

"*I was afraid you'd ask that, but when you didn't show up the Council members were embarrassed and angry. They don't want to see you again.*"

"That's not fair. It wasn't my fault."

"*I know, but they don't care whose fault it was, Stump. They just think it makes them look bad in front of the voters.*"

"But if I don't get my program approved, it's those very people who lose out."

"*That may be true, but it didn't look as if they were going to approve your presentation anyway.*"

Stump wrinkled his brow. "Why not? Everybody should want to have safer houses."

"*Some of the folks thought the home improvements were going to be free. Others thought they were going to be forced to make repairs even though they didn't have the money to do it. With all that opposition, the Council won't bring it up again. It's not good politics.*"

He would have liked to scream a profanity or two in Ms. Delgado's ear but he'd already been reprimanded a couple of times for blaming the wrong people for his troubles. "Well, would you mind checking with them again in a few days? Maybe they'll change their minds."

"*Not without a game changer, they won't. I'm afraid you'd just be wasting your time.*"

"Well, we're screwed then, cause I don't have anything like that."

"*I'm sorry, Stump. You're a nice young man and I enjoyed working with you, but I think we struck out.*"

Too tired to argue, Stump slammed the phone down and went back to bed.

CHAPTER 49

It had been a couple days since the priest and nuns whisked Francisca away as if she were a deposit in one of those pneumatic tubes in the drive-up banking lanes. Fortunately, Delores sent said tube directly to Carlsbad, and now Francisca was safely residing with Yolanda Vigil. It was time for Delores to have another chat with both of them.

When Delores arrived, a short, mature Hispanic man with a straw hat was watering the flower garden. She brushed some loose hairs off her forehead before she popped out of her Audi.

"They're beautiful," she said as she sniffed at the thick inland air. He smiled but said nothing as she strode past him toward the living quarters near the back of the lot. This time Yolanda Vigil was quick to greet her.

Inside, Francisca was seated at the small kitchen table with a new half-moon-shaped gash near her eyebrow. Delores had a pretty good idea where it came from.

"Pepsi?" asked Yolanda. "I bought them with the money you gave me."

"Thank you," Delores said, thankful they'd eliminated the gross tap water from the discussion. She both admired and pitied these women. On the one hand they were incredibly brave. They'd left their families and former country behind in hopes of building a better life in America, just like millions of other immigrants had been doing for centuries. But, through no fault of their own, they'd encountered Dixon Browne and ended up in a quagmire that they neither expected nor deserved. Delores placed her hand on Francisca's arm. "You are safe here."

Francisca's eyes were filled with cautious hope, her nod timid.

"My real name is Detective Delores Sanchez," she said, mostly to Francisca. "I've been living in Cal-Vista under a different name so that I could learn about the bad things that your husband does. That's why I came down here today. I need to ask both of you some specific questions."

Yolanda nodded, but Francisca was more stoic.

"I need both of you to help me show that he does the same bad things to different people. You can understand that, can't you?"

Since neither Yolanda nor Francisca replied, Delores pointed to Francisca's wound. "Can I assume that Dixon did that to you?"

Francisca placed her hand on top of her Pepsi can as if she didn't want it to hear what she had to say. "I admitted to Mr. Dixon that I had been lying about taking the birth control pills." She hung her head, "and that I'm three months pregnant."

Delores resisted the urge to groan and placed her hand lightly on Francisca's arm. "Oh, my goodness. What did he say?"

"He got really mad and threw a plate at me."

"I'm so sorry. At least you're safe now."

"That's when I knew I was just saying I loved him because I was afraid to have my baby by myself."

"So you went out and stood by the new roses?"

"Yes. At two o'clock, just like you said. I don't want my baby to live with that man."

"That was very brave." Delores swirled her hand in a

little circle. "The three of us have to stop him from doing the same kinds of things to other women."

Neither woman jumped at her proposal, but they didn't say no either. Delores took a sip of her soda and leaned toward Francisca. "How did you meet Mr. Browne and come to be his wife?"

Francisca glanced at Yolanda, who nodded as if it were okay for Francisca to speak. "I lived down the street, but needed a cheaper place to stay. He said I could do some work for my rent. The next month his other wife went away and he said I could live with him for free and become a legal American."

It was the same basic story that Dixon had told Delores when she was pretending to be Lorraine Martinez.

After a few more questions Francisca loosened up. She said that Dixon had been doing the same thing with various women for a number of years. It usually ended with some paperwork, presumably to lend a scary formality to it all.

Delores shook her head and leaned toward Francisca. "I have something I have to ask you. I wouldn't even ask, but it's very important. Is that okay?"

Francisca's eyes swung to Yolanda, who tipped her head approvingly.

"I need to know if you wanted to sleep with him or if you just thought you had to."

Francisca hung her head. "At first, I just did it because I had to, but then I wanted the baby."

"You wanted to have *his* baby?"

"My baby would have to love me."

Delores understood the feeling perfectly. A baby doesn't want to exploit you or feel you up or dump you for somebody better. "In the beginning, when you didn't like it, did he make you do it anyway?"

"A lot at first. But later it depended on how much he was seeing other women."

Yolanda nodded her head.

Delores raised her eyebrows. "Did he make you do anything else that made you uncomfortable?"

Francisca stared straight at Delores, who realized there was more. "I'm sorry, honey, but we need to do this."

"He made me watch movies of him with other women. Then he wanted to take pictures of me too. I didn't want to but he got very angry and made me do it."

Delores wanted to spit. Although she'd just verified something Dixon had said earlier and could add sexual exploitation to his eventual charges, she sure didn't feel any glee. Nonetheless, if these two ladies could hold up under the harsh cross-examination of a ruthless defense attorney in court, she could probably get a conviction, but she doubted they'd testify without more support. Furthermore, DA's tended to cut deals with defense attorneys so Dixon might get off with the equivalent of a swat on the wrist. Delores still needed more. "Do either of you know the names of his other wives or how I can find them?"

Francisca covered her can again and mentioned Inez Quintana and Rosalie Ortiz who lived near Cal-Vista, at Casa De Lucero. They acknowledged that there were others but neither Yolanda nor Francisca had names or addresses.

"Juanita might help you," Yolanda said at the last minute.

"The cleaning lady? Dixon mentioned her. Do you think she'd talk to me without letting Dixon know I'm asking questions about him?"

"I don't know, but Manuel hates Dixon because Dixon steals money from them."

"Oh really?" That was interesting. If Manuel and Juanita really hated Dixon, they might be useful when Delores moved her investigation on site. Having sensed she had extracted all the info she could for the time being, it was time to bug out of there. "I want you both to know you've been very helpful."

"Are you going to arrest him?" Yolanda asked.

"Not right now. I have some other people to talk to first. I need both of you to keep our little conversation between us. Then when the time is right I'll need you to help me."

Francisca's shoulders rose up as if she was trying to cover her ears. Delores assumed Dixon had scared the hell out of them but she'd deal with that later. For the time being she could take comfort in knowing these two ladies were safe and beginning to open up. She rose and handed each one a business card. "If either of you think of anything else I should know, please call me," she said.

Yolanda rose and wrapped her arms around Delores; then Francisca joined the hug-a-thon.

Outside, the straw-hatted gardener laid his hose down, picked up an incredible rose and offered it to Delores. He beamed when she took his offering. Her stunned eyes were drawn to the bright yellow petals in the center that glowed like the sun. A half-inch ring of pillowy-white petals encircled the yellow and both rings were inside a double ring of the darkest and richest pink petals she could imagine. But as gorgeous as the incredible tri-colored rose was, it had an even better quality: A giant whiff revealed it to be the most glorious-smelling flower Delores had ever encountered. "Oh, my goodness," she said, while taking a deeper whiff. "What's this called?"

The man beamed from ear to ear, tapped her arm and pulled a pencil and small note pad from his pocket. He scribbled two words, then handed it to her: *Double Delight*.

In spite of the fact that the man obviously couldn't hear, he and Delores had communicated perfectly. "Beautiful and smells good," she mouthed.

He removed his hat, held it to his chest and nodded.

As Delores walked to her car, she again smelled her special rose and allowed the aroma to temporarily become part of her. As she savored her gift, she pulled away and waved to the man who stood, hat in hand, in her mirror.

Somehow the aroma of the flower cleared her mind.

Regardless of her own troubles, there was no way she was going to let Dixon Browne beat her, which meant she had to think about rent day, which meant that Dixon would surely be coming by Lorraine's apartment very soon, and not merely to say hello.

CHAPTER 50

Stump tugged at his knee brace as he and Myles left the shopping center—only this time Stump wasn't driving. "I can't believe you bought me a new iPhone, Myles. Thanks a lot."

"Sure. Someday you can do me a big favor and we can call it even."

Any other time Stump would have been overwhelmed by Myles's generosity, but Cal-Vista was dead ahead and he was worried about Maria. Last he knew Dixon was at her house and had probably told her mama all about what they did. In addition, Stump would likely lose both his job and thirty bucks an hour.

At Cal-Vista, Myles and Stump made their way to the bike rack and Ol' Ug'. Myles wrinkled his brows, knelt down and pointed at the tires. "These things aren't slit. Somebody just let the air out of them."

Stump shook his head. "Either way Dixon's a piece of shit."

As usual, Myles ignored the profanity. "Before we jump to conclusions, let's go talk to him."

The hair on Stump's neck stood on end. If Myles were to find out about the couch action, Myles would be backed into that awkward corner that he'd clearly said he wanted to avoid: He'd either have to abide by his duty and turn Stump in, or ignore his responsibility. "To tell you the truth," Stump said, "I'd rather handle this on my own."

Myles nodded and tugged lightly on Ol' Ug's handcuffs. "Then give me the key to these things and I'll load the bike in the truck while you do what you need to do."

So far, so good, but Stump suspected everything would get worse in mere minutes. While he scooted past the pool and toward the boss's office, his eyes gazed across the courtyard. Maria's curtains were open. He could only imagine how disappointed her mama must have been. That sucked more than anything else. It reminded him of something his mother used to say: *You should have thought of that before you got yourself into this mess.* His mom was always wiser than he gave her credit for. Regardless, he had to make arrangements to get his final paycheck.

When Stump arrived at the half-flight of stairs that led down to Mr. Kraft's office, it looked like a form of much-deserved punishment. He grabbed ahold of the handrail and hopped down the stairs. At the bottom he limped to Mr. Kraft's office where the door was ajar and the light was out. Stump nudged the door to find Mr. Kraft lying on the couch.

"Oh, Stump," Mr. Kraft said. "I've been waiting." He sounded like crap. Stump flicked on the light and noticed a partially empty glass of water and two pill bottles on the main desk.

Mr. Kraft rose and moved slowly to his chair. "Looks like you're worse off than I thought."

"The doctor said it's a severe sprain." He pointed at Mr. Kraft's bottle of Percodan. "They prescribed some of those."

"Must have been pretty bad." Mr. Kraft raised one hand slightly. "I know how much that meeting meant to you, and I hate to pile on, but I think I've decided to let you go."

Huh? Stump had expected to get fired, but there was something peculiar in Mr. Kraft's tone and the particular words he used. "*I think I've decided*" indicated there could be some wiggle-room for a conversation. "I can tell you're disappointed in me—"

"Disappointed? You don't know the half of it. It's not like you. Now I've got to file an insurance claim and clean up my tenants' cars. I just don't have the energy for things like this."

Insurance? Cars? "I'm sorry, sir, but I really don't know what you're talking about."

"Don't play coy. I know you slopped that paint all over the parking lot, and on tenants' cars too. I can't ignore that."

The parking lot? "I don't mean to argue with you, sir, but I did a pretty good job painting those stripes. This doesn't make any sense."

"For crying out loud, Stump. You must have been out of your mind to make a mess like that."

Stump scrunched his brows and tried to recall anything he did to warrant this conversation. He may have been temporarily distracted by Maria, but he didn't spill any paint on the lot or cars or anything else. "I recognize that you don't feel very well, but would you mind showing me what you mean?"

"No use, Stump. The damage is done."

"Please, Mr. Kraft. I promise I don't know what you're talking about."

Mr. Kraft looked Stump in the eye and then sighed. "Oh what the hell. I guess you deserve that much. Some fresh air might do me some good."

As Mr. Kraft and Stump limped to the back lot, Stump tried to remember how he could have been so careless. "There it is, right there," Mr. Kraft said just past the halfway point. "Don't tell me you don't remember doing that."

The pavement looked as if a thousand yellow stars had spread across a black sky. "I didn't do that." Stump pointed to the area a little further out. "Look over there. That's my work. I'm nowhere near that sloppy."

"Well, these things don't happen in a vacuum."

Stump looked more closely, then bent over and pointed.

"Look at this. There's a bunch of big drops right here, close to my feet, but the drops get smaller and farther apart as they get farther away." He pointed three feet to his left. "Look here. It's the same thing. Whoever did this was standing right here, where I am now and flung that paint out there on purpose. I wouldn't do that."

Kraft glared at the splatters near Stump's feet. Then his eyes moved to where the smaller splatters fanned out.

"Who else has access to the maintenance room?" Stump asked, already knowing the answer. Of the four people who had keys, Kraft could obviously eliminate himself and Juanita because she wouldn't have the strength to lift the heavy paint bucket nor any reason to resort to vandalism. That left Dixon and Stump.

"I respect you too much to do something like this, Mr. Kraft. Besides, I need this job."

Kraft stared up the courtyard for a moment. "Alright. I think this warrants further thought. For now, you take the weekend off. Then call me on Monday, around this same time. I'll let you know what I decide."

"Yes sir, I'll call you then. But I promise, I don't know anything about this."

"Just call me on Monday, like I said." His tone indicated the conversation was over, which was fine with Stump. He had another stop to make.

He would have rather gone to a dentist than face Maria's mama, but he had to explain that the couch time wasn't Maria's fault. He wondered if the fact that he used a condom would make any difference.

After limping all the way to Maria's place, he knocked and took a step backwards, out of hitting range. Then the door pulled inward. As expected, it was Mama. Stump braced himself for the rage that was sure to come, but she smiled and called for Maria. Nothing was making sense.

Seconds later, Maria came to meet him and tugged him into the hallway, where she kissed him on the cheek. "Hi.

What happened at the meeting?" she asked. "Why haven't you called me?"

What the—why wasn't anybody yelling at him? "I sprained my knee and never got there."

She gasped and looked toward his knee. "You want to come in? Tell me what happened."

"In a minute," he said as he rested a hand on her shoulder, "but I'm worried about you. Did you get in a lot of trouble?"

"No," she whispered. "I don't think Jerk-wad said anything to Mama."

Stump wrinkled his forehead. "That's weird. I don't think he said anything to Mr. Kraft either."

"He's probably afraid you'll kick his butt."

Stump shook his head. "I don't think that's it. I'm just glad that you're still talking with me."

Maria grabbed Stump's hand. "Of course I am. We love each other."

"That's good. Anyway, I'm really sorry for taking you into his office in the first place."

"Don't be silly. I knew what I was doing. I'm not a little girl, you know."

"So you don't regret what we did?"

"Well, I didn't like getting caught, but we love each other and I want to do it again."

Holy shit! Stump's skin tingled. "You do?"

"Of course I do. We're boyfriend and girlfriend. Maybe it will last longer next time."

"I want to do it too, but I can't do it today, because my dad's here with me."

Maria grinned. "I didn't mean right now, silly. I just meant sometime—pretty soon."

"What about tomorrow? I should be able to bend my knee by then."

"We'll just have to wait and see."

"Sunday or Monday are good days for me."

She chuckled. "It sounds like you're trying to make a

doctor's appointment. I don't want to set a time. It should just be natural."

Natural? Stump nodded as if he understood, but as far as he was concerned, sooner was much more *natural* than later.

CHAPTER 51

ANOTHER DAY, ANOTHER DOLLAR in the hole. Thirty of them per hour to be more precise and Stump knew where to place the blame. He wobbled over to his dresser for his copies of Dixon's notebook. It was too difficult to concentrate. There had to be something else he could do.

He snagged his new cell, hobbled into the living room, and called Juanita. "Hi, this is Stump," he said when she answered. "I was thinking I could make a couple calls to people who used to live at the complex. Do you know how to reach them?"

"New tenants fill out an application before they move in, and many provide their forwarding information when they move out. All those records are in the file cabinets in Mr. Kraft's back room."

"They're probably alphabetized. Can you check them out and call me back?"

"I'm not going in there after what happened with Dixon's notebook. You have a key. You do it."

"I'm at my place and can barely walk. You don't have to take anything. Just make sure Mr. Kraft's car isn't there and make it look like you're going to clean his office. Once you're inside, the window in that room looks right into the courtyard so you can see anybody who is coming. Just scan the files of a few people you think are most likely to help us. Then call me back with their numbers. I'll take it from there."

"I don't think I should—"

"If we can force Dixon out of there, you can work directly with Mr. Kraft, and you'll get full payment for your work. You guys deserve that much."

She sighed and hung up, which suggested she was going to do it. Satisfied that he'd done about all he could for the time being, Stump took a shower and borrowed Myles's electric shaver for his bi-monthly shave. As he splashed on some cologne Juanita called back.

"That was fast," he said.

"Mr. Kraft's car was gone. I was scared, but I've got three people for you."

Stump grinned and grabbed a pencil. Investigating was sorta fun. "Who's first?"

"Erlinda Romero. Dixon used to see her every week. Then one day, I heard them fighting about her children. The next day she moved out and left most of her things behind."

"Okay. That's a good possibility. Who's next?"

"Ronnie and Betté Herrera. I don't know exactly what Dixon did to them, but it had something to do with Ronnie's brother. Dixon got out his gun and made them leave."

"That sounds good too. Who else?"

"The last ones are Jorgé and Mary Salazar. I heard that Dixon tried to get her into the bedroom and that Jorgé was really angry, so Dixon made them move."

"Good. If you think of any others let me know."

After they hung up, Stump shuffled excitedly around his living room. Even though he'd never really investigated anybody, he seemed to be catching on—and liking it.

He wasn't exactly sure what to say to the people, but he figured the best thing to do was jump right in there like he did when he knocked on doors with Myles. Erlinda Romero answered almost immediately.

"Hello?"

"Hi, Erlinda. My name's Stump. I want to know about Dixon Browne at Cal-Vista." He barely finished the sentence when he heard a click followed by a dial tone.

He redialed and got another quick answer. *"Stop calling me."*

"I'm just trying to find out if Dixon Browne ever hurt you."

"Who'd you say you are?"

"My name's Stump. My girlfriend's mother got beat up, and we think Dixon did it. We want to know if he did the same thing to you."

"I don't like getting calls from strangers. How'd you get my number?"

"Juanita got it for me."

"The cleaning lady? She's nice, but I don't want to talk about this. Don't call me back. Okay?"

Stump sighed. Erlinda obviously knew what Dixon was like, but he didn't do a very good job of drawing her out. He made a note in his iPhone to try her again later. Then he made another note. *Ms. Romero loosened up when she heard Juanita's name.* That was a good lesson. People might be more inclined to talk with him if they liked a common acquaintance.

He called the next number and got a recording. "Hello, my name is Stump. I got your number from Juanita at Cal-Vista. We're investigating Dixon Browne and she told me you had an interesting experience with him. I'll try to call you later. Thank you." He hung up. Even though he hadn't connected with a real person he was proud of how he handled the contact. He'd used Juanita's name and made the call sound important. He even used the word "we" to make it sound as if there was an entire organization of some kind doing the investigating. He added another note to his sleuthing lessons. *Make it sound like you're with a big team.* He dialed the final number.

"Hello?"

"Hello. My name's Stump. Juanita at Cal-Vista gave us your number. Is this Mary Salazar?"

"Yes."

"We think Dixon Browne beat up one of the women at the apartment building. We're trying to find out if other people might know of other bad things he's done."

"The police? Good. I hope you put that peeper in jail where he belongs."

Police? She thought Stump was with the police! Wow! He was on a roll. "A peeper, huh?" he asked, trying to sound as official as possible. "What did he do?"

"Oh, yeah. He walked in on me in the shower. He said somebody reported a scream from our apartment, but I could tell by his eyes he just wanted to catch me naked. I told Jorgé. He got real mad and wanted to kill Dixon, but I was afraid of that gun so I didn't want to live there anymore."

"We don't blame you," he said.

"Do you need me to sign some papers? 'Cause I will."

Just then another call came in. Stump checked the read-out. Betté Herrera was calling back. "That won't be necessary right now," he said to Mary Salazar, "I've got another call coming in. I'll get back to you if we have any additional questions."

"Okay by me."

Stump grinned and clicked to the other line. "Stump here." His name sounded cool when he said it like that.

"Hello. I'm Betté Herrera returning your call."

"Yes ma'am. Thanks for getting back to us. As I said on the message, we're doing a background check on Dixon Browne. Did he ever hit you or anybody else you know of?"

"Mr. Dixon wouldn't have done anything like that to us. He was afraid of my husband and his brother."

Juanita never did say what Dixon did to the Herreras so Stump hoped he could draw it out of her. "Yeah. We heard he really screwed you guys over. What's your version?"

"Mr. Dixon said Umberto could stay with us for an extra hundred dollars a month, but then he raised it to two hundred. Ronnie and Umberto said no, because if he raised it once, he'd do it again."

"So what happened?"

"Mr. Dixon said we had to move and we wouldn't get our damage deposit back."

"What? He screwed you over and then kept your deposit too?"

"We haven't told Umberto yet because if we don't get it back, Umberto will want to do something very bad to that man and won't care if he has to go to jail. That's why I called you back. Can you get our money for us?"

"Well, er, no. I'm afraid that's not my department. Maybe you could take him to small claims court."

"What's that?"

Stump barely knew what it was, but he was proud for thinking of it. "I suggest you call the main line at the police station. They should be able to direct you. Can I ask you one more question?"

"I guess so."

"Do you know anybody else who we should call to see if Dixon Browne has hurt anybody else?"

"Yes, there's one lady who probably still lives there. A long time ago he used to get drunk and hit her when he got mad. Her name's Inez."

Holy shit! That was Maria's mom! This meant that Maria was probably right. If Dixon had hurt her mama before, he easily could have done it again. Stump was excited to have uncovered such a significant clue, but he stayed focused. "Did you mention any of this to anybody else?"

"Nobody ever asked me."

That was another great lesson. "Okay, then. You've been a great help. We'll call you back if we have any more questions, and good luck with that small claims court matter."

As Stump hung up, he could barely contain himself. Betté had good information that she was willing to share, but nobody ever asked her. He made a note. *Ask if they know anybody else who can help.*

He hobbled into the bathroom and beamed at himself in the mirror. Among other things, he learned that nobody could tell how young he was if he asked his questions over the phone. He decided to do a quick Google search about interrogations.

244

CHAPTER 52

ON FRIDAY MORNING, when Stump first awoke, the word consequences danced in his head, but since he'd already missed two days of school another day wouldn't matter. He called the attendance office, said he was supposed to stay home for another day. Even if he did get caught, it would be worth it if he could get back at Dixon.

He could see much better so he fetched his copies of Dixon's notebook and picked up where he'd left off a few days back. There were still forty pages to translate and this was the day to make a big dent in it.

Once again he wrote out the alphabet and numbers one through twenty-six. He began by changing a few numbers to letters because that might spell out words. He got a couple hits and smiled as he followed his instincts and worked on a group of characters with an equal number of letters and numbers. A tale unfolded right out of his pen. Before long additional scrutiny revealed certain abbreviations: The letter D meant Dixon. H stood for husband, W for woman or wife, B for boy, and so forth. Some of the entries were more wordy: D had H paint hall; 2-103 pd 300 for 2 weeks. More words formed and sentence fragments came forth and ultimately the excrement of a dark soul emerged.

The earliest entries were several years old, mostly monetary in nature, and consistent with the things that Stump and Myles learned when they first examined the building. Dixon cut side-deals with tenants each month, mostly allowing extra people to live in the apartments in exchange for a hundred bucks or so in cash.

Stump assumed that Mr. Kraft never knew what was going on because there were so many legitimate tenants coming and going that there was no way the man could keep track of everything and considering Dixon's usage of multiple receipt books Mr. Kraft wouldn't see a paper trail.

Several pages and a long hour passed before something unusual popped up. When translated, it said, *3K to bank.* Stump grinned. He had gone beyond the reaches of petty sums. The term embezzler came to mind.

Another strange grouping referred to the days of the week: Friday-200, Wednesday's B-day. None of those made much sense, but that didn't deter him from going on.

As the minutes became hours, he dug through more pages. If it weren't for the sleaziness of Dixon's activities, Stump might have admired the accomplishment. No single misdeed was big enough to draw attention to what Dixon was doing, but tens of thousands of dollars had successfully escaped from Mr. Kraft's business and slithered into Dixon's bank account.

Stump shook his head. While he and others were busting their asses to earn a measly ten bucks here and there, a corrupt turd with false teeth was dancing around Cal-Vista, picking up hundred-dollar bills as if they were rectangular palm leaves. Nobody should get away with that, especially at the expense of a nice man like Mr. Kraft.

Stump considered going to the big boss with what he'd learned, but he had been told to stay away until Monday and the best he could hope for was that Mr. Kraft would fire Dixon. He'd decide what to do later. For the moment, he only had a couple hours before James was supposed to drop by so he wanted to use what time he had left to translate as much of Dixon's code as possible.

He persisted, looking for something different, something more substantial, monetary or otherwise. Then after lunch he caught a break. It came from three years earlier. To somebody else, it was just a bunch of jumbled letters and numbers separated by commas, but after he translated it, it said, "*Y only had 1K must work til Feb.*"

It appeared that Y was somebody's initial, and whoever it was had paid Dixon a thousand bucks, but owed him even more. The important thing was, it confirmed that some of Dixon's transactions were substantial, which justified working it all the way to the end as soon as he could. That noted, he heard James honk.

The previous evening Mr. Connors called to say he had a job for a few guys at four o'clock the next day and wondered if Stump might like to help out. Stump shared the news about his knee and recommended James.

"Thanks for getting me the job, Dude," James said as soon as Stump wiggled himself into the Subaru. "How's your knee?"

Stump scoffed. "I can tell you this: Jiggle Jaw deserves a big-time smack-down, not just for what he did to me, but I found out some other shit about him and Maria's mom too."

"Good for you, Dude. I bet you'll get him. What about this job? What does this Connors guy want me to do?"

"Sounded like somebody got arrested and abandoned one of the apartments. You have to get the furniture and stuff out of there so they can rent the place to somebody else."

"Don't they already have guys that can do that kinda shit?"

"Probably, but Connors said he likes to help younger people too. He probably wants to help us go to college or something."

"College? You? You never said nothing about going to no college."

"I never thought about it much until recently. Do you think I'd make a good detective?"

"I dunno. I guess you're pretty good with solving puzzles. They're kinda like clues."

"And seeing messages in license plates and phone numbers."

James scoffed. "Thank God you don't do that no more."

"I still see them. I just don't say much cause it bores everybody else."

"True that," James said as they came to a detour off the main drag.

"Speaking of clues," Stump said, "I found a couple other people who have dirt on Dixon. One lady said he used to beat up Maria's mama a long time ago."

"A long time ago? Is there a statue of limitations?"

"I think they're called *statutes*, Dude, with an extra *t* sound at the end. They're not statues in a park."

"Whatever. You gonna turn him in or not?"

"Not sure what Maria will want to do." Stump grinned. "But I have some other news for you, and you ain't gonna like it. What do you and the last bottle of olive oil have in common?"

"I dunno. What?"

"Remember when school started. We were both complaining that we were probably the only virgins left in our class? Well, now you and olive oil are the last two virgins." He sucked in a ridiculously huge deep breath so his chest would swell to its fullest size. "I got laid."

James's head swung Stump's way. "No shit? You and Maria?"

"Yep. Not only that. She wants to do it again, but don't say anything."

James banged on the steering wheel. "I don't believe this shit!"

Stump smiled and nodded at the same time. "Just before I was supposed to go to the meeting. In the owner's office."

"You wild dog," James said, obviously impressed.

"There's one little problem though. When we were done, I told her she was my first, but she didn't say anything like that back to me. Do you think I should ask her if—"

"If she has a history? What do you care, as long as you get what you want?"

"I dunno. It just seems like it should matter."

"It wouldn't matter to me none."

Stump paused a moment. "Maybe you're right. I guess it's none of my business unless she wants to talk about it."

"Agreed. When a loser like you catches a hot chick, he shouldn't look for ways to make a problem out of it."

Stump smacked James on the arm. "Look who's talking. The only virgin," he said, just as they reached the police building and lot. He pointed. "Hey, look. There's Myles's truck. The one with the 49ers decal in the back window."

"Yeah, I see it. You wanna stop?"

"Naw. I don't want to be late for our appointment with Mr. Connors and I was hoping we could stop at the bank and Target first." He looked back over his shoulder, wondering what Myles was doing at the police building.

CHAPTER 53

After introducing James to Mr. Connors, Stump called Maria expecting to hear that Dixon had finally ratted them out, but he discovered otherwise. She agreed to meet Stump outside.

Stump grabbed a gift he'd bought for her at Target and wobbled his way to poolside. While he waited, he snagged his iPhone and began a new list consisting of his business contacts. He had a couple dozen names identified when Maria walked out of her building and quickly scooted his way on those lovely long legs of hers. He was surprised she kissed him on the lips. "How's your knee?" she asked.

Liking the sympathy, Stump sat and rubbed it more than it needed. "A little better, but I'm wondering why Dixon hasn't said anything about us to your mama."

"Maybe he's just being nice."

Stump scoffed. "He doesn't do nice things unless there's something in it for him."

"Have you found out anything we can use against him?"

"A few things, but don't worry, I'm going to find a way to bury him." He smiled. "Without hurting you or your mama, of course."

"You're the smartest person I know," she said, patting his arm.

"I bought you something." He reached under the table, then handed her the bag. "Sorry I didn't have any wrapping paper."

She tilted her head. "An early birthday present?"

"Nope. Just 'cause I like you."

"Like?"

"Okay. Love," he said, shifting his foot.

A huge smile washed across Maria's face as she opened the sack. "A purple candle." She took a huge whiff. "You're so sweet."

"It's lilac, my mom's favorite flower. And you know what else?"

Maria held the candle to her nose and inhaled. "Hmmm?"

"This proves I love you 'cause it cost me three times as much as it would cost somebody else."

Maria took another sniff of her candle. "How can that be?"

"'Cause if I saved the money instead of buying the gift, Myles would have matched it and so would my trust. I gave up all of that just for you."

"I don't understand all that, but I do know that you deserve a *special reward*."

Stump's heart jumped. If she meant what he thought she meant, they needed some privacy. He didn't dare take her to Mr. Kraft's office again. Maybe the kissing van? No. They could get caught there too. Too bad he didn't have his own car. Suddenly, Maria's eyes focused on something over Stump's shoulder. Instinctively, Stump turned just as Dixon reached them and laid a small white box on the table in front of Maria.

"Here you go." He pointed his jaw toward Stump. "I was looking out the window and noticed he just gave you a candle. I thought you might like this better."

The nerve of that bastard. What the hell was he doing?

"I don't want nothing from you," Maria said, abruptly, causing Stump to smirk.

"Go ahead; open it," Dixon urged. "Consider it an early birthday present. I never told you that I have a daughter your age. I know that dating can be confusing for young women."

"Leave us alone," Maria insisted.

Right on! Go away, old dude.

"Your mama likes it."

Maria paused, twisted her head to the side. "Mama saw it?"

"Sure. She wants you to have it."

Maria raised the little carton to eye level. "Well, the box is pretty," she said, before carefully removing the lid.

Damn that Dixon.

"A bracelet!" Maria removed a delicate golden chain that contained a handful of pinkish stones spaced an inch apart. She flashed them toward Stump's face. "Isn't it beautiful?"

"Not just any bracelet," Dixon said. "Those stones are a rare agate, your birthstone. You can tell by all the swirling colors."

Maria tilted her head and beamed. "How do you know my birthstone?"

Dixon looked square at Stump. "You'd both be surprised by what I know."

Stump clenched his jaw. Were boyfriends supposed to know about birthstones?

Dixon returned his attention to Maria. "There's a special poem just for young ladies who were born in June. Would you like to hear it?"

Maria smiled. "If you want to."

Dixon nudged Stump over and sat on the edge of the bench, then looked adoringly at Maria.

> *"She who comes with summer to earth,*
> *and owes to June her hour of birth,*
> *with stone of agate near her hands,*
> *health, wealth and long life commands."*

Stump rolled his eyes while Maria reexamined the bracelet. "Well, it's nice but I don't want it," she said, putting it back in the box, "because I don't like you."

Stump almost laughed out loud.

"You have to be more selective," Dixon said while pointing a thumb at Stump. "Guys like this will say anything to get what they want."

"He's a better man than you are."

Stump grinned. On second thought, he was actually enjoying Dixon's company for a change.

"You're too young to understand, but trust me. You can do much better."

"You're just jealous 'cause he's nicer than you are."

Stump agreed and folded his arms across his chest.

"I'm just saying you should hold off. That's all. There will be plenty of other guys later—with careers and college educations. The kind that don't lie to their girlfriends and bosses." Dixon rose, scooted the box back toward Maria and lowered his voice to a near whisper, "I want you to keep it," he said before he turned and walked away.

Stump waited for Maria to throw the box at the jerk-wad, but instead she reclaimed the bracelet from the box. "Agate, huh? I didn't know that was my birthstone."

What the hell just happened? Stump eyed the bracelet. "Wait a minute," he said. "Let me see that thing."

Maria tilted her head, shrugged her shoulders and laid her new bracelet in Stump's palm. "Pretty, isn't it?"

"I thought so," he said pointing to one of the settings. "See this? It's scratched. Look. Here's another one. This bracelet is used. I bet he stole it. What kind of present is that?"

Maria took it back and looked it over. "Yeah, I see what you mean, but if that's true, it must be pretty valuable." She put it on her wrist.

"But it's like lying to you. He wants you to think he spent a lot of money on it, but he really didn't."

She slid it up her arm and then back down to her wrist. "Isn't that what you did when you said you paid three times as much for the candle?"

CHAPTER 54

Stump wouldn't have thought it possible to hate Dixon Browne any more than before, but he sure as hell did. His blood sizzled as he limped back to Mr. Connor's building to wait for James. Finally on the ride home, "It's not about a candle," Stump said, "but the bastard loves to tear people down."

James shrugged. "That's life, Dude. Everybody has power but us. We're the ones who do the grunt work and they're the ones who rake in the big bucks."

"Well, this time, I'm gonna do something about it," Stump said just before James dropped him off.

Myles was already home from work when Stump limped into their apartment. Myles turned immediately. "This morning, I got another call about my mom. This time she got lost in her own building and ended up in somebody else's apartment. When they found her, she was crying because she didn't know where she was. It's looking more and more like she's going to have to be relocated."

"No problem. Bring her here."

Myles paused a moment then, "You've said that before. Are you sure you'd be okay with it?"

"Of course, Dude. She's your mom."

"What about the inconvenience?"

"How many time do I have to tell you? None of that kind of shit matters."

"If she catches you talking like that, she might make you wash your mouth out with soap."

Stump wondered if people really did that.

They threw a frozen pizza in the oven and finished it off before Myles left for his nightly AA meeting, which lent Stump a chance to get back into the copies of Dixon's notebook.

After a group of routine pages he came upon an interesting, off-pattern entry: *m's coll acct 2 chase.* Stump stared at the data for several minutes. He'd seen plenty of hidden comments in license plates and phone numbers. He should be able to figure this out too.

Acct was a common abbreviation for *account* and he knew of Chase Banks, so those two could have been connected. *Coll* could have something to do with coll—ecting money. The *m* might have stood for money or a name or a man or a mom. The best possibility was *Manuel's collection account to Chase Bank*, but as far as Stump knew, Manuel didn't do any collecting around there. Regardless of the mystery, Stump was inspired to keep going.

As he progressed through the copies, a new pattern emerged. Two years earlier, there was an escalation in the number and types of Dixon's scams. That was about the same time as Mr. Kraft took ill. Stump couldn't imagine why anybody would rip off such a nice man, especially considering Mr. Kraft's health.

Stump plowed on. More phrases emerged and some names that Stump recognized appeared. J and M together had to be Juanita and Manuel. F was for Francisca. K stood for Kraft. Stump's pace accelerated. Then, with only three pages to go, the oddest entry popped out: *M's acct 20k showed IQ.*

Stump sat back, gazed at the paper. *20K* could have meant twenty thousand, but it was different in that it was the biggest monetary amount in the entire book. But *IQ?*

What did money have to do with somebody's smartness? And who or what was *M this time*? Dixon's mom? Manuel? Stump added M and *IQ* to his notes. His mind's eye played around with various combinations. I and Q went together, with no space between them. Maybe IQ stood for something besides intelligence quotient.

Then, in a split second something came to him. Dixon had been showing up at Maria's place at odd times and concerned about things that seemed to be none of his business. IQ could've easily stood for Inez Quintana, in which case M surely referred to Maria. That would mean that Dixon's earlier entry of *m's coll acct 2 chase* could have been an account for Maria. If that was accurate, *coll* could have meant college, as opposed to collection as he previously suspected. This was beginning to take shape. Stump raised one eyebrow.

There could only be one reason why Dixon Browne would do all of that for Maria. It explained everything. Maria said she and her mom lived at the complex ever since she was born. Why would anybody hang around that long if they didn't have to? It could also explain why Maria's mama did so many favors for Dixon. And why Dixon knew about Maria's birthstone. It explained why Dixon was so pissed off when he caught them in Kraft's office. And it clarified why Dixon kept encouraging Maria to wait before getting entangled in a relationship with Stump.

And most importantly, it explained why Dixon hadn't ratted Maria out to her mama. For once in Dixon's miserable life he had a soft spot for somebody and that somebody was Maria. She had to be his daughter.

A flush of adrenalin washed away the pain in Stump's knee. He leapt to his feet and twirled around. "I got you, you son-of-a-bitch, I got you," he bellowed, before he suddenly stopped and sat back down and scowled.

Maria had always believed that her father was a Mexican hero, but if Stump told her the truth he could break her heart. On the other hand, if he didn't say anything, and he eventually sent Dixon to jail, Dixon might level with her or she might lose her college fund.

On yet another level, if Stump didn't keep the pressure on Dixon, Maria would surely wonder why Stump didn't care enough about her mama. And just as irritating was the ugly fact that Stump would have to abandon his own goal to shove a heaping helping of red-hot vengeance down Dixon's throat.

What the hell should he do? Regardless of whether he continued his investigation or not, Maria was going to end up disappointed. Now he wasn't feeling so good. About all he could hope for was that he'd made a mistake.

CHAPTER 55

DELORES, DRESSED AS LORRAINE, wrinkled her nose and waved her hand in front of her face. Monday mornings were both useful and problematic. Anticipating a visit from Dixon Browne, she arrived at Cal-Vista fairly early. Given the recent humidity and the heat, her sham apartment smelled like a locker room. She flicked on the air conditioner and opened a couple windows.

While she situated the recorder-pen on top of the fridge and placed her gun and a small wad of marked bills she'd accumulated under her bedroom pillow she thought about the previous evening, when she had located Rosalie Ortiz, Dixon's wife from some four years earlier. It was pretty much the same story. Rosalie didn't want to talk about her relationship with Dixon, but squirmed uncomfortably when Delores mentioned some of the patterns she'd uncovered. On its own, Rosalie's information didn't add much except that it would help to prove the "serial" part of Delores's serial rape by deception argument.

Basically ready, Delores set one of the folding chairs near the large window facing the courtyard and waited for her prey to prey on her. Just as she was about to turn her cell off it vibrated. She checked the readout. "Hey, Myles. What's up?"

"It's Monday morning," he said. *"You going to be okay?"*

She looked into the courtyard. "I think so. I'm at the apartment right now, waiting for the dreaded weekly grab fest. Did you check those sites we discussed?"

"That's why I'm calling. There isn't much, but according to Ancestry-dot-com, there was an article in a Des Moines newspaper almost twenty years ago wherein one Dominik Braun was charged with felony domestic violence for beating up his brother's wife."

"And?"

"They cut a deal. Dominik pled guilty to misdemeanor assault, got six months' probation and all was forgotten."

"Okay, so?"

"Just before the six months were up, Dominik Braun changed his name—"

"Don't tell me," Delores butted in. "To Dixon Browne."

"You got it."

"Well it's not much, but there's no telling what other aliases he might have used."

"Or what other cases he may be involved in. What about Stump? You think he's in any danger?"

"Don't think so. He seems to stay out of Dixon's way. But if that changes, I'll get him out of here and let you know."

"I'd appreciate it, Detective. What about you? What's your plan for today?"

"Just trying to hold Dixon off for another week or so. I'm not sure exactly how I'll play it until I find out what his gambit-of-the-week is. Did you have any luck with Victoria?"

"Not really. I stopped by there and said I was considering hiring Dixon for a manager's job in a bigger complex. She seemed more concerned about the prospect of him getting away than happy that he might be leaving."

"Okay that's what I suspected. She's probably more worried about feeding her son than anything else."

"That's the way I read it too, so I elected to back out of there, without making a big deal out of it."

"Good. At least I know not to talk with her for now. I'm going to hate to end her meal ticket, but this is just another example of one of his victims." Some movement across the courtyard caught her eye. "Uh-oh. I gotta go, Sergeant. He's headed this way with a paper sack."

A minute later, Dixon tapped on her door, walked right in, set his paper sack on the feeble kitchen table and closed the curtain. "It's been a week."

"I know," Delores said while moving to the edge of the kitchen, toward the refrigerator. "Can I get you some water?"

"I brought some wine and cheese. I thought we might go for a little hike up in the San Gabriel Mountains. It's supposed to be cool up there today."

Hmm. While such a trip might draw out some incriminating conversations, the last thing Delores needed was to be alone with Dixon in a remote place. "Couldn't we just stay here?" she asked, trying to think of something Lorraine might say. "I can turn the air conditioning way up so it'll be just as cool."

He placed his hand under her chin. "I think you know that the weather isn't the only reason we're going up there."

"I know I owe you some money, but—"

"Perhaps you'd like to get rid of that debt right now. It'll only take a little while and you'll be done for the day. Might even get some overtime at the restaurant."

She scrambled for something else to say. "I could kiss you like before."

"Good idea." He pulled her to him, wrapped his arms around her neck and kissed her, but kept his tongue to himself. Then he eased his hands to her backside. "But it's going to take a little more than a kiss this time," he said.

"But I don't want to—"

He gently nudged her against the wall and kissed her again, this time with tongue, then lightly thrust his hips toward hers. His breathing quickened and he raised his hand up her side toward her breast. Yikes. This had the potential to get ugly. She pushed his hand aside. "I don't want to do anything dirty."

"Listen to me. I've been covering you for a whole month, without a legitimate commitment from you. This has to be a two-way street. I want something new and substantial." He tapped her breast. "Starting right here."

Instinctively, her arm shot upwards, pushed his hand away. He was lucky she didn't knee his 'nads, but that probably wasn't what Lorraine would have done.

"Which is it?" he asked, while facing her fridge-pen, "We're either going to get it on right here or up in the mountains."

Her heart bumped as a whirlwind of emotions rushed through her. This was as bad as the things Tio did to her when she was little and that made her want to run away. But the detective inside her wanted to bring down a perv. For the time being she had to set aside her own apprehensions and focus instead on the invisible women who didn't even know they were counting on her. "If I let you touch me for a few seconds, can we say that's enough for today?"

He sneered and shook his head. "A few lousy seconds? No way. If I'm letting you off the hook for the whole week, it's going to take a lot more than that." He reached for her breast again, but she scooted backwards and gazed into his eyes. His eyebrows were drawn down like Tio's used to be.

"I have another idea," she said with a feeble smile. "I've got a surprise for you."

He grabbed her arm and squeezed. "I don't want no damn surprises. You know what I want."

"I know, but you'll like this. I promise. It's in the bedroom."

Dixon hesitated. "The bedroom, huh? Now we're talking." He loosened his grip slightly. "This better not be some stalling tactic 'cause I—"

She twisted out of his grip. "I'll be right back," she said as she bolted to the bedroom and locked the door. She grabbed both her small pistol and a thin wad of cash she'd scraped up by selling some of her clothes to a consignment store. She stuffed the gun in her panties and returned to the living room with the cash in hand to see that Dixon had taken off his shirt and shoes.

She held out the bills. "I can pay you a week's rent. Then we don't have to do anything until next week."

Dixon gazed at the bills and wrinkled his brow. "Where the hell did you get money? How much do you have?"

"Almost two hundred. I pawned my grandma's brooch. You can have it all for yourself. Just give me another week."

He hesitated. Then, "You must think I'm stupid. You're just trying to buy me off with money you'd owe us for rent in a few days anyway."

"I know it seems like that, but that brooch was important to my family. I could have hidden that money from you but I didn't. I have to get something extra out of it or I could never forgive myself."

He grabbed the wad, slowly counted the money. "It's only one-seventy."

"I know, but it's all I've got. Please take it. You deserve it."

He thumbed the wad again. Then he threw it on the ground and stepped closer. "Naw. I want to play with your tits."

OMG!!! She took a quick step toward the door but he grabbed for her wrist. "You ain't going nowhere."

Oh, yes she was. She spun around, twisted out of his grip and ran out the door. The stupid bastard was lucky she didn't kill him.

CHAPTER 56

IT HAD BEEN TWO DAYS since Stump discovered that Dixon Browne was Maria's biological father but he still couldn't figure out what to do about it. No matter what he said or did there was a high probability that Maria would be deeply disappointed. It was all so damn confusing he felt as if he were living in the Penrose optical illusion where he'd walk up a flight of stairs, turn onto another flight, then another and another only to end up right back where he'd started. There was no progress and no way out.

Fortunately, he avoided his dilemma on Sunday because he and Myles spent the better part of the day at a Dodgers game, and getting in several more hours of practice driving, which left Stump just a few hours shy of qualifying for his full-blown license.

Then on Monday, right after school, Stump called Mr. Kraft as instructed, and was relieved to learn he no longer needed to wear the tattered clothes of the unemployed.

Mr. Kraft didn't say why he changed his mind, but it was obvious to Stump that Dixon was behind the paint spill and Kraft probably suspected the same thing. Regardless, it was a delightful twist of justice to know that Dixon was the one on defense for a change.

But all of that was in the past and now, it was Tuesday,

post-school. Most of the swelling and pain in Stump's knee had subsided and he was anxious to get back to work. At Cal-Vista he hustled to Mr. Kraft's office.

"Look who's here," Mr. Kraft said, his tone less upbeat than his words.

"Thank you again for giving me my job back. What do you want me to do today?"

"The first thing is to clean up those paint splatters. If the tenants think we don't give a damn about this place, why should they?"

Made sense. Stump thought back to the time when he got caught stealing a pint of vodka and was sentenced to remove graffiti from a government building. "I've removed paint before," he said, hoping he wouldn't have to elaborate. "Is everything in the maintenance room?"

"Yep. Picked it up this morning. Just read the label and don't get too close to the fumes." Mr. Kraft opened his desk drawer and handed Stump an envelope. "Here's your paycheck."

Cool. It couldn't be a lot because Stump had missed quite a few days, but every bit helped. "Thanks. I needed this."

"Nearly everybody does. By the way, you'll have to be careful in the maintenance area. Yesterday morning somebody left an old Queen Anne bed frame by the dumpster so I had Manuel put it in there until we clean that area up. As soon as I'm feeling better I'm going to have an expert tell me if that bed's worth repairing."

"I'll be careful. I promise." As soon as Stump reached the maintenance room he stepped inside where a previously messy room had gotten worse. Several support boards leaned against the Queen Anne bed frame as if to make a giant M, which made Stump think of Maria.

He smiled as he opened the pay envelope. A miserable two hundred and five bucks. He couldn't even pay all his bills off. He thought about his mom. She was always short of money too, even on payday. He shook his head, grabbed the paint-removing gel and some supplies and headed for the parking lot.

At the back of the lot, he spread some gel on the splatters and waited for it to agitate the paint. Then Maria showed up wearing the damn new-used bracelet that Dixon gave her. "Are you going to be able to see me when you get off work?" she asked. "I'd like to know how our investigation is going."

This was a good chance to soften her up for the news about Dixon's real role in her life. "I can talk with you for a moment while the paint loosens up," he said. "I got through most of the notebook and found something interesting."

She lifted to her tiptoes. "Really? Like what?"

"Mid-way through the pages, Dixon started pulling off more scams, and making a lot more money than he did previously. That's why he could buy that car of his."

Maria ticked her teeth with her tongue. "I don't care about that car. I want to know if he hurt people like he did Mama."

"He hasn't said anything like that, but I wasn't done there. I had Juanita get me some names of former tenants. I figured they might know of some things he's done."

"And?"

"One lady, Erlinda Romero, wouldn't tell me what happened between them, but I think she knows something along the lines you're talking about. I'm going to check back with her later."

Maria grinned and threw her arms around Stump's neck. "I knew you could find something."

Stump rubbed his hands on a rag. This was a good chance to eliminate one of his unanswered questions. "Before I get back to work, do you mind if I ask you about something completely different?"

"Of course not. You're my boyfriend. You can ask me anything you want."

Some boyfriend he was. Sooner or later he was going to have to disappoint her. "The other day, I was trying to remember what you said about your papa. What did you say his story was?"

She turned her head. "But I already told you."

"So tell me again. You're not ashamed of him, are you?"

She sighed. "Heck no. Mama said he was the bravest man in a big gunfight with the drug lords. He killed nine of them before they got him."

"What if none of that is true? Would you be disappointed?"

"Of course it's true. Why would Mama lie to me?"

"Have you ever seen any pictures of him, or newspaper articles about the gunfight?"

"No. I was just a baby. Mama said we had to run away or they were going to kill us too."

"What about your papa's family? Have you ever gotten any letters from them?"

"No. The bad guys killed them all."

"But what if it turns out that your papa is somebody else or still alive, or something else?"

"That's stupid. Mama wouldn't lie to me."

"She might be wrong. People make mistakes you know."

Maria shook her head and put her hands on her hips like she did whenever she was aggravated. "Mama isn't wrong."

Stump hesitated, smiling. "I can tell you're real proud of your papa." He pointed at the ground. "I gotta get back to work. I'll see you around six-thirty."

Maria tapped his nose. "How would you like to buy us all a pizza for dinner?"

A whole pizza? For all three of them? That would cost at least twelve bucks, times three. He sighed. Why not? According to Dixon, Stump was a rich boy.

After Maria left, Stump lowered his head and worked hard until his shift ended. After he cleaned up, he went to see Juanita and Manuel. Juanita answered. "Come in. Manuel is over at Dixon's but he should be right back."

Stump filled her in on the leads she'd given him a few days

earlier. "Most of them were glad to hear that Dixon was being investigated," he said.

Juanita shrugged. "It might not matter after what Mr. Kraft's doctor said."

"What? Is he worse than we thought?"

"According to Dixon, Mr. Kraft only has a few months."

One of Stump's stomach boots kicked him. He hadn't known Mr. Kraft very long, but the man had become one of his favorite people. "I didn't know it was that bad."

"He'll be getting sicker and sicker. It's supposed to be a secret." Just then the door flew open. It was Manuel.

"That damn cabrón did it to us again."

Stump's mind was in a fog about Mr. Kraft, but he knew enough Spanish to know that somebody screwed Manuel over, and it wasn't too difficult to guess who it might be.

"Why? What happened?" Juanita asked.

"He only paid me half of what he owed us for the last paint job. He said I took too long and he had to teach me a lesson." Manuel threw some money on the table. "One of these days, somebody's going to teach that cabrón a lesson of his own."

CHAPTER 57

THE NEXT DAY, Delores was hoping that Dixon had cooled off. She'd always known that making a case against him would be both difficult and dangerous. Men like him and Tio could be very intimidating. Many rape victims, even full-blown citizens, didn't want to talk about what happened to them for concern they'd be ridiculed and told they'd essentially asked for it.

As far as her case was concerned, no one victim was willing to be the first to speak out against Dixon, so Delores reasoned it was best to set up a team-like situation in which they could speak collectively.

To do that, she needed some additional players and she had a couple ideas that she'd not yet acted upon. But before she could go in that direction, she needed to employ her alter ego, Lorraine Martinez, to return to Cal-Vista, tail between legs, and patch things up with the grabaholic.

She removed her makeup and drove to her usual parking spot a few blocks from Cal-Vista. She waited for the bus to go by to imply that she'd just gotten home from her job at the restaurant before she slipped into Lorraine's apartment.

As expected, the wad of money that Dixon previously eschewed was long gone. In the bedroom, her clothes and bedding were disheveled, indicating he'd rummaged through it all. Back in the kitchen, her pen was still in its place. Then a note on the counter caught her eye:

I want to talk to you.
D

Good. She wanted to talk with him too. As she moved through the courtyard toward his apartment she thought about men who could steal a woman's innocence without giving a damn that afterwards those victims found it difficult to sleep, difficult to trust good men and difficult to experience real love.

At Dixon's apartment the curtains were wide open. A TV was on. As soon as he saw her he sprang to the door and swung it inward. "Come in, Lorraine," he said with a smile. "I was expecting you."

She forced a faint smile of her own and stepped inside, while he closed the curtains. "You're looking beautiful tonight," he said softly.

Delores cautiously eased into a side chair where there was no room for him to wiggle next to her. "My money is gone," she said.

He sat on the couch. "Let's be honest, Lorraine. We both know you're here because you need me." He leaned forward. "That's why I keep urging you to move in with me. It will make everything easier for you."

This was exactly the temperament she had hoped for. He was calmer but still motivated to advance the relationship. "To be honest," she said, "I've thought about it, but I shouldn't have to do anything right now. You have my money. That should take care of everything for a week or so."

Dixon shifted his teeth and shook his head. "Even if I let you get away with it this time, the next rent cycle begins in two days and you're going to be right back in this same boat. Then what? Have you thought about that?"

She paused a second and then lowered her head just enough to feign shame. "I don't know what to do."

"Look, Lorraine," he said. "You have to accept the fact that I know what's best for you. I've seen these situations before. I know how they play out. You need something permanent. That's why we should get married. Six months will fly by and this problem of yours will never come up again."

She waited before answering, then, "I guess I don't have much choice."

His eyes lit up. "Now you're talking. Let's get your things and you can move in right now."

"But I can't. We're not married yet."

"That's just a minor detail. First you have to show me you're serious—as a good faith gesture—then we can make it official."

The detective hiding inside Lorraine almost smiled. Dixon may have been an excellent poker player, but when it came to the possibility of making love with Lorraine Martinez, he had a major tell of his own: He wanted a lot more than a one-time fling and that sexual appetite could be used against him. "But I don't want to do it that way. I promised my mama that I would never do anything like that until I got married. Then we can do it."

"Do you know how juvenile that sounds?" he asked. "None of the other women I've done this with were like that."

"I'm sorry but I want the papers first. I don't want to do it if we're not married."

He scoffed. "Alright. Alright. I've got a friend at the County Clerk's office. If I take you there, and we get the damn license, that's it, right?"

"Except for one thing. The rent isn't due for a couple days. I might still be able to get the money."

"We already went through that. I'll call my buddy. He can have the papers ready by Thursday morning. Then we'll go make it official. You just tell your boss you need the day off."

Yeah. She could do that, all right. In fact, she was looking forward to finding out how Dixon persuaded his wives that he could streamline their paths to citizenship. Just as importantly she wanted that information without giving him anything in return. The best way to do that was to round up some rent money. She needed a loan.

CHAPTER 58

THE PREVIOUS EVENING Stump shared a pizza with Maria and her mama, who actually helped Stump get over his gloominess regarding Mr. Kraft's health. She even lit the candle that Stump gave Maria and made sure Stump got half the pizza. It might have been a perfect evening if Maria hadn't been wearing that stupid bracelet that Dixon gave her.

Before leaving Stump thanked Maria's mom, then he and Maria stepped out in the hall. "Can I ask you something?" he said. "Does your fondness for that bracelet mean you're willing to give Dixon the benefit of the doubt and drop the investigation?"

"Heck no," she'd said. "I just wear it because it's pretty."

As before, Stump ended that evening unsure whether he should say anything about Dixon being her biological dad or not.

Now, Stump was busy fixing a couple lounge chairs by the pool when Dixon approached. "Just so you know," Dixon said, "I'm still thinking about calling the cops about your escapades in the boss's office."

"Leave me alone."

"Don't you know you both have to be eighteen in California to do what you did?"

Stump turned away, tightened a screw in a chair.

"If I turn you in, you'll have to register as a sex offender for the rest of your life. If I'm going to keep it quiet you owe me, big-time."

Stump slammed his screwdriver into his back pocket, faced Dixon. "What a crock of bullshit. I have friends who hook up all the time and they don't go to jail. I've looked up the law too. Even if they do get caught, it's no big deal as long as they're similar ages."

"Bottom line is, I don't want you around this place anymore. If you don't quit, I'm going to run you out of here one way or the other."

Stump shook his head. "Ain't happening, Dude. Besides, you're the one who has to worry, not me."

"What's that supposed to mean, rich boy?"

"I know you let the air out of my bike tires just to screw me over."

Dixon scoffed. "Bicycles are for you children."

"You were pissed off because I got the line-painting job and you wanted to give the work to somebody else so you could skim off some money for yourself. Then, when you knew I had an important meeting you saw your chance to mess with me."

"You're out of your mind, rich boy."

Stump hated the *rich boy* comment. "You're the one who could go to jail. I almost died by the river. That's endangering a minor. I looked that up too."

Dixon hooted. "You're full of shit."

"Oh, yeah? Am I full of shit when I say that I know you're really Maria's father?"

Dixon stopped dead in his tracks. His eyeballs bulged as seconds lapsed. Then, "Like I said, you don't know shit."

"That ain't all I know. I found your notebook."

Dixon stepped to within inches of Stump's face. "I thought so, you little thief. I'm gonna have my cop buddies haul you off."

Stump scoffed, "You ain't gonna do that because I've

already figured out your code: letters are numbers and numbers are letters—it was easy."

Dixon's jaw muscles pulsed like waves and his face went red. "You're fucking with the wrong guy, rich boy."

"So are you. I've known you've been swindling tenants and Mr. Kraft since the first day I met you. The notebook just proved it. So I've made extra copies and if you cause me any trouble, I can fry your ass. Who do you think the cops will want more, a kid who has a girlfriend or a jiggle-jawed thief who's stolen enough money from innocent people to buy himself a pimp-mobile?"

Dixon looked toward Maria's building and then back. "Have you told Maria?"

Stump crinkled his nose. "That would disappoint her. We both know that she thinks her daddy is a Mexican hero, and for some reason you want her to keep thinking that."

Dixon nodded. "Looks like we have an impasse."

"Yes we do. Furthermore, you never said anything to Mr. Kraft about me and her because she's the only person you care about and you didn't want to embarrass her. But now you and I both know if the truth comes out, her world gets turned upside down, and neither of us wants that, so I propose we make a deal."

Dixon reared back his head and scanned Stump up and down. "A deal? I'm listening."

"You leave us alone. If she wants to be with me, that'll be her choice. If she doesn't want to be with me, I'll leave her alone, but either way, she decides for herself."

"What's in it for me?"

"I'll back off, forget about my notes, and won't tell her who her real daddy is. Oh, yeah. I won't say anything about that college fund you set up for her either. That way the cops won't confiscate the account or throw your ass in jail."

Dixon's jaw wiggled. "Oh, you know about that too?"

"I told you I translated the whole notebook, Dude. Like I said, neither of us wants to hurt her. So that's my offer. We can destroy each other or we can tolerate each other for her sake. I won't rat you out if you leave us alone. But the important thing is she makes her own choices."

Dixon stared into Stump's face.

"There's one more thing," Stump added. "No more gifts. It makes her think you're a nice guy and we both know better."

Dixon chortled and then agreed just as Stump's phone rang. "I gotta go now." He took the call. "Hey Myles. What's up?" Stump asked as Dixon walked off.

"Bad news," Myles said. *"My mom has gotten worse. If you're still okay with her living with us, I'm going to fly out to Oklahoma on Saturday, rent a moving van and bring her things back here."*

"Of course. We've already agreed."

"Okay then. There's a morning flight. I'll take the bus into LAX. That way I don't have to deal with my truck when I get back. You'll have to get by on your own for a few days."

A few days on his own? That opened up some extremely promising opportunities. "Sounds like a good plan to me," Stump said, hoping he didn't sound too excited.

CHAPTER 59

When Delores last spoke with Dixon he said he had a secret contact at the County Clerk's office that could streamline some of the paper work. If that proved true this buddy could be pulling similar scams with other landlord-types and her case could broaden into an uncontrollable monster and require the assistance of the L.A. department. Some of those guys would try to shove her aside and break up the ring of bad guys without her. Then she'd be stuck in an ugly turf war that she couldn't possibly win.

In the meantime she needed to round up some money so she could pay Lorraine's rent on the first and hold Dixon off long enough to wrap up her investigation. Unfortunately, the only people she knew well enough to approach for a loan of that size were her mama and Tio.

On her way to El Centro, she wondered about the sanity of that frazzled woman in her rear-view mirror who was so pissed off at a current perv that she was willing to overlook the actions of a former perv, provided the former perv would give her the money she needed to incarcerate the current perv. The pretzel-logic made her bowels nervous.

As miles passed, Delores wondered how to beg for money from somebody she hated in the first place. Unsure of exactly what she wanted to say she grew more and more frustrated until she finally reached their block and desperately needed their bathroom. She checked the clock on her dash. She'd gotten there so quickly she must have been speeding the whole time. She rushed up their sidewalk.

"Hello, Delores," Tio said upon opening the door. "You're early."

"The traffic was lighter than usual," she fibbed as she stepped over the threshold. "I need to use your bathroom."

Just then Mama came down the hall. "Hello, Delores," she said in a cold tone before they hugged in what felt more like a rushed obligation than affection. "Let's go into the kitchen."

"I need to use your restroom first."

"Go ahead, but I didn't have time to straighten it up."

Delores finished her business, then returned to the kitchen where Mama was wiping down the counters and Tio was seated at the table with his back to the window. If only she could say how difficult her life had become because of him. But she couldn't afford to piss them off. That *kindness-over-correctness* tactic that Dr. Moreno liked seemed wiser. "Can I help you clean up, Mama?"

"Why don't you just tell us why you wanted to see us? This is unusual."

Delores had hoped to ease into the conversation more gradually. She glanced at Tio and had second thoughts about borrowing money from the man. He'd hold it over her forever—even after she paid him back. However, these were the only people who could help her burn Dixon. She changed her mind—and then changed it back again.

Suddenly, Mama slapped a dishrag on the counter. "Dammit, Delores. I know you forgot my birthday. Are you here to apologize?"

Good God. What brought that on? Apparently Tio wasn't any good at keeping secrets. "I admit I forgot your birthday, Mama, and I'm ashamed of that, but it has nothing to do with why I'm here. Can't I just come because I love you?"

Mama shook her head. "Hogwash. I bet you want something. You never come unless you want something."

Delores's stomach tightened. She'd be damned before she'd let Tio and Mama ignore who was really the problem in the family. "Do you know why I don't come around, Mama? Do you know why? It's because I don't want to hurt you. That's why."

Her mother looked at Tio and back to Delores. "You're not going to bring up those fairytales again, are you?"

"They're not fairytales, mama. They're real. I remember when Simone told you about Tio touching us, but you didn't believe us."

Tio scooted his chair back and shook his head. "It wasn't like that, Delores."

"Oh bullshit, Tio. You know damn well what you did. Do you know how helpless we felt?"

Mama put a hand on her hip. "I saw him around you girls, and he never did anything like that."

"It was late at night, Mama, when you were sleeping. He made us be quiet. How do you suppose we felt when you didn't believe us? I've lost my sister because of you two."

Her mama scowled. "How dare you blame us! Simone had a boyfriend and ran away with him. That wasn't our fault."

"I need you, Mama. Don't you know that? I might be married some day, and have babies. But I can't bring them around this monster."

Tio jumped to his feet and pointed to the door. "That's enough, Delores. I want you out of our home."

"Screw you, Tio," she said with no hint of Dr. Moreno's kindness in her tone or mood. "I'm not done yet." She looked at her mama again and flipped a thumb Tio's way. "I know about men like this. They don't care who they hurt. I can't even tell you what I have to do to block out the pain he's caused. That's why I don't call you or come by very much. It hurts me too much when I think of all he's done to all of us, including you."

Her mama threw the dishrag in the sink. "We go to church every week. That proves he's a good man. Jesus forgives everybody. You'd be a better person if you did that too."

The veins in Delores's neck pulsated. "Forgive him? I can't believe you're even saying that. We're talking about big-time crimes here. You're both lucky I don't have him arrested for what he did. I'll never forgive him."

Tio pointed to the door. "I said get out."

With tears forming in her eyes, Delores rose and turned toward him, "You're just a goddamn animal, Tio. You ruined our family. Your entire relationship with Mama is a lie. Someday she's going to figure that out and you're going to rot in hell for what you did."

Delores ran to her car and slammed the door. Seconds later she realized she'd rushed out too quickly, but she wasn't about to ask them to use their bathroom again. They'd hold that against her too.

CHAPTER 60

Delores blew right past Dr. Jeanine Moreno and flopped into her usual seat. "I got thrown out by a perv. I'm a cop. I should have been the one throwing him out."

"Thrown out of what?" Jeanine said, as she settled into the remaining chair.

Delores launched into the details of her visit with her mother and Tio. Ultimately, she said, "By the time I got out of there, I was so angry I never got around to asking them for the loan."

"Did you try to choose kindness over being correct?"

Delores scoffed. "I tried to, but it didn't work. I swear, I could screw up a one-piece puzzle."

"Alright then. If you didn't choose kindness, what did you choose and what were the results?"

Oh, crap. Jeanine had a way of getting right to Delores's secrets. "I'm ashamed to say it, Jeanine."

"Well, we can talk about the weather if you think that will help you solve your problems." She smiled, kindly. "Do you know why there aren't many clouds in the desert?"

Delores sighed. "All I got out of it was a bad bout of diarrhea. Tio was damn lucky I didn't shoot him for that too. After I got home I took a shower, washed out my clothes and then went to a bar."

"A bar? To get drunk?"

Delores shook her head and brushed some stray strands of hair to the side. "I hate being out of control, Jeanine. I thought I could get my mind off what happened if I could pick somebody up."

"Fascinating. Did it work?"

"Hell, no. I'm too ugly."

"Oh, baloney. You're an attractive woman. You should be able to cull a horny dude out of a bar any time you want."

Delores looked directly at Jeanine. "To tell the truth, I had a couple chances but I was so bitchy I hated myself. Apparently nobody else liked me either."

"Have you ever done that before? Felt out of control and then tried to pick somebody up, I mean?"

A vision of cowboy Clint flashed through Delores's mind. She covered her face with her hands and bobbed her head up and down.

"Can you tell me about one of these situations?"

Delores sat back and dug her fingers into the arms of the chair. "A couple weeks ago, at the beach, I was angry with myself for being such a coward and pushing Gordon away."

"Gordon? The English gentleman we talked about last time?"

"I didn't tell you everything, Jeanine. After I ran away from Gordon, I needed a power trip of some kind to prove I wasn't a coward. To tell you the truth, it felt like revenge."

"Revenge? Revenge against Gordon?"

"Not against Gordon. I was angry with myself for getting scared in the first place."

"So to convince yourself that you weren't really a coward you did something that you thought was brave and reckless?"

"I know it sounds stupid, but I can handle the risk of recklessness way easier than the risk of romance."

"Alright then. Tell me what happened."

"I got all whorish and went to a cowboy bar and met a big guy. We went to dinner and then to his hotel."

"How'd that make you feel?"

"Powerful. When he found out I'm a cop he started asking me all these questions about whether I'd ever done it in a jail cell or with my uniform on, things like that. To tell you the truth it was kinda exciting to know I aroused him. That meant I was the one with all the power as opposed to when I was with Gordon and I couldn't know if he'd use me and then dump me."

"I see—"

"But when we got back to his room, he wanted to tie me to his bed and I realized I'd gone too far. I told him I changed my mind and made him take me back to the bar."

Jeanine unfolded her legs. "So you didn't actually have sex with him?"

"No. I felt guilty for leading him on."

"But you've done this other times and actually went all the way?"

"A few times."

"Alright, let's go back to what caused all this and see if I can summarize it. If I remember correctly, when Gordon said he wanted to get to know you better, you recalled the helpless feeling you had when you were a little girl and Tio fondled you and your sister; since you couldn't know if Gordon was using you in the same way, you felt out of control, so you panicked and ran away. But later, you knew that cops shouldn't be cowardly. So you had to prove to yourself that you're not afraid of the unknown, so you went to a bar. But then, when you found somebody you could manipulate, he got a little too creepy so you changed your mind. Do I have it right?"

Delores shook her head. "I told you I'm a nut case."

"I wouldn't say that. I once had a patient who dealt with similar problems by burning herself with cigarettes. She had dozens of wounds and said the physical pain was easier to deal with than the psychological pain."

"Poor thing."

"Life isn't always easy, Delores. Now, I'd like to fast-forward to the mini-war you had with Tio. After the blowup with him and your mother, you went to a bar again. Was that revenge too?"

Delores nodded. "I was angry with myself for losing my cool and never getting around to why I went there in the first place."

"Okay. So you lost control again and wanted to distract yourself from your anger by going to a bar, but when it came right down to it, you *got ugly*, as you called it. Why didn't you play nice, pick up some good-looking man-prize and go have a wild time?"

"I dunno, Jeanine. I'm so damn confused."

"The common theme throughout all of this is control. When you become angry or meet somebody you'd like to trust, you feel out of control and to escape that feeling you find somebody else and let him think he is picking you up, but it is actually the other way around. You become the manipulator as opposed to the manipulatee. You are the one who has the power. Does that sound like anybody else you know?"

Delores glared at her shrink. "Oh my God, Jeanine. I'm doing the exact same things to men as Dixon and Tio do to women. I'm no better than they are."

Jeanine nodded slowly. "At least you're not stealing anybody's dignity."

"Yeah, that's true. I just want revenge."

"Or control. But, there's something else you should know. All this bizarre activity is not really retaking control at all."

"It's not? What is it then?"

"It's just another version of the same thing. You're still allowing the guys you don't like to control you."

"How can that be? They're not even there."

"Oh, yes, they are. They're deep inside your head. Anytime you react to something somebody else says or does, whether it's run away or seduce a cowboy or anything else, you are allowing others to manipulate you, even if they're not in the room."

"Oh, my God, Jeanine. You're right."

"When it comes to relationships, there are very few guarantees. You might indeed discover that the Gordons in your life only want a physical fling. You might even get dumped by a few guys. Love isn't always emotionally tidy. But what's the alternative? Denying yourself real love? Running away from nice guys? Going to sleazy bars? How has that worked out?"

Delores pinched her lips together.

"I know it's difficult, but the next time you meet a man you like, try to remind yourself that Tio doesn't get to control you anymore. Tell yourself that you're not going to run away and you're not going to manipulate others. Excuse yourself if you have to. Go to the restroom and get in touch with your IMT like we practiced. Ask yourself if you really want to get to know this guy or not. And then kindly act on that information."

"I see what you mean. It's so obvious."

"Not always. If it were, I'd be out of work. The bottom line is it's usually best to neither force nor avoid your relationships. Just do what's natural—unless, of course, you become interested in a married man, in which case run like the wind right back here. That can be the worst situation of all."

Delores grinned. "I've got enough troubles without going there."

"Good." Jeanine glanced at the clock on her desk. "We still have a little time. Would you like a couple other pointers before you leave or have you had enough of my nagging for one day?"

"Please."

"For starters, I'm pleased with the outcome of your last two trips to the bar compared to the previous times when you actually had sex with strangers."

Delores lifted her head high. "Are you sure, because I felt like I'd failed again—this time for not following through?"

"But who had control? You or Tio? In a sense, you were finally acting differently than him and that's a good sign. Next, I suggest you look for some new hobby that you can use to soothe your anxieties. Something external."

"External?"

"As opposed to reading or cooking or driving where you're alone with your thoughts. You already do those things. To balance things out, consider reaching out to others. Volunteer to work at a seniors' facility or in a maternity ward or a soup kitchen. Anything where you're a helper and a leader. As you hand out support and wisdom you'll gain confidence and feel good about yourself."

"That sounds good. I like children. There are a few grade schools in my community."

"That's the idea. Any school would love to have a law enforcement officer come around and talk with their young girls."

Delores smiled. "Okay. I should be able to find something fun to do."

"Good. Now, let's discuss your mother's IMT for a moment. What if down deep, she truly knows you and Simone were correct all along? What if she really does know that Tio did all those awful things to her girls? What if she was so afraid of how she'd raise her girls in his absence that she couldn't bring herself to face what was happening?"

"I've thought about that."

"It's a form of deviant behavior. That is, she *deviated* from what most people would do in that situation. It doesn't mean she didn't believe you. It means she was scared more than you could ever imagine."

"She must have been secretly happy to see us leave, for our own sake."

"That's certainly a possibility. I think she loves you more than you realize. I think she says certain things to encourage you to stay where you're safer. What if a woman who loves you that much knew you had been doing risky things with strange men? What would be her IMT?"

Delores nodded. Jeanine understood her better than anybody else. "She'd be extremely worried about me."

"Doesn't a person like that deserve kindness more than being corrected?"

PING!

CHAPTER 61

Like a jet plane with a flat tire, Delores was on the verge of an incredible journey, but couldn't get off the ground. All she needed to gather the necessary evidence she needed was a measly seven hundred bucks. Basically out of options, she'd checked public records to find out who owned the Cal-Vista apartments. His name was Rodger Kraft.

When she found out the man hung out at the complex she placed a two-birds-with-one-stone type of call. Her first objective was to find out just how much Kraft knew about Dixon's antics and/or if the man was in on any of it; the second issue had to do with seven hundred dollars.

Expecting Rodger Kraft any minute, Delores was always aware of her youthful appearance. She dressed professionally and attached her badge to her belt. The visitor arrived and shook her hand. She recognized him as an elderly white guy she'd seen around the property. "I haven't been in many police buildings," he said.

She pointed to a chair and sat across from him, then flicked on a small recorder. "Thanks for coming in, Mr. Kraft. Can I get you something to drink?"

"No thanks. I just finished some water." He tilted his head. "You look familiar. Do I know you?"

"We've never met," she said decisively.

"You still haven't told me why I'm here."

"I need to ask you a few questions. We know you own the Cal-Vista apartments. Do you own any other buildings?"

"One property is enough for me. Why do you ask?"

"I'll get to that, but I need a little background first. How would you rate Mr. Browne as a manager?"

"Dixon? Outstanding, especially back when the economy was better."

"Oh? How did that affect you?"

"The rising interest rates caused financially challenged people to lose their homes. With tens of thousands of extra homes on the market, prices dropped and builders had to shut down. Many of our tenants, and others like them, relied on those construction jobs and couldn't pay their rent."

"I see. What do you do when that happens?"

"It can get pretty ugly, especially if they have children. I don't want to evict them, but we can't let them stay for free either. We collect as much as we can, but we usually let them stay a couple extra weeks for free before evicting them."

"That's not how I hear it. My sources tell me that Mr. Browne makes those people pay him about half the going rate, under the table, for those so-called free weeks. I'm wondering if you're pocketing some of that money too, maybe to avoid the IRS?"

Kraft wrinkled his brow. "I don't mean to be rude, Detective, but there are plenty of legitimate tax deductions without doing things like that." His eyes were steady, his hands and facial expressions at ease.

"Okay. That may be true for you, but what about Mr. Browne? I hear he cuts side deals with your tenants. Doesn't it bother you when he gets money that should go to you?"

"I know he charges tenants ten bucks here or there for doing them favors, but I don't make a big deal out of it because the economy has been difficult for him too."

Delores's eyes narrowed. "Ten bucks? I've heard it's more like thousands."

"Dixon wouldn't do that. We go back a lot of years. He knows I'm sick and how badly the building is doing."

"Weren't you suspicious when he got that nice new car?"

"Why should I be? His family sold a vacation house up by Lake Tahoe and he used his share to buy the vehicle. So what?"

"Did you check it out?"

"Check what out? There's no reason to distrust him."

"Did you know that his real name used to be Dominik Braun?"

"Are you sure we're talking about the same person?"

"I'm sure, alright. I'm also sure that we're talking about some very serious crimes, such as rape."

"Rape? No way. He doesn't have to rape anybody."

"Didn't you find it odd that he had so many women living with him?"

"Not really. He's a bachelor and a lot of nice-looking eligible woman come around a property like Cal-Vista. A fellow in that situation doesn't need to rape anybody."

"Did you know he married quite a few of these same women?"

"He used the term *married* from time to time, but the women came and went so often I thought it was just his way of saying he was sleeping with them."

"Oh, it's much more than that. He charges them a lot of money to live with him, and to be his wife. Any idea why he'd do that?"

Rodger Kraft stared at her as if he'd suddenly realized there might be something to her allegations. "I didn't know he was charging them anything. I probably should have gotten that money. Just how many marriages are we talking about?"

Delores hesitated. Rodger Kraft's manner and compassion were not the signs of a guilty man. He wasn't smug or avoiding eye contact. It was time to level with him. "At least five," she said. "Maybe as many as twelve."

"Twelve marriages?" Kraft frowned. "Quite honestly, I doubt that. Where'd you get your information, anyway?"

"A couple months ago, I went undercover and rented one of your apartments." She tugged on her blouse. "I dress differently when I'm there."

"Oh. I thought you looked familiar."

"The truth is, Mr. Kraft, Dixon Browne has been taking advantage of you. I'm afraid your old buddy is going away for a long time. It would look a lot better for you if you were on our side."

Kraft lowered his head, sat silent for a few seconds. Then, "I'd say this is hard to believe, but now that I think of it, Dixon has been causing trouble lately. He even threw paint all over the parking lot just to blame it on somebody else. He's never done anything irrational like that before. I guess I should have paid better attention, but I was too distracted by my own problems. Cancer does that to a guy, you know?"

"I'm sure it does and I'm sorry about that, but now we've got us a mutual problem and I need you to put together a list of all the women with whom Dixon might have had intimate relations. I need names and contact information."

Kraft blew out a deep breath. "I'll do whatever I can, but I looked upon a few of them as long-term house guests so I never made them fill out any paperwork."

"Alright, get me what you have and let me know if you think of anything else that might help to track these ladies down."

"Certainly."

Delores made a note, then raised her head. "Just a couple more things before I let you go. I need you to keep this meeting to yourself until we make our move. We don't want him to get spooked."

"Sure. When is that?"

"We don't know yet, but not long."

"No problem. This is a bit of a shock, but I guess he deserves whatever he gets."

"I'm glad you think like that, because I have another favor to ask of you. As you know the rent is due."

"What of it?"

"I'm expecting him to come see me very soon and I don't want him groping me as he's done before. It would make things a lot easier on me if you'd advance me the rent money. Naturally, we'll note the serial numbers and I'll give you a receipt."

"Of course, Detective. Whatever I can do to help."

"Good. Thanks. I'll give the money to Dixon and hopefully he'll give it back to you."

Kraft stared aimlessly at the floor. "Those poor women."

CHAPTER 62

It had been two weeks since Stump wracked up his knee and was essentially forced to give up on his desire to help people make their homes safer. After that he missed so much school there was a genuine chance he wouldn't pass the tenth grade. He tried to knuckle down, but he still had other, bigger problems distracting him.

After school, he pedaled Ol' Ug' to Cal-Vista and found the big boss at the office. "Hello, Mr. Kraft," he said as he filled in his time card. "What do you have for me today?"

Mr. Kraft spoke of the meter room, down the hall. "Each of the seven buildings has a similar room and none have been painted since the building was new. The first thing you need to do is straighten up the room and then paint it. After you're done, move on to the next building and do the same thing. By the time you finish the last one, you should be ready to paint the trim on the outside of the buildings."

More painting? Oh, well. About 40 minutes later, Stump was well into his work when he heard the building's main door open. "Couldn't keep your mouth shut, huh?" Dixon said. "The old man says you blamed the parking lot paint on me."

"I didn't have to blame anybody. Mr. Kraft is smart enough to figure out you did it."

"Look here, rich boy. I can turn some powerful people against you. Trust me. You won't like that."

"We already went over that. You got more to lose than I do so you ain't gonna do nothing." Stump stood toe to toe with Dixon and smiled. "You should have never made that notebook, but I guess you weren't smart enough to keep track of your activities without it. That's too bad for you."

The muscles in Dixon's jaw tightened. His face reddened. "Trust me, you're going to be sorry." He spat at Stump's feet and spun to walk away.

"Good riddance."

Seconds later and alone Stump was pleased with himself for standing up to Dixon. He threw a rag on the spit puddle, kicked the rag to the side and went back to work. In the meantime he had to figure out what, if anything, he should say to Maria about Dixon being her biological father.

Each time he imagined the dialogue he arrived at the same conclusion: There was no way she was going to believe him without proof and a few scribbles in a notebook wasn't enough. Then Stump had an idea.

He grabbed his cell. As usual, Google had the information he wanted. He rolled up the rag with Dixon's spit in it and stuffed it in his back pocket.

Later, when his shift ended, he met Maria at the picnic table near the pool. "There's something I want to talk about," he said. "It's something important. In fact, it might be the biggest piece of news you'll ever hear."

"Good news?"

He hesitated. Then, "You always want me to be honest with you, right?"

"Of course I do. Why wouldn't I?"

"It has to do with you and Dixon."

She scrunched her eyebrows. "I hate that guy."

"I know you do, but there's something you need to know about him that might change your mind."

"Not even if he kissed a hundred babies."

"Okay, then, here it is." Stump swallowed and shifted in his seat. "I found something in his notebook that has to do with you."

"Me? He never did anything bad to me."

"He never would. In fact it ties into why he gave you that bracelet with your birthstone in it." Stump's forehead felt hot. "I guess I might as well just come right out and say it. The truth is Dixon is your biological father. Your real dad."

"Ha ha. Nice try, but I ain't falling for your little joke."

"It's no joke. Honest. I confronted him and he admitted it. Trust me. It's true."

She shook her head. "Impossible. I already told you about my papa."

"I know how we can prove it."

"I don't need to prove nothing. I know the truth."

"Just hear me out. Would you, please?"

She rolled her eyes and sighed. "This is ridiculous."

"I know it seems like that, but I did a Goggle search and found a home DNA test that's designed just for things like this."

Maria folded her arms across her chest. "I don't care what you say, I'm not related to that man."

"We could prove it, one way or the other, within a week." Stump tugged the rag out of his back pocket. "I've already got his DNA. Saliva. I just need you to give some too."

Her eyes bounced off the rag, then back at him. "Eeeew. That's disgusting."

She was cute when she said things like that. "I'm not asking you to touch it. Just go along with me. I'll take care of everything. A lab will analyze the results and we'll know for sure."

"It's a waste of time."

"But what if you're wrong? You might change your mind about having Dixon arrested."

"I've already told you what I want." Her voice grew louder. "How many more times do I have to tell you?"

What could Stump expect? "Before you make a final decision, there's something else you should know."

She put her hands on her waist. "You never give up, do you?"

Stump looked over his shoulder, then back. "Dixon's been saving up money for you to go to college."

Maria turned her head. Looked deep into Stump's eyes. "That's not very funny."

"It's no joke. I promise. It's at Chase Bank. It was all in his notes. Pretty cool, huh?"

She looked at the ground and then into his eyes. "How much is it?"

"Over twenty thousand dollars. That's enough for a small college if you live at home and pick up a grant or two."

"I have twenty thousand dollars?"

"Either he's your father and you have a lot of money or neither of those things is true. That's why I have to get your DNA. I can get the kit here in a couple days. You just have to give a sample of your saliva."

"Spit? You want me to spit?"

Stump grinned. "You just wipe the inside of your mouth with a swab, that's all. It's easy."

She hesitated and then sighed. "I still think this is stupid, but okay. You can order the kit."

"Great. There's just one more thing. The kit is ninety-eight dollars. I don't suppose you have any money to pay for it until my next payday?"

CHAPTER 63

LIKE MOST BRIDES-TO-BE, Delores was excited about getting a marriage license, but she may have been the only woman who'd ever hoped the procedure would terminate her relationship with her fiancé. Dressed as Lorraine Martinez, Delores had just watched Dixon waddle up the courtyard toward her apartment. He wore a nice shirt and long pants for a change. "You ready?" he asked without dillydallying.

"Where is this place?" she asked.

"Registrar's Office." He rested his hands on her shoulders. "But first I want a kiss from my bride."

"But you might get carried away."

"Look, all I want is a single kiss—to start the day off right. You're not backing out, are you?"

"No, but I want to get started," she fibbed.

He grinned and leaned in. "I'm glad to hear that. We'll make it quick."

It wouldn't look good to deny him a single kiss on their big day. She closed her eyes and let him kiss her. Predictably his claws went right to her rear end. She cringed and reminded herself that other women had to do worse things with him. She secretly counted to ten and then pulled away as gracefully as possible. "Okay, let's go."

In the Caddie, with her recorder going, Delores figured that Lorraine would be nervous and prone to ask questions and some of them could lead to some useful information. "How long does it take to get a license?"

"Not very long. Then we can go back home and *finalize* the deal."

She winced at the thought.

"What about an ID?" she asked. "I don't have a driver's license."

"Won't need it."

Additional questions generated similar curt and confident replies, which indicated that Dixon had employed his formula before. Words such as fraud and conspiracy came to mind. She avoided smiling.

An hour and a half later, they rolled into a parking lot inland from Santa Monica. Delores recognized the four-story office building but had never been in it. After parking, Dixon made a call from his cell. "We're here," was all he said.

He took her hand and led her inside to the cafeteria and then to a corner table, away from other customers. Five minutes later a tall, pepper-haired white guy in his fifties joined them and introduced himself as Louie. "Let's make it quick. I've got a lot to do," he said, placing a thin packet of papers on the table. He eyed the top sheet and addressed Delores. "I take it you're Lorraine Martinez?"

She nodded and wondered if this guy really worked in the building or if he came from someplace else. "Don't you have an office where we should do this?"

"He's doing us a favor," Dixon said. "It's best to do this right here."

Louie looked at Dixon. "You're *Devin D. Brown* with no *e*, correct?"

"Yep. Devin D."

Hmm. That was interesting. Another one of Dixon's aliases. She wondered how many other names he and Louie might have used. "Devin?" she asked. "But I thought your name is Dixon?"

"Dixon is my middle name."

She shrugged as if she bought his explanation.

Louie asked a few additional questions about Lorraine's date of birth, her parents' addresses and so forth but he didn't ask whether she or Dixon had ever been divorced. Too bad, 'cause she was curious how Dixon would answer that one. A few minutes later Louie reached the back page of his custom-made packet and stamped it with a notary seal indicating his name was Lewis Drabble. "Okay, that's it," he said.

Amused by the brevity of the ritual, Delores looked at Louie. "A friend at work told me that the license is just *permission to get married*. She said there would be a separate ceremony by a judge or priest. When do we do that?"

Louie looked at Dixon, who took over. "Ceremonies are optional, and too expensive. We're not going to waste the money."

"What about a ring?" Delores asked, holding back a mischievous grin. "My friend said I'm supposed to get a big diamond."

"It's on order," Dixon said.

Louie glanced around the room before sliding his hand, palm up, toward Dixon. "You got those other papers?"

Dixon nodded, reached in his back pocket and slipped his friend a sealed envelope, presumably Louie's fee for making everything look almost official.

"What's that?" she asked.

"Nothing that concerns you."

Louie stuffed the envelope in his shirt pocket, rose and moved toward the door. Delores waited until he reached the hall before she sprang to her feet and turned to Dixon, "I gotta go to the bathroom." She hustled out the room and into the hallway in time to see Louie press the "up" button on the elevator. Good. It shouldn't be difficult to find him later.

From there, she found the restroom and made a call to Rodger Kraft who agreed to watch for her and Dixon to return to the Cal-Vista in a couple hours.

As she and Dixon returned to Palmdale, Dixon drove quickly, spoke excitedly and made exaggerated hand gestures. He reminded her of a twelve-year-old on his way to Disneyland. At the Cal-Vista parking lot, she observed Rodger Kraft's car and hoped he was standing by. Once parked, Dixon grabbed her hand and led her toward his apartment, but there was no sign of Rodger Kraft.

At Dixon's apartment, he disregarded the tradition of carrying the bride over the threshold and opted to pull her inside like a caveman. He quickly pulled the curtains closed then twisted the deadbolt and reached for the buttons on Delores's blouse. "Let's begin our honeymoon right now."

With still no sign of Rodger Kraft, she pushed Dixon's hand away and clung to her purse. "Wait. I have something to say."

"This ain't no time for conversations."

"But my priest said that what we did today wasn't really getting married. It was just permission to get married."

Dixon's scowled. "What priest? He must be talking about a church wedding. Ours wasn't that kind." He sounded like a big kid on the playground who was ridiculing a younger kid who didn't know the rules to a game. He reached for her blouse again. "You owe me and I'm done waiting."

She hugged her purse. "But I got some money from the church I can give you."

Dixon stood motionless for a few seconds and then looked her in the eye. "You've been sandbagging me again." He nudged her backwards. "Won't work this time. We're going to the bedroom." His tone was firm and eerie; saliva had gathered at the edge of his lips.

Out of time, Delores reached for the top of her purse and access to her gun just as a loud knock came from the door. "Dixon. It's me. Rodger. You in there?"

Thank God. Dixon placed his hand on Delores's mouth. "Keep quiet. He'll go away."

But she pulled loose. "Yes, we're in here," she said loudly to the back of the door. She rushed over, pulled it open and mouthed thank you to Rodger.

Rodger stepped inside. "Sorry to butt in, but I saw you just got back. I'm going to the bank and wanted to see if you have any other money for me to take while I'm at it?" Delores reached into her purse for the money Mr. Kraft had given her previously. "I was just paying him my rent money," she said. "I have it right here. The full seven hundred."

Dixon glared at her and then looked at Rodger.

"I won't need a receipt," she said as she slipped behind Rodger and out the door. "You both know that I paid."

CHAPTER 64

THERE WEREN'T MANY rich people in Palmdale. Fewer still lived in the Valley Elementary School area, which made it a perfect place for Delores to do some volunteer work. She could relate to these students because both she and they were Hispanic and of modest backgrounds.

Contrary to her usual practice, she wore her uniform in hopes of showing the kids that they didn't have to fear the police.

The school itself was comprised of two attached buildings. Stonework and deep-red bricks lent the older section a certain majestic coldness that was typical for nearly all the official buildings that were constructed a century earlier when the railroads sprawled across the country like daddy longlegs.

Later, perhaps in the late '50s, another section had been added. Constructed of blonde bricks and smaller windows and doors, it lacked the architectural charm of the original structure.

The final bell had just rung and the departing students enabled Delores to bypass the security buzzer. She was told she could find the art teacher, Carlton Fayes, in the so-called "newer section," by a cluttered bulletin board. Loud kids rushed through the stuffy narrow hallway with enough happy noise to remind her that there were plenty of positive experiences in life to offset some of the ugliness that she frequently encountered. Her quickened pace and swinging arms made her realize that Dr. Moreno was correct about finding something external to work on. Delores already felt good about being there.

A minute later, the wider halls, lower ceilings and brighter overhead lights indicated she'd reached the new section. Two doors down, she saw the cluttered bulletin board and its heading: *Warning! Creative Minds at Work*. Beneath the title, dozens of pictures of students, stapled one on top of another, competed for a piece of the board's fame.

"Uh-oh. I guess I'm busted," a man said from behind her. She turned to see a tall, thin man with an ivory smile that would light up a room. "Hi, I'm Carlton Fayes," he said. "Principal Haley said there was a policewoman looking for me?"

"Oh, yes. I'm Delores Sanchez. I'm actually a detective but I sometimes wear a uniform so the kids know the police are their friends."

"Good idea," he said, pointing to his classroom. "Let's step into my office."

Inside, the walls were packed with paintings, drawings, posters and quotes of all types. Only a few boasted of genuine artistic talent, the remainder being just a notch above the kind of thing one might see on the refrigerator in the home of any normal student. The odd thing was, every single piece had a bold A+ on it.

Carlton twisted two student desks so they faced each other. "Have a seat," he said, as he squeezed his lanky body into the farthest one. "So, I understand you want to do some volunteer work. Do you know any of these students?"

"No. I'm not a mom or anything like that," she said, peeking at his bare ring finger. "I'm not even married. I'm just looking to be a positive role model for some of the girls because I know how difficult life can be for them."

Carlton nodded, stretching out his legs. "Well, you hit your first nail perfectly. What did you have in mind?"

"I'm flexible, but something after school. I thought it should be fun, as opposed to studious or strenuous. That way we might get more participation."

"We already have art class, so I don't think they'd want to hang around after school for more of the same."

"Well, I know a lady who does magical things with her fingernails. I could probably get some pointers from her and help the girls do their own nails."

He curled his lower lip and cocked his head to the side. "That might be a problem. We don't allow the students to wear nail polish in school. I don't actually know why. But even if we could get an exception, they'd have to remove it before the next school day. Do you know any activities that would include the boys? We try to do things that include everybody."

"Not really. I can't sing or play an instrument. I guess we could memorize some poems?"

He curled his lip again. "Possible, but that sounds like extra schoolwork. What would you think of decorating cupcakes? I might be able to get Mrs. Carbone in the cafeteria to mix up a batch."

Delores's heart jumped. "I'm not real creative but it sounds fun."

"And who doesn't love a cupcake once in a while? Maybe we could even sneak in some information about cupcake history."

Delores grinned. That sounded exactly like something a teacher would say. "I'd have to do a little studying myself," she admitted. "I don't know anything about cupcake history or decorating them or anything like that."

"I've got a secret for you," Carlton said while leaning forward. "You just have to know enough to stay one step ahead of the students. They'll be happy that somebody is spending time with them."

Delores thought it would be good for her to be around a handsome, single man in a safe environment. "I don't have any of the pans or tools, do you?"

"I'm not sure what they have in the cafeteria, but it can't be very difficult," he reassured her. "Why don't we do a little research? I'll ask Principal Haley and Mrs. Carbone if we can use the kitchen. If I get the all-clear, we can get what we need and see if there's any interest in the idea. If it works out, maybe next year we can expand it somehow, perhaps for the holidays."

"That would be wonderful, but I have to be honest. I never know when I get called away on a case. I might have to miss a meeting in an emergency."

"No problem. I can take over if that happens, but I bet the kids will be disappointed if you're not there."

That sounded a little like flirting. Maybe because she'd made that stupid comment about not being married. "At least the messes won't be as permanent as if we spilled nail polish," she said, grinning.

Carlton matched her smiling face. "Trust me. We'll still have our hands full."

CHAPTER 65

As EXPECTED, MYLES did indeed go to Oklahoma on Saturday to get his mother. Stump put in a long day painting the fence between Cal-Vista and the Connors' property, then he spent some time with Maria before he and James went to the Target store and then to see the new Harry Potter movie.

Now it was Sunday morning and Stump had just jumped out of the shower. He was looking forward to a catch-up day. No work; no driving lessons; just a few hours to make some progress in his long-neglected schoolwork and then a few hours with Maria, hopefully at his place and all alone. Just then Maria called. "Are you checking up on me?" he asked, hoping she'd say something to the effect that she couldn't live without him.

"There's been an accident," she said, breathing hard. *"Mama was making sopapillas and splashed hot oil on her hand. I need to get her to a doctor."*

"Oh, no. Does she need an ambulance?"

"It's not that bad, but it stings. The people at the medical center want to get some salve and a bandage on it before she loses too much skin. Dixon went somewhere with Manuel, and it's Mr. Kraft's day off. Can you come get her?"

The law required Stump to have a twenty-five-year-old licensed driver with him until he obtained his own license, and he didn't like to borrow Myles's truck without permission, but this was an emergency. "I'll be right there."

"Please hurry. We'll meet you outside in the parking lot."

Stump threw on his clothes and bolted to the truck. Behind the wheel, he cautiously hurried to Cal-Vista where he picked up Maria and her mother, whose hand was wrapped in a wet towel.

"It's not super bad," Maria said as she buckled her seat belt, thereby revealing she was still wearing that damn bracelet that Dixon gave her. "Mama just needs something for the pain."

"Thank you for helping me," Maria's mama said. "You're a good young man."

"No problem. I know where that place is."

Stump rushed Maria and her mama to the center and waited until Mrs. Quintana was escorted into an exam room for treatment. He tugged on Maria's arm. "It's going to be a while before she's done. Let's go to the truck. I have an early birthday present for you."

Maria smiled. "You do? What is it?"

"You'll see." He grabbed her hand. "It'll just take a minute. C'mon."

At the truck, Stump handed her a small bag he'd gotten from Target the night before. "I think you'll like this," he said.

Maria pulled out a small white box, removed the lid, and screeched. "A bracelet. I can't believe you."

"That's gold over sterling silver," he bragged, "and a brand-new diamond, not a used rock like Dixon gave you. This is a better bracelet, isn't it?"

"It sure is," she said with a full smile. "It's the nicest thing anybody's ever given me." She hugged Stump's neck, then kissed his cheek.

"You deserve it," Stump said without mentioning a word about it costing him all of his last paycheck—and two-hundred additional dollars that he authorized himself to *borrow* from his joint checking account with Myles. All he knew for sure was he'd given Maria a nicer gift than Dixon gave her and it felt great to one-up the bastard.

Maria's mama was released a little later, sporting a large white bandage. They said she could expect a near-perfect recovery with minimal scarring. Once in Myles's truck, Maria showed her mama her new bracelet, then suggested they go see the doggie park. "Stump made it for his own mama," she said proudly.

Stump probably should have returned Myles's truck but this was a good chance to impress Maria's mama. "I guess it wouldn't hurt," he said with feigned modesty, "but don't expect too much."

Minutes later, they pulled into a good-sized parking lot where a large stone slab was engraved with *Jean Randolph Park*. "It's lovely," Maria's mama said.

They walked down a short path to a life-size bronze sculpture of a woman and a young boy holding hands and facing two large fenced-in areas. Maria looked at the statues and lifted her hands to her mouth. "Oh, my God. That little boy is you."

"And my mom," Stump said, grinning. "We're facing east so we can see the sunrise every day."

Maria's mama tapped Stump's arm affectionately.

Maria grabbed Stump's hand and read the plaque that lay near the base. "*This park is dedicated to Jean Randolph and Rachel Louise Johnson. RIP*," she said. "Who's Rachel Johnson?"

"The assistant principal at my school. They thought she committed suicide, but when I proved she was actually murdered, her grandmother felt a little better and gave me a reward."

"And you used that money to build this park?"

"Kind of. When I said what I wanted to do with the money Granny was so pleased she donated this land too. So, we both played a role."

Maria squeezed Stump's hand. "That Granny must be a very nice woman." Her mama nodded.

"She was, but she passed away just after the park was finished. The weird thing was, she didn't have any other kids or anybody else to give her money to so she gave some of it to me."

"So that's the trust money that you've mentioned?"

"Yeah, but I don't really get it until I'm 21—unless Myles says it's okay." He pointed at the fenced areas where there were over a dozen leash-free dogs running around and sniffing each other while most of the people gathered near a large cement picnic table.

He plucked a leaf from one of the bushes. "My mom loved the smell of lilacs."

Mama grabbed Stump's arm with her good hand as the trio watched several enthusiastic dogs of various breeds teach a tall man how to throw a saliva-drenched tennis ball. Stump was both happy and sad. This park never would have existed were it not for his mother, and for her death.

"We better take Mama home," Maria said while grabbing Stump's hand. Then she turned to her mama. "Would it be okay if Stump and I go see Harry Potter this afternoon?"

Stump turned his head. He'd already told her that he's seen the movie with James, so there was a pretty good chance she was actually thinking the same thing that had been going through his mind.

* * *

A few hours later, Stump pulled his numb arm from under Maria's head, causing her to stir. Then, "Oh, my God," she gasped. "It's almost seven. Mama's going to kill me."

They jumped out of Stump's bed and into their clothes and hurried to the truck. "What am I going to tell Mama?" she wondered out loud. "I'm supposed to call her when I'm going to be late. She's going to know that we didn't go to a movie."

"You're only off by an hour," he said, rushing along.

"Only an hour? That may not be a lot to you because your dad lets you come and go, but Mama worries about me."

Stump considered defending Myles, but that wouldn't soothe Maria's feelings. "Tell her it's my fault."

"I don't want to blame you. I'll just tell her the first theater was sold out so we went someplace else for a later movie."

Stump nodded. Up ahead, at Cal-Vista, a familiar red Cadillac was about to pull out of the lot and onto the street. Stump zipped around it and rushed to the rear of the lot.

Almost instantly, Dixon backed alongside them and jumped out. "Where the hell've you two been?"

"That's our business," Stump said.

Dixon bobbed his head toward Maria. "Not when her worried mother comes knocking on my door and asking for my help."

Maria sighed. "I don't have time for this." She kissed Stump on the cheek. "Call me later."

"A movie, huh?" Dixon said to Stump. "Who you trying to fool, rich boy?"

Stump stepped back. "Leave me alone."

"I knew you couldn't be trusted. Now, I've got all the cards and I want you to quit seeing Maria."

"I ain't doing that."

"The hell you aren't. It's either that or I'll see to it you lose your job; then it'll be hard to get another one. It's up to you, rich boy."

Stump scoffed and pushed Dixon's hand aside. "As usual, you're full of crap. I ain't quitting and I ain't gonna stop seeing Maria. I still know all your scams and I can find copies of that notebook anytime I want and send you to prison."

"You're in way over your head, rich boy."

"Screw you, Dixon. If you hurt me or Maria or her mama or anybody else I care about, I already have a plan to take you down." Stump climbed back in his truck. "Just remember, you have a lot more to lose than I do."

CHAPTER 66

While Stump pumped enough gas into the truck to bring it back to the point where it was when Myles left town, he felt guilty as hell over all the money he'd *borrowed* from Myles without ever telling him about it. What a butt-head.

Back home he parked carefully and checked the mailbox on his way inside. There, he discovered an envelope addressed to him from Inspect Enterprises. Inside the envelope, there were two sheets of paper, including a hand-written note: *Stump, Sorry they wouldn't let me knock off more. Geoff.* Stump's gut tightened. He'd forgotten all about the home inspector.

He flipped to the back page. Three hundred dollars? Damn it! He was hoping for a bigger discount. He threw the damn papers onto the floor. He shouldn't have to pay a bill that came in so damn late, especially when the case was over and the power-hungry City Council wasn't going to approve his plan anyway.

He clumped around the apartment for a few more minutes blaming and damning everybody, before he remembered who really screwed everything up. "Damn you, Dixon."

* * *

Monday after school, still gloomy and ashamed for having spent money that didn't belong to him, Stump made it to Cal-Vista on time by bike. It took his full shift to haul a shit-load of trash out of an abandoned apartment. As he threw remnants of somebody's life into the bottom of the pit, it occurred to him that there were many decent people who lived on the verge of despair, yet they didn't resort to stealing other people's money as he had.

At the end of his shift, Stump and Maria met at the picnic tables. Almost instantly Myles called to say he and his mother were back from Oklahoma and he needed Stump to help unload the U-Haul truck.

Before leaving, Stump told Maria why it was important for him and Myles to take Grandma Pauline in. "She used to teach History and Current Events in a high school. But now, her brain is slipping."

"Is she crazy?" Maria asked.

"Not crazy. It's the early stages of dementia. Myles said she's usually okay in the mornings. But as the day moves along she forgets simple things, like what day it is, or to take her meds. Sometimes they call it Sundown Syndrome."

"But how are you going to help her and work and still see me?"

"We'll take shifts. Myles hired another lady to stay with her in the daytime and he'll stay with her until I'm done working, then I'll watch her while Myles goes to his nightly meetings."

"Sounds complicated."

"I just have to do a little of it. I can still see you plenty."

Maria kissed his cheek. "She's lucky to have you. You know that?"

The ride home flew until Stump reached the stretch in the river where two weeks earlier he'd nearly lost his life. He thought about his mom and Grandma Pauline. They didn't deserve their fates. Neither did Maria's mama or the struggling tenants at Cal-Vista. Meanwhile other people were beneficiaries of good fortune. For instance, Dixon drove a flashy Caddie around that he certainly didn't deserve and Stump had a trust worth several million. It made him realize that Myles was right about his earning the money for his own car.

A little later when Stump's apartment building came into view there was a mid-sized U-Haul truck at the back of the lot. He looked forward to seeing Grandma Pauline again.

Inside the apartment, Myles met him almost instantly with a finger pressed to his lips. "Shhh. She's taking a nap." He motioned for Stump to join him in the dining room.

"Is she okay?"

"I didn't realize how often she takes side trips to Looneyville," Myles said. "Last night, in our motel room, she kept thinking we were in somebody else's apartment."

The compassion in Myles's tone reminded Stump of the days following the fire, when Stump's mother died and Myles wanted to adopt him. Myles blew out a deep breath. "I'm exhausted and need a quick shower."

"Go ahead. I'll cover you."

After Myles slipped into the bathroom, Stump heated some canned chili and settled into their recliner for a little TV.

"What smells so good?"

"Grandma Pauline!" Stump rose and hugged Myles's mother. "How are you?"

"I'm hungry," she said. "Who are you?"

"Don't you remember me? I'm Stump. We've met before."

She stared at him and said, "Oh, yeah. I thought you looked familiar." She pointed toward her temple. "I keep forgetting. I used to be a teacher, you know?"

"History and Current Events. Right?"

"Were you one of my students?"

By that time, Myles had gotten out of the shower and was rustling around in his room. Grandma Pauline tilted her head. "Where's my daughter?"

"Aunt Ellen's not here," Stump said. "We're in California. She lives in North Carolina."

"Oh, yeah. That's right. She's selfish, never visits or calls. I have a good mind to pull a Ruby on her."

"A Ruby? The red stone?"

Grandma Pauline scrunched her face. "Not a stone. The man. Jack Ruby."

"Who's Jack Ruby?"

She shook her head. "Don't you kids remember anything I teach you? We discussed this in class last month."

"But we're not in school. You're retired now."

She stopped and studied Stump's face. "Oh, yeah. Sometimes I forget. The gangsters hired him, you know."

Ruby sounded interesting, but it would be easier to learn about the guy online. Stump made a note in his phone to Google *Jack Ruby* when he had a breather.

"You got one of those portable phones, huh? What will they think of next?"

Stump let her look at it. "It's an iPhone. I just made a note in it."

"A note in the phone? Did you know we used to have a party line?"

"A phone just for parties?" Stump asked.

"We shared it with the Wynns and those other people up the road. I forget their name, but their kids hogged the lines."

Sounded weird. Stump made a note to look up *party lines* when he had a chance.

"I needed that," Myles said, returning to the action. "Everybody okay in here?"

"They remodeled." Grandma Pauline said before she faced Stump. "Students aren't allowed in the teacher's lounge you know."

Stump and Myles exchanged glances.

"I'm Stump, Grandma. This is our apartment."

She turned to Myles. "Did you tell him I caught you drinking beer?"

Myles grinned and said to Stump, "I was eighteen. Boys will be boys." He turned to his mother. "If we give you some chili, will you be okay while Stump helps me bring in your things?"

"Sure. You boys go ahead. I'll be fine."

Outside, Stump spoke first. "I'm glad you brought her here. She needs us."

"She's on again, off again. I'm just hoping that all this moving around doesn't make her worse." Myles opened the back end of the U-Haul. He turned his head and then back. "Did you wash my truck?"

A chill raced up Stump's back. He wished he hadn't taken advantage of Myles. Maybe he could come clean—at least partly. "I did something I shouldn't have, so I wanted to do something nice for you—as an apology."

"Oh, really?"

"I borrowed some money from our checking account."

"For what?"

Stump grabbed a box of Grandma Pauline's belongings from the storage area. "I know it's stupid, but Dixon gave Maria a bracelet, which made me look bad, so I had to buy her something too. I just got carried away."

Myles shook his head. "Carried away? Is that what you call it? I call it stealing."

"I wasn't stealing it. I was just borrowing it. It's my account, too."

"But you already spent all the money you put in there. The rest was my money. Just like our apartment. You're welcome to use it, but you don't own it."

"Well, if I'm welcome to use it, that's what I was doing with the money. Using it until I could pay it back."

Myles's head bobbed back in mocked surprise. "Exactly when and how were you going to pay it back? You haven't even paid me for your tires yet. How much did you take?"

"After I pay Geoff Harrington, who charged me way more than you said he would, there's about four hundred left."

Myles eyes ballooned. "You've got to be kidding me, Stump. That means you took hundreds that didn't belong to you, and you had to drive my truck without permission or a driver's license to get it cleaned. What the hell were you thinking?"

"That's why I wanted to do something nice for you. You already told me I could take my driving test in a few days, so I just jumped the gun a little bit."

Myles shook his head. "That was stupid. You know that? You're lucky you didn't have an accident."

"This is your fault too, you know."

"How the hell do you figure that?"

"If you'd let me use my trust money, we wouldn't have these misunderstandings."

"It's not a misunderstanding, Stump. It's dishonest. There have to be some consequences this time."

CHAPTER 67

DELORES WOULDN'T ORDINARILY VISIT a school without an appointment, but the lure of a cupcake caper with Carlton Fayes was too intriguing to get bogged down in formalities. This time, dressed in street clothes, she would simply tell Carlton she had just finished some other police work nearby and had some news for him.

She entered the lot, bypassed the bike rack and the short-term parking area, and eased her Audi into the larger section where there was a mish-mash of smaller-sized vehicles, including an unpretentious pick-up that she assumed to be Carlton's. The spot next to it was open.

She reached across her seat and grabbed a sheet of yellow construction paper on which she'd pasted a collage of cupcake pictures along with a few comments and facts about the treats. She popped open her trunk and stashed her gun before taking another look at the silly poster she'd made. Nobody else would get a kick out of it, but Carlton probably would.

She rang the entrance buzzer, checked in and was halfway to the art room when the final bell went off. In a split second, the frenzied activity in the hallway was as if she were inside a giant beehive that had just been invaded. She grinned. All kids loved the end of the school day. She hadn't been this enthusiastic in weeks.

Carlton was with two ten-year-old girls at the back of his classroom straightening a few pieces of art on the wall when she arrived. She tucked her silly homemade poster behind her back and walked up behind him. "American Cookery," she said in one of the few indoor voices she'd heard in the last couple minutes.

Carlton and the girls turned around.

Delores held up her yellow poster and read some of the script she'd added at the bottom. "The first mention of cupcakes was in 1796 in a book called American Cookery. They got their name because they were made in small individual pottery cups about the size of a teacup."

Carlton grinned, "Detective Sanchez. I almost didn't recognize you without your uniform." He reached for her poster and looked it over. He turned to the students. "I'm sorry girls, but this is a policewoman and I need to speak with her, now."

One girl giggled. The other looked at Delores suspiciously. They both seemed to sense that she had a little more than ordinary police work on her mind. Delores smiled and watched them leave before she gestured to her poster. "Icing had already been around for nearly 30 years. Do I get an A?"

Carlton shook his head. "Not quite." He strutted to his desk, grabbed a big red marker from his drawer and scrawled a giant A+ in the upper corner. "Anybody who shows creativity around here gets the highest grade possible."

Delores raised both hands to her heart in a playful gesture of pride. "I'm sorry I didn't call ahead, but I had a few things to talk to you about."

"No problem. I was getting ready to call you too, but I need to follow up with Mrs. Carbone in the cafeteria. If you have time, we can go see if she's still in."

Delores would have preferred to close the door and continue their private chat, but that would be too forward for the moment. "Sure. I can tell you about a store that I found."

"But we can't leave without finishing your project." He handed her the yellow poster. "Put your name in the lower corner. It's going on the wall."

"Really?" Delores understood why the students were so fond of Mr. Fayes. He made the little things seem fun. She reached in her purse for a pen. "Should I be Delores Sanchez, or Detective Sanchez?"

"How 'bout both? Detective Delores Sanchez."

They tacked her poster to the back wall, among the others, and made their way toward the cafeteria. If it weren't taboo on a couple of levels, the giddy schoolgirl inside her would have liked holding the teacher's hand.

At the cafeteria, Mrs. Carbone, a slim, slightly greying woman, was on her way out. "Mrs. Carbone," he said, "I'd like you to meet Detective Delores Sanchez." He turned toward Delores. "We could never get by around here without Mrs. Carbone."

"I assume you're here about the cupcake wars," Mrs. Carbone said in a matter-of-fact tone. "You know that boys like to show off. They'll make frosting balls and toss them around. Who's going to clean up their messes?"

Carlton put his hands to his mouth in mock surprise. "Why, Mrs. Carbone, don't you know that all of our students are perfect little angels?"

"Yeah, right. You do realize that I'll be checked out and the janitor isn't going to want to clean up a big mess?" She turned toward Delores and flipped a thumb toward Carlton. "He already does more than his fair share around here."

Delores grinned. "I figured as much. I'll help him. He's doing all this for me anyway."

"All right then, if you two are willing to take responsibility, all we gotta do is get the cupcakes. How many kids you expecting?"

Delores and Carlton traded glances. "Twelve to twenty," he said, apparently guessing.

"Okay, I'll need enough ingredients to make three

dozen." She turned to Delores. "Nice to meet you," she said and walked away.

Carlton faced Delores. "If it wasn't for a couple tiny problems, we could go get those ingredients right now."

"What problems? Maybe I can help."

"First, I rode my bicycle today."

She should have guessed. "I could drive. My car is like a giant purse but I could move a few more things into the trunk."

"I wish that was all, but I'm embarrassed to say I don't have any money until my check clears in a couple days."

Delores snickered, "I'd offer to advance the money, but I'm in the same darn boat. Doesn't the school have a petty cash account we could use?"

"Not for something like this. I usually have to fund these things on my own, but I like the kids, so I do without some of the frills in life."

"Admirable," she said, nodding.

Carlton looked over to the kitchen area. "I doubt Mrs. Carbone would mind if I put on a pot of coffee. We can work out our plans and pretend we're in a fancy restaurant."

"I'd like that."

They moved toward the kitchen. "When we get those ingredients," he said, "we should double the order. That way a certain broke art teacher and an equally poor policewoman could have their own bake sale and split the profits."

Delores nodded, thinking about Gordon the Brit, Clint the cowboy and Dr. Moreno. Somehow this felt like progress.

CHAPTER 68

"Duck down," Stump said as he and Myles drove past Stump's school. "I don't want anybody to see me with you."

Myles grinned. "Ain't going to happen, but I want you to know I'm proud of you. Now you've got a full-blown driver's license to show for all your efforts."

"The instructor said I needed to work on defensive driving."

"Well, we all do. And just to show you that I can be a nice guy once in a while, after we go home and I introduce you to my mom's new caregiver, I'm going to let you use the truck to go to work today—"

Stump's heart jumped. Adulthood may have had extra responsibilities but it also contained some rad benefits.

"That's not all," Myles added. "I've decided to give you ten bucks an hour whenever you take my mom places."

"But I already told you, I don't want no—"

"I know, and I appreciate that, but there's a difference between hanging out with somebody and taking them places such as the doctor's office or the park. Those things are extra and more like work."

Made sense. Stump nodded. "What about tripling it?"

Myles's smirked. "Straight to work and straight back afterwards, got it?"

"Well. You can't blame a guy for trying. Do I have to come right home after work 'cause—"

"I should cut you off because of your bank-robbing episode while I was gone, but you've shown me a lot of compassion too. So the deal is you can hang out but you gotta get home in time for me to get to my meetings." Myles raised a finger. "And no other driving in between. If you can handle that, then next time we might open up other possibilities. How does that sound?"

Of course, it sounded great.

A few minutes later, Stump and Myles arrived at their apartment where Grandma Pauline was watching TV and Stump was introduced to Katherine DeLong, a professional caregiver. In her late thirties, she had stunning Asian features including gorgeous eyes, bobbed black hair, and a pretty smile. She insisted that everybody refer to her by her first name.

"How'd you do?" she asked Stump when he walked in.

"I passed."

She hurried to him and gave him a warm, unanticipated hug. "I'm so proud of you."

"Gee, thanks," The embrace was unlike any other he'd ever experienced. Naturally, other mature women like his mom and Aunt Gerry had hugged him before, but they were family and that was before he'd gotten serious with Maria and became aware of some other things. Katherine's breasts were larger than Maria's.

Katherine grabbed a package from the table. "This came for you while you were gone."

Stump turned it around. It had to be the DNA kit he'd ordered.

"What is it?" Myles asked.

"Just a small teddy bear for Maria's birthday." Stump said, not wanting to get into another uncomfortable conversation about his recent spending habits and why he needed a DNA test.

Myles flipped him the keys to the truck. "Remember what we talked about. No side trips."

A little later, with the DNA test on the seat and savoring his adult-like status, Stump called Maria who agreed to meet him in ten minutes. When he made it to Cal-Vista he parked Myles's truck toward the front of the lot where people might see him driving; then he went right to Mr. Kraft's office.

"You're early, today," Mr. Kraft said. "What's going on?"

"I passed my driver's test and got my license. My dad even loaned me his truck. I drove here by myself."

"Oh, I see. That first drive is a big deal for a young fellow."

It wasn't really the first drive, but it was the first completely legal solo drive. "I can't wait to get my own car."

"Considering that deal you worked out with your dad, you must have a nice little nest egg already."

"I've decided not to be so picky."

"Good idea. The nicer cars depreciate too much." Mr. Kraft rose and opened his wallet. "This won't buy the entire car," he said, handing Stump a twenty, "but it might help with that first tank of gas. Consider it a bonus."

"Really? Gee, thanks." Stump had always liked Mr. Kraft. It wasn't the money per se, but the fact that the man had faith in him. That must have been what grandfathers were like.

"Glad to do it. I'm not going to be around forever and I can't take it with me." Mr. Kraft pointed a thumb toward the hallway. "I saw you finished up that back fence. That means you can replace all the light bulbs in the hallway. There's a case of the new spiral-type fluorescent bulbs in the maintenance room."

"Will do."

When Stump opened the door to the maintenance room, he damn near tripped over the box of bulbs and noticed a new mattress leaning against the ladders and the Queen Anne bed. He flashed back to the old days when he was oblivious to the messes in his own bedroom. Now he knew why his mother got so frustrated with him.

After the bulbs were replaced, Stump spent the rest of his shift straightening up the maintenance room, without being told to do so. When done it looked twice as big.

After work he took the box of used light bulbs to Maria's apartment, where she answered the door wearing a beautiful pink polo shirt. "How do you like my new blouse?" she asked as she opened the top button. "Mama got it for me."

"I noticed it right away, but you always look hot when you wear bright colors."

She smiled. "I do? Why didn't you say so before?"

"I thought it was obvious."

"Well, nobody else ever told me that." She pointed to the box he'd brought with him. "What are those for?"

"My boss said I could give them to you."

"What's wrong with them?"

"Nothing. We just changed to a different kind and he likes them all to be the same so he said I could have these. They still work and there's no use wasting them, so I thought you might want them."

"How sweet." She turned her head toward the center of the apartment. "Mama. Come see what Stump gave us."

Mrs. Quintana, still nursing a bandaged hand, came and took a peek. "Light bulbs. We'll think of you every time we use one," she said, mirroring her daughter's grin. It was another good lesson for Stump. Presents didn't always have to be expensive.

Free to hang out together for a few hours, Stump and Maria meandered out to one of the picnic tables near the pool where Stump told Maria about the restrictions on his use of Myles's truck. "Another thing," he said. "The DNA test arrived. I think we should deal with it now so I can take it right over to the post office."

Maria put her hands on her hips. "Since you paid for it I guess I have to, but I'm telling you, it's a waste of time."

"We'll see," Stump said while he opened the box. "All you gotta do is swab your mouth."

"Afterwards, will you buy me an ice cream cone?"

"I'm not supposed to do that." He was proud of himself for showing some restraint for a change.

Maria touched his lower lip. "You might get a reward."

He tapped the swab. "Well, are you going to give me your DNA or not?"

Maria sighed, grabbed it and dragged it extra slowly across her tongue. "There. Happy?"

"It's better if you wipe it on the roof of your mouth."

She stuck her tongue out, farther than before, and seductively wiped the swab across it again, this time even slower. "Take it or leave it."

Stump loved her playful nature. "Okay, I'll take it," he said as he packaged the items back up for the lab. "I'll drop it off at the post office after school tomorrow. They ought to have the results posted online by Tuesday."

"Isn't that the last City Council meeting? Are you going to try again?"

"Can't. After what Dixon did to me, everybody hates me and I've moved on."

Maria grabbed his hand. "Too bad we can't take your truck to some secret place."

He observed her wide-open eyes and mischievous stare. He may not have been the world's most experienced lover, but he got the hint.

CHAPTER 69

Maria's not-so-subtle hint that she was open to making love was the highlight of Stump's day, but they couldn't do it right there in the front of the Cal-Vista lot. "I've got an idea," Stump said, grabbing her hand. "Follow me." He led her toward building six.

"That's where Mr. Kraft's office is," Maria whispered. "I don't want to do it in there again."

"We're not going there. I've got a better idea."

They went around back and tiptoed down the stairs in the direction of Mr. Kraft's office but stopped one door earlier, at the maintenance room. Stump put his finger to his lips. "In here," he said softly while inserting his key. "I just cleaned it up and nobody comes in here after hours." Inside he flicked on the light and pointed toward the Queen Anne bed. "See. It's even got a new mattress. I'll lay it down."

Maria shrugged. "I guess it'll do."

Stump reached for the mattress, just as a deep cough came from Mr. Kraft's office. Maria and Stump swung in the direction of the noise. "What's he doing here so late?" Maria whispered.

"Don't know. He's usually pretty tired by this time of day." Just then Stump heard somebody coming in the outer door. Stump flicked off the lights, as the person descended the stairs and opened the door to Mr. Kraft's office.

"I want to leave," Maria whispered.

Stump nodded. "Just a second. We gotta make sure they're not coming right back into the hallway." He moved from the door to the common wall between Mr. Kraft's office and the maintenance room and stuck his ear to the wall.

"Have a seat," Mr. Kraft said to his visitor. "This invoice shows we received two stoves and two refrigerators last week." Stump couldn't hear real well, but Mr. Kraft's voice was stern.

"Yeah. So?"

Stump's eyebrows rose. "It's Dixon," he said softly to Maria before returning his ear to the wall again.

"A few days ago, you said you were going to have a couple guys take both a stove and refrigerator to that vacant apartment in building four," Mr. Kraft resumed.

"What's all this about?" Dixon asked.

"The appliances were a different brand than I usually order, so a couple hours ago I went over to check them out. I was surprised to learn the place wasn't vacant after all."

"Oh. If you'd said that in the first place I could have told you I just rented it yesterday. I told them they could stay for free until the end of the month, then their rent would start."

Stump raised a proud fist in the air. This was the type of crap he uncovered both the first time he and Myles visited the property and throughout the notebook. It was about time Dixon got called out for it.

"What about the boxes?" Kraft asked.

"Boxes?"

"Yeah, considering they just moved in yesterday, as you said, I'd expect to see a few moving boxes—or at least some bags around. Instead, they've already unpacked, put their things away, been to the grocery store, cooked a meal and left some dishes in the sink. People can't do all that in one day. So where are they?"

"How should I know? They probably put them out by the trash last night, and somebody else must have taken them. Happens all the time."

326

"Yeah, right," Kraft said sarcastically. "That's not the only issue. They still had their old appliances so after I left, I looked everywhere for those new appliances and couldn't find them. Some paint is missing too. We can go next door to the maintenance room right now to have another look if you don't believe me."

Maria's hands shot to her face.

"It's okay," Stump whispered. "They won't come. Dixon knows that stuff is gone."

"Is that what all this is about?" Dixon said. "It's no problem. I heard there were some guys going around the neighborhood, late at night, breaking into maintenance rooms to steal tools and pawn them off. So just to be safe, I had a guy I know return those things to the store."

"That's interesting. Then where's the paperwork that shows I got a credit on my account?"

Good question. Answer that, you lying pile of poop.

Maria tugged on Stump's sleeve. "I can't take this. I'll meet you by your truck."

"Okay. I'll catch up in a minute."

"He hasn't brought it back yet," Dixon said, "but he should bring it around by tomorrow."

"Cut the b.s., Dixon. I may be ill but I'm no idiot. I've been doing a little research and I'm very disappointed in some of the things I've discovered."

"Oh, I see. It's that Stump kid, isn't it? He's been making up shit about me ever since he got here. I told you he was no good."

"Don't be passing your troubles off to him. He has nothing to do with this. I'm giving you fair warning; between radiation treatments and my meds I ain't in no mood for this type of activity."

Stump scrunched his ear closer to the wall.

"You'd have a hard time finding anybody who'd put up with all the crap around here," Dixon replied. "And we both know it."

"I'll tell you what we both know," Mr. Kraft said in a louder voice. "We both know that you've learned to bluff your way through life, but this time you're up against a better hand. You'd best heed my final warning lest you lose everything you've got. Now get out of here and watch your back 'cause I'm on to you now."

Stump felt like applauding but he waited to hear Dixon leave before he too scooted out the building and hustled off to his truck where Maria was waiting. "Sorry I left," she said, "but I don't like it when people yell at each other. What happened?"

Stump unlocked the truck. "You would have loved it," he said as they slid into the seat and turned on the radio. "Dixon almost got fired."

"I'm glad he's still here so you can make him go to jail instead."

Stump wondered if she'd think that way when the DNA test came back. "We'll see," he said, as his thoughts returned to that other activity he had in mind earlier, but there was no way Maria would go back to the maintenance room now.

Just then, the kissing van pulled into the lot and Manuel piled out with a shoebox-sized red and white box. He appeared to be chewing on something that looked like a piece of chicken. Stump watched Manuel walk up the sidewalk on the opposite side of the complex from where his apartment was. It was like being at the movies. Stump took Maria's hand. "Too bad we don't have some popcorn."

"Do you love me?" Maria asked Stump as she laid her head on his shoulder.

"I think of you all the time," Stump said as Manuel tossed his chicken in a trashcan, causing Stump to wonder if there was anything wrong with the trashcans on the other side of the complex.

"You do?" Maria continued. "What do you think about?"

Returning his attention to Maria, Stump was still interested in the kinds of physical activities that lucky boys and girls do on occasion. "For one thing," he said, "I know our relationship is special."

"Oh, really?"

"Yeah. I like being with you. Doing things. Being alone. You're an interesting person." Anybody who'd spent her entire life happily believing in a Santa Clause type daddy would be plenty interesting. "You're also one of the most loyal people I've ever known. You're loyal to your papa even though you've never met him. You miss Señorita. You stood up for your mama and me. You're usually very happy, and you're a great kisser."

The gleam in Maria's eyes was essentially an invitation. Stump leaned her way. He liked being with Maria, even if it was simply in a used pickup truck at the back of a parking lot.

Another glance at the courtyard revealed that Manuel had disappeared and Dixon was near the pool and coming their direction. "I hope his rear-end hurts from that butt-chewing he just got," Stump said.

Maria looked up. "I hate that jerk-wad. Let's not talk to him."

If Myles hadn't forbidden him from side trips, Stump might have driven off. "Don't worry, I can handle him," he said, rolling down his window. Dixon came right to him, wagging a finger in Stump's face. "I want you to get off this lot when you're not working, rich boy."

"Go away." Maria said. "Tenants can have guests and he's my guest."

"I wasn't talking to you," Dixon turned to Stump. "I know what you're up to and I want you out of here."

"Okay with me," Stump replied as he hopped out of the truck and reached back for Maria's hand. "We'll just go for a walk."

Maria stepped down, looked at Dixon and said, "We don't like you!"

CHAPTER 70

Barely a block away from Cal-Vista Stump and Maria walked past a motorhome and Stump glanced at the large chrome bumper. "I gotta tell you something," he said, "but whatever you do, don't turn around."

"Don't tell me the jerk-wad is following us."

"You guessed it, but don't let him know we're on to him. We can lead him on a wild goose chase."

"What's that?"

"It's almost like *ditch 'em*, only he doesn't even know what's happening. It'll be fun. The first thing we have to do is walk a little faster."

Maria giggled. "Okay, maybe his teeth will fall out."

Stump grabbed her hand and they sped up ever so slightly. At the corner they turned and walked even faster. For the next fifteen minutes they went quicker and quicker, making several illogical turns. Finally a little out of breath, Stump peeked out the corner of his eye. "He's still back there, but farther than before."

Maria blew out a breath. You're in better shape 'cause of riding your bike."

Stump pointed up the street to the road construction area near the police building. "There are some bulldozers and construction equipment in the field behind those stores. Let's go back there. We can ditch him."

Maria nodded. "Okay. I hope he has a heart attack."

When they reached the string of neighborhood stores, they cut around the back to the employees' parking lot. As Stump expected, the field behind the lot contained a portable outhouse and a dozen pieces of heavy equipment such as excavators, Bobcats and dump trucks. "See," Stump said, looking around. "These things ought to slow him down."

"I hope so, 'cause I'm tired of this."

Before bolting out to the field, Stump glanced to the back of the businesses where it appeared the door to the flower shop was ajar. "Quick, let's go over there."

Maria sighed and they hustled toward the door. Stump leaned against it. "I think we can hide in here."

"What? That's crazy. We might get in trouble."

Stump glanced around. "There aren't any cars back here. I don't think there's anybody around."

"No way. They probably have alarms."

Stump looked to the top of the building for any sign of surveillance cameras. "I don't think so. They would have already gone off."

"I'm not going in there. Let's just tell that jerk-wad we're going to call the police if he doesn't stop following us."

Stump glanced to the corner of the buildings. Dixon would arrive any minute. "You stay here. I'm going inside to check it out."

"No! I don't want—"

"I'll be right back." Stump hustled inside. The place was dark, delightfully chilly and smelled nearly as good as bathroom spray. He hurried down a hallway, passed a bathroom on one side and a work area on the other and ended up in the sales area where there was a fairly tall L-shaped counter and quiet music came from overhead. Seeing no sign of surveillance equipment, he snickered. Who'd want to steal flowers? He rushed back toward Maria. "All clear."

"I don't care. I don't want to go in there."

Just then sandals flapped around the corner.

"It's Dixon," he whispered, snagging Maria's hand.

"But—"

He pulled her inside before quietly closing the door. "Shh. We can watch him from this room over here." He tugged her into the work area, where they huddled behind a small window.

Just then Dixon helicoptered into the area and hovered for a moment before squatting down and looking under the big vehicles.

"See what I mean?" Stump said, beaming. "He's caught us in Manuel's van and Myles's truck so he probably thinks we're hiding inside one of those big cabs."

Maria smiled, grabbed his hand. "You're smart."

Just then a brown and white cat rubbed up against Maria's leg and meowed.

She smiled and picked it up. "She looks a lot like Señorita."

Stump nodded, checking the tags. "Says her name is Sassy. She likes you."

"Well, I like her too," Maria said, rubbing her cheek against Sassy's coat and earning a gentle purr.

For the next five minutes they giggled, petted Sassy, and watched Dixon buzz from vehicle to vehicle like a bee in a field of flowers. Finally, Dixon rushed around one of the dump trucks and smacked right into its rear-view mirror. He snapped his hand to nose, then bent over, picked up a rock and slung it at the mirror, causing broken glass to rain down.

"I don't like that man," Maria said for the hundredth time.

"Look," Stump interrupted. "He's taking a leak."

Dixon was facing them, rubbing his nose with one hand and attending to Little Dixon with the other. Maria giggled. "What's wrong with that man? There's a Port-a-Potty right behind him."

"He's a piece of work alright," Stump said as Dixon finished up and shook his little friend around.

"Ewwwww!" Maria's hand shot to her mouth. "That's gross. Now where's he going to wash his hands?"

As if on cue, Dixon rubbed his hand on the side of his Bermudas before walking back toward the corner of the building.

"Look. He's leaving," Maria said while petting Sassy. "You were right. We ditched him. Now we can wait a few minutes and get out of here."

The show basically over, Stump tugged Maria's hand into the main sales room where a large ceramic cat clock on the counter had the time at eight-twenty. On the floor near the cat clock a large trash can with a dozen or so discarded yellow flowers sat on a thick carpet. "Look. It's like a private fort back there. We could stay here all night if we wanted to."

Maria's eyes darted to the floor. "No way. I'm not doing that. Mama expects me home in an hour."

Stump grinned. "I didn't mean it literally." He reached in the can for the nicest of the discarded flowers and handed it to her. "I meant nobody can see us, even if they come to the windows. This is a good chance to, well, you know."

"Oh." Maria looked in his eyes and then at the front window.

* * *

After Stump and Maria made love, they put their clothes back on and leaned against the back of the counter.

"You were right," she said. "This place is nice. I mean with the clean aroma and the music and Sassy."

Stump smiled, "And the privacy." He slid a yellow flower behind her ear. "Sometime I'll buy you a dozen brand-new roses."

"This isn't a rose, silly. It's a tulip."

Stump shrugged. "Same difference. I just want you to have pretty things. You make them look even better."

Maria grabbed his hand and leaned her head on his shoulder. A moment later the ceramic clock meowed.

"Nine already," Stump said. "I guess we better be heading back." He pointed to the remaining discarded tulips. There are a couple more nice ones. Would your mama want them?"

"I wish we could, but she'd want to know where I got them."

They took their time getting back. Stump knew he'd never forget that night. "Do you think we'd make good PI's?" he finally asked.

"What's a PI?"

"A private investigator. They're like detectives only they mostly work for private people."

"Oh, yeah. I've seen people like that on TV. You might like it, but sneaky things make me nervous."

"I dunno. I think it's exciting." He checked the time on his cell. Nine-twenty. They'd be right on time.

Suddenly flashing red lights came from behind them. "Oh, no," Maria said. "They found out what we did. We're going to jail—"

"Can't be. They would have come right away," Stump said as a cop car whizzed passed them. Up ahead, he saw additional red lights flashing on the treetops. "Looks like something's going on at your building. Let's hurry."

Moments later they'd reached Cal-Vista, where the cop car they'd seen earlier was parked on the street. They entered the courtyard. At the other end of the pool a small group of people stood over a male's body lying on its side and facing away. Although Stump had played a key role in solving several murders, he'd never actually seen a dead body, not even at the mortuary when his mother passed away. "You'd better go to your apartment," he said to Maria. "I'll come tell you what's going on a little later."

"You're not going over there, are you?"

Stump glanced back toward the pool area and noticed

bystanders gathering in the shadows. "I have to, but you should go inside so you don't have nightmares."

"Alright," she said as she leaned in and kissed him, "but promise me you'll be careful."

"I will." He pivoted and moved toward the action. A few people, including Manuel, Juanita and Mr. Connors from next door were standing above the body, but Dixon wasn't around. He looked closer. The dead man wore shoes and long pants. It wasn't Dixon. Stump passed the first two buildings and a trashcan with a KFC box inside. At the halfway point he could see the back of the body, dripping wet and motionless. A glance toward the windows in Dixon's apartment revealed mostly darkness.

Now, just a few yards from the body, Stump could hear the conversation. "It looks like somebody hit him with a baseball bat," one of the males speculated.

"Mr. Dixon is the only one I know who'd kill anybody," Juanita said.

She had a good point. Dixon had a string of enemies and could have been drawn into some sort of quarrel. Stump made his way around the small group and peeked back at the body. Almost instantly his stomach boots kicked him so hard he thought he might puke. The dead man was Rodger Kraft.

CHAPTER 71

Rodger Kraft was like a grandpa to Stump. The man was wise, generous and fair, but most importantly, Mr. Kraft believed in Stump. Stump wiped away a tear and observed a deep gutter-shaped indentation, high up, on the back of Mr. Kraft's skull. Did Dixon do it, and if not, was the killer here now? Stump looked up and down the lines of windows inside the complex to see if anybody appeared suspicious.

Just then a car door slammed in the parking lot. Was that the killer, getting away? Stump rushed toward the lot to get a plate number, just in case. Seconds later, he reached the sidewalk and saw a pudgy, 50ish male open the back door of a black sedan and grab a wrinkled sport coat that he flung over his white shirt and loose-fitting tie. Stump immediately recognized the man from several years earlier. His name was Sergeant Byrdswain.

Before Stump could reintroduce himself the sergeant wobbled into the courtyard. Stump followed along like a duckling trailing its mother.

When the sergeant reached the body he put on rubber gloves, glancing at the group near the body. "Who's in charge here?" he asked. This seemed to Stump like one of those situations in which Dixon would be underfoot. Stump checked out Dixon's windows again. As before, there was no sign of him.

"I'm the maintenance man," Manuel said.

Mr. Connors tipped his head respectfully to the sergeant. "I'm Clyde Connors. I own the building next door."

Sergeant Byrdswain crouched near Kraft's head. "Who's the manager of this building?"

"Dixon Browne," Manuel said. "He's in his apartment. I think he's the killer."

Very possible, especially after the blow-up that Stump and Maria had heard earlier. Their dispute could have easily resumed after Dixon followed Stump and Maria to the flower shop. Stump wiped another tear from his eye and returned his attention to the sergeant.

Byrdswain felt Mr. Kraft's neck for a pulse. "Anybody know the victim?"

"He's Rodger Kraft," Mr. Connors said. "The owner of the property."

"How well did you know him?"

"We've been neighbors for years, but we both tend to mind our own business. I just came over a little bit ago when I saw the red lights."

"Who found the body?"

"I did," Manuel said. "About a half-hour ago. My wife here is the one who called the police."

Juanita nodded and Byrdswain rose. "How'd he get out of the pool?"

Once again, Manuel moved first. "He was in the water when I got here. I pulled him out in case I could save him. But there was no breathing. No movement. He was gone."

"What time was that?"

"About nine."

Byrdswain gestured toward Mr. Kraft's head. "Any of you see anything around here that could have been used to hit him?"

Good question. If Stump weren't so distracted by his own

grief, he would have appreciated Byrdswain's techniques and how the people responded to the questions, both verbally and with their body movements. Stump scanned the courtyard for a potential weapon.

"Nothing like that around here," Manuel said. "But Dixon could have something in his apartment."

The sergeant rose. "We'll have a closer look after we get some pictures. Did any of you see anybody suspicious hanging around when you got here?"

"There were a few folks gathering when I got here," Mr. Connors said, "but it was dark and I wasn't paying much attention until I saw the body."

Sergeant Byrdswain glanced at Stump and then turned to Juanita. "What about you, ma'am? Any of the people watching us right now look suspicious to you?"

Juanita shook her head but didn't speak.

"Most of these people are good folks," Manuel said. "They're just trying to get by without any trouble."

"Which apartment is Dixon Browne's?"

Manuel lifted his jaw toward Dixon's apartment. "Building one, Unit 101. He was out here earlier but went inside."

"You said he could have killed the victim. What makes you think so?"

That too was a great question. Stump could have given the sergeant a list of reasons why Dixon was capable of such a thing, but he elected instead to hold his tongue until he heard what others thought.

"I heard Dixon and Mr. Kraft arguing," Manuel said. "They were always fighting. The owner said he was losing money and knew who was taking it."

That was more or less what Stump thought, but Stump wasn't aware of any previous battles between Dixon and Mr. Kraft. Of course, Stump was only on site a few hours a day and Kraft usually left the premises shortly after Stump arrived.

Just then Stump heard several cars come into the parking lot. Byrdswain paused for a moment as if he'd heard them too. He returned to Manuel. "Who else, besides you and Dixon, might have seen something?"

"Any of the tenants," Manuel said as three car doors banged shut in the lot. "There are eighty-four apartments. Most of them have two or three people living in them."

Several lingerers pivoted toward two men and a woman who joined the courtyard and moved toward the body. "Forensics," Byrdswain said before addressing Manuel and Connors again. "I need you guys to stay close by for a couple hours."

Connors nodded while Manuel pointed across the courtyard. "Juanita and I live on the second floor of that building."

"Good enough." Byrdswain reached into his pocket, "Here's my card in case you think of anything else I should know."

As Connors and Manuel headed off, Byrdswain swung Stump's way. "Don't I know you?"

"Yes, sir. My name's Stump. I helped you solve some murders three years ago."

"I thought so. You're Cooper's kid, but you're bigger now. Did you see what went on?"

"No, sir. I wasn't here when any of this happened. I was with my girlfriend."

"Girlfriend, huh? I should be so lucky." He nodded at Stump. "I gotta get back to work, but I want you to know you did an impressive job on the dog park."

"Thank you," Stump said looking back to Mr. Kraft. "He was a nice man."

Sergeant Byrdswain turned toward the new arrivals. "I need you guys to tape off the scene, get some pictures and order an autopsy. I'll check back with you after I have a talk with the manager." He pointed his finger at Mr. Kraft. "Oh, yeah, when you're done, cover him up."

The sergeant pulled a cellphone from his coat and tapped at the screen as he went to the quiet end of the pool.

*   *   *

The read-out on Delores's phone indicated that her incoming caller was Sergeant Byrdswain. *"We've got something hot,"* he said the instant she answered her phone. *"I thought you'd want to know."*

The excitement in his tone filled her with child-like curiosity, but the trained expert inside her urged restraint. She sat forward. "What's going on?"

"I'm over at Cal-Vista. The owner is dead. The maintenance guy and his wife think your buddy, Dixon Browne, did it."

Delores's free hand shot to her cheek. "Rodger Kraft? Oh my God! What happened?"

"A blow to the head, followed by a late-night swim. I would have called you when the call first came in, but I wanted to see what was going on first."

"No problem. Why was Rodger there so late? He usually goes home in the afternoon."

"Maintenance guy says he heard Browne and Kraft arguing over money. A little later he found the victim, pulled him out of the pool but Kraft was already dead."

"Is Dixon still there?"

"I think so. I'm seeing him next."

"You want me to come help?"

"Not just yet. If you come around now, and Browne didn't do it, he'll recognize you and that'll be the end to your investigation. We can wait a bit."

"Thanks, boss. It's nice to know you've got my back."

"On the other hand, a murder has to take priority over your case. How close are you to arresting Browne on those other charges?"

"Ideally, I'd like another week, but I could do it now if we want to tuck him out of the way."

"He'd probably just lawyer-up. We don't want you to be shuffling paperwork on a lower-priority case that can wait. Let's hold off for now. I don't want to jeopardize either one of these cases."

"I'm for that."

"Alright, here's what I think we should do. I'll knock on some doors around here and try to figure out which way the wind blows. You stay close by in case I need you. If we're lucky we might solve a murder and catch Mr. Browne all in short order. Regardless, if Dixon is our murderer, I'll make sure you're in on the arrest. You deserve that much."

"Thanks, boss. I'll have my cell."

"Okay then, if you don't hear from me tonight, meet me in the office first thing in the morning. One more thing. I saw that Stump kid hanging around. You ought to call Cooper. He may want to get his kid out of here."

"Will do. See you in the morning if not before."

"Roger that. Oops. Poor choice of words."

CHAPTER 72

Inside Dixon Browne's building, Sergeant Byrdswain caught a whiff of fresh-brewed coffee. He knocked forcefully on Dixon's door. "Palmdale Police. Open up."

Seconds later a misshapen eye filled the peephole. The sergeant simply held up his badge.

Dixon Browne swung the door inward. He had a bath towel in hand. "I was expecting you," he said, tossing his towel on a chair.

"You were? Why?"

"C'mon Sergeant. It's obvious. The owner of the building is killed. I'm the manager and you're a detective. Just makes sense."

Byrdswain nodded. "I understand you got a close look at the body."

"Yeah, but there wasn't much I could do, and I was sweaty, so I decided to take a shower while I could."

"I see." Byrdswain sniffed at the air, then pointed to the kitchen. "I don't suppose I could bother you for a cup of that coffee."

Dixon snickered. "Serve yourself."

Byrdswain seized a mug and filled it. He stared at Dixon, sipped down some coffee and raised his cup. "Now, that's what I needed."

"I'd offer you some creamer and sugar but you ain't staying that long."

"That's a nice shiner you've got there. I suppose you ran into a door?"

"Something like that."

Byrdswain took a couple steps down the center hall. "You mind if I look around?"

"My apartment? What for? I ain't got nothing of interest to you."

"I just might find a baseball bat with the victim's hair on it. Or blood in your tub. You got anything to hide?"

Dixon waved his hand. "Why would I have those things?"

"Seems a little odd that you'd leave a crime scene just to take a shower. You sure you're not destroying evidence? We can find traces of blood in the tub you know."

"Nothing like that, Sergeant, I assure you. I went for a walk, worked up a sweat and simply figured it'd be a long night."

Byrdswain moved down the hall, glanced in the bedroom, bathroom and Dixon's office before he returned to the living room. "Nice trophies."

"Just lucky."

"I didn't see any signs of a woman."

"My wife bailed on me. Is that a crime?"

"If it was," Byrdswain snickered, "we'd all be in jail."

Dixon pointed toward the courtyard area. "How's it look out there? Any clues?"

"Just the dent in Kraft's head. Did you see it?"

"Sure didn't."

"Where were you between seven and nine o'clock?"

"Like I told you, I went for a walk."

"Can anybody verify that?"

"I didn't talk to anybody, if that's what you mean."

"I see. When did you first hear about the victim?"

"When I came back from my walk. There were already some guys standing near the body. I saw he was dead and came inside to call the cops. Then I jumped in the shower."

"What time was that?"

"Around eight-thirty."

"How many people live in this complex?"

"Never really counted them, but I'd guess there's a couple hundred. Why?"

"Do you know all of them?"

"Makes the job easier," Dixon said, sarcastically.

"It must give a guy a feeling of power to be in charge of so many people," Byrdswain slid his cup on the counter.

"It's just a job."

"But an important one, nonetheless. Must piss you off when things don't go your way."

Dixon shrugged. "Not as much as when people don't rinse out their dirty coffee cups."

Byrdswain grinned. "You'll get over it. Your job must pay pretty well to own a Cadillac."

Dixon scoffed. "What are you getting at, Sergeant? We both know you don't give a damn about what car I drive."

"True, but I've always put a lot of faith in instincts, first impressions. If you'd lie about a car, you'd certainly lie about killing somebody. I'm wondering if your boss caught you with your hand in his cookie jar and threatened to turn you in so you ballpeened him to keep him quiet."

"I'm afraid you're fishing in an empty lake, Sergeant."

"We'll see. One more thing. I need you to put together a list of any troublemakers around here, anybody who's been arrested, people who argue a lot or have aggressive visitors."

"Why would I do that?"

Sergeant Byrdswain stared in Dixon's eyes. "Because it makes me think you're trying to help rather than trying to get away with murder. That's why."

"Fair enough. I guess I can put in a few minutes for my friends at the almighty Palmdale Police Department."

"That's better. If I find you left anybody off the list who should have been on it, it'll mean I can't trust you and you don't want that. Got it?"

"Now why would I do that?"

CHAPTER 73

THE NEXT MORNING AT SCHOOL, Stump slouched down in his seat. Filled with sad thoughts, he found it difficult to concentrate. Then the heavy door at the front corner of the classroom swung open and the Assistant Principal approached the teacher who quickly looked in Stump's direction. "Neal. It looks like you need to go with Mr. Dunlap."

Stump shrugged and made his way to the front and then out into the hallway where Myles and Grandma Pauline were waiting. "Sergeant Byrdswain wants to see you," Myles said.

"Is it about Mr. Kraft?"

"I think so. We'd better get going."

At the truck, and almost by habit, Stump slid behind the wheel. "I'm glad you brought Grandma Pauline."

"Had to. Katherine had a doctor's appointment."

"Is Detective Sanchez going to be there, too?"

"Oh," Myles said lifting his hand off his lap. "I didn't know you remembered her."

"I saw her at work one day but couldn't remember how I knew her. But then James and I drove past the police building and saw your truck. I still didn't put it all together until last night after I spoke with Sergeant Byrdswain. I can tell you one thing. She's hot."

"I use to get hot flashes too," Grandma Pauline said.

Both Stump and Myles grinned.

"It's a weird coincidence," Stump said.

"What is?"

"What are the chances Detective Sanchez would be living at the same building where I work and where a murder took place?"

Myles sighed. "It's no coincidence, Stump." For the reminder of the ride, Myles filled Stump in about Detective Sanchez's investigation of Dixon for rape. Finally, "And that's why I tried to get you to look for another job. Now it looks like you'll have no choice."

Stump thought about Mr. Connors's offer, but there'd be plenty of time to kick that around later. For the moment he wondered what the meeting with Sergeant Byrdswain might be like. He hoped he wouldn't have to say anything about him and Maria hiding out in the maintenance room. "What have they found out so far?" he asked.

"All I know is Sergeant Byrdswain has been working on-site and Detective Sanchez is lying low."

"Mom used to say life is short. Now I know what she meant. Even though Mr. Kraft was ill, I didn't see this coming. Now I hate Dixon even more for causing me to miss that last City Council meeting."

"Don't be so hard on yourself. Your mom would be very proud of your effort."

"Effort? What good is effort, without results?"

"We should mind our own business," Grandma Pauline said.

Stump almost grinned. "Thanks, Grandma. I'll try to remember that."

They made their way to the lobby of the police building. "The conference room is upstairs," Myles said, heading for the elevator.

"I'm taking the stairs," Grandma Pauline said. Myles and Stump looked at each other and followed her just in case she lost her balance.

At the top, Myles pointed off to the right. "You guys go in the conference room. I'll tell the others we're here."

Stump and Grandma Pauline took seats at a large table where she pointed to a picture on the wall. "Oh, look. That's my neighbors' house."

Stump's eyes flashed to the picture. "In Oklahoma? I don't think so."

"Oh, yes it is. I recognize those windows."

Stump rose, examined an engraved brass plate attached to the bottom of the frame and read it out loud. "In appreciation of Gregory and Wilma Wellstone for donating their family farm to the City of Palmdale. The Wellstone raised four of their own children and countless foster children on this site."

Grandma Pauline shook her head back and forth. "They're wrong. That's Sheila and Ted's house, after they got their money from the county."

"Look who's here." The voice came from over Stump's shoulder. He pivoted. "Hello, Detective Sanchez."

She smiled at Stump as she and Myles took a seat. "How've you been?"

"Sad, but okay. I saw you a while back, but didn't recognize you at first, but now that I think of it, Mr. Connors said somebody else was investigating at his building. That must have been you too, investigating the same scams."

Grandma Pauline waved at Detective Sanchez and said, "Did you know Myles is my son?"

Detective Sanchez smiled. "Yes, ma'am. He told me that."

"Do you know Ted and Sheila? That's their home on the wall after they got their new windows."

Stump sighed.

"No, I didn't know them," Detective Sanchez said.

Stump addressed Detective Sanchez. "Did Dixon kill Mr. Kraft?"

"That's what we're trying to figure out. A killer must have motive, means and opportunity."

"A MOM!" Stump said.

"A mom? What's his mom got to do with it?"

"I just made it up. If you rearrange those three words so that it's motive, opportunity and means, it's an acronym that says MOM. Every killer has to have a MOM."

Myles and Detective Sanchez traded glances. "Clever," she said. "I never thought of it that way."

Just then, Sergeant Byrdswain came in and sat down. "Hello, everybody. You can ignore me. Just go on with your conversation."

Detective Sanchez turned back to Stump. "You were talking about Dixon scamming people. What scams?"

"Lots of 'em. He charges tenants money, off the record, for getting them jobs or for doing favors for them. Stuff like that."

"What makes you think so?"

Stump certainly didn't want to admit that he had Juanita steal Dixon's notebook. Maybe a different truthful answer would work. "I discovered it before I started working there. My dad and I considered buying the property and when we looked around, I saw a suspicious receipt book."

Detective Sanchez nodded. "Okay. Did you ever say anything about these discrepancies to the owner?"

"I mentioned them, but Mr. Kraft had known Dixon for a long time and I didn't want to make waves and risk losing my job."

"What about after you started working there? Did you see more examples of Dixon cheating people?"

"Not exactly, but I knew he was doing it."

Sergeant Byrdswain shuffled in his seat. "Did Dixon just confess to you?"

Stump's stomach tightened. He'd hoped that he wouldn't have to discuss everything he discovered and some of the follow-up investigating he did, but now that the cops were involved anyway, this could be his chance to get them to take over his own *Case of Did He or Did He Not*? "My girlfriend suspected that Dixon might have raped her mom, and she wanted me to find out if he'd done anything like that to anybody else. Then we could turn him in without her mama having to talk to the police."

Byrdswain shook his head. "Why would they tell you something like that as opposed to reporting it to us?"

"Simple. They're scared of both Dixon and the cops. Everybody around there avoids you people because they don't want to risk being deported. Besides, if you started asking Dixon questions it could piss him off. He could make things even harder on Maria and her mother, just like he did to me when I wanted to talk at the City Council meeting."

"So you spied on Dixon?"

Stump nodded. "I learned a few simple things and then I heard about his secret notebook."

Byrdswain and Myles traded glances.

"What notebook?"

Stump sighed. "Dixon kept it in his desk. He ripped off so many people he had to keep track of them all. That's why I agree with Manuel. Mr. Kraft must have figured out that Dixon was stealing from him and Dixon killed Mr. Kraft to stay out of jail." Stump was pleased with himself for getting that idea on the table without revealing he and Maria were hiding in the maintenance room when Mr. Kraft and Dixon were arguing about this very topic.

"Where's this notebook now?"

"I copied it and threw it away."

"Where's the copy?"

"At school. It's in code, but I figured it out."

"I'm going to need that notebook."

Anxious to end the meeting, Stump rose. "Okay, I'll go get it."

Byrdswain pointed at Stump's chair. "I didn't mean right now."

Detective Sanchez asked the next question. "Did Dixon admit in that notebook that he raped Maria's mom?"

"No, but it said he was Maria's real dad and that he had over twenty thousand dollars hidden away for her."

Myles sat back and crossed his arms.

Grandma Pauline pointed to the wall. "That house is Sheila and Ted's after they got their grant from the county."

Myles placed a finger on his lips. "Shh."

Sergeant Byrdswain tapped at the table. "So you were messing around with Dixon's daughter, and Dixon must have found out his notebook was missing. Did he confront you about these things?"

"Yes, sir, but I denied knowing anything about it. That's when he let the air out of my tires and almost killed me and made me miss a meeting with the Mayor and the City Council. Now a whole neighborhood is dangerous because of him."

"I thought the City Council had another meeting coming up?" Detective Sanchez said. "You could try again."

"It's the day after tomorrow, but I can't go back because they think I'm a flake."

"We're getting off track here," Sergeant Byrdswain said. "Let's get back to last night and our victim. Where were you from seven-thirty to eight-thirty?"

A bolt of adrenalin raced up Stump's spine. "Am I a suspect, cause I don't have a motive and I liked Mr. Kraft. He was like a grandpa to me."

"Grandpa? Is my husband here?"

Myles shook his head. "No, mom, we're talking about somebody else."

"But you were at the building earlier in the evening?" Byrdswain continued. "True?"

"Yes. I got my driver's license and my dad let me take his truck over there."

"What time was that?"

"I worked until seven."

"Then what did you do?"

Ugh! Stump didn't want to say he took Maria to the maintenance room or the flower shop. "Maria and I went for a very long walk. She can verify that."

"We'll ask her. What time did you get back?"

"Just about five minutes before you got there. I saw you park on the sidewalk."

"So you didn't see or hear anything between seven or so when you left the property until you got back, at the same time I arrived?"

"We weren't there when Mr. Kraft was killed, if that's what you mean."

"Alright, that's enough for now. But in the future, I want you to call Detective Sanchez and me before you go sticking your nose into police business. Okay?"

Stump sighed. "I wanted to."

CHAPTER 74

THE NEXT DAY, STUMP DRAGGED HIMSELF to school and got drawn into more conversations about the murder. Yes, he knew the victim. No, he wasn't there when it happened. Yes, he saw the body. Yes, he'd missed a lot of school lately.

Then at lunch, he sneaked into the restroom and hid in a stall, just to have some peace. He pulled out his iPhone and sent a brief "I miss you" text to Maria. Then he remembered the notes he'd previously left himself. He checked out Maslow, party lines and Jack Ruby. He found it interesting that Grandma Pauline knew so much about a mobster from decades earlier but could easily forget where she was at any moment.

Another note regarded the comment Grandma Pauline made about her neighbors in Oklahoma. He couldn't take anything Grandma Pauline said at face value, but she seemed pretty certain that her friends got a grant for their windows. He wondered if other places, such as Palmdale, had anything like that. He tweaked the key words a couple times before he nearly fell off the stool.

Rebuilding Together

Through our Home Modification Program,
we aim to improve safety and accessibility within
and around the home for Seniors, Disabled People,
Veterans and Low-Income Families.

Holy shit. Words like *low-income families* and *safety* sounded perfect for his old neighborhood. He quickly dialed the number and worked through several prompts before a real person came on. *"Rebuilding Together. Help you?"*

"Yes, please," he said drawing on his earlier experience about sounding mature on the phone. "My name's Neal Randolph. I'm in Palmdale. We're wondering if you guys have any grant money to fix houses."

"I'm sorry. Where'd you say you are?"

"Palmdale, California."

"We're in a hundred and sixty places. Let me look it up."

A hundred and sixty places? Wow. That was good odds.

Seconds later the lady returned. *"Nope. Sorry. I have no listing for anyplace named Palmdale. Is it near a bigger city?"*

"Yes. It's a suburb of Los Angeles."

"Oh. That's different. Hang on. Okay, here it is. Yes, it looks like Palmdale qualifies under the L.A. program."

Stump's heart damn near jumped through his chest. "No kidding. What all will you do?"

"Practically anything that improves safety or assures energy savings. Furnaces, painting, windows, insulation. You name it. Don't you have a lot of stucco homes out there?"

"Yes. Old ones."

"A lot of those can use new roofs and gutters and air conditioning. We can do all of it if the home owner qualifies."

Good God, this was too good to be true. "What do we have to do to qualify?"

"How much money do you earn?"

"It's not for me. It's for my neighbors. Some of them are pretty poor."

"Well, each person will have to fill out their own application, but it's quick and easy to qualify. I can email some information."

"I'm trying to help a whole neighborhood. Is that too big for you?"

"Not really. We complete an average of 10,000 homes every year."

"Do you provide carpenters and electricians?"

"No. No. We work with the community to get volunteers, but we have nearly a million of them. The only thing you have to worry about is the availability of the funds. Our grants usually dry up pretty fast. How soon would you need the funds?"

"I don't know yet—maybe a month or two."

"Well. That's cutting it pretty close, but if you can get the applications in within a couple weeks, I can put you on the list."

"I think I can do that."

"Before you go, there's another program in your area you might be interested in. It's called Neighborhood Improvement Program. It offers free painting, landscaping, driveway work, roofs and trash removal, but there's a limit of six thousand dollars per household. Would you like me to send you a link?"

"Yes, but I can't deal with it right now. I'll call you back later." He sprang to his feet. Grandma Pauline was correct. Everything fit. "Thank you. Thank you. I love you, Grandma." He sat back down and made another call.

"Danielle Delgado here."

"Hello, Ms. Delgado, This is Stump. Do you remember me?" His words were flying off his tongue at nearly twice their usual pace.

"Of course I do, Stump. You sound excited. What's up?"

"You have to get me on the City Council agenda tomorrow."

"I'm sorry Stump, but we discussed this previously. They won't reschedule you because of what happened last time. Besides, it's way beyond the deadline and they have a full docket. They're just not going to do it."

"But they have to. I've got fantastic news. I can get those unsafe houses fixed for free."

"It doesn't really matter now. They've printed up the agenda already and they have too much to do. Besides, the neighbors made it clear that they didn't want any part of a program like that. The council members want to get re-elected. They're not going to fight that battle."

"But there are government programs, with money for just what we need. You can look it up on the internet."

"That might have helped before, but the Council simply doesn't have the time or inclination to discuss the project with you right now. It's bad timing."

"But they have to. If we don't get it done now the money will dry up. We've got to try. Can't you call the Mayor or at least Mrs. Crumpler? Maybe they'll reconsider."

She sighed. *"I doubt it'll work, but I guess I could put you on hold and call Mrs. Crumpler on the other line. Don't get your hopes up."*

"Thank you, I'll wait." With his iPhone glued to his ear, Stump flushed the empty stool out of habit. He moved into the sink area and paced until finally he heard the click.

"I'm back. Mrs. Crumpler said it's impossible."

"Didn't you tell her it's important?"

"Everything is important to somebody, Stump, but the Mayor's going to give an end-of-term summary and the schedule is too full. She wouldn't even consider it. The matter is closed. Maybe you can try again when the next term begins."

"That won't work. I'd have to be twenty-one to get on the agenda and the grant money will be gone. I've got to do it now."

"I'm really sorry, Stump. I tried, but they're definitely not going to budge."

The finality in her tone convinced him he was shit-out-of-luck. "Yeah. Right. Everybody is always sorry." Angry and frustrated, Stump went to his last two classes but didn't pay attention. Why bother? His grades were going to stink anyway. Eventually the bell rang and he climbed on Ol' Ug' and pedaled to Cal-Vista to be with Maria.

When he pulled into the lot and then the bike rack, he observed an ugly mark near the top of the fence that he'd painted not long ago. Somebody must have parked near the fence, then tried to pitch something over the top and into the Connors's dumpster on the other side. It reminded him of the times when his mom would get upset with him because he'd come home and make messes without even noticing she'd just cleaned the house.

He slumped his way into the courtyard where Maria was at one of the picnic tables. "Hi," she said. "You look sad. What's wrong?"

"Everything. I'm a loser. People die. I can't do anything about it." He sat and plopped his elbows on the table. "I'm so far behind at school, Myles is gonna kill me. My life sucks."

"Would you like to go to my place and watch some TV? Mama might make us some popcorn."

"Not in the mood for TV."

"What about a walk? We had fun the last time."

"Naw. Ain't in the mood for that neither."

"How about an ice cream cone? Mama might give me enough so we could split one."

"Nothing sounds good right now."

She patted his arm. "Well, you still have Mama and me, and I love you. That has to count for something."

"Yeah. I know, but Mr. Kraft's dead and Dixon is still running around. Just doesn't seem fair."

"Maybe you'll feel better when he goes to jail."

"I don't think that's going to happen either."

"Why not? Everybody knows he did it."

"Not really."

"Why not? He's the only one who had anything to gain by killing that nice man. He had to do it."

Stump sighed. "Can you keep a secret?"

"Of course. Why?"

He looked over his shoulder. "I figured out that Dixon isn't the killer. Mr. Kraft was killed when Dixon was following you and me. I'm going to have to tell the cops."

"How do you know that?"

"The cops asked me where I was between seven-thirty and eight-thirty. They must have determined that was the time of death. But Dixon was following you and me at that time."

She slapped her hand over her lips. "We don't have to say anything. He deserves what he gets."

"I thought about that, but if we get caught withholding evidence everything will be worse. I don't think we have much choice." He rose. "I'm really sorry, but I think I'd better just go home. I'll call you later."

"Okay," she said, wrapping her arms around his neck. "I love you."

"Yeah. Me too."

Some twenty minutes later, at home, Stump dragged his sorry ass into the living room and sagged onto the couch next to Grandma Pauline, who was watching reruns of "America's Funniest Home Videos." He sighed. "This sucks."

"You want to change the channel?" she asked.

"It's not that. Everything is going wrong and I can't do anything about it."

Grandma Pauline tapped the back of his hand. "The interesting boys always have important things to do."

Stump smiled slightly. "You know something, Grandma? You must have been a great teacher. You know what to say to make people feel better. You're pretty smart too. You knew about your neighbors' windows; and before that you taught me about party lines on telephones and Jack Ruby."

She tilted her head. "Jack Ruby? Sounds familiar. Was he one of my students?"

"No, he was just somebody else you knew about."

She pointed her finger to her head. "My noggin' isn't what it use to be."

Stump held her hand. "You're still a smart woman." He laid his head on her shoulder. "You make me miss my mom."

She wrapped her arm around him. "Would you like to go to the nurse's office?"

If only he could.

CHAPTER 75

After another restless night, Stump forced himself to get to school, but he simply couldn't concentrate on his subjects with so many loose ends. It would have been easier if he didn't have to clear Dixon, who was essentially free as a bird and there was no telling who would take over at Cal-Vista. Mr. Kraft's family might just leave Dixon in charge. That would make everything worse.

Then there was the unresolved DNA matter and the last City Council meeting. It was just a matter of time before somebody else would have a bad accident. That would be his fault too.

Frustrated like never before, he considered doing something drastic, such as dropping out, or getting his tongue pierced or getting a tattoo, but he wasn't old enough to do anything cool without permission and Myles was always a buzz kill.

At lunchtime he grabbed a tray of gross school food and sulked into a quiet spot near the corner of the cafeteria. As he picked around the edges, James showed up.

"You better not sit here," Stump said. "I'm a jinx."

James set his tray on the table. "What's that supposed to mean?"

"Mr. Kraft's death was my fault. Everything was fine around there until I got that job."

"Yeah, that's a downer." James nibbled at a bite of the greyish substance the school called chicken. "There's never any justice for guys like us."

"I finally got to the point where I could hang Dixon without bringing attention to Maria's mama, but then I figured out he didn't do it."

"Maybe you made a mistake?"

"Naw. They got the time of death pinned down. The dude was following me and Maria when it happened. He couldn't have got back there in time."

James gnawed another chunk off his drumstick, leaned forward and whispered. "If you're the only ones who know, why not keep your mouths shut?"

Stump smirked. "Trust me. We talked about that. All I can do is let the bastard squirm for a day or two before we clear him."

"Good for you, Dude. At least clamp down on his balls while you've got them in a vice."

Stump sighed. "That's not all I've messed up. I finally found a program that would help everybody in my old neighborhood, but the City Council won't even let me in the damn room to tell them about it. Do you think I'd look good with pierced ears?"

"Yeah," James said enthusiastically. "Get those big barrel-shaped ones. I hear they whistle when the wind blows through them."

Stump smiled.

"It's another justice problem, Dude," James said, pointing his drumstick Stump's way. "You played it straight. Did what you were supposed to do, but those big-government types only listen to old rich dudes."

Stump nodded and then paused. His body froze before his eyes zeroed in on James. "Say that again."

James tilted his head. "I said people listen to rich dudes."

"And that was brilliant," Stump blurted as he jumped to his feet. "Loan me your keys. I need your car."

"What did I say? What about school?"

"I'll deal with that later. Now give me your keys."

"No way. I'm going with you." James took another big bite of his chicken and threw the bone in a trashcan as he and Stump rushed out the cafeteria door.

Suddenly, Stump stopped just as abruptly as he'd risen a few seconds earlier, causing James to bounce into Stump's back. "What the hell you doing, Dude?" James asked.

"You threw your bone in there."

"Of course I did. What else would I do with it?"

"It was the closest trashcan, but Manuel didn't do that and now I think I know why not."

"What the hell are you talking about?"

"Holy shit, Dude. This is big, but we gotta hurry."

"Okay, but let me go first in case you decide to stop again."

They rushed to James's car. "You drive," Stump said. "I gotta make a couple calls. I just hope we're not too late."

"Gotcha. Where to?"

"Cal-Vista," Stump said as he punched in his first number. Then, "Hello, can I talk to Mr. Irv Wedlock? My name's Neal Randolph. He knows me."

Stump listened to the receptionist, then said, "Okay then. Would you have him call me back as soon as possible? I have a big, big scoop for him, but he has to hurry."

James turned his head toward Stump. Minutes later they parked near the back of the Cal-Vista lot. "C'mon. Follow me," Stump said as he rushed into the courtyard and then up the sidewalk. "Please be there. Please be there."

A couple dozen more steps and Stump stopped at a full trashcan. "This is it."

"What's going on, Dude?"

Stump looked around the courtyard again before he grabbed a loose piece of paper and dug into the can, past the top items, "I got it," he said, pulling out what he wanted.

"A greasy chicken box?"

"It's KFC," Stump said. "I got the idea when we were in

the cafeteria and you threw your bone out. Why was he on this side of the complex?"

"Who? You lost me, Dude."

"I'll explain it later, but this is evidence. We gotta put it in your trunk."

James shook his head. "Whatever."

They hustled right back to James's car and stashed the trash, after which Stump quickly closed the trunk. "Now I gotta talk to Mr. Connors. Hurry."

"You're weird, Dude. You know that?" James said as they rushed around the fence.

Mrs. Connors was out front pulling weeds. "Sorry to bother you, Mrs. Connors," Stump said, breathing briskly, "but I need to ask Mr. Connors a big, big favor."

"He's inside. If I let you in, will you pull this old root out of the ground? You boys are a lot stronger than me."

"Sure," Stump said as he grabbed hold of an old vine root of some kind and yanked it out of the ground so hard he almost fell backwards.

"Thank you," she said, wiping her forehead. "We're getting too old to do all this work." She pointed inside. "My husband is downstairs."

Seconds later, Stump and James found Mr. Connors in the laundry room. "Hi, Stump. How's the investigation going?"

"They're not done yet, but it looks like Dixon is innocent."

Mr. Connors shrugged. "These things can take a while. What can I do for you? You looking for that job, 'cause—"

"Tonight is my last chance to get City Council to help people get their homes fixed up."

"Oh, yeah. I remember you talking about that. I thought they said they couldn't help you."

"They did, but I found two programs where the residents can get grants for the money they need, and I don't want to give up."

Mr. Connors nodded. "So why are you telling me all this?"

"If I bring a couple adults to the meeting, especially if one

362

of them has experience with housing issues, I would have a lot more credibility." Stump wrote some notes on a piece of paper. "These are the names of the programs I mentioned and the people who are in charge of them, along with their numbers. It would mean a lot to me if you'd call them and learn as much about the programs as possible, then come to the meeting and tell the council members what you found out."

"Me?" he took the paper looked it over. "You really think I can help?"

"You're the only person I know who they could relate to."

Mr. Connors looked at James and then back to Stump. "Well, I suppose I could do that for you. It'd be nice to see something good happen to somebody around here for a change."

"Thanks, Mr. Connors. You always try to do the right thing."

Mr. Connors nodded. "My offer still stands, you know. If things don't work out over there, you can always work for me."

"I might be getting back to you on that, but I gotta go now." Stump turned to James. "Hurry."

As they returned to James's car, Stump saw a blackbird land on the fence at the back of the lot near that ugly scar that somebody made in his paint job. It was as if he'd been slapped in the face. His mind raced to answer a string of questions as fast as they entered his head. He pointed toward the bird. "Dude! We gotta go back over there, and look in Mr. Connors's dumpster."

"But we just came from there. Why don't you make up your mind?"

"C'mon, Dude. This is important."

Minutes later, "Son-of-a-bitch," Stump said, knee-deep in Mr. Connors's trash dumpster. "Just as I thought."

"What'd you find?" James asked.

Stump wrapped a piece of paper around a four-foot long

piece of wood. "This." He said pulling it out. "Don't touch it."

James pulled his hand back as if he was avoiding an electrical shock. "What is it?"

"Just the murder weapon. That's all."

CHAPTER 76

As EXCITED AS HE'D BEEN in a long time, Stump climbed out of Mr. Connors's dumpster and examined the board he'd just found. "I knew it," he said to James, "Put it in your trunk. I gotta talk to Maria's mama before Maria gets home."

"Next door again? Wait a minute, Dude. Slow down. You're driving me nuts. Who did it?"

"Manuel. I'll tell you all about it later," Stump said over his shoulder as he rushed off. "I'll see you in a few minutes."

"Yeah, and we'll probably go next door again."

Stump rushed into the front entrance of building four and knocked on Maria's door. Her mama answered with a dishtowel in hand. "Maria's not here."

"I know, but I'm here to talk with you, not her." She stepped aside and let him in.

"I need your help," Stump said as he hurried into the living room. "You don't know how much Maria loves you and I understand why. You're a kind woman."

"You want a cookie?"

"Not right now. I'm afraid I have a big, big problem and you're the only person who can help me."

She slid a cookie his way.

"Please don't get mad at Maria, but she knew Dixon hurt you and she couldn't stand it. She believed Dixon did similar things to other women and asked me to find out if that was true, but without making you talk to the police. Only now it's all blown up."

"About Mr. Kraft?"

"That's part of it." Stump hesitated. Then, "The truth is I discovered that Dixon is Maria's papa."

Mrs. Quintana stared into his eyes but it was as if she didn't care what he knew.

"But now everybody thinks Dixon is guilty, only Maria and I know he's innocent. I'm going to have to tell the police."

Mrs. Quintana barely flinched at Stump's revelations. "Some of us don't want Dixon to get away," he continued. "I know a lady who can help us send him to jail. I haven't told her anything about you because I promised Maria I wouldn't, but you would do me a huge favor if you'd talk with her. Her name is Detective Sanchez."

Mrs. Quintana finally shook her head from side to side, "I don't like to talk to police."

"I know you don't, Mrs. Quintana, but Detective Sanchez is on our side. I promise. My dad told me she's trying to catch Dixon too, and she's talked to some of the women who used to live here, but they are just like you. They don't want to talk to the police either."

"Dixon does many bad things."

"I know he does, but somebody has to talk first. Those other women respect you. If you'd be willing to tell Detective Sanchez what you know about Dixon, she can get the other women to talk too. That way everybody can gang up on him." Stump looked her in the eye but she was difficult to read. "I know you're worried about being deported, but things have changed—"

She nodded. "That's what Maria said, too."

"She's right. The government is not like they used to be. They don't deport good people now. That's why you should talk with Detective Sanchez. She knows about these things and can help you. Honest."

Mrs. Quintana appeared to be thinking it over, but she wasn't anxious to speak. Stump needed to raise the stakes. "I don't want to hurt you or Maria, but I don't know what else to do. I need your help right away for something else I'm working on for my own mom. I can't do it unless you help me. If you'll do that, I can get the newspapers and a TV station to show how bad Dixon has been. Then the police will have to arrest him."

"I don't know."

Stump sighed and decided to use his last power point. "I wasn't going to tell you this, but Dixon has a college fund for Maria. There's over twenty thousand dollars in it. We might be able to transfer that money from his name to Maria's."

Once again, she was unmoved by his statement. "You knew that already, didn't you?" he said.

She nodded. "If we turn in Dixon, they'll take the money away."

So that was the roadblock. Mrs. Quintana wanted Maria to go to college. "If they take it away we can get her a grant. And if that doesn't work, I can get her some money from my trust. I have plenty. I won't even make her pay me back."

Mrs. Quintana smiled shyly. "You're a nice man. I saw what you did for your mama. You've been nice to Maria too."

"Thank you. Does that mean I can call Detective Sanchez?"

Mrs. Quintana nodded. "Okay, but she has to come here. I don't want to go to the police station."

Stump's heart nearly jumped out of his chest. "Thank you so much, Mrs. Quintana. I'll see if I can get her to come here pretty soon. I'm sorry to be so abrupt but now I have to get home to help my grandmother," he said as he scooted for the door.

She smiled and nodded.

Outside Stump rushed back to the parking lot where he joined James in the car. "We're making awesome progress, Dude," he said as he punched a phone number into his cell. "Let's go."

"Detective Sanchez here."

"Detective Sanchez, this is Stump. I know you told me to stay out of it, but my dad said you needed a witness who isn't afraid to talk to the police about Dixon and I found one. I think Dixon raped her. She said she'll tell you everything."

"Really. Who is it?"

"My girlfriend's mother."

"Inez Quintana? Great. I want to talk with her and the sooner the better. Can you get her over to the police building where nobody will see us talking?"

"I'm sorry but she specifically requested that you go to her house. I don't know why she was so insistent, but I wanted to make it easy for her."

"You did the right thing. I can sneak in the back door of her building. I know she's in building four. What's her apartment number?"

"It's 102. Will this be enough to arrest Dixon?"

"It depends on what she says. If it's as you say, and she agrees to testify, I think I can get other women to fall in line. That would be enough."

"Good. Then I need a big, big favor from you."

"I'll try. What's up?"

"If Mr. Kraft was killed between seven-thirty and eight-thirty, I know for certain that Dixon didn't kill him. Dixon was following Maria and me at the time, but I need you to wait until tonight to tell Dixon that I've become his alibi. Then you can arrest him on the other charges."

"That's interesting. You sure you've got the time right?"

"Yes, ma'am. One hundred percent. Maria can verify it too."

"I guess it won't hurt anything to let him sweat it out for a while longer. Why do you want to wait?"

"It's a timing issue. Tonight is the last City Council meeting and I think I can force my way onto the agenda if I can come up with something dynamic to say."

"Alright. I don't know how all this ties together, but I know

how hard you've tried to help the people over there. You can count on me, but keep me posted. I don't want to get this close and then fumble the ball."

"Yes, ma'am. I'll call you just before my meeting. I gotta go now. Bye."

Stump flipped his phone in the air, and then slapped James in the arm. "I got him, Dude. Dixon's gonna fry."

"That's rad, but why didn't you tell her about the chicken box and that board we found?"

"I will, but this ain't the right time. I have to play it out differently."

James whistled. "I hope you know what you're doing. What's next?"

"I've still got some more calls to make, but I can do them on my own. For now, just take me back to my bike. I'm going home and acting like nothing is going on. I need you to lie low until tonight when Myles goes to his AA meeting. Then come pick me up and take me to the City Council meeting. I'll probably bring Grandma Pauline with me."

"Your grandma? Why do you need her?"

"I don't, but she needs me."

CHAPTER 77

DELORES HAD BEEN DELAYING her discussion with Inez Quintana, but Stump's call changed everything. She dressed down to look like her alter ego, Lorraine Martinez, hid her badge and gun in the bottom of her purse and parked in her usual spot, a couple blocks from Cal-Vista. She strode to the complex and eased into the back entrance of building four.

A gentle rap at the door produced a smallish woman about forty. "Hi, are you Inez Quintana?" she asked before looking around and lowering her voice to a whisper. "I'm Detective Sanchez. I believe you're expecting me," she said.

Inez let her in. "I made cookies. You want one?"

"That would be nice. Could I bother you for a glass of water too?" Delores followed her hostess to the kitchen and sat at the table. "Are we alone?"

Mrs. Quintana nodded. "I sent Maria to the store."

"Good. First off, thank you for agreeing to see me like this. I was going to talk to you soon anyway but this makes it a little easier."

"Stump asked me to. I trust him."

Delores began. "As you probably know, I'm here to talk about Dixon. I'm particularly interested in his relationship with his past wives. I understand you were married to him?"

Mrs. Quintana was slow to respond. Then she said, "We lived together sixteen years ago."

"I've already spoken with Francisca, Yolanda and Rosalie. They're all angry with him for the nasty things he did to them. You might not know it, but most of what he did to them was illegal and I want to punish him for it."

Inez glared as if she were sizing up Delores.

"The problem is," Delores said, "nearly everybody is scared of Dixon, but they look up to you because you've been around here so long. You know the kind of things Dixon did to them, don't you?"

Inez's nod was barely perceptible.

"That's why I need your help. If you're afraid of being deported, I can assure you that it simply won't happen. You've been in the U.S. for too long."

There being no indication that Inez was ready to volunteer any information, Delores elected to try something else. "As a Latina, myself, I know exactly how it can be. May I tell you a story?"

Inez offered an emotionless nod.

"When I was a little girl, I had an older sister. Her name was Simone. We lived with my mama and stepfather in El Centro. Do you know where that is?"

Inez nodded, seeming to relax slightly.

Delores continued with a story about her background, until, "After my sister ran away I hated Tio, but I was scared of him. Just like other women are afraid of Dixon. But eventually, I decided I was going to be brave. I asked somebody to help me and I'm feeling much better now. You can start feeling better too."

Inez smiled for the very first time.

"The one thing I know for certain," Delores continued, "men like Dixon Browne need to be stopped. You and I can do that."

Inez rose and got them each another cookie. "What do you want me to do?"

"I need you to testify. Then the other women will do it too. When all of you say the same thing, I can send him away for a long time."

"But what if he gets out? He can come back."

"I wouldn't worry about that. There's a new law that will make it very, very difficult for him. I can assure you if he does get out, it won't be for at least 20 years. By that time he'll be an old man."

Inez broke a cookie in half. "That's not enough, but I know what is." She rose yet again. "I have to get something."

Delores waited until Inez returned with a paper sack and pulled out a colorful piece of material. Inez carefully wiped at the front, as if to be rid of any dust or imperfections. "It's a blouse," she said just before handing the scrunched-up material to Delores.

The blouse had deeply imbedded creases, indicating it had been wadded up for a long time, probably at the bottom of a drawer and covered by other items. Delores carefully unfolded it to find a sealed plastic bag that contained what appeared to be an old, folded-over newspaper article. "May I take the paper out?"

"Be careful."

Delores slowly opened the bag and eased the clipping out. Slower still, she unfolded the fragile paper to discover a black and white picture of a female body lying on the road and wearing a blouse with a busy pattern. It was dated 1996. She checked the headline. "Woman found at side of road." She looked at Mrs. Quintana for some sort of clue.

"She's my sister, Lupe. That monster killed her."

What the—Delores's hands bounced to her mouth. "Do you mean Dixon killed your sister?"

Mrs. Quintana's head bobbed up and down, much more animated than before. "Right after Maria was born. I was the cleaning lady. I saw Dixon drive off with Lupe, but she didn't like him. So I waited for them to come back. Then very late that night Dixon came home, alone, with a bag in his hand."

"A bottle of liquor?"

"No. That was when he was first going gambling. I was worried. I ran to him and asked where Lupe was but he was drunk and denied even being with her. The next couple days I worried and waited for my sister to come home but she didn't. I couldn't read English but I watched the trash for newspapers that people threw out, and then I saw this article and picture. It was my sister. I could tell by the blouse." Inez pointed at the blouse Delores was holding. "It was just like this one. We bought them at the same time."

"Oh, my goodness. I'm so sorry to hear about Lupe."

"We never had any cameras so this is the only picture I have of Lupe. I knew he killed her, but I had to keep quiet because the government deported people who made trouble. I even saw him have people taken away."

"That must have been very scary for you."

"After that, I had to stay close to him until my Maria grew up. But now Maria is a woman and I can tell you what happened."

Delores shook her head and re-examined the blouse in her hand and compared it to the one in the picture. "I can certainly look into it, but I doubt if this will be enough to get a conviction."

"That's not all." Mrs. Quintana said. She opened a door under one of her lower kitchen cabinets, extracted a large cooking pot and placed it, upside-down, on her counter top. Then she got a broom from the corner and dragged a kitchen chair near the cooking pot. Then, with broom in hand, she stepped on the chair and then the counter. Getting a hint of what was next, Delores leapt to her feet and moved toward Inez in case she slipped. "Be careful."

Inez took the final step. Balanced on her cooking pot, she raised the broom over her head and scraped the handle across the top of the upper cabinet to pull forward a dusty paper sack with something heavy in it.

"Here, hand it to me," Delores said, reaching for the sack.

Mrs. Quintana did as requested and stepped all the way down. "A few days after Lupe disappeared, Dixon made me clean his apartment. I saw this on a shelf in the back room. I think it's what he had in his hand that night when he came home late."

Delores opened the bag to find a small but heavy gambling trophy.

"I didn't really know what it was," Mrs. Quintana continued, "but it had some playing cards on it. I left it alone for a few years and then he won more trophies, bigger ones, and he put them on the shelf too. Then one day I was dusting them and saw a dark spot on this one." She twisted the trophy to show Delores. "It looked like dried blood, Lupe's blood. Now all I have of her is this little drop of dried-up blood, and the picture from the newspaper."

Delores couldn't believe her ears. After all this time of trying to catch Dixon, she finally had something that would seal the deal.

"I don't even know what happened to my Lupe," Mrs. Quintana went on. "But now that Maria is all grown up I might be able to find out. I don't care if I have to go to jail."

Delores shook her head. "You won't go to jail, honey. About all you did wrong was withhold evidence. Under the circumstances it was completely reasonable. I'm sure I can get the DA to give you full immunity if you'll help us."

"What's immunity?"

"It means you won't get in trouble because you didn't do anything wrong."

CHAPTER 78

After checking with Sergeant Byrdswain and the DA, Delores met the sergeant outside the police building. "Sorry I'm late," he said. "Everybody else will meet us at Cal-Vista."

"Fantastic," she said, wearing nicer clothes and more make-up than she usually sported around the complex. "I'll drive. I'm tired of parking down the street."

A few minutes later they pulled into the lot on their way to arrest Dixon Browne. "You've been working hard on this case," he said. "You deserve your glory. I'm going to stay out of it unless you need me."

"Thanks, Sergeant. I appreciate that. I'd also like you to hang back out of sight in the beginning if that's okay."

Seconds later, Dixon checked the peephole and quickly opened his door. "Lorraine! You look fantastic. What gives?"

"Just this," she said. She wrapped her arms around his neck and kissed him on the lips. Just as he got into it, she pulled back.

He grinned. "I see you've made your choice. Which is it? Monday Girl or wife?"

"Neither," she said while stepping back and shaking her hair before she pulled her badge from her back pocket. "Surprise! My real name is Detective Delores Sanchez and that may be the last kiss you'll ever get from a woman. I just wanted it to torment you for the rest of your miserable days."

He scoffed and wiped his lips. "Well that explains a few things, but why all the secrecy? I haven't done anything wrong."

"In that case, you wouldn't mind if I read you your Miranda rights just in case you make some gigantic confession."

"If you're trying to turn me on, it's working."

Good. The bastard was underestimating her again. She patted her pockets before pulling out a tiny booklet. "Here it is," she said as if it was the first time she'd ever read it to anybody. "Do you mind?"

He chuckled and nodded.

"It says here you have the right to remain silent. Oh, and anything you say can and will be used against you in a court of law. Number three says you have the right to an attorney. Here's another one. If you cannot afford an attorney, one will be appointed to you." She exhaled and flipped the page. "Knowing and understanding your rights as I have explained them to you, are you willing to answer my questions without an attorney present?" She looked up as if she'd barely gotten through it all.

Dixon smiled. "Sure. I'm enjoying this."

She faced down the hall and hooked a finger. "Ready for you, Sergeant."

"Hello, Mr. Browne," the sergeant said as he reached Dixon's door. "I said I'd be back. Step inside like a good boy. My partner wants to have a talk with you."

Dixon jiggled his teeth. "Partner, huh? You guys are wasting your time. I was following that Stump kid when Kraft was murdered."

"Keep moving."

Inside, they directed Dixon to his couch. The sergeant folded his arms and stood guard at the door while Delores pulled a chair from the kitchen and sat just a few feet from Dixon. This time she was the one in control. "I have good news and very, very bad news for you. First, the good news. Stump's an honest kid. He verified your alibi. We know you didn't kill Mr. Kraft."

"So why all the theatrics? Do you need the practice?"

"Turns out Stump got me some information I desperately needed to convict you of rape."

"Me? Rape? You people are out of your minds. I've never raped anybody in my life."

"Quite the contrary. In fact you may become famous for what you did, or should I say infamous? Either way, you get to be the first serial rapist in our little city."

Dixon turned his head to Sergeant Byrdswain, "Is she insane?"

"Quite honestly, sir, I think she's got you by the balls."

"You know that string of wives you put together? None of those women would have had sex with you were it not for your false promise to get them citizenship. Thanks to a new law, each time you screwed them it amounted to rape by deception. How many women did you do that with anyway?"

"Those women wanted what they got."

"I don't think so." Delores said. "So far, I've spoken with Yolanda and Francisca and Inez and some others. They're all willing to testify about your little marriage-go-round. That makes you a serial rapist of each woman and a serial rapist of the group."

The color went out of Dixon's face.

"Not only that, we're talking to your pal Louie, at the Registrar's office. He'll sing his heart out to avoid being charged with accessory to serial rape. That is, of course, if he's not actually your brother, but we'll figure that out later. The point is, now you're the one who's screwed. I have to tell you, I just love the irony."

Dixon watched her, silent for a change.

"But I've got a lot more," she said. "For instance, there are all those things you admitted to in that notebook of yours."

"That little turd."

"I assume you're referring to Stump, but he's the least of your worries. Manuel and Juanita are ready to skin you and Mr. Connors, next door, says you waved a gun at him. But my favorite witness is sweet little Inez Quintana. You can't even imagine what she told me."

"You can't believe anything she says. She's just angry 'cause I never loved her."

"We'll just overlook the list of rapes for now, including the recent one, and talk about an old gambling trophy of yours. You might have forgotten about it. Mrs. Quintana thinks you used it to kill her sister about sixteen years ago." Delores smiled coldly. "That's the one that pisses me off the most. You see I lost a sister too because of a pervert like you."

Dixon's eyes shot to Sergeant Byrdswain, "I don't know what she's talking about, but I was covering for Inez."

"Covering?" Delores said. "How so?"

"Inez killed her own sister. I forget her name."

"Lupe. You'll probably never forget her name again."

"Whatever. Anyway I just won some money and Lupe wanted to help me spend it, so I figured why not have a few drinks and bang her while we were at it."

Delores smirked, "Are you sure you didn't hit her over the head when you were done with her and then throw her on the ground? 'Cause that's where she was found — sizzling on a road."

"Don't be ridiculous, I ain't no caveman. I was happy to split a bottle of wine, and snag a goodnight kiss or two before I porked her." He glared at Delores's chest. "You're a pretty good kisser. I bet a bottle of wine has loosened you up a time or two, huh Detective?"

"Nice try, but you ain't getting under my skin. You said you were covering for Inez — how so? What happened that night?"

"Me and Lupe just got out of the liquor store when Inez walked up behind us and before I knew it that crazy Inez hit her sister over the head with a hammer. Poor woman was out of her mind with jealousy."

"A hammer? Are you sure, 'cause the investigating officers said it was something with a sharper edge—like a gambling trophy, for instance."

"They're mistaken. When she did it, I turned around, shocked. Then Inez dropped the hammer. People like her don't own guns or other kinds of weapons, you know."

"Where was this place? They might have some old surveillance videos that would corroborate this tale of yours."

"They were closed down a few years after that to make room for a new highway ramp."

"How unfortunate for you. Inez doesn't drive. How did she get to the liquor store?"

"How should I know? Maybe she had somebody else take her."

"Who? Did this mystery chauffer drop her off or wait until she clonked her sister and then take her back home?"

"Whoever it was must have left 'cause she asked me to help her get rid of the hammer and the body. But that's not murder."

"No, but it probably won't surprise you to hear that Inez has a completely different story."

"Well it's her word against mine and you know how women are—their emotions overtake their ability to think rationally."

"But the wound was on top of Lupe's head."

"So what?"

"You said you just got out of the liquor store and Inez walked up behind you. Inez was shorter than her sister was. If she hit Lupe while they were both standing up as you said, the wound would be somewhere around the back of the skull, not on the very top of the head."

"Well, Lupe's head was bent forward."

"Nah. Ain't buying it. You said Inez came from behind but based on where that wound was, the perp was quite a bit taller than Lupe. I'd say you're a full nine inches taller than either one of those two." She glanced at Sergeant Byrdswain and then back. "There's another reason I don't believe you. We have the real weapon. Your trophy. There's a dark brown glob in the corner of it. Inez thinks it's her sister's blood."

"Coincidence."

"I don't think so. You were the only one who had access to that trophy. In fact I'd bet it never left your hands from the moment they gave it to you. We also have time of death, and I'm betting it came shortly after you were awarded that trophy. You had a MOM too."

"A mom? My old lady's been dead for years."

"Means, Opportunity and Motive; and motive is the only thing we haven't discussed, but I've got that covered too. Lupe liked her wine and had a tendency to talk too much when she was drunk. She also knew that you didn't want word to get out that Maria was your daughter. Maybe she even threatened to spread the word. But you couldn't risk it, so you did what you had to do and lied to Inez about what happened. As long as Inez bought your lies, all you had to do was keep her happy so she wouldn't take Maria away, so you gave Inez some work and kept them both around. Too bad for you, Inez knew exactly what happened and now she's happy to tell the story."

A knock came from the door. Byrdswain opened it and a uniformed officer entered the doorway. He addressed Delores, "We're ready for you."

"Thank you, officer," she replied as she pulled her handcuffs from behind her belt. She turned back to Dixon. "We've got a surprise for you outside, but first you're under arrest for the murder of Lupe Barbados, and for serial rape by deception of Inez Quintana, Francisca Diaz, and Yolanda Vigil. Now turn around. I've got a set of bracelets that are just your size."

Dixon hung his head.

Delores turned to the officer. "Apparently this sick-o has taken unauthorized videos of his victims. Would you find them and secure them so they don't cause any additional troubles?"

"Gladly."

Detective Sanchez led Dixon outside where a small crowd of noisy people, including Francisca, Yolanda, Inez and Juanita heckled him. "Some of your friends wanted to see this for themselves," Delores said, grinning.

Francisca stepped forward and spat on him. Inez kicked his shin.

"Assault," Dixon screamed in the direction of Sergeant Byrdswain. "That's assault."

Byrdswain motioned at one of the uniformed officers. "You'd better restrain these big bad women."

Delores got right in Dixon's face. "By the way, I'm twenty-six, you perv."

CHAPTER 79

WHILE STUMP'S CLASSMATES were anxiously counting down the last days of the school year, Stump was taking a final of his own making. He had to get into the last City Council meeting and to do so, he relied upon something Myles taught him: To get what he wanted he had to give them what they wanted.

As agreed, James came by at seven-fifteen, when the City Council meeting was underway and Myles was with his AA pals. Stump dropped a note on the table telling Myles where he and Grandma Pauline would be.

Some minutes later, when Stump, Grandma Pauline and James arrived at the meeting place, the parking lot contained quite a few cars and a small van belonging to KLAC TV. One thing Stump had learned about the media types was they were always looking for a fresh story.

"Looks like a good turnout," James said.

Stump nodded. "Last meeting of the year. They have to pack a lot in. That's one of the reasons they shut me out."

"Assemblies are fun," Grandma Pauline said.

Although many of Grandma Pauline's comments were off the wall, Stump was glad she was there. As before, she reminded him of how important his own mother was and why he was doing all of this.

When the trio opened the meeting room doors, a cameraman was in the middle aisle filming the goings-on. Heads turned as Stump led Grandma Pauline down the outer aisle toward the back where TV reporter Irv Wedlock was seated. Stump urged James and Grandma Pauline to scoot into one of the back rows, leaving the aisle seat for him. He waited as the leaders worked through the schedule.

Finally, at a quarter after eight, Mayor Curtis pointed at the clock. "Looks like we're a little late, but there being nothing else on the agenda for this year, I wish to thank—"

"Excuse me Mr. Mayor," Stump said as he and James bolted to their feet and James began to video Stump with a cell phone. "There is one last thing before you close down for the season." Eyes rolled and the cameraman pivoted toward Stump as he stepped up the side aisle toward the front of the room. Mr. Barella, Stump's councilman, folded his arms.

The mayor leaned into his mic. "I'm sorry. We know who you are and you're not—"

"That's right," Stump said as he reached the lectern. "I'm Neal Joseph Randolph." He pointed to the TV correspondent. "Two months ago Mr. Wedlock invited me to keep him posted regarding my progress with this City Council. Therefore, I am the one who invited him to join us tonight."

Mr. Wedlock nodded.

"Great," the mayor muttered.

Just then Myles came in, scanned the room and took Stump's vacant seat next to Grandma Pauline.

Stump turned back toward the council members. "I promised Mr. Wedlock that I would give him two good stories tonight. I told him that even though you have a full docket, and even though I let you down once before, you are the kind of people who will always put the citizens of the community before your own interests. I said that you would gladly be late to your end-of-term party if you could help the residents." Stump pointed to his own councilman. "Mr.

Barella has always said that very thing, haven't you, Mr. Barella?"

The cameraman pivoted to catch Barella's reply. Barella sat up and nervously straightened his tie. "Er. Yes. That's exactly what we've talked about. Neal and I go way back. I think we should let him speak."

"Alright, alright," the Mayor grumbled. "But make it quick. These good people want to go home."

"Thank you, Mr. Mayor," Stump said, "and everybody else too. Many of you may know that there was a murder in our town a few days ago. The victim was Mr. Kraft, my boss at the Cal-Vista apartments. At this very moment, the police are at that building and arresting the man who some believe committed the murder. His name is Dixon Browne."

The end-of-meeting buzz that dominated the room minutes earlier had calmed to low whispers as the cameraman, James and most of the attendees focused on Stump.

"Interestingly," Stump said, "I can prove that Mr. Browne is both innocent of the killing and guilty of a rape." The buzz picked up as Stump pulled out his cell. I'm going to call the detective in charge right now and you can listen to her make the arrest." Stump turned to Mr. Wedlock. "My girlfriend is taking video of it all so you can put the story on TV." Mr. Wedlock nodded.

Pleased with himself, Stump set his phone on speaker and held it to the microphone at the lectern. "But the most important part," he said, "will come at the end when I reveal something that the detectives don't even know — who the real killer is."

Heads bobbed enthusiastically and a hush settled on the crowd.

Stump tapped his auto dial and everybody waited through the first couple rings, then, "*Hi, Stump.*"

"Hello, Detective. I'm at my meeting, like we discussed. I've told everybody about Dixon Browne's crimes. Are you ready to make the arrest?"

"I'm sorry, Stump, but things didn't work out quite like we discussed."

Oh, no. Stump's stomach tightened as nervous mumbles of doubt replaced the precious silence of mere seconds ago. Embarrassed, he shifted his feet. "Er. Why not? I thought you believed me. Dixon didn't do it."

"Relax, Stump. I'm just down the hall from you right now. I came to see you all in person. Okay. I think I've got the right room." Just then the outer doors opened and Detective Sanchez walked in. She looked around and then joined Stump by the lectern and faced the council. "Good evening, everybody," she said as she put away her cell. "I'm Detective Delores Sanchez. I came here tonight because I owe Stump here a big thank you. I can assure you all that Stump was correct about the key points he made. As he said, Mr. Browne did not kill Mr. Kraft as previously thought; but something else came up so my boss thought we needed to act quickly."

Whew! Stump secretly blew out a deep breath while Detective Sanchez continued.

"In addition to the charges Stump suggested, we also charged Mr. Browne with murder in a very old case. Stump's girlfriend was able to get that part on video for the TV people."

Wow! This was working out okay. Now was Stump's chance to impress the hell out of everybody. "That's very interesting, Detective Sanchez, but I have a news flash for you too. Do you have two sets of handcuffs?"

The cameraman swirled to catch Detective Sanchez's reply. "Of course. Why?"

"I told you earlier that I could prove that Dixon Browne didn't kill Mr. Kraft, but now I can tell you who actually did. It was Manuel Alvarado. The maintenance man."

"What?" Detective Sanchez said with her eyes wide. "Are you certain? What makes you think so?"

"I'm not only certain. I've got proof. Maria and I heard Mr. Kraft and Dixon Browne arguing around 7:30. Then we saw Manuel come home and dump a chicken box on the opposite side of the complex from where his apartment is. I didn't think much of it at the time, but after that Maria and I went for a walk and when we got back, Mr. Kraft was already dead."

"Oh my goodness," Detective Sanchez said with her hand to her mouth.

"Then today at school, James finished a piece of chicken and threw the bone in the closest trashcan just as anybody else would do, but it was radically different from what Manuel did. But this time when I thought about Manuel's actions I knew the time of Mr. Kraft's death and it all fit. Between statements by Maria and me, plus the receipt in the chicken box and Manuel's fingerprints on the box we know that Manuel was there just minutes before Mr. Kraft died. That's why James and I went back to the complex and got the chicken box."

"Oh, my God," Detective Sanchez said, both hands to her face. "I wish you would have called me."

"There's more. I also saw a big mark on a fence that I'd just painted and we looked in the neighbor's dumpster where we found a board that was clearly the murder weapon and all of this proves that Manuel had both the means and opportunity to kill Mr. Kraft."

"But evidence shouldn't be removed and it has to be handled carefully."

"Don't worry. The board and the chicken box are both in James's trunk. We didn't get our own fingerprints on them."

Detective Sanchez grimaced. "At least that's one good thing." She moved toward the door. "I've gotta get back there."

Stump stepped forward. "Don't you want to know the motive?"

She stopped in her tracks and raised her head. "Well, yes. What is it?"

Stump looked at Myles, who was grinning and shaking his head. "Two reasons. It was a combination mercy killing, and a chance to frame Dixon Browne."

Detective Sanchez grabbed at her hair as if she wanted to pull it out. "Well, you've been correct about things like this before. I'll have to go talk with him right now." She turned to Myles. "Can you secure that evidence for me?"

"Will do," Myles said, still shaking his head as she ran out of the room.

Stump proudly faced the Mayor and a healthy smattering of applause blended with a few cheers, James being the loudest.

"Quiet down, everybody," the mayor said into his microphone. "Quiet, please. Quiet." Finally the noise eased and the mayor addressed Stump. "That was all pretty interesting, Neal, but it's not our department. Now, we can finally—"

"Wait a minute, Mr. Mayor," Irv Wedlock said from the side of the room. "Neal here said he had two stories for me. After that show, I'm sure everybody here wants to hear what else he has for us."

"Yes. I understand that, Mr. Wedlock," the Mayor said, "but we're running very late and these good people—"

"These good people, as you say, are here because they care about their community and I'm sure you want our story to illustrate that the Palmdale City Council is a first-class example of what all city councils should be like. I'd like to say you're always interested in doing what's right for the citizens, no matter how unorthodox or inconvenient."

The Mayor sighed and turned back to Stump. "Alright, Neal, did you have something else you wanted to say?"

Finally. "Yes, sir. I definitely do." Stump took a deep breath, reached in his pocket and grabbed a small piece of paper containing his notes.

CHAPTER 80

With the full attention of the City Council and the TV camera, Stump began his story. "As many of you know, three years ago, my mom died in a house fire in the oldest part of town. She got trapped in a room with bars on the windows, bars that had no safety latches. Later, I found out that there are lots of unsafe homes in that area, mostly because they were built before there were good building codes like there are today. It didn't seem fair to me that poor people have to live in unsafe homes.

"So I came to a previous meeting to try to help my mom's neighbors upgrade their unsafe properties. Unfortunately, I had an accident and missed the follow-up meeting, and for that I'm sorry. Afterwards, I found out that some of the citizens simply didn't have the money to do the things we were talking about."

Stump looked directly into the camera. "Things like removing asbestos insulation, unsafe wiring, lead-based paint, fixing leaky roofs and plumbing—and of course, windows that don't allow for safe passage in emergencies." He turned back toward the council members.

"Since that day, I've continued to do research." He pointed to Grandma Pauline. "And thanks to that very special lady back there, I've discovered some brand-new information that all of you should know about."

"Alright. Get on with it," the Mayor said.

Stump nodded. "To help me, I've asked Mr. Clyde Connors, a very successful local businessman who specializes in housing matters, to explain it to you." Stump turned and nodded at Mr. Connors.

Mr. Connors approached the microphone. "Hello, everybody. I own the apartment building next door to where Stump works. I came here tonight to share with you two programs, which I have personally investigated. Earlier today, I spoke with representatives from both agencies, so the information I am about to share with you is very fresh. These organizations were established precisely for the type of things Stump here is talking about. Roofs, furnaces, windows. All of it. But the remarkable truth is that there is no cost to the residents to upgrade their homes. I repeat. All of these repairs are free to homeowners who qualify." Stump glanced around. Silent people seemed stunned.

"Are you certain about this?" the Mayor asked of Mr. Connors.

"As I said. I checked it out today. Any of you can look it up on the internet right now. It's called Rebuilding Together. They get their money from federal grants and have funds as we speak."

Several people began tapping at their phones.

"I have some of the application forms here so you can see just how simple they are," Mr. Connors added.

"I found it," somebody said.

Another guy held his cell in the air. "Me too!"

Councilwoman Torrez showed the Mayor the read-out on her cell phone.

"I'll be damned," said a different voice.

Others mumbled in amazement while Mr. Connors plopped the applications on the side table and returned to his seat.

"Well, Neal," the mayor said. "I have to admit this is very interesting. Exactly what were you expecting from this committee?"

"Thank you, Mr. Mayor. If we do this right, we won't have to pass a new law and force people to do things they don't want to do, but we can help everybody who wants it. The key is we need to get the word out to make it more official. That's where the Council can help. You guys have much more credibility than a sixteen-year-old like me."

The Mayor snickered. "I wouldn't say that after what we've seen here today, but we don't have a lot of manpower."

"I thought about that, but if we work together we can do it. The first thing we have to do is inform the residents of the programs. We just need some brochures to deliver door to door." Stump pointed toward his councilman. "Mr. Barella is a nice man. He helped us before. I'm sure he'd provide these brochures too, in the name of the City Council, and help me and my friend, James, deliver them."

James jumped up. "I'm in."

The cameraman bounced back to Michael Barella. "Err. Ahh. Yes. I can do that," Barella said, while adjusting his collar.

Stump grinned. "We could have two meetings that will explain it all. One at night, after dinner, and one on a Saturday. That way everybody should have a chance to come to one or the other." He pointed toward the side of the room. "That's my attorney over there. Ms. Delgado. I've asked her to oversee all the details so you'll know that somebody responsible is in charge of all the legalities."

Danielle Delgado rose. "Not only that. If councilman Barella and the City Planner will help me, I'll chair a committee that will look into getting funds from the county and some merchants to improve Main Street. We'll see if we can put in a nice island and some foliage so people will be glad to live here, and visitors will think of our town as a nice place to spend their money." She looked at Barella. The camera zoomed in again.

"Why, yes," Councilman Barella said with a half-smile. "Why not?"

The cameraman spun to the side table where Mrs. Crumpler beamed at Stump for several long seconds before nodding in approval. "You can count on my department."

James raised his clenched fist high into the air. "Yes."

"I hope they'll also put in safer sidewalks for bicycles and the elderly," Stump added.

The Mayor nodded. "God knows we could use the jobs. Where would you hold these meetings?"

Stump shuffled his feet, "Well, to tell you the truth, I haven't exactly—"

"Excuse me." Stump knew the voice. "My name is Myles Cooper, Mr. Mayor. I'm Neal's dad and I know several local law enforcement officers who I can call upon to help out with the meetings. We can provide an interpreter and maybe get some refreshments. The detective who was here earlier has a contact at the grade school. I'm positive we can use the cafeteria."

Mr. Connors rose. "I'll donate five hundred dollars to cover the refreshments and miscellaneous costs."

Grandma Pauline clapped her hands. "This is a good play."

Myles held her hand.

A giant smile stretched across Stump's face as he addressed the Mayor. "I rest my case."

"This isn't a court, Mr. Randolph," the mayor said. He paused for a moment before he banged his gavel. "I'm going to call a quick recess to have a conversation with the panel. We'll reconvene in five minutes."

After the council members went out in the hall, Stump joined Myles in the aisle next to Grandma Pauline. "I'm sorry I didn't tell you what I was up to, Myles, but I was afraid you'd stop me."

"We'll talk about that later, but for now we're all working for your mother. Now get back up to the front of the room where you belong."

Danielle Delgado wandered over. "I'm sorry I threw in that part about sprucing up Main Street, but I just couldn't help myself. It's so ugly over there."

"I'm glad you did," Stump said. "Especially getting Mr. Barella involved. You made him look like a hero."

Irv Wedlock tapped Stump on the shoulder. "Great job, Stump. We'll see if we can't plug your program on the news."

Other people took turns patting Stump on the back and encouraging him as he moved back to the lectern.

A moment later, the outer doors burst open and the cameraman got the shot of the councilmembers as they returned, in single file like a jury, to their seats. Mayor Curtis checked his microphone. "Everybody please be seated. We're already very late and we'd like to wrap this up. The committee has discussed the matter as proposed." He pointed at Stump. "Now if Mr. Randolph here doesn't have any additional jobs for Mr. Barella to do, can we proceed with the vote?"

Stump leaned into his microphone and grinned at Mr. Barella. "I was hoping he'd stand on the corner with one of those spinning signs and direct traffic to the meetings."

The audience laughed and Barella wagged a friendly finger at Stump.

"Okay, then," the Mayor said. "I will ask each panel member, one at a time, whether they agree that the City Council should promote and advise the community of the importance of upgrading their homes based on the terms and conditions we spelled out earlier, all of which is now of record." He banged his gavel and looked to his right. "Let me begin with Victoria Hennretti. Do you vote yes or no?"

"Yes."

"William Goode. How do you vote?"

"Affirmative."

"It's my turn, and I vote yes," the Mayor said as he turned his head to his left.

"Carmen Torrez?"

"Yes."

"And finally we come to tonight's man of the hour. Mr. Michael Barella. And how do you vote, sir?"

Ever the showman, Mr. Barella grinned and stalled, enjoying the moment and the TV camera. A hush filled the room as everybody anticipated his reply. Then, "I don't know how I got roped into all this, but I say, hell, yes."

Wild cheers overwhelmed the room while the camera perused all the happy faces.

"It's unanimous and the measure passes," the Mayor yelled into his microphone. "Now let's get to that party."

CHAPTER 81

As soon as the meeting was over, a group of well-wishers encircled Stump. Naturally, Michael Barella stood wherever the camera was aimed. After the excitement wore off Myles offered to take his mother, Stump and James for a slice of pie. They called Detective Sanchez and invited her to meet them.

Once seated at the restaurant, Stump was able to see the door.

"I can't eat that much," Grandma Pauline said.

"You haven't even seen the menu yet, Mom," Myles said.

"They always give me too much."

"Don't worry, Grandma," Stump said. "If they give you too much, I'll help you."

The waitress came by and Myles ordered apple pie for everybody.

"There's Detective Sanchez now," Stump said, pointing to the entry door. He waved her over and scooted around the booth to make room. James slid too, and Detective Sanchez eased into the new space.

"I'm surprised you could make it," Myles said.

"I probably shouldn't have, but I'm starving."

"I hope you like apple pie. We all ordered the same thing."

"Right now, I'd eat liver and onions."

"Gross," Stump said. "What happened to Manuel?"

"It was sad. After he heard we had the weapon and a chicken box full of his prints he folded like an old sheet. I think he was feeling pretty guilty and just wanted to get it over with."

"Was Juanita in on it?" Stump followed up. "I wasn't sure."

"Don't think so. She was pretty broken up. I had to get somebody to stay with her for the night."

"Consequences," Grandma Pauline said.

Stump turned her way, wondered if she knew she'd made a relevant comment.

"Dixon's having a rough time," Detective Sanchez said. "He thought he'd gotten away with that old case, but he's mad as hell. He's hired an attorney, but it isn't going to do him much good. There's too much physical evidence and too many witnesses."

"Well, I can tell you this," Myles said. "If Stump's mom knew what he pulled off tonight, she'd be damned proud." He looked sternly at Stump. "But you should have told Detective Sanchez or me what you were up to. The way you played it was too risky."

"We considered that," James said, "but Stump wanted to give the TV station a scoop."

Stump shrugged. "I know I didn't do everything just right, but it was the only way I could force them to listen to me."

"Gotta admit it worked out well," Myles said. "What made you think of getting the TV station there?"

"You taught me about giving people what they want. So I thought about Mr. Barella and the others. What's the one thing they want more than anything?"

"To get reelected," James said.

"Right. It's all about image to guys like that, so the best way to get their attention was to give them what they craved, and the best way to get the cameras there was to give them something they wanted too."

"Look how fat that guy is," Grandma Pauline said, pointing to a customer in the next booth.

Detective Sanchez cringed while Myles shushed his mom, and then turned back to Stump. "You said my mom helped. What did she have to do with anything?"

"Two ways. First she was the only one who knew that there are grants available for people to upgrade their houses."

"Did you know Ted and Sheila?" Grandma Pauline asked Detective Sanchez.

"No ma'am. I haven't had that pleasure, but we're all glad you knew them." She turned to Stump. "What was the other way this smart woman helped?"

Stump smiled at Grandma Pauline and looked at Myles. "When she first arrived from Oklahoma, she was thinking about changing her will without your sister ever knowing about it. Her idea was, by the time your sis figured it out, it would be too late. She called it a Ruby."

"Where is Ellen anyway?" Grandma Pauline asked. "She never comes around anymore."

"She's at her house, Mom," Myles said. Back to Stump. "A ruby?"

"She was talking about Jack Ruby, the guy who killed Oswald for killing JFK. I had to look it up."

"Jack Ruby?" Grandma Pauline said. "He was one of my students."

Myles patted her hand.

"What about Ruby?" Detective Sanchez asked.

"There are several theories surrounding the President's death. One of them was that the mob tricked Oswald into killing JFK. But they didn't trust Oswald to keep his mouth shut, so they hired their loyal friend, Jack Ruby, who ran a bar in Texas, to kill Oswald."

Myles nodded. "I saw that on TV, but I thought a committee proved Oswald acted alone."

"There were several theories, but none of that matters for our purposes. The relevant point has to do with Ruby's health. He was very ill and expected to die within a year. Other than the mob, nobody knew the details of the assassination except Oswald and Ruby but Oswald was already dead and Ruby wasn't going to be around very long because of his illness so he had nothing to lose by killing Oswald. It was brilliant."

"But Manuel wasn't ill," Myles said.

"No, but Mr. Kraft was." Stump said. "Manuel hated Dixon, but couldn't do anything about it without becoming a prime suspect. But then word got out that Mr. Kraft was dying. The first time I met Manuel he told me that he'd seen his own uncle suffer through the same thing and he didn't like it. Manuel figured he could carry out a mercy killing on Mr. Kraft and frame Dixon all with one swing of a heavy board. If he was lucky, he and Juanita might even get Dixon's job, or at least get paid what they were worth."

"It almost worked," Detective Sanchez said. "If Stump hadn't seen Manuel's out-of-place chicken box..."

Stump nodded. "And the scar on the fence. After James and I checked that out and found the support board from the bed frame, I knew Manuel had the means, opportunity and motive to kill Mr. Kraft."

"A MOM," James said.

Myles nodded and said to Stump, "I still wish you wouldn't go off on your own like that."

"To be perfectly honest," Detective Sanchez said, "Stump found out some things nobody else knew, like that Mrs. Quintana had been raped recently. More importantly, he persuaded her to talk about it. That enabled us to arrest Dixon and find out about that old case. I'm not sure we could have done all that without him." She looked directly at Stump. "Regardless, I'm glad we all got reunited."

"When I figured it out, I wondered why I didn't recognize you earlier, 'cause I always thought you were, well, you know."

"You thought I was what?" Detective Sanchez asked while folding her arms. "In over my head?"

"No, nothing like that."

"I know what he means," James said. "He thinks you're hot."

Stump thumped James on the arm. "For an older woman, Dude. I said she looks good for an older woman."

Detective Sanchez chuckled. "Older woman, huh? You don't know how good that is to hear. If you weren't Maria's boyfriend I might just be tempted to scoop you up myself."

Myles grinned and pointed toward the kitchen. "Thank God. Here comes our pie."

"I can't eat that much."

"It's not even here yet, Mom."

CHAPTER 82

It had been several days since Delores arrested both Dixon Browne and Manuel Alvarado. She'd had her fill of interrogations, reporters, paperwork and attorneys, but those weren't her only problems. Except for a few quick phone calls, she'd essentially abandoned Carlton Fayes, the art teacher, which meant he'd had to attend to nearly every detail of what he came to refer to as The Great Cupcake Extravaganza.

All of this proved two things: one, Mrs. Carbone was correct when she said that Carlton usually did more than his fair share of the chores; and two, now that the day for the Extravaganza had arrived, Delores looked forward to it as much as any of the students did.

Delores took the afternoon off, donned some blue jeans and a short-sleeved pullover sweater, and arrived at the school just before two. Inside, she immediately noticed her yellow poster on the entrance wall along with several others, all of which boasted of the cupcake decorating party that was to be in the cafeteria right after school.

"I'm Detective Sanchez," she said to the receptionist. "I'm supposed to meet Mrs. Carbone."

The grin on the receptionist's face was a little friendlier than Delores expected. "Oh, yes, we've heard all about you. Go ahead."

As Delores wandered toward the cafeteria she noticed poster after poster, all with an A+, promoting the event. There had to be a spot in heaven for a guy who could inspire kids like that.

In the cafeteria, a handful of adults were busy taping balloons, crepe paper and additional posters to the walls. "There she is," Mrs. Carbone said, pointing to Delores. "C'mon back. You can help in the kitchen."

"I didn't expect to see so many helpers," Delores said as she smiled her way past the other workers.

"You don't know the half of it. One of the ladies is from the office. The others are parents." She grinned. "We're going to need every one of them."

"Why? Carlton and I should be able to handle—"

Mrs. Carbone waved off the comment. "It's been a wildfire around here. When word of a cupcake party got out, all sorts of people wanted to come. We even heard from the superintendent's office. She's sending over a representative to check it out."

"Oh my gosh, Mr. Fayes didn't say anything to me about all of that."

"Course not. He said you were tied up on that big case— congratulations, by the way."

"Oh. Thank you, but I was just doing my job."

"We're expecting somewhere around 50-60 people and every one of them is supposed to make two cupcakes. Mr. Fayes calls one a Me Cake; the other one is a Friend Cake to give to somebody else. It's about the pleasure of doing nice things for others."

Delores's eyes widened. "What a wonderful idea."

"If you'd like, you can help me whip up the batter. We're also making an extra fifty cupcakes, just in case."

"Gladly. Where do I start?"

For the next hour Delores traded niceties with the helpers and mixed batter, cooked cupcakes and spread decorating utensils among the tables. Then for the final twenty minutes

Mrs. Carbone showed everybody how to use the icing tubes so they could pass the information along to the kids when the time was right. "We'd like one adult at each table," Mrs. Carbone said. "Don't expect a lot, artistically. Our objective is merely to show these kids that school and learning and trying new things can be fun."

Delores nodded. That was precisely what she'd hoped for the first day she met Carlton Fayes.

As the final bell approached, it appeared as if nearly everything was ready. "Don't worry about the loose ends," Mrs. Carbone said. "You guys just enjoy yourselves and spread that attitude to the children."

It occurred to Delores that Mrs. Carbone was actually friendlier than she originally seemed.

By the time the final bell went off the whiff of chocolate cupcakes filled the room. Parents and students worked their way into the cafeteria. Some sniffed at the air. Others took seats. A couple boys grabbed the icing tubes and pretended they were laser pointers. Then Carlton Fayes walked in.

He deserved to make a grand entrance for all he'd accomplished but instead he simply eased in, apparently leaving the others to enjoy their moments. He moved quickly to Delores. "I'm glad you could make it."

"Me too." She said, tempted to kiss him on the cheek.

"If you'll excuse me, I'd like to get this function going." Carlton moved close to the kitchen and banged at the bottom of an aluminum pot with a large cooking spoon. "Wow!" he said in an outside voice. "We had no idea there would be so many of you here today. It's so good to see you all. Before we start decorating I'd like to thank Mrs. Carbone and everybody who volunteered for the various jobs. Let's all give each other a hand." After the applause died down, he resumed. "Okay, the table captains will show you what to do. We'll have a short hour to ice up our cakes before we call it a day. So everybody have a good time and don't be afraid to ask questions."

After the announcements, Delores took a captain role at a table facing Carlton, who sat at the next table over facing her. She showed the kids how to squeeze the icing tubes and spread the icing evenly, all along trading glances with Carlton and enjoying each new finished cupcake at her table. Icing globs found faces, hair and the floor. She hadn't heard that much giggling and laughing in a long time. She silently thanked Dr. Moreno.

This was precisely the type of activity Delores needed to remind her that life is not all about bad guys and their victims. Then Carlton rose and Delores glanced at the clock. It seemed like mere minutes had passed but the hour was nearly over. He clanked on the pan again. Some whines of regret indicated that nearly everybody else was enjoying themselves as much as Delores was.

"Okay, everybody," Carlton said once the noise subsided. "I don't know about you people, but I've had a wonderful time. Before we start cleaning up we've got one more exercise and this should be the most enjoyable part of our afternoon."

Kids quieted and looked his way as if it were difficult to believe that anything else could enhance the fun.

"This entire project was the brainchild of Detective Sanchez over there, but there's a little more you should know about her. Not long ago, she arrested two very bad men and sent them to jail. This is the kind of thing she does every day. Then in between all of her dangerous work she came to our school, just to do something nice for all of us. Why don't we show her how much we appreciate her and all these cupcakes?"

Carlton led the applause while Delores humbly rose and mouthed several *thank yous* to her new friends.

"Now, for that other exercise I spoke of," Carlton went on. "In a minute we're going to give away our Friend Cakes. To start things off, I'm going to give my Friend Cake to Detective Sanchez." He showed his cupcake to the kids. "As you can see, I put a big gold star on top." He walked over to Delores and handed her the cupcake.

She nodded, and mouthed another thank you.

Almost as if she'd been cued, Principal Haley rose and gave her Friend Cake to Carlton Fayes, saying, "You bring out the best in us."

Just then the janitor joined the group and Mrs. Carbone grabbed one of the spare cakes and gave it to him. "Nobody ever thanks you, but you keep our school clean and we appreciate that."

"Okay, everybody," Carlton said. "You get the idea. Let's take a few minutes to share our good feelings."

The janitor took a bite out of his cake and grinned while students hurried around the room handing cupcakes back and forth. Carlton nudged Delores toward the batch of extra cupcakes. "Help me make sure every student gets at least one extra cupcake."

Delores reached for the tray but was interrupted. "Here, this is for you," a young girl who appeared to be about seven said as she handed Delores a cake covered in red, white and blue icing. "My mom says the police are heroes."

"Take mine too," one of the boys said handing a simple white-covered cake to her. "I'm not very creative."

"It reminds me of a fluffy cloud," Delores said. "I love it just the way it is."

Before she knew what happened, Delores had a small stack of Friend Cakes in front of her and Carlton had drifted across the room where he was busy handing out the extra cupcakes and making everybody feel special. She took a deep breath and knew this was precisely the lesson Dr. Moreno wanted her to learn. This truly was an *extravaganza*.

CHAPTER 83

THE DAYS IMMEDIATELY FOLLOWING the City Council meeting left Stump awash in mixed feelings. While he was pleased with himself for solving Mr. Kraft's murder, and proving that Dixon Browne raped Maria's mama, and identifying a pathway for low-income people to live in safer homes, there was also a new set of issues tormenting him.

Even though Mr. Kraft's remaining days would have become more and more miserable due to his illness, it saddened Stump to lose one of the most influential men he'd ever met.

Then there was Juanita and Manuel Alvarado. They too were decent people. In a way Manuel was a compassionate man for sparing Mr. Kraft from a gruesome death. But now Manuel was locked up and Juanita had to raise their daughter without him.

All of this left Stump wondering what would happen to Maria and her mama and all the others at Cal-Vista now that the most influential people who worked there were long gone.

In addition Stump was extremely concerned about his schoolwork. He'd cut so many classes that the only way he could expect to pass the tenth grade was to do well on his finals. He'd been studying the best he could and finally took all his tests, but he knew he didn't do all that well and Myles had already warned him that there would be consequences if his grades didn't improve.

Now it was all over and all he could do was wait for the results to come in the mail. In the meantime he had no job, so he went home to check on Grandma Pauline and Katherine the caregiver.

Once at his apartment, Stump was surprised to see Myles's truck in the parking lot. "What are you doing here?" Stump asked when he first saw Myles in the living room. "Is everybody okay?"

"Couldn't be much better," Myles said. "The women are in the kitchen putting a puzzle together. I came home a little early because I have a congratulatory gift for you."

"Really? Rad. What is it?"

"It's out in the truck, wrapped in white." Myles tossed Stump his keys. "Go get it."

"Okay." As Stump hurried to Myles's truck, he thought about their history. Sometimes Myles was a hard ass, but overall he was a nice guy. After all, the dude adopted Stump when Stump was at his all-time low. Myles deserved big cred for that. But when it came to gift giving, Myles was a bit of a tightwad.

Underneath the carport, he opened the truck door and glanced around. There was no gift in sight. He looked in the glove box and behind the seat, but nothing. He stepped back outside, checked the truck's bed. There was no gift of any type, wrapped or otherwise. Bummer. He returned to the apartment. "Somebody must have stolen it. There's nothing out there."

"Oh, really," Myles said. "Sometimes you look right at things, like your dirty underwear on the floor, and just don't see them. You'd better go look again. It's definitely out there."

"I looked pretty good. Where is it exactly?"

Myles sighed. "For crying out loud, Stump. I guess I have to do it myself." Stump watched from the picture window as

Myles hurried out to the truck, stuck his head in the cab and bolted right back. "It's there, alright. Just like I said. Damn thing was right under your nose."

"Under my nose? But you said it was under the roof."

Myles shook his head. "If it's under one, it's under the other." Myles pointed out the window. "In fact, I can see some of the wrapping from here."

Stump peeked again. Then, "You sure you ain't been drinking?"

Myles grinned and pointed off to the side of the lot. "Let me make this easier. See that shiny SUV over there? The black one with the luggage rack."

Stump looked. "Yeah. So?"

"Who would need a vehicle like that?"

"I dunno, maybe a family or somebody whose car wore out."

"What about a family that got bigger?"

"Sure. A mom has a baby and needs a bigger car. So what. What's that got to do with what we were talking about?"

"New babies aren't the only way a family grows," Myles said before chin-pointing toward Grandma Pauline.

Stump looked at Grandma Pauline, then studied Myles and finally it hit him. "No shit? You bought new wheels. Can I drive it?"

Myles nodded. "Just picked it up a couple hours ago, but that meant I needed to do something with my old truck. What color would you say it is?"

Stump's eyes shot to the old truck again, then back to Myles, who wore a shit-eating grin. "It's all yours, and this time you don't have to pay me back."

Stunned, Stump's smile stretched all across his face. "No shit?"

"You boys shouldn't use words like that," Grandma Pauline said from the other room.

"I've been thinking about it for weeks," Myles added, "and almost didn't do it after you did so many sneaky things without telling me or the other detectives. But then I looked in my mirror. Even though I specialize in other types of crimes, I knew if I had been in your shoes I probably would have done the exact same thing. It doesn't make it right, but at least I understand why you did it. I filled the tank, but you have to buy your own insurance and gas from here on out. That fair?"

"Hell, yes, that's fair. Thanks a lot, Myles." Stump reached out for a handshake, but Myles pushed Stump's hand aside and grabbed him.

"We can hug this time," he said.

Stump wasn't accustomed to hugging men, but it felt pretty darn good...for a couple seconds. He pulled away. "I gotta show Maria."

"Speaking of Maria," Myles said, "you've been seeing an awfully lot of her lately, but you must be ashamed of your grandma and me because you haven't made any attempt to introduce us. Would it kill you to bring her and her mother around for dinner sometime soon?"

"I can't eat that much."

Stump looked at Grandma Pauline and back at Myles. "I'd rather we all go to a restaurant because Grandma Pauline shares her apple pie with me."

"Okay then," Myles said while nodding. "Go ahead and see if you can set something up. And on that other matter, just so we understand each other, there'll be no more messing up, or I'll make you forfeit your keys. I really mean it. Is that clear?"

"No problem. There won't be any more troubles. I promise."

"Okay, then. I'll see you after my AA meeting tonight."

Stump's heart throbbed as he rushed outside and leapt into his very own brand-new, super-cool pick-up truck.

CHAPTER 84

IN HIS NEW TRUCK, Stump immediately replaced the stupid country music station with one more worthy of high volume and cranked it all the way up. He sat tall and headed for Cal-Vista and Maria.

When he arrived, head bobbing, he found Maria sitting by the pool with tear tracks running down her cheeks. "Hi. What's the matter?" he asked.

"Everything."

"Oh, really? I thought you'd be happy, now that the dragon has been slain."

"Mama lied to me."

"I know. But now we don't need the DNA results for the proof."

Maria shook her head. "That's not it. She's never told me anything about me having an aunt."

"Oh, that. It was a surprise to me too. But she must have had a good reason. Did she explain it to you?"

"No. I just ran away. Now she's crying. She said something about being poorer than ever."

Stump recalled how worried his own mom used to get when she said things like that. "I know how she might get some money."

Maria's face lit up. "You do? How?"

"That college fund we talked about. After the DNA test proves—"

"You never give up, do you?"

"I checked the website this morning. The results are supposed to come out later today. Then you'll be one step closer to the money. Maybe she'll feel better and tell you the truth about everything."

"I keep telling you that's not possible; therefore there won't be any money for me or Mama."

"But Dixon admitted it in his notebook. Let's at least go talk to her."

Maria sighed. "Okay, if it'll shut you up, but don't blame me if she throws you out of our apartment."

Minutes later Stump and Maria entered her apartment where Mrs. Quintana was huddled on the couch, her eyes red, her face blotchy. A trashcan full of crumpled tissues was near her feet.

Stump sat next to her. "Hello, Mrs. Quintana. Maria said you've been pretty sad since Dixon was arrested. I'm sorry I made you feel bad."

She sniffled. "It's not because of him. I don't know how we're going to pay our bills."

"That's what we wanted to talk to you about. I know you didn't want Maria to know that Dixon is her real papa and that he has hidden some money for her that—"

Mrs. Quintana waved Stump off and glared at the floor. "He wasn't Maria's daddy."

"See!" Maria said. "What did I tell you?"

Mrs. Quintana blew her nose, and then looked at Maria. "I guess you deserve to know everything now."

Maria looked somber.

"Your daddy was exactly who I told you he was. His name was Eduardo. He brought me up here from Mexico when the drug wars reached our town. He stayed with me for a couple weeks and then he went back to get his mama and brother."

Maria folded her arms across her chest, rolled her head toward Stump. "See."

Stump wasn't buying it. Dixon's notes were more believable. It sounded as if Stump's only means to convince Maria of the truth was the same as before: wait for the DNA results.

Mrs. Quintana lowered her head. "As soon as Eduardo left, Dixon showed interest in me, but I said no. The next week I got the message that bad men killed your daddy's family and ours too."

"Oh, my God." Maria wedged herself next to her mama.

"A few weeks later I realized I was pregnant. I had no way to support us. I had to think of something." She looked deep into Maria's eyes and then hung her head and wept. "I let Dixon have me—several times." She wiped at her tears. "Then a couple months later I told him he got me pregnant so he'd pay our bills."

Maria gasped and covered her mouth with her hands. "But Mama, that was dishonest."

Stump rolled his eyes and was tempted to speak, but thought better of it.

"I know, but I couldn't go back to Mexico because everybody was dead. Dixon suggested an abortion, but I didn't want to lose your papa's baby and I already loved you."

Tears had formed in Maria's eyes.

"Dixon was afraid that his first wife and his children would find out what he did, so he didn't want me to tell anybody. As long as he thought he was your papa and he wanted to keep it quiet, I was willing to go along with everything." She took a deep breath. "As soon as I started to show, he did that awful thing to Lupe. I couldn't say anything to you about it because you were just a child. If you slipped up and accidently said something to anger him he might have thrown us out. I'd seen him do that to other people and couldn't take a chance because I had no other money."

"Oh, Mama. I'm sorry you had to deal with that animal." Maria's tears and tone suggested she believed every word of her mama's tale.

"I would have moved in with him if I had to, but he liked to be with other women—which was better for us—as long as he kept providing a way to pay our rent." Tears rolled down Mrs. Quintana face. She almost deserved an Academy Award. "I never loved him, but I've always given him what he wants because I had no other choice."

Stump sighed. Maybe this was one of those times when it was best to leave things alone. Maybe he should just keep the results of the DNA test to himself.

"When you were about seven, my body began to change and from then on, he only used me in that way when he couldn't find anybody else. But I always did whatever he wanted just to be sure he still supported us."

Maria threw her arms around her mama's neck. "Oh, Mama. I love you more than ever."

"He made me get rid of Señorita too." She looked at Stump. "I knew that the money we got belonged to Mr. Kraft, but I told myself that he wouldn't miss it." She hung her head. "Dixon may not have been a good man but I needed him to help me raise my beautiful Maria." She wiped her nose. "But now he's gone, and I don't know what we'll do."

At least that was true. It was difficult for nearly everybody around there to get a job. Stump had an idea. "I'll be right back," he said as he reached for the door. He stepped outside hustled next door and rang the bell. A minute later, Mr. Connors answered.

"Hi Stump. I hoped I'd see you before long. Did you come for that job we spoke about?"

"After you and everybody else helped me at the City Council meeting, my dad gave me his truck. I have to pay for gas and insurance so I was thinking maybe I could start sometime next week."

"Glad to hear that. I'll hold a spot for you."

Stump shuffled his feet. "Mr. Connors, I had another favor to ask. I wouldn't bring it up but—"

"What's on your mind?"

"Well, Dixon used to give my girlfriend's mama some work so she could pay their rent. You and Mrs. Connors have said you could use some help around here. Is there any chance you could hire Mrs. Quintana to help you?"

"Strange you should ask that. We were just talking about something along those lines. Why don't you have Mrs. Quintana drop by and we can talk about it."

"Really? I can go get her right now."

"It just might be the push we needed."

On the way back to Cal-Vista and jubilant, Stump decided to check if the DNA test results had been posted. But now he wasn't sure if he'd show them to Maria. A couple of clicks into his cell and his pulse quickened. They were in. He clicked the link and instantly saw the answer. *Negative*? How the hell could that be?

He looked toward Maria's apartment. There could only be one answer. Maria's mama was telling the truth. Maria wasn't related to Dixon after all. The only person who'd ever out-bluffed Dixon Browne was the last person anybody would expect. A humble woman of limited means had been manipulating the great poker player non-stop for sixteen years. This was priceless. Stump sat down on the curb and laughed until it hurt.

CHAPTER 85

Delores spent the last few days tying up loose ends but still had a couple unfinished stops. She pulled her Audi into the Cal-Vista lot and grabbed a padded envelope that she'd brought with her.

As she moved toward building four she thought about the bond she shared with Inez Quintana. Each had lost a sister and endured a lot of pain because of an evil man. As she reached the back corner of the building Maria emerged with a laundry basket full of heavy pots and pans, which she set next to a white pick-up. Just then, Stump backed out of the building holding one end of a sofa. James followed Stump and they loaded the sofa into the truck. "Hello, everybody," Delores said.

"Stump got Mama a job," Maria said. "It might be a little harder but at least she won't have to rely on Dixon."

"It's right next door," Stump said. "With Mr. and Mrs. Connors."

"That's wonderful. You guys deserve a fresh start. Is your mama home?"

Inside, Inez Quintana had stuffed a lifetime of items in boxes and bags. "Hi, Inez. I brought you something," Delores said, holding out the padded envelope. "I thought you might appreciate this."

Inez smiled and opened the package. "It's Lupe's crucifix," she whispered as she touched it to her cheek.

By that time Maria and Stump and James had wandered in. "They'd usually keep it until after the trial," Delores said, "but I insisted they have more evidence than they need to convict Dixon." Delores tapped Inez's arm. "As you know I had a similar problem. That makes us like sisters."

Maria sprung to her tiptoes. "Does this mean you're like an aunt to me?"

Delores grinned. "Why not. I'd really, really like that."

"What do I call you? Aunt Detective or what?"

Stump grimaced.

"I guess you can just call me Aunt Delores," she said before turning to Stump and James. "But I'm still Detective Sanchez to you gentlemen."

Maria grabbed her aunt's hand and stuck her tongue out at Stump as if she'd won a big victory.

"I hope you can find your sister someday," Inez said.

"After all that's happened lately I've hired some professional people-finders to see if they can do any good. I'm keeping my fingers crossed."

"I'm glad Mama doesn't have to worry about the police any longer," Maria said.

"That's one of the good things that's come out of all this. There's something else too. I found out where the county buried Lupe. She's in a nice cemetery in east L.A. I thought you might want to go there—to be reunited—at least you'll know where she is and can visit from time to time. I've taken the morning off so I can take you there right now if you'd like."

Inez and Maria traded glances. "Can I go too?"

Inez nodded, then looked at Stump.

"Go ahead. James and I will finish moving the furniture. Then I can come back later and help with the rest of it."

*   *   *

That afternoon, after returning from the cemetery, Delores invited Carlton Fayes to go with her to the office of Dr. Moreno. "I'm sorry I didn't set an appointment, Jeanine," Delores said as soon as the doctor stepped into the waiting room, "but, I've told Carlton so much about you and I just had to drop in and say thank you."

Jeanine shook Carlton's hand before turning back to Delores. "I saw you on the news when you made the arrests. That was quite a night."

"So many things have fallen into place since I met you, Jeanine. I don't know where to begin."

"Can I assume you had your cupcake party?"

"We called it an *extravaganza*," Carlton said.

Delores grabbed his hand. "He did practically everything. There must have been fifty kids and teachers and parents and even somebody from the superintendent's office."

"Impressive."

"Carlton had everybody give away one cupcake to anybody they wanted, just to be nice."

Jeanine smiled.

"We worked in some extras," Carlton said, "so everybody would get at least one extra cupcake." He gestured toward Delores. "Ms. Selfish here got seven of them."

"You were so right, Jeanine," Delores said. "Nothing has ever lifted my spirits like that party."

"*Extravaganza!*" Carlton said teasingly. "It was an *extravaganza.*"

"Tell me about your case," Dr. Moreno said. "That must have been very gratifying."

"It sure was. Once we found somebody who was willing to talk, it all fell into place, just like I expected. I even got the DA to charge Dixon with serial rape by deception. He said that Dixon's crimes prior to the new law wouldn't count but we could still use the witnesses to show a pattern. Overall, it isn't as powerful as the murder charge but it makes a darn good statement to the other cops. But that's not all. I tried that

IMT thing you taught me and decided to leave Mama and Tio alone as long as Mama is happy."

"That sounds like *kindness over being correct* to me."

"Yeah. I guess it does. You were right about that too."

"I'm happy for you."

Delores grinned. "You know that other thing we talked about? It worked itself out, too." She kissed Carlton's cheek. "Thanks to my very own cupcake man."

CHAPTER 86

"That's the one I was looking for," Stump said to James as they flopped a mattress on top of Maria's mama's bed. "The last piece."

"Good. I'm beat. Now you can take me back to my car."

They locked up and went outside where James pointed toward the bike rack. "Hey, Dude, check it out."

Stumped turned to see two boys about age ten, messing around with the bike tires. Suddenly Stump heard fizzing. "Those little bastards must be the ones who let the air out of my tires." He ran toward the boys. "Hey you guys—"

The youngsters looked at Stump and ran away.

All Stump could do was shake his head and turn back to James. "I didn't recognize them. Did you?"

"Nope, but they must be from the neighborhood, somewhere."

"I wouldn't be surprised if they found my old phone too," Stump said as they climbed into his truck and he inserted his key. "Did I tell you that Detective Sanchez said I should become a detective?"

"You just listen to her 'cause she makes your pecker pucker."

"It's not that, Dude. In fact, she's not the first person to tell me that. I never took it serious before, but I kinda like investigating and figuring things out."

"I think you watch too much TV."

"I'm serious about this. It's exciting to ask questions and sneak into places and learn things other people don't know. If I hadn't got my hands on Dixon's notebook or ended up in the maintenance room with Maria, I wouldn't have been able to solve the case."

"I bet the cops would have figured it out sooner or later."

"Probably, but that just proves that I think like they do. Furthermore, I wouldn't have been able to help those other people improve their homes if I didn't figure out how to get Mr. Barella on my side. I even liked going door-to-door."

"It was my idea to ditch school and to trick BigBunz. That was pretty rad."

"No shit. Did you see her smile at the end, when we needed her? Maybe we both have a knack." Stump pulled into the parking lot of his apartment complex and parked near Myles's SUV. "I owe you a favor, Dude," Stump said.

"That's another thing you're good at," James said. "Getting people to do favors for you."

Stump wasn't sure if that was a good quality or not, but he was glad to have such a good friend.

"Hello, people," Stump said to Myles and Grandma Pauline when he and James entered the apartment. "We're worn out."

Myles muted the TV and rose. "Just the gentlemen I wanted to see." He pointed to the kitchen table. "You got some mail. Which do you want first, the good news or the bad?"

"Huh? I like good news."

"I like good news too," Grandma Pauline said.

Myles handed Stump an envelope. "Looks like it's from Irv Wedlock at the TV station."

"Really?" Stump ripped it open and read out loud. "Neal, Congratulations on your recent successes. I always knew you had the type of mettle that makes for great leaders. If you're interested, I might be able to get you a nomination to one of the military academies. Otherwise, I expect to see you in law enforcement someday. Either way, I hope you'll stay in touch. Your friend, Irv Wedlock."

Stump curled his bottom lip and grinned. "Wow! This is rad." He looked at Myles. "I've heard of military academies. What do they do?"

Myles took the envelope. "There's West Point, and the Naval Academy and the Air Force Academy. They give you a great college education for free and make you into an officer."

"It'd be pretty cool to fly those big jets, Dude," James said.

"Sure would." Stump turned to Myles. "You think that's possible?"

Myles shook his head. "I doubt it. A guy has to belong to clubs, do things for his community and—"

"I got the City Council to—"

"As I was about to say before you interrupted," Myles continued, "you won't get in those places without good grades, which brings us to the next piece of mail." Myles picked up a different envelope and slid out the letter inside. "It was addressed to me. It's from your school. Shows you've had a serious attendance problem that I knew nothing about."

Stump shuffled his feet. "Oh, that."

"I called the school to find out why they never said anything to me about all the absents. As near as I can tell, you two cooked up some scheme to cover for each other."

"Uh-oh," James said. "I gotta go."

Myles nodded and James disappeared faster than one of his infamous farts in the wind.

"I guess you thought you were smart," Myles said. "You assumed you could cut corners but it turns out you're not quite as brilliant as you thought you were." He picked up another envelope. "Your report card was addressed to me too. You got an F in Literature, another in Biology. Damn near flunked Spanish too. You know what this means. It's summer school for you."

"How about Trig and History?" Stump asked, fishing for something good to offset the bad.

"Not much better." Myles handed the paper to Stump. "Everything else was I's and D's. Any worse and they would have held you back."

Stump lowered his head. "I'm sorry, but I didn't have much choice."

"I know how hard you've worked, so if grades were your only problem, I might be inclined to cut you a little slack, but there's something else here. Even worse," he said while handing Stump a larger brown envelope. "This one was also addressed to me. Go ahead, open it."

What the heck could be worse? Stump pulled out the contents. The heading said it was from the County Court. The words "speeding" and "traffic ticket" stuck out like dress clothes in a swimming pool. Twenty miles an hour over the posted speed limit. How could that be? He'd only been driving for a few days. Maybe it was another one of Myles's pranks.

"Keep going," Myles said. "Look what's behind it."

Stump flipped to the back page where there was a super-clear picture of him and Maria and her mama, from when Myles went out of town.

"You stole my truck," Myles said, hands on hips. "Were you out of your ever-loving mind?"

"Well. It was an emergency. Maria's mama had to go—"

"Bottom line is I didn't say you could take the truck. And you know it."

"This reminds me of when you got drunk in high school," Grandma Pauline said, looking at Myles. "You sure got sick."

Stump grinned. Sometimes Grandma Pauline was an unintended ally.

"Not now, Mom," Myles said. "We're talking about Stump, not me." He turned back to Stump. "What other secrets are you holding from me?"

"Nothing else. I promise."

"That's what you said yesterday and before that. You always say there won't be any more problems, but the words are barely out of your mouth before something new happens."

"I said I'm sorry."

Myles shook his head. "Not good enough this time, Stump. You stole my truck and messed up big-time at school." He tapped the first envelope. "Summer school begins next week. It says here you're already enrolled."

Summer school? "James said they have make-up classes online. I can just—"

"Oh, no, you don't. That might be alright for somebody who went to class in the first place, but since you couldn't be bothered to get your butt into the classroom, I think you should try it again so you don't get the impression that you're getting away with anything."

"Good character is borne out of the pain of our mistakes," Grandma Pauline added.

Stump smiled at her, then returned his attention to Myles and exhaled. "Alright. I guess that's fair."

"Good. And you have to get B's. Nothing worse. That deals with school. Now, why don't you tell me what should happen to a guy who sneaks around behind his parent's back and steals cars and ditches school?"

Fair question. Stump pursed his lips, then pulled his truck keys out of his pocket and handed them over. "I don't get to drive for a week."

Myles shook his head. "Throw in your cell phone and make it two weeks."

"Okay. It's a deal," Stump said, turning toward his room.

"Not so fast," Myles said. "While we're clearing the air, we still have this matter of your unpaid bills. When you took money that didn't belong to you, you were doing the same type of thing that Dixon Browne did."

"But I was going to pay it back."

"That's what everybody says, but sooner or later they get in over their heads and end up making matters worse. You're going to get another job. I don't care if you have to work for minimum wage. But you're going to pay me back every damn dime before you get your keys back."

"But that will take at least six weeks and we just said I could drive again in two weeks."

"You still can if you pay me back. Otherwise, you'll have plenty of time to think about what you did."

"Alright. Alright. Mr. Connors has offered me a job. That way I can see Maria too." He laid his head on Grandma Pauline's shoulder, having no idea what her future would be like, but he'd already planned to be a big part of it. "I'll use the rest of my time to get to know Grandma Pauline better," he said. "She's one of my best friends."

In the meantime, if he could figure out a way to pay off Myles all at once he could be back behind the wheel in two weeks. He grinned mischievously. Good thing James had a savings account.

OTHER AWARD-WINNING BOOKS

By David A. Thyfault

(see below to get FREE eBooks
for your devices or computer)

NON-FICTION

Instant Experience for Real Estate Agents
A fun and interesting non-textbook slant on the real estate profession. Features jokes, true stories and an explanation of why agents should be their own best clients.

Stop Flushing Your Money Down the Drain
Find out how and why the typical adult loses nearly a half-million dollars in buying power during his or her lifetime. Easy to read. Packed with good tips.

FICTION SERIES:

The Making of Detective Neal "Stump" Randolph

Episode One: Three Deadly Twins
A trio of twins causes deadly trouble on one side of town while 13-year-old Stump endures the tragic death of his beloved mother in a nearby neighborhood and ultimately discovers he has the knack for detective work.

Episode Two: Monday Girl's Revenge
Unknowingly, both 16-year-old Stump and young Detective Delores Sanchez get drawn into the same unsavory world of

a serial sexual predator at an apartment complex. By the time a body is discovered, Stump is well on his way to becoming an effective, self-taught investigator.

COMING UP

Episode Three: Grandma's BFF Does Coke
While establishing a funky breakfast restaurant, Stump, now 19 and enrolled in a college of criminology, teams up with a mysterious truck driver to investigate a dementia patient's claim regarding a lost family treasure. Gunshots and corpses prove the patient knew a lot more than originally thought.

Note: Among other places, readers can find these books on Amazon, Smashwords.com (where the eBooks are FREE) and the author's website: DavidThyfault.com.

ABOUT THE AUTHOR

Like most Americans I liked my career of several decades but I have to admit that I didn't always approach the mornings with wild enthusiasm.

But then, I retired and discovered something I never would have guessed: When the day is mine, I love to get up even earlier. Now I'm the guy who wakes up the rooster. I still work as much as I ever did, only I now work on things that bring me a different form of compensation. Like writing books.

Some have asked me where I get my ideas, but it's no mystery. I had a storied youth with six sisters and a wild family. When I wasn't engulfed in that world, I spent a fair amount of my time wandering the alleys and streets of our neighborhood. A fellow learns a lot from all of those people even before he arrives for his first day of school. If he has the ability to recall the characters and the activities in which they engaged, and blend that with a dash of make-believe, there's a goldmine full of fodder from which to draw his inspiration.